Journey Sisters

Four Girls turn into Women

Julia Jacobs

P ROLOGUE

"Nikki!!! God no, Nikki! Break the window, Nikki!" You could hear the desperation and horror in their voices. But Nikki was the only one who had already given in to her inevitable death. She knew it, they knew it, but they were still hanging on to some crazy idea that a miracle would happen and she would be saved. Nikki looked at them and finally understood how much she loved them all.

Lizzie was still stopping cars in a frenzied attempt to find someone who could do something about the whole situation. She was not going to give up. As long as she could still see the car on top of that cracked ice, she was going to fight for everybody's life in that car, Nikki's above all.

"Oh, dear Nikki, what have you gotten yourself into this time. I'm so sorry I wasn't strong enough to stop you from running away with that bunch of losers. I knew they were too high to even know which way they were actually going. They didn't even have boots on, just freakin' flip-flops in the middle of the winter, pretending they didn't feel the frozen winter air because "their spirits will keep their bodies safe for as long as they still want to continue their journey in this mortal world". I guess their spirits concluded they are lunatics and decided to bail on them. End of the journey for them! Maybe, but not for Nikki. Not as long as I'm here and I can do something about it!" Lizzie thought out loud while jumping in front of every car that was crossing the bridge in hopes someone will know what to do, or have enough rope for her to safely get to that car with a hammer and free everybody from that awful death. Especially Nikki. She saw Nikki's face as she turned and put both her hands on the back window in an attempt to reach out as the car was flying off the safety of the road. She couldn't erase that sheer panic she could read all over Nikki's beautiful face.

Lizzie shook her head and started yelling off the top of her lungs "Does anybody know anybody who can help them and can get here faster than the fire department or the police? Can you think of something that can help? Come on people. This is a life and death emergency happening right here in front of your eyes. Wake up! Think! Help me! Help them!"

Her throat was hurting from screaming. Nothing happened. Nobody said anything. Nobody did anything but watched the car that had Nikki in it, slowly sinking into the river.

"What a bunch of idiots. Watching this like it's the circus. Like this was some kind of entertainment. Maybe Nikki was right, maybe the world is doomed, especially if these people right here were representatives of our human race. God, I'm starting to think like her and look where all that thinking got her. I need to be productive. Come on, think, what else can I do? Maybe throw rocks to crack a window? But the car is too far and I can't see any rocks on this stupid bridge. Ok, what else? I need another idea. Come on, Lizzie, think! Think!"

Julie and Sasha were on their cell phones frantically trying to get some help, any help, fast. They were staring at Nikki both with tears in their eyes trying to send their love and hope and not to look as freaked out as they were. Wasn't that what Nikki always said to them? That she can feel the emotions of other people when they are looking at her? Let's hope she really does.

Sasha exclaimed "She just needs to hang on until help comes."

"I'm going to miss you all! See you in our next lives!" whispered Nikki almost to herself as she closed her eyes and accepted what was coming with as much serenity as she could muster. Sam's serene face appeared in front of her as she kept her eyes shut.

"Sam! I want to say goodbye to Sam! That's all I want!"

"Where's my cell?" asked Nikki knowing nobody will give her an answer. She started jamming her frozen fists into her pockets hoping to find it. Nothing there was big enough to be a cell phone. Her mind started racing, "I just need my cell and one last call to Sam. Just one last call!"

A tear started trickling down her left cheek. "Please, I just want to say goodbye to Sam."

She could hear the thin layer of ice giving way under the weight of the car. Soon, the frozen waters of this grandiose river she used to swim in every hot summer day when she was a child, will take her away forever from the people she loves and cherishes. How strange, that some of those clichés, that this society she's been running away from all her life, are proving to be right. Wasn't it said that right before you die the most important moments of your life flash before your eyes? That's what was happening to her, at this very moment. She finally understood how much her family and true friends actually love her. And she always was sure she was alone. How wrong she was.

It wasn't too easy to tune out the other four people in the car with her that were still trying to get out, banging the frozen windows of the tiny little old Volkswagen with their bare hands and feet. Their hauling cries were ripping her heart apart.

"Stop it!" Nikki yelled. "Joel, Anna, Crystal, Ben!!! All of you, stop and accept it! This is the end of our lives in these bodies. It's ok. Death is a wonderful thing! It's like an escape from the limits of this world. Weren't we looking for an escape from this mundane world, from its selfish, self-destructing inhabitants? What changed? We're looking death in its eyes! Don't turn around and close your eyes. Don't fight it. It has us in its grip. Now let's smile back at it, so it'll make the transition easier for all of us."

Nikki was trying to convince herself as well, by saying all that out loud. Did she believe it?

Somebody's foot smacked her right in her nose. She couldn't tell anymore whose feet were where. Arms and legs were flying agitated in the almost nonexistent space in that car. Their bodies were all crashed together like sardines in a can, but when they picked this small car they didn't think they might need more space to gain enough velocity to smash a window in case one of the tires of this old coffin would just literally fall out of its place, making the car jump off the bridge and into the river. Yeah, they didn't see it coming. Maybe the price tag should have been a clue. Maybe driving a car- that was cheaper than her last meal- on snow packed roads should have given her a hint. Well, not that they could have afforded more anyways. They spent all their money on that sweet stash for the party tonight. They were so sure that cheap car was a sign from divinity. It was a sign all right, a sign that it was time for all of them to go to heaven, if any of them believed in such a place.

Her nose was bleeding. Nikki remembered her hands being frozen solid but with all this last breath agitation, her blood was flowing rapidly all throughout her body. What was the point of trying to stop the bleeding? It was such a normal reaction to reach for the first piece of cloth she could put her hands on and try and stop the bleeding.

"Funny!" thought Nikki. "I'm going to die any second now and I'm wasting my time and energy trying to stop a nosebleed. Isn't that how life usually goes by anyway? We waste our time taking care of the small immediate and trivial things automatically, without even thinking, while the actual important things in our lives tend to be left to chance? And then if life doesn't turn out the way we want it to be, we complain and blame everybody else except ourselves."

A noise penetrated the madness in the car and Nikki's hand went right to the source of that sound. Finally, her cell phone. She looked at it and her heart stopped beating, it was Sam.

Chapter 1

The phone rang. Sasha looked at her mom and muttered "Go, pick it up. It's for you, my friends only call me on my cell. And no matter what you do or what you say, I'm still going to my friend's house, so get out of my way!"

Her mom literally barricaded the entrance door with her own body impeding Sasha from going out.

"If I have to hit you, I will, if you don't get out of my way! Now!" shrieked Sasha trying to physically push her mom out of her way. Her arms were wrapped around her mom's arms pushing her in an attempt to make her mom lose her balance, while Sasha's left foot was strategically placed behind her mom's rear foot, so she would fall backwards, away from the door and from Sasha's way to freedom.

The next second her mom fell down like a sack of potatoes. Sasha couldn't believe her plan worked. Finally, her two years of judo paid off. Now she wished she would have paid more attention to what she was taught there because that stuff actually works. Ha! Who would have thought that? I'll have to look into going back to those classes, they might one day save my life.

Ok, first things first. She was escaping her paranoid crazy mother. Sasha jumped over her mom and jolted towards the door. Her hand was on the doorknob when suddenly the door opened into her face! Ouch! Who the hell... who are those people?

"Mom, what have you done this time?" Sasha asked looking at those three big men all dressed in white.

"That's her" said her mom pointing at Sasha.

And that's the last thing Sasha could see, as two of the men grabbed her and held her while the other one was putting a rough straight jacket on her and a black sack over her head. She couldn't believe this was happening. This time her mom went too far. Hopefully her dad will return from his trip soon enough so she won't get that shock therapy she heard people in straightjackets get. Sasha knew she was somehow going to outsmart those people and manipulate them into not giving her shock therapy, but her dad needs to get back soon and rescue her before she goes crazy for real.

"By the way, if you think you can rely on your naive daddy to come and rescue you, think again, because he's gone for 4 months this time. He has this complicated corporate case in a place far away from civilization and the couple of times he'll be able to call you, I'll just tell him you're at a surf camp or something" finished her mom with what Sasha imagined to be a disgusting smirk on her evil distorted face.

Sasha listened to her mom trying to decipher if she was telling the truth or just bluffing. But she knew that tone of voice way too well, her mom wasn't lying. "Can I at least see your face so I know you're not lying to me" said Sasha wanting that bag off her head. She agreed.

"Ok, time to panic" murmured Sasha under her breath. She started walking away with those men, pretending that she was more than compliant, then, right before the elevator doors opened, she jerked from the men's grip and ran towards the stairs. She was free, free at last. She was running and those men were far behind her. They will never catch her. They can't catch her, she won't let that happen. It's her life at stake here.

"I'll just have to find a cell phone and call my friends, or steal one if need be. Do I know how to get to Jill's place if I have to walk there? I bet I can find it. But first I..." Sasha couldn't finish her thoughts as she felt a hand on her right shoulder. She was trapped in that hideous straight jacket, so her movements were limited. She twisted as fast as she could from one side to another, so she could lose the guy, but as she was trying to shake him off, she lost balance right at the top of the stairs and fell forward and couldn't even hold her arms up to protect her head from that fall. She was falling down the stairs head first and saw the ground approaching fast... she was going to break her neck and die.

"Nooooo" she screamed in horror.

"Sasha, wake up. Wake up Sasha. It was just a dream!"

Lizzie was holding her in her arms. "I'm not going to let go, you're here with me and you're ok. I promise. Open your eyes please. Just trust me and open your eyes. "

"I see you're holding yourself tight. I guess it was the same nightmare you've been having since I've known you. I'm so sorry honey. We're all here for you and we love and care for you. You're safe. What's in the past remains in the past. Your trial-happy mom cannot really hurt you anymore. She's out of your life and has been out of your life for a while now. She can try to take you to court for another of her imagined reasons, but she has no ammunition - she doesn't know you anymore and doesn't know anybody who knows you or who can tell her anything about you. We're here to support you in every possible way. She will never be able to take you to court again. Ok? Now look at me. Can I hug you?" finished Lizzie opening her arms wide for Sasha to fall into.

Julie and Nikki were in the doorway. They were woken up by Sasha's screaming.

"Are you alright?" asked Nikki. "Let's go and have a smoke. It will calm you down."

Sasha looked up at Nikki. "Yeah, let's go for a cigarette. I need to smoke this excruciating dark memory out of my consciousness. I was only 12!"

Both of them moved to the balcony. Nikki had the pack of cigarettes already in her hand. Even if Sasha wasn't a smoker like Nikki, when she woke up sweating like that from a nightmare usually involving a memory which included her mom, a cigarette with Nikki, small talk or just silence . . . and it all made sense again, slowly. Everything was alright.

"You 3 are my family now. The family I've never had and how odd is the fact that we found each other at a teen rehab, we bonded in hell, and look where we are today, living together, following our lives' dreams and keeping each other sober and clean" said Sasha while exhaling slowly looking at the deep fall night.

They said nothing for a while.

"Too bad they're no stars in Manhattan!" Nikki broke the silence, her emerald green eyes staring at the dark sky.

Julie came out on the balcony with couple of blankets and soon after Lizzie followed with a cup of her hot chocolate for each one of them.

"I thought coffee would just keep us awake, so I made my special hot chocolate for us!"

Sasha's eyes were glittering with tears "You are my family and I love you all so much." They all hugged and the whole moment became very emotional.

"Just look at us! We're a bunch of crybabies," said Sasha.

The air was crisp, the moon was high up in the sky throwing a clear light over every single object around. There were no visible stars, but just knowing that they existed and were all looking down on everybody and everything made the four girls feel safe and cared for.

Grabbing unto those soft fleece blankets, sipping hot chocolate from Disney colorful mugs that Lizzie bought for all as their first year living together anniversary gift, they were all looking faraway, lost in their own worlds.

It was quiet. Even the non-stop traffic of this lively city slowed down and just disappeared after a while. The wind was flowing through, taking the last leaves of the trees that heroically seemed to have kept some of them attached to their branches until the last days of the season. The streets beneath the balcony were invaded only by the shadows of what was left behind after the people who busily populated them during the comfort of daylight went to their homes, to their soft warm blankets, hot chocolate and loving family.

Out of nowhere, a high-pitched laughter cracked the tranquility of the night. Shortly after was followed by an unmistakably male deep heartfelt chuckle.

"What do you know?! There's actually life on this planet after all," said Nikki with a smile, pulling her long curly brown hair away from her face.

"And it seems to be life worth preserving. Observe how happy they are. They must be in love ... "added Lizzie with a sigh.

"Well, then. Let's skip this planet for now and go destroy another one, if the consul agrees" followed Julie, trying to sound like a scary five foot two blonde Darth Vader.

"And it better be the planet on which my mom lives and we better not miss it this time!" concluded Sasha with a seemingly straight face.

Two seconds later they were all laughing. They had no idea what they very really laughing about but they couldn't stop. It was like that tiny little snowball that accidentally started rolling down the hill. Nobody knew why it began moving, but every second that passed it gained velocity, strength and rapidly grew in size. It had a life of its own. And so the girls were laughing so hard at this point that they started tearing up. They were laughing at themselves, at the world, at the ugly situation Sasha was in, at all the mistakes they've ever made in their lives, at life itself. And they couldn't stop laughing.

Julie was the first one to stop laughing and was once again lost in her worries, thinking about Joe. "Why hadn't he called? He said he would call her later. Maybe something happened to him. No, nothing like that. I'm just pissed at the fact that if something would ever happen to him, I would never find out. His friends don't know I exist, nor does his family and we've been together for more than a year. Is he ashamed of me? I understand there's a pretty big age difference, but I don't care. I love him and I know he loves me back. Or does he? Yes, yes, what's wrong with me, of course he loves me. He told me so himself. But only after I did. He did not lie. I know he cares; I can feel he cares every night we're together. But then in the morning he just jumps on his feet and goes about his day like we had never shared all that love the night before. Then he never answers my calls. He only calls me when he feels like it and it's usually at night ... Am I just a bootie-call even after so long and after sharing so much and after helping him so much? I give, give, give. When am I going to receive? Oh, look at that couple down the street, they seem to be so happy. I want to be that happy. Why aren't I? When am I going to be that happy? Well, at least my mom doesn't want to hurt me like Sasha's mom. I know my mom loves me in her own way. And I have her and my dad and my brothers and sisters, and my roommates and Joe. Poor Sasha. "

Sipping from her hot chocolate, Lizzie was dreaming about the love that couple they were staring at shared. "It must be the warmest feeling on earth, and sweet and comforting, just like this hot chocolate on a cold night "said Lizzie out loud. "I know I'm going to find the perfect man for me, the perfect love and get married right away and have children and be happy for the rest of my life. I know it! I only need to find him and my life will be perfect," smiled Lizzie with satisfaction. Then she turned towards Sasha and felt like giving her a big hug. "Poor Sasha, it's a good thing she has us. We all love her." this thought she kept to herself.

"Sasha, you are so brave, I'm so proud of you. We are all proud of you. Our love is real. Do not forget. We're not asking for anything from you and we love you unconditionally. We are all fighting your mom in that court tomorrow. You are not alone. You are safe. Relax!" said Nikki taking Sasha's right hand in her hands.

"You are safe" followed Julie and Lizzie putting their hands on top of Nikki's.

Chapter 2

The smell of wood polisher was still floating faintly in the air as they all walked into Mrs. Clifford's office. She was supposed to be the best attorney on the island of Manhattan. Julie's grandfather took care of everything, so the girls never had to worry about research, money or bribed officials. You can never be too careful when it came to Sasha's mother.

"Sit down girls. I have no time for pleasantries, so I'll cut to the chase" uttered Mrs. Clifford rapidly. "Your mom," she said looking at Sasha, "Mrs. Brooks, filed her papers yesterday. I was able to get her statement and I'll read it out loud to all of you in a second, but first of all I want you, Sasha, to know that your mom put a restraining order under your name. You can't get within two hundred feet of her except for when you are in court and that's the only exception. Now, do you know why she's suing you?"

"She claims I hit her and stole my grandmother's diamante bracelet" replied Sasha sternly.

"Exactly right," continued Mrs. Clifford, "and based on your history which is so well archived in the legislative system and with this paper trail of all your former trials with her, this trial shouldn't take long at all, but we need to make sure she won't do this again in the future. I'm going to find a way so she can never drag you in court again."

"Is that even possible? Can this be the end of my nightmare? Oh, if you can do that, I will be grateful to you for the rest of my life. Girls, I am going to finally have my life back, for good! I dreamt about this all my life! Can this be real" asked Sasha with tears in her eyes, turning to face her friends.

Lizzie started wiping. "It has to be true! You deserve it! You will have your life back! I know it's possible! Let's do this! That stupid, hateful woman will disappear from all our lives and especially from yours!"

"Here's what Mrs. Brooks statement says," interrupted the attorney:

"On the night of May 12th, 2008, I caught my daughter, Sasha Brooks, stealing from my home. She was clearly high, and considering all her addiction history, that is part of who she is, so I tried not to get in her way too much, but being her mom, I just wanted to help her with her problem because I love her so much. As I was saying, on that night I was asleep and a sharp noise woke me up. I heard whispers and movements in my house. I knew I was being burglarized, but I thought I had heard my daughter's voice, so I didn't want to call the police on her.

I went to the living room and turned on the light. There was my daughter, alone, all dressed in black, looking high and desperate. She had a huge bag with everything she was stealing from me, her own mother. By her look, I knew she wanted to sell all that to get money to get high again. My heart was hurting, I am her mom and I had to help her, so I begged her to stop stealing and getting high. I told her I would give her all I have if she becomes a good and respectful girl. I told her I loved her and I wanted all the best for her.

My daughter though yelled back at me with hatred and she had a crazy look on her face and I became afraid of her. Sasha took a glass and screamed at me "I'm going to kill you with this, get out of my way now!" Then she grabbed me by the hair and pulled my mother's diamond bracelet off my wrist.

I was physically afraid for my life. I don't care about all the other things that she stole, but my mother's diamond bracelet has been passed on from generation to generation and it belongs in the family not in a pawn shop somewhere lost in the world. I want to give it to my daughter after she gets clean and lives a normal healthy life, when I know she's not going to sell it for drugs."

The room was quiet for a split second.

"What a lying bitch!" screamed Sasha. My God she can come up with stories at the drop of a hat. I was there that night because she invited me for dinner, but not in the middle of the night! We had a fight, like we always do and I told her that her drinking will kill her, while pointing to the glass of wine she had in her hand, not me. Drinking makes her crazy, steals all her self-esteem and she starts pointing fingers, coming up with stories and suing me. And that diamond bracelet that she was talking about", added Sasha catching her breath, "she never had it. My grandmother gave it to me at my 18th birthday. My grandma never gave it to my mom and my mom always hated me for that too. My roommates are my witnesses, they were there when my grandma gave me that specific bracelet."

The attorney looked directly at the other girls with her left eyebrow raised in a question. "So, I am sure that all of you are ready to write a statement confirming that, right?"

"Definitely. Just give us a pen and a piece of paper" replied Julie promptly. "This nightmare has to end as soon as possible!"

"Thank you, girls. Thank you for being here for me, thank you for caring and I'm sorry if I haven't said thank you before as often as I should have. I'm in my head so much, especially with all this going on, that I forget to be grateful, I forget to follow my recovery plan. But you don't seem to forget about me, you don't seem to forget to care for me, and show it to me every day. You keep me on my path and that's more than I could ever ask from anybody in this world. I love you guys! I love you so much". Tears were making their way down Sasha's perfect cheeks. She was one of those girls who never needed makeup. She was voted most likely to age beautifully out of her entire university class. All that stress and lack of love that she grew up with and she still did not show any of that on her gorgeous face. Her hair was straight and well-conditioned, naturally black which complimented her dark brown eyes contoured by long luscious eyelashes. Mascara was a waste of money and time for her. She didn't need it. All in all, nature was extremely generous with her, too bad the motherly genes were inexistent in her mother.

Mrs. Clifford was the first one to break the silence. "Sorry to interrupt, but I need those statements right away," she said going around her heavy desk. She opened a drawer, pulled out some paper with her firm's logo and information on it and handed a sheet to each girl. "Take a pen and write in detail what happened the night Sasha got that diamond bracelet from her grandmother. I need names, times, date, places, colors, smells ... everything you can remember. Sasha, you need to do the same thing" added the attorney while pointing at a large somewhat oval shaped expensive looking marble and gold pen holder. Everything in this office screamed money. Big money. Probably that's why Julie's grandfather was paying and not Sasha. She could have never afforded anybody like this. "Mrs. Clifford must be very good at what she's doing" thought Sasha, starting to trust her new attorney and her ability to end this craziness as soon as possible.

"I need to be in court in 5 minutes, so when you're finished with your statements, sign them, date them and give them to my assistant. I'll call you if you need to come in today. With the new evidence and your statements, we might not even have a trail. I will let you know when I know. Goodbye girls, it was nice meeting you all." And with that Mrs. Clifford swiftly walked out of her office with a slim and elegant leather briefcase in her hand.

"Wow, how professional does she look, speak and act! I want to be her when I grow up. All that confidence. I love it. I want to put a picture of her in my room and pray to my Higher Power every night that I become her one day!" said Sasha in admiration.

"Yeah, maybe, but without that nose and inexistent lips and cankles," added Nikki with a laughter.

"There you go again picking on every little imperfect thing. Can't you ever just see the whole picture, Nikki? And you're wondering why you can't find joy and are on a constant journey to find your happiness. I read couple of the books that you gave me to read and between the two of us, I think you're the one not paying attention to what's written in those books." Nikki said nothing. She preferred not to fight Sasha right now. Sasha was in a bad place.

Stop searching Nikki! If you're looking for happiness, stop searching for everybody's weak points. The glass is half full, not half empty. Just take a look at us. Do you see how much we love you? Trust me, there's nothing else in this world that matters, that could make you happier than true love, and you have it here" finished Sasha and pulled herself back in her chair looking back at the piece of paper she had in her hand. "Now this whole thing that I'm going through is crap and we all know it. I should start blaming, screaming, yelling and seeing the whole world black and bleak, but I don't."

This had to stop. "Oh, so I should learn from you, the queen of bottling everything up, blocking the natural flow of energy through my body and having emergency room worthy migraines? I prefer feeling and expressing my emotions."

Lizzie stepped in, "Come on girls, it's not the time, nor the place". She wanted to say more but she finally saw Julie signaling to butt out and let the other two figure out where they were going with this nutty duel.

"Feel them and express them as much as you want to, but let them go too" retorted Sasha.

"I let them go while I express them. I always say out loud what I think and therefore let them go."

"If you were letting them, go you wouldn't be so focused on the ugly part of things. And by the way, what you find ugly others might find beautiful. Weren't you the one who said that life is a matter of perspective, that two people might look at the same thing and see it totally different, yet both of them would be right? And I don't always need to know your perspective especially when is so callous, cold, mean and insensitive!"

"Oh, well, listen to yourself. You just went back on your own argument. If you find my way of looking at things so callous, cold, mean and insensitive, maybe it's just a matter of perspective. Maybe I see it warm, nice and thoughtful" said Nikki purposefully pressing on each and every word.

"Nikki, you're impossible! I hate you sometimes! You can drive me crazy! I stop thinking straight with you because you know exactly how to spin my words around, so I seem incoherent even to myself. Just let me be! Let me be" repeated Sasha softly, staring right through the carpet in front of her feet "Don't you see that I'm in deep shit right now and I can't pay attention to you and your little games. Can't you see how screwed up I am? My own mom who's supposed to be on this earth just to love me and to care for me is so oblivious to her duties, feelings and reality that she hurts the most precious thing a person can ever have in this world ... her own child" added Sasha finally crying, crying hard. "I still love her and I want her to love me back! So badly! I want her to wake up from her own craziness and see me, remember she's supposed to love me and protect me and take me into her arms, kiss my forehead, rock me and telling me how much she really loves me" said Sasha sobbing so hard the girls could barely understand what she was saying.

"Let yourself really feel it, Sasha. Go through the whole emotion. Don't stop it, so you can finally let it go, honey."

Sasha kneeled on the floor, her chest bent over her thighs. She was finally feeling, finally loving and hating her mom, finally not trying to make sense of the whole mess and her mixed feelings, just letting them flow right through her.

Five minutes later, the other three girls stepped out of the office giving Sasha space to finally deal with what was in her heart. They knew her for almost four years now. It might not be too long of a time for a normal relationship to develop such depth that it has between the four girls who met in unusual circumstances – at a teenage rehab. They helped each other survive through all that and then pushed each other to stay with the program and live one day at a time, sober and clean. They opened up to each other in a matter of days. They talked about their hopes and fears, about their dreams and nightmares, about everything that was and was not. They all knew the worlds they lived in before they ended up at that luxurious little hell called rehab. They all learned to respect it but they never cared too much for it. Julie was a veteran there by the time the other three girls rolled in, but they bonded faster than Julie was able to bond with anybody in the 10 months she lived in that rehab. She was supposed to be out after 45 days, but she had no place to go thanks to her parents who were in worst shape than she was, so her grandfather paid good money to keep her safe and away from harm's way. "A little too late" she thought, but was very grateful when her grandfather bought her an apartment in Greenwich Village to move in with her now best friends for ever Nikki, Sasha and Lizzie. They were all trying to piece their lives together, figure out the future and live healthy, supporting each other every step of the way.

After a little bit over forty-five minutes, Sasha came out of the attorney's office with her written statement in her hand. Her face was all flushed, she looked exhausted, but put a smile on and said "All done. Hopefully forever" handed the statement to the young gentleman behind the only desk in the waiting area and walked out towards the elevators. When she couldn't hear anybody following her, she turned around and signaled the girls that it was time to go. They all obliged her without a word.

Lizzie couldn't help it but say "You are so kind for letting us use your boss' office. So understanding, sweet and handsome" sighed Lizzie staring at Mrs. Clifford's assistant with her cold ocean water blue eyes, biting her lower lip. "I took the liberty of writing my cell phone number on the statement. Please feel free to use it."

"Was that a wink? Were you just flirting with him in front of us. Lizzie!?!" inquired Julie jokingly.

"Bravo! I have never seen you so bold before. You're always Miss Shy and Precious. Nicely done! You've finally grown some balls. Very proud of you!" added Nikki.

Lizzie was blushing already, pressing the elevator button repeatedly "He can still hear you guys. Keep it down!"

The minute the elevator doors closed, Lizzie looked at her reflection in the metallic doors, playing with her stylish short hair with uneven bangs, and nervously asked "Do you think he'll call?"

Sasha was the first one to start laughing. She was laughing so hard they couldn't help but join in.

By the time the elevator got to the lobby they were all laughing so hard the people waiting in front of the elevator to get on were startled when the doors opened and the loud laughter sounds came out of that little box, filling the entire lower level of the sophisticated modern building where Sasha's attorney's office was located.

Those people's startled faces only made the girls laugh even harder.

On their way out of the building, a huge artsy black and white poster caught Nikki's attention. She stopped and read it while the girls are walking away apparently not observing Nikki's impulsive quick stop.

"Guggenheim Museum has the honor of hosting one of the world's most popular exhibits: A Life in Pictures - Louise Bourgeois.

In Bourgeois's universe, art is a recuperative practice; it can invoke and heal the deepest emotional wounds. [...]

For only three days! ..."

"Oh my God! I have to see it! I have to go and today is the last day! How come I didn't know about this? Have I fallen off the planet? This is huge! This is a sign. Girls, want to come? I'm going and I promise you this is going to be a very awakening experience. Just look ..." Nikki stopped as she turned around and saw this bald short man with a long thin mustache looking at her like she was from another planet.

"Excuse me" whispered Nikki going around the man and rushing through the doors to catch up with her friends.

They all saw the entire scene from outside and were laughing uncontrollably. Sasha was leaning against a black marble pillar tearing up from all that laughter. Julie tried to stop and let Nikki know they were laughing at her this time, but all that came out while cracking up, bending and putting her hands on her knees trying not to fall over was: "you ... and we were ... and you ..." pointing to where she was standing next to the poster.

Nikki turned around and saw the little man that she seemed to have scared away. She finally saw how hilarious the whole situation was and all that contagious laughter made her join them.

"So, what were you talking about in there in front of that poster?" asked Lizzie trying to compose herself.

"Oh, that yeah! It's an awesome exhibition at the Guggenheim Museum. We all have to go and today is the last day, so unless you have other pressing obligations that I don't know about, I'd love for all of you to join me in this experience of a lifetime. I promise you it's going to be good. If you really enjoy my work, this will blow you out of your socks ... your pantyhose to be more exact" Nikki added after looking at all of them wearing the "courthouse" skirt suit outfit!

"Let's go see it," said Julie. "Should I hold on to my pantyhose? I really love this pair and it's so hard to find ones that I like "she added bursting out loud.

***

Five minutes later they were all in a cab on the way to Guggenheim Museum.

They all got out right in front of the museum, still laughing. There were a lot of people waiting to get in.

"Wow, this must be something really extraordinary. I haven't seen so many people at a museum in a very long time. I'm intrigued. Good job Nikki!" exclaimed Sasha. "What do you know about this artist?"

"My favorite art professor, Mr. Pullock, introduced us to this artist. I can't remember too much, unfortunately, but what grabbed my attention was that the professor told us about the impact of childhood trauma on her art. The way she used all that to make her art and also through her art she was able to channel and release these tensions." Nikki pointed to the white and black poster that was prominently positioned right in front of the museum's door.

"In Bourgeois's universe, art is a recuperative practice; it can invoke and heal the deepest emotional wounds."

"Now that's something we can all identify with: childhood trauma. This should be interesting" said Julie walking inside the museum with enthusiasm and curiosity written all over her face.

"If this woman was able to get over her childhood problems through art, and heal herself completely, I'm going to quit what I'm doing and change my major to art. I'll come to classes with you Nikki."

"I believe there's art involved in anything we do, Sasha" responded Nikki, "you just need to let yourself see it. What you are doing at your job is art. Those projects you are working on at the U.N. are pure art. Takes a lot of courage, skill and creativity. Just like my paintings and drawings. You are awesome at what you do and shouldn't quit, ever. You believe in it and that's why you're so good at it. Keep helping those women who need your help. That's your art in this world!"

"I'm just an intern, it's not a job. Well, not yet. I wish it were, but first I need to finish school. Working for the Human Rights division sounds just right up my alley, especially for the women's rights. Too many of them don't see or know their rights. Just like my mom, she doesn't know how important she is to me and other people, how much I love her and rely on her, she has no self-esteem, so she turns to lawyers and courts to prove to herself that she has "the power". If I can't make her see the reality and fix her and give her some self-esteem back, maybe I can do it with other women. Women should know how beautiful, smart and important they are "sighed Sasha trying to come back to the present, to where she was, in a museum with her friends enjoying an art exhibit.

Lizzie started reading out loud: "This might be an unusual exhibition. It's the story of her life, which is documented in this exhibition with photographs, journals, and identification cards from her personal archives ..."

"Lizzie, do you mind reading it to yourself? People really seem to be into it, nobody's talking except you" said Julie trying to be considerate of others, just like usual.

"Sorry, of course"

The girls kept quiet and started moving slowly through the entire exhibition fully taking in the whole thing, reading about adultery, nurture, rage, guilt, fear of abandonment, looking at pictures, reading her journal pages, staring at her art, going through the artist's life, one big moment at a time, feeling her feelings, tasting her bitter anger, caring for her sick mother. There were people who were actually crying while going from room to room, being part of the story of Louise Bourgeois' life.

There were over a hundred works part of this exhibition that the artist created over seven decades, from the wooden constructions which made Louise Bourgeois famous, to drawings and prints, couple of her notorious "cell" installation, and significant sculptural works in marble, bronze and fabric. The museum did an incredible job at putting the exact amount of light and positioned it just perfectly to dramatize each and every peace and pair it up with the corresponding journal pages and description.

Later on, they met in front of the museum. They were all silent.

"Let's shake it off by walking in the park. Who's with me?" said Julie breaking the silence.

They crossed the street and stepped into the park.

It was one of those last warm sunny days of the fall. People were taking advantage of it, walking their dogs, taking a ride on their bicycles or just walking alone or with friends. There was barely a breeze moving the yellow, red and brownish leaves, breaking them free from the branches they were born and grew on, moving in what seemed to be a dance towards the ground where kids would play with them, pile them up and jump on them or just grabbing a whole bunch for their art class or just as a souvenir.

Couples were sharing this sweet pleasant afternoon sitting on a blanket and reminiscing the good old summer days that were gone and planning for the future, already thinking of Christmas gifts and last New Year's Eve party.

Lizzie was staring at an old couple that was walking on the alley in front of them. "That is the most romantic thing ever. There's nothing more romantic than a couple of old people hand in hand, smile on their face and love in their eyes. Look at them! That's exactly what I want from life: a man to love and be loved by, share our lives together and grow old together walking side by side, hand in hand."

"I agree, honey. That looks very romantic. I should paint it. I should draw it. That definitely has a lot of potential." Nikki stopped for a second. "That gave me an awesome idea that is starting to grow on me. I'm going to have a series of romantic works. I'm going to start my "love" collection. The love we all want and deserve in our lives. What do you think?" asked Nikki contemplating her new idea.

"That's the best idea you've ever come up with" blurted out Lizzie, before anybody gotta say anything, "and we should flood our apartment with all those pieces from that new collection of yours in order to flood our lives with all that love you're talking about, the love that we want and deserve in our lives. That sounds fantastic! When are you going to start working on it? I'm going to repaint the whole apartment so it goes perfectly with our new love collection. Is there anything I can do to help out so we can start this love flood?"

"Love flood?" pondered Nikki. "That actually sounds good. Thank you, Lizzie. That's what I'm going to call my love collection. Love flood! Sweet!"

Two little boys were trying to fly a kite despite the fact that there was no wind to help them get it high in the sky. One of them was holding on to the kite and the other to the thread and they were running and laughing one after another, not bothered by the lack of wind or futility of their efforts. They seemed to have fun just by trying, enjoying the whole process without worrying about the results.

"We should definitely learn from them," said Julie "I envy their innocence, their ability to enjoy the present moment with no expectations or worries."

The unmistakable broken music sounds of the ice cream mobile stand interrupted Julie. Lizzie was already rushing towards it. There has never been a time when any of them were able to take a walk-through Central Park and just pass by an ice cream stand and not buy some delicious "pick-me-up". That's what the girls called their favorite dessert and they had to have it no matter the temperature outside. They all loved this tradition and enjoyed it through and through, no guilt, no worries, no second thoughts.

Savoring their ice cream, they found a vacant bench right in front of the playground.

"Perfect! We get to enjoy our delicious dessert and look at happy faces, playing and laughing like nothing's wrong in this entire universe. It couldn't have been better if we had planned it ourselves" declared Julie while licking the drops of melted chocolate ice cream that were trickling down her fingers.

The freckles on a sweet tiny girl's face were in an unusual pattern and with the sun brightly shining right on her pretty little face putting her carrot red hair on fire, the pattern seemed to move and change shape and attracted Sasha's attention.

"It might be the warmth and the fact that this ice cream is pretty much the only meal I had today, but are the freckles on that little redhead migrating from one cheek to another?"

"Sasha, you should definitely eat more. That's funny. Migrant freckles! Next thing you know there will be migrant pimples, wrinkles and cellulite – and boom the world's biggest problems can migrate away at the flip of a switch. Now the only problem remaining is: where will we migrate all those to?" asked rhetorically Nikki. "Hey, Julie, how about you hold on to my wrinkles and cellulite tonight. I have a hot date! Can I migrate them to you or do you have plans also? And if so, who's staying home? Who can we migrate all those pimples to while we're out on a date?" Nikki pondered jokingly.

"Funny, Nikki. You are so funny. Ha! Ha!" replied Sasha, turning her attention to that red haired little girl. She seemed to be friends with everybody on the playground. They were all sharing some interesting stories that the girls couldn't hear and giggling like there was nothing in the world funnier than what they were just saying. Four of the kids split from the big circle and headed for the blue wavy slide. Waiting for their turn, they each climbed up those plastic stairs and sat neatly on the slide and let themselves go. Their giggles were filling up the afternoon air. Sounds of real happiness.

Second round came, then the third and they weren't bored and still kept going, nicely waiting for their turn and then giggling all the way down the slide.

"Make me do the same thing over and over again after waiting in line for it and I'll complain, ask for a raise and whine about how monotonous my life has become. But look at them! What happens to us later in life? Do we develop short term memory? They seem to miss that bug completely" philosophized Nikki again.

Seconds later after she said that, the redhead girl must have felt courageous and in mood for something different and she plunged full speed head first down the slide. It seemed like the world stopped breathing for a second waiting for the finality of this foolish bravery. It did not end well. She landed on her chin in the sand below the slide. For a second there was silence, she tried to pick herself up, then blood started gushing from an opened cut on her chin. The next second she was crying so hard and loud, couple of kids around her got scared and started crying as well and running to their parents.

A mature version of the little carrot head girl, rushed towards her. Picked her up, kissed her and tried to assess the situation as fast as possible, while calming her daughter in her arms with visible love.

"Hmmm! Only if things worked that way when we are older. We pay the consequences of our stupid actions." Julie didn't seem to feel too much compassion towards the little girl with a cut chin.

"Come on, Julie, where's your heart? Did you forget to bring it with you today? I can't believe you just said that" commented Lizzie. "We only learn from our own mistakes and you know that. I bet on everything I own – which is not much – but I still bet it all that that little girl will not try that stunt again. That's how we all learned. We never do what we are told to do, especially by our parents. We are little Dora the explorer when we are that age and want a taste of everything just to learn, just to experience it. And parents are there to make it all better at the end. Did you see how that mother rushed and help her in her arms and kissed her? No harsh words. And according to "mature" wisdom, what the little girl did was stupid. We could have predicted that ending, she didn't. But she will from now on."

Sasha's eyes filled with tears sitting on the bench next to her friends.

"What's wrong Sasha? Are you ok? Did I say something to offend you? I'm sorry for the lack of compassion I showed a minute ago. It must have been more envy than anything. I had to take care of myself at her age, I had to know what's best for me and what the consequences were for my actions. I seem to be a bit callous when it comes to happy children living their happy childhoods sometime. Forgive me!" begged Julie, looking through her purse for a tissue for Sasha.

"Don't worry Julie, it's not you. And just for the record, I'm on the same side with you unfortunately. I'm just envious as well. Looking at the whole scene it hit me what witch of a mother I have. Mothers are supposed to care, love us and protect us unconditionally. Why was I given a rotten mother? I can't even call her mother. She doesn't fit the description. The only time we were close was when she carried me for nine months and she probably hated me then as well. What did I do wrong? What debts do I have to pay that I have to have that woman as my mother? It's so unfair. It hurts so much. I just want this hurt to go away somehow."

"It will go away, we are here" said Julie kindly.

"Sorry, but it doesn't seem to matter. All I can think now is how good it felt to be numb, to not feel a thing. "

"Red alert!" exclaimed Lizzie. "You're not thinking what we think you're thinking? It's good to feel. It's the only way to work through all those emotions and troubles you have inside. You know what? Let's go to a meeting tonight. I think tonight there's an awesome meeting on relapse prevention only couple of blocks away from our apartment. Ok?"

Sasha did not say anything. She was just staring blankly in front of her.

"I'm coming too. Let's all make it a date" offered Julie.

"Sasha, you have to go. You have no choice in the matter. We are your family and we know what's best for you right now. I won't be able to make it, because I have a late class, but I might be there for the last part of it. In any case, you are going and we're all going to be there with you ... sooner or later, when it comes to me, but you are going and that's that" concluded Nikki.

"So, it's all settled then. We are all going to this relapse prevention meeting. Good! I haven't been to a meeting in a while now with my crazy schedule, but it is time to go. Let's go home then, so we can get a chance to eat, take a shower and change before we go. And Sasha, you are eating with us. You need to keep your body nurtured, so you can nurture your mind. It's all one. One will not function well without the other. You know that. Let's move it!" Julie pushed herself off the bench and waited for everyone to join her.

Chapter 3

Nikki was going as fast as possible through her salad. She had ten minutes left until her class started. She grabbed her stuff and ran out the door.

Pizza and salad. Dinner for the champions. Fast, easy and partially healthy.

Julie was playing with the melted cheese on the slice of pizza that she had on the plate in front of her. She picked it up and played with it like that string of melted cheese was spaghetti, lifted the slice of pizza way above her head, having those threads of cheese touch her mouth and slowly started chewing on that cheese until she got to the actual slice.

"Stop playing with your food" said Lizzie jokingly. "You just make me want to do it too and it gets too messy."

"It's not messy at all. That's if you do it right. I dare you! Come on! Pizza becomes the most interesting food on the planet when you eat it this way and plus, by the time you get to the actual slice you can barely contain yourself not to devour it in one bite, because it feels like it's the prize you won after a long and arduous journey ... the journey of the ever-moving melted string cheese," ended Julie with what seemed to be a bow. "Let the games begin!" said Julie with a deep voice as she grabbed another piece of hot pizza, lifted it over her head and tried to catch the strings of melted cheese with her tongue while her mouth was wide open in case the cheese volunteered to just drop into her mouth without much of a struggle.

The whole scene looked hilarious as Julie was trying to talk the cheese into giving up and surrendering her mouth. Lizzie and Sasha snatched the last slices of pizza and followed Julie in her crazy playful game.

"Let's see who's going to finish first after doing this whole thing correctly…from strings up to the slice" barely articulated mouth wide opened Julie while fighting to catch those moving cheese strings.

Sasha was already chewing on her cheese strings, halfway to her slice of pizza and she was watching the other two girls from the corner of her eye. The cheese strings were already cold but still full of flavor. The basil, and marinara sauce were infused in the cheese so deeply that she could smell them even though those strings were very thin. She was already drooling, inhaling the sweet and spicy marinara sauce that was sliding down the last piece of cheese. When she finally got to the slice, she raced her way through it like she was a malnourished woman that was left in the desert with no food to eat for days and days.

"Done" she screamed pushing the last piece of the slice into her already full mouth. The sudden burst of air that was needed for her to get the word "done" out, took with it half eaten pizza and sprayed it all over the table and her other two friends. They all followed suit as they burst into a core shaking laughter.

Tears were rolling down Julie's face, she was laughing so hard. The sounds echoed into their hallway and that made them laugh even harder.

Julie's phone started ringing loudly interrupting them. Wiping off her tears, Julie opened her purse to get her phone. "Today was a very dramatic day for us. I can't remember the last time we cried and laughed so much in one day."

Her whole demeanor suddenly changed once she saw who was calling. She seemed to be serious yet very excited. There was a special little light in her eyes and she looked like she was barely able not to jump out of her skin.

"It's Joe!" said Lizzie and Sasha in unison watching Julie shutting her bedroom door after her.

"This means it's only the two of us. We'll be going to this relapse meeting even if the hell freezes over!"

Sasha smiled at Lizzie "You are such a great friend. I understand if you chose not to go tonight. Everybody else bailed. It's ok. I can take care of myself."

"Are you crazy? I'm not going for you as much as I'm going for myself, so you would do me a huge favor if you'd accompany me. I am the one who really needs this. Now let's get ready" said Lizzie pushing Sasha off her chair. "I need to use the shower first, so do you mind cleaning up here really fast and I'll take care of what's left to do while you shower. Cool?"

"And don't tell me you won't shower. You need to. We both need to clean our auras before we go to the meeting. We need to brush off all the negative energy we got through the day. And especially this last one ... this asshole Joe character. We're both thinking about killing him every time he calls or doesn't call. But let's not think about this anymore and just clean our auras!" added Lizzie on her way to the bathroom.

"You sound just like Nikki!" yelled Sasha, so Lizzie could hear her.

"Well maybe she's onto something!"

***

"Hey, it's me" said Joe with a sweet low voice. "How are you?"

"I'm good, I'm laughing with the girls over a silly pizza contest we had" replied Julie. She was sitting on the soft carpet at the foot of her bed, her heart screaming with joy at the fact that Joe called.

"Ah, so you already ate. I was thinking about what I'm going to have too because I'm so hungry."

"Well, I didn't eat that much. I can always eat a bit more. Maybe a fruit salad or something" said Julie hoping he was going to ask her to come by and eat or go out and then go to his place.

"Are you sure?"

"Of course. You know me, I can always eat a fruit salad. I love fruit. Don't worry about it, really. I'll have a fruit salad or something" said Julie rapidly crossing her fingers hoping Joe will want to ask her out. Anything just to see you. Be around you. I missed you. Please invite me already, thought Julie. Just play cool, Julie. Play cool. Don't scare him off.

"Ok. How long will it take you to get here? I'm kind of hungry. I played ball with the guys after work and I'm actually starving."

"I'll jump in a cab and be there in half an hour, maybe less" offered Julie. "So, you played basketball with Dennis and the guys? Where? At that court in your neighborhood?" tried Julie to make conversation and connect a bit more to her man. "It sounds like you had fun. Good for you!"

"Yeah, ok. We'll talk when you get here."

"Sure. Of course. See ya. Bye"

"Bye"

Oh man, what am I going to wear? I wonder where we're going. Probably that sushi restaurant we both like so much, next to his building; the one owned by his friend Matt. Then I should wear something casual but still a bit sexy, so his friend would approve of me. My man can show me off and feel all manly. That's a good idea! But I can't look like I tried too much.

Minimal makeup, that pair of faded light blue jeans Joe likes so much and a top.

I need help with the top.

As Julie walked to the kitchen, she saw Sasha washing the dishes they all ate pizza on. "Oh, thanks for doing that Sasha" said Julie quickly. "When you have a moment can you please come to my room to help me out with something?"

Seeing that Sasha was continuing on her task, Julie grabbed her left arm and said" "Now, please. I'm in a hurry. Could you please help me? It will only take one second, I promise" and put on her begging puppy face that she knew worked with Sasha.

"Ok, fine. I'll help you, but stop manipulating me. You promised never to use that face with me again unless it's a true emergency and you truly are helpless."

"But this is an emergency ... for me" added Julie after looking up at Sasha's untrusting face. "I'm really sorry I used that face. I promised I won't use it. I'm sorry, but it's not manipulation this time, I swear. I just really need your help."

"It is manipulation if you talk me into doing something you want me to do when you see I'm doing something else. And especially when you feel that I should do it. You do feel that way, don't you? You're going to throw a fit if I say you crossed my boundaries, which you have, by the way, if you stop for a second and think of others except yourself."

"What's this? The third degree? Gosh! I only want your advice on the top to wear and it has turned into step work and boundaries and promises and manipulation." Julie couldn't believe how far this whole thing was taken. "If you don't want to help, just say so. I can do this alone, I just thought it would be nice to get your input because you have such good taste and know me so well. That's all."

"I'm sorry, too. I overreacted. Let's see those tops" sighed Sasha as she followed Julie into her bedroom.

There were a multitude of tops and dresses on her bed, so Sasha picked a green dress that was closest to her and handed it to Julie. "Go green" announced Sasha smiling.

"Ok, Nikki, you can stop now. I'm not a tree hugger" commented Julie sarcastically.

"He loves green, he told you so, remember? It's his favorite color. And you look really good in it. Get that dark purple push up bra and you're ready to go. I guess you won't wear jeans tonight."

After thinking about it for a split second, Julie took the dress from Sasha's hand. "Thank you. See how quick it was? And you helped me a ton."

"Just don't put that "I'm a ghost" makeup on. I know he kind of likes it, or so he told you once, but it kind of freaks me out. I like your lips pink, as nature intended them to be, not white. "

"Ok, thanks. I'll take that one into consideration."

"Into consideration?" asked Sasha and turned back to Julie. "It's one thing to make him like you and from time-to-time wear stuff you know he likes and it's another to do everything the way he likes it every single time. You're not doing anybody a favor, not yourself, not him. You'll lose all your respect in his eyes as he sees that he can play you like a toy. Please listen to me or at least promise me you'll think about it" finished Sasha and walked out the door feeling defeated.

Then started mumbling down the lobby into the kitchen.

"I hate that man and the way he plays with her. She acts like such a loser when it comes to him. I don't understand her at all. She's one of the strongest women I've ever met in my entire life. I hate him, but the problem has to be with her. I need to figure it out and help her out somehow. What is it about that emotional vampire that she likes so much? I want to shake her out of this relationship. And that's another problem. I think it's a relationship only in her head. If he uses her like this and calls her only at night when he gets lonely and horny, she must not be relationship material to him. Just a bootie call. That's what she is. And she cares about him so much. Ahhh, it infuriates me!"

"Wow, who crashed your party, girl?" asked Lizzie walking out of the bathroom with a towel wrapped around her head and one around her body. Her skin was still wet and smelling of sweet gardenias, her favorite body wash.

"Joe! He..." sighed helplessly Sasha trying to continue her thought.

"No need to say anything. He's a charming bastard. Every time he comes around, I can see why she has fallen head over heels for him. He's definitely one of the most charming guys I've ever met, but he uses his powers for evil" said Lizzie smiling a bit at her own joke. "No really, I have to remind myself how many times I've seen Julie cry over his incapability of acting like a boyfriend. They've been seeing each other for over a year and he can't call her girlfriend, he doesn't have her meet his friends, even though he met us, he seemingly never calls back unless he wants something, usually sex, at night ... To his defense he did tell her he was emotionally unavailable, but that kind of nonsense is served as appetizers in any relationship, right at the beginning when you're not sure if you want to see the other person regularly, or commit in any way. But he seems to somehow make her forget all about that when they see each other and she forgives his huge shortcomings every single time.

"She either has the brains of a chicken, which we all know she doesn't, or she's slowly going to stop caring about him. No one can hurt a person over and over again without any consequences, no matter how gorgeous he is," concluded Sasha with confidence.

"She's soon going to figure out she doesn't love him anymore and not know when all that happened or started. She just needs a little help from us to make that happen sooner rather than later. She also doesn't know when enough is enough and tries to rescue all the sick emotionally unavailable puppies out there, as she's tried to fix her family and was never able to. Now she looks to fix the world, one bastard at a time" finished Lizzie catching her breath. "Is that what's been bothering you?"

"Yeah, pretty much. I should let it go or do something about it, right?"

"We have to come up with a plan. We'll figure something out. Now I need to take another shower as I let that Joe poison my aura again" and with a short smile, Lizzie re-entered the bathroom.

Chapter 4

"Welcome to our monthly relapse prevention meeting" was written on a big worn-out sign right outside the medium sized ballroom of the hotel that has been hosting this gathering for as long as the seventy something year old woman at the front desk could remember.

The slightly musty smell of the room was just a reminder of how old this hotel was. Who knows when it was renovated last, maybe never, but by the looks of the perfectly glued wallpaper and functional light fixtures, you could assume they have been working on giving the hotel a new fresher feel. Good for them.

The meeting seemed to be more successful than the last time the girls attended it, when their sponsors coerced them into making a presence. They were all thankful they didn't have to make a commitment to this meeting. There was something about just the word 'relapse' that made all of them feel uncomfortable. It was more like cheating or screwing up big time. They only promised their sponsors they would come when one of them seemed to absolutely need it and Sasha seemed to fall into her past pattern of hating her 'unfair' life because of her mother, so they knew this was one of those times when they needed to come, no matter how uncomfortable they felt or how much they disliked the whole place.

The two girls set down in the back of the room, away from where usually the whole action seemed to take place. They got there late enough so they didn't have to read anything out loud, like the 12 steps, 12 traditions, what is an addict or any of those that were freely passed around in the room about 10 minutes or so before the meeting. They just wanted to be invisible, if possible, learn what they came here to learn and move on.

Less than a minute after they set down the meeting started. The cheerful young man leading the meeting did a great job keeping everybody's spirits up with his jokes and his enthusiasm while they all went through the beginning of the meeting routine.

"Really, who pays attention to all this part anymore. We all know it by heart. Can't we just skip to the speaker part and the shares?" whispered Sasha impatiently.

"We're doing it as a reminder for ourselves and especially for the new people. It's good for you" whispered Lizzie back. "Just focus on the words and stay in the moment. You'll understand it better that way, and plus, staying in the moment is the core message in our entire recovery program, so follow it. You can do it!"

A gorgeous young man was the first speaker of the night. He was tall, well built with big bouncy shiny curls all around his olive skin face, accentuated by piercing green eyes and luscious full lips.

"Hello, my name is Eric and I'm an alcoholic" he started.

"I hope he's at least eighteen or my thoughts about him right now would get me in jail in no time" joked Lizzie.

"I've been sober for three years now, that's if you don't count my last year's relapse. So, really, I've been sober for only 10 months."

"What can be wrong with his life. He's a gorgeous young man, looks like he has more than enough money, he doesn't seem stupid at all, quite the opposite ... I hate this stupid disease. It's screwing up one of the most perfect male specimens on the planet. I hope he can stay sober so we can have lots of babies together" whispered Lizzie again.

"Shhhh, Lizzie! I want to hear what he has to say" Sasha murmured back.

Both turned their heads back to the speaker as he seemed to be looking straight at them. "When they say that denial is the first symptom to reappear in the relapse process, they are right. And relapse was a process for me. It did not happen overnight; I didn't just come from a meeting one night during my recovery program and decided to taste some tequila" he paused as the audience understandingly started laughing at the idea of an alcoholic 'tasting tequila'. "I didn't all of a sudden got loaded. There was a series of progressive destructive thinking and behavior that pushed me over the edge where the only solution was to use. After being in the program for almost two years, I thought I was ok, I was cured, I didn't have to go to a meeting five times a week, I could have a normal teenage life, with all my other friends and classmates. I started skipping more and more meetings, then I stopped calling my sponsor daily and soon after I was convinced, I wasn't an alcoholic, that at this point I knew how to control myself and could drink a beer or two at the parties I was going to as a normal teenager. Well, the next thing I remember was being half conscious in the hospital, seeing my parents crying next to my bed. I've never felt as sick as then and later on I was told I was in an alcoholic comma and barely came out of it. That was a wakeup call for me. Now I know I'm stuck with this disease for the rest of my life, but I have the tools to defeat it one day at a time and be in control of my life, a healthy, joyful, sober life."

Everybody started applauding as Eric went back to his chair and set down.

A pamphlet was being distributed among the participants, while another speaker was invited to tell her story.

Triggers activate cravings, unattended cravings can lead to relapse! Stop the disease in its tracks; recognize those triggers.

• *Thought triggers – romanticizing the times you were using, magical thinking*

• *Feeling triggers – involve the five senses: seeing, hearing, touching, smelling and tasting*

• *Behavioral triggers – chugging, snorting sugar, shooting water*

• Situation triggers – stressful situations or relationships that happened while drinking/using

"Wow, I am definitely falling under the fourth trigger. At least I'm aware of it. It's kind of scary, but I have you guys, my sponsor, my program tools, I'm going to make it through this one too. I just have to remove this trigger and the only way to do it is to somehow remove my mother from my life for good, or at least until I become indifferent to this trigger. I need a lot of help. I don't want to relapse. I will not give her this power, "said Sasha firmly.

The moment she finished saying that she heard the second speaker say: "And I know now I need to live in the present. It's the only way to stay happy and stop worrying so much. I also learned to still wish for things and do the work for all my dreams not matter how big or small, but let go of my attachment to the outcome. That's what brought me the most disappointments and painful moments in my life. Let go and let God! Right? God or any other Higher Power that you believe in! And it works, it works so well. You should try it!"

"Exactly what I need and exactly what you were telling me Lizzie. Now that's a sign for me! I don't need more than two people to tell me the exact same thing in one day without taking it seriously! This is what I need to work on. Stay in the present, do the work and let go of the outcome. Sounds simple enough!" whispered Sasha.

The meeting ended with the serenity prayer.

"Hey girls, I came in a bit late and there were no chairs left, so I just chilled outside waiting for you, thinking about my new 'love flood' exhibition" said Nikki still contemplating that whole idea. "Lizzie, I know you're getting all excited about this but I don't want you to start pushing me, I need to do this on my own time, my own pace. Can you handle that?"

"Of course, whatever you need. You are the artist. Just let me know when you're done with your first pieces so I can start redecorating the house accordingly."

Sasha smiled at the entire conversation. Lizzie appeared to be so excited at the whole idea that she was literally glowing.

"So, what is your vision on this collection? What do you think your first pieces will be? Are you thinking drawing, painting, photographs …" she couldn't finish her enumeration because Nikki planted herself in front of Lizzie and said: "No, we're not talking about this unless I'm bringing it up. Remember? My own pace, my own time!"

"Ok, ok. I'm sorry. I didn't mean to get in your face like that. I was just curious, wanted to start planning what kind of paint to use for the walls, how to rearrange the furniture, what to buy, what to toss to go with your collection. It was just the control freak in me speaking … sorry!"

"No worries. Just wanted to make sure you're cool."

"Tell me about the meeting, did it do the trick? Maybe you should call your sponsor as well. I know you have us, but …" Nikki's eyes started searching for something or someone and then she finally asked "Where's Julie?"

"Better not ask" muttered Sasha between her teeth and then she twisted her sealed lips to the right.

"Oh. You don't even have to say it!"

***

"Joe, I'm here. Hello, Joe?"

I wonder where he is, he always leaves the door to the house open when he knows I'm coming, but most of the times I have to go look for him everywhere, and it's not a small house, or property for that matter. I guess is part of the fun! But I still don't want him to think that I'm sneaking up on him, so I should probably call his name couple of times while I'm tracking him down.

Let's see. Maybe he's in his master bedroom. Or maybe taking a shower ...especially after playing basketball with the boys, maybe he waited for me to take a shower and when he saw my cab pull into his driveway, he jumped in the shower to surprise me. Nope, nobody's in the bathroom.

Ok, maybe he took his dog for a walk. He had all the time in the world as it took me over 45 minutes to get here.

This is totally insane.

"Joe, honey, where are you? I thought you very starving, let's go! Are you ready?" yelled Julie rapidly crossing the beautiful dining room with a heavy crystal chandelier, placed perfectly above an ostentatious dark and heavy cherry tree designer dining table, with matching chairs. The red wall across the table was hosting a big inviting fireplace that was waiting for the cold nights of winter to warm up the lucky people that happen to be around it.

That fireplace brought great memories to Julie.

First time she came to Joe's place, was a freezing late fall rainy day. She was all wet and he made the fire just for her to warm up while her clothes were put in the dryer. He was a perfect gentleman, offered her dry clothes and a glass of wine. She couldn't remember what they talked about, but it must have been pretty innocent. All she recalls is that somehow, she ended up giving him a massage on the soft fluffy carpet in front of the fireplace. But nothing else happened. She still remembers the sexual tension. It was so magical. And when it was peaking, she asked for her clothes, got dressed and went home in the pouring rain not caring about anything but the happiness she felt inside. "This one has to be a winner! I'm sick and tired of all the losers I've been dating! He's so warm, and thoughtful, and such a gentleman!" she told herself while hailing a cab.

Julie was staring at the fireplace recalling that day. She snapped out of it as soon as she saw Joe crossing the kitchen and coming towards her.

"Great, you're here. Let's go into the hot tub babe, my muscles are so sore from kicking those guys' butts at basketball today. "

"I think I'm ok. I just took a shower, so I don't really want to get in the tub with you. Is that ok?" said Julie thinking she didn't want to spend another evening indoors with him, even if it were in bed. She knew what hot tub and his "only naked in my hot tub" rule would lead to. She wanted to go out. Go to dinner, have a decent conversation, in public. Maybe run into some of his friends and finally meet them, wouldn't that be lucky!

"As long as you keep me company, you don't have to get in the tub with me. I missed you; I want to talk to you."

Julie's heart jumped with joy; her eyes were getting moist with tears of disbelief. "I missed you too."

"Baby, can you please open up a bottle of wine and bring me a glass downstairs to the hot tub. Get yourself some juice or water or something - check the fridge."

"Sure. Of course. Does it matter what kind of wine?"

"Anything you want. You know me, I like all my wines or else I wouldn't have them in the house" finished Joe with a smile and winked at Julie.

"Go get yourself comfortable, I'll get the wine."

While carefully coming down the steep stairs with a generous portion of quality wine in her left and water in her right hand, she heard him talking. She peeked and saw him on the phone, in the hot tub.

"Hey, buddy, how are you? .... Good, good. And Jenn? You're still together, right? .... Glad to hear it. Well, hey, listen, I called you to see if you guys would join me and my girlfriend for dinner tonight."

Julie's jaw dropped to the floor. She couldn't believe her own ears. Did he say girlfriend? And he wanted his friends to meet her and go out together? Was it real? Was she asleep? She was grinning and rapidly kicking the floor with her feet like a soccer player at practice. She felt like she was going to get out of her skin.

"Oh, maybe some other time then" she heard Joe say.

"Shit, no other time, now! Come on ... Joe's buddy and his girlfriend, Jennifer, let's go out. I beg of you. This is a miracle and it has to come true. Please, God, make them come. Her heart sank as she heard Joe hanging up.

She tried to put the "I have no clue what just happened" face on and walked onto the terrace where the hot tub was with the glasses in her hands. Out of a sudden, a quiet evening, even out with just him wasn't enough for her. She wanted to meet his friends. She wanted him to make her feel he really cares about her, loves her and wants his friends to know she exists and meet her.

Now that he actually made that step, she knew she won't be happy again until they really do go out with some of his friends, any of his friends really. He lifted the expectation bar up all by himself. Oh, this is going to be a sucky evening. Damn it! In a way she wished she had never heard that phone conversation.

"Good choice in wine" said Joe after taking a nice gulp from his glass. She looked at him wishing he'd drink a little bit less. She was not sure he was an alcoholic, because he always stopped before getting completely smashed —like an alcoholic would do, but she definitely knew he had a problem when it came to wine...or beer. That part of him reminded her of her dad, but her dad also did a lot of coke, so the resemblance stopped there.

"It's your wine, of course it's good."

"Yes, that's true, except that wine that you gave me once, from Europe or something. That was just shitty, you know that, right? I wouldn't even have my enemies drink that. How embarrassing" finished Joe taking another gulp of his wine.

"I called a friend of mine to go out to dinner with us, but his girlfriend and he are tied up in something tonight, so they can't make it. I thought it would be nice if the four of us would go out to dinner, but it didn't work out" spilled Joe without any introduction.

"You look beautiful tonight, babe."

"Thank you" replied Julie blushing. She didn't know why the simplest compliment from Joe made her feel more special than anybody on earth. He was on a roll tonight. He was so sweet and loving and even called his friends to all go out together and called her his girlfriend. Too bad that didn't work out, but this has to be the beginning of the beautiful, loving relationship Julie was dreaming about and knew Joe being capable of. This was it. After fighting for over a year for his love, he finally gave in. It was all worth it.

She sipped a little bit of the water she brought down for herself and stared far away daydreaming.

"Are you sure you don't want to join me. It's not the same in here without you" said Joe with a sweet inviting voice.

"Yes, I'm sure" said Julie firmly, standing up. "Come on, let's get moving. I'm kind of hungry now. Weren't you starving?"

"Give me a minute to shower and I'll get ready so we can go. You are right, I am starving."

***

"Hey, girls, is there any of that pizza left? Some friends of mine are going to join me later on, so we can work on a project" announced Nikki.

Sasha looked at Nikki in disbelief "Again? You're having those people come to our place again? I told you she watched 'Pay it forward' way too many times" said Sasha to Lizzie with frustration.

"At least that boy in the movie was under the age of ten for God's sake. What is wrong with you Nikki? Bringing homeless people in our house? That's just insane and totally dangerous. They are strangers! You can bring them in your own house when you live alone, that's totally your choice but don't you dare put us in danger and take those chances and decisions for us."

"Maybe I will move by myself, away from you all. I can't believe you're so prejudice. Especially you, Sasha, interning at the U.N. for the Human Rights Committee? That's a load of crap. What? It sounds great to help them on paper, but when it actually gets to the real part of the Human Rights you back down and wash your hands? You're a total hypocrite!" yelled Nikki at Sasha.

"I'm sorry, but I think you're the one who's the biggest hypocrite in this crowd. You preach about good auras, positive energies, clean, sober and safe time that we all need to keep ourselves away from drugs and alcohol and learning a new safe, healthy way of life. What positive energies do those people have? When their lives are all screwed up. You're trying to keep me safe from my mom who's only a predictable mental danger, yet you bring the unpredictable eminent physical danger right in my living room. Maybe with a bottle of vodka and some drugs to use right under our noses, just to add the flavorful mental and spiritual danger to their resumes. I wish I could help, but none of us are able to do that. We are barely able to keep ourselves out of trouble and safe and sober."

"Fine, if that's how you see things, maybe I will move out. As a matter of fact, I'm going to see what I can find tonight. Why wait" threw Nikki at Sasha.

"Are you crazy?"

"Maybe I am. Maybe that's what it takes to actually care about what's going on around us. Crazy! We all need to be crazy to live in a harmonious world, full of trust and hope and love. If we don't start this trend who will? Every person who does something for the better matters. Don't you want to rid this world of hate and despair; of mom like yours who are just not supposed to be moms?"

"Don't you dare attack my mom like that! I don't wish for her to die. That's just mean and cruel. I can't believe you just said that. Who or what exactly makes you the right person to decide who lives and who dies, who's worthy to care for on this planet and who we should get rid of? What makes you God? Or Hitler?"

"Oh, so now you're calling me Hitler? Nice, Mrs. Human Rights! Very diplomatic of you."

"You're the one who want to get rid of people" replied Sasha underlining every single world. Then she stopped and took a breath and said "What I just called you was wrong. I apologize; I got carried away because I care about you. And I don't want you to leave us. We care about you and don't want you do move out! Please!"

"Are you begging me to stay?"

"Yes. In a way ... begging" barely murmured Sasha.

"Can I bring my gypsy friends with me?"

"Oh, so they are gypsies this time. Since we've known you, you always dreamt about traveling with the gypsies and now you finally found a bunch you're ready to live with? I'm happy for you, in a way, but you're magical thinking again. You are not ready to give us up and the program and go travel to every corner of this world, being with gypsies, random troubadours, gurus, missionaries ... whatever. You still need the structure of the program in your life. You need us as we need you!" finished pleading Sasha.

"That's very sweet of you to say, but I made up my mind. I love my new friends and they need me more than you need me. And to tell you the truth, they are much more fun than all of you put together. I know it will be better for me to go with them. Their life is much simpler, they learned how to enjoy simple things and they are going to teach me to do the same. I won't have to remember and focus on my own problems, my past, or any of your problems. Don't you see? We should all split and have friends like them and learn to put our past where it belongs, in the past. That's all we need to move on?"

"Move on from what, Nikki? We have a disease. We can't put it in the past. We'll always have this disease. We're addicts in recovery.

Remember, for us 'one is too much and a thousand is never enough'?! And it will always be that way. What you call past, is the things we went through that made us resort to alcohol and drugs and we have to dig it out and bring it to light, in order to be destroyed. We need to deal with our past, so it never has to bother us again and take us back to addiction. But more than that, we need to have people around us who do understand what we're going through one day at a time, and that's us: me, Lizzie and Julie."

Lizzie seemed to have finally something to say "Nikki, honey, Sasha is right. And you know she is or you would have been long gone. Even if your addict voice is fighting everything we say, the Nikki that wants the best for you, is there inside telling you not to go, to listen to us, because we do care, we do love you. And you are safe with us. We keep each other clean, sober and safe. We are a family for God's sake, we care about each other. We know each other's' secrets and corks and smelly farts," she stopped Lizzie for a second waiting for a reaction from Nikki, and after seeing her smile, she continued " We know how to take care of each other. We are a family. Don't break this family, please."

The smile on Nikki's face completely disappeared and was replaced by anger "Are you telling me that I am responsible for keeping all of us together. That if I leave, we all fall apart? Are you putting that kind of pressure on me?"

"Wow, you took that all wrong"

"Did I? How come? Maybe you can explain it better to me."

Sasha stepped in "Nikki, you need to take a time out, a deep breath or call your sponsor or something."

"I do now, don't I. And how would you know, princess know-it-all?"

"Because you don't seem to be in your right mind"

"And what's my right mind? Please, I might need to know for future reference" replied Nikki sarcastically.

"Look, clearly, we can't help you right now. We tried, but we can't."

"I can't?"

"No, you won't listen to us, so you need to use your tools to get a hold of yourself and get over this. This will go away, just give it a chance. Please, call Marie, call your sponsor, she'll be able to help you, you always love talking to her, just give it a try."

"That's not it."

"What's not it?"

"Whatever you're doing, you're just trying to control me. To make me obey, give me a sedative. But what you don't seem to understand is that you're taking me away from my dream. This is all that I've ever wanted, to travel the world. This is my dream and fulfilling my dream will make me and keep me happy, so I don't need the program anymore. I needed the program to find myself and to find my way in life, but now that I have, I'm free to follow my dreams."

"Your dreams?" asked Lizzie puzzled. "How about your school? Your art? The "love flood" collection you were talking about. Aren't those part of your dream, part of your path, big part of what makes and keeps you happy?

"A part. Yes, I won't give that part up. I'll continue my art wherever I go. It can only be better, while I experience the world. And if need be, I can always come back and finish school at a later time. Right now, a unique opportunity has shown itself to me and I'm going to take it. Please be happy for me!" and with that, Nikki ran into the night.

Chapter 5

"Julie, please call us as soon as you get this. Nikki ran off ... again" sighed Lizzie. "We're really worried and we never got the chance to get some information on what she was going to do and who those people are that she's hanging out with. You usually have a better idea than us about her way of thinking. Plus, she talks to you more than she talks to us, so maybe you have a better idea than us on where she could be and how to approach this whole thing. Please call us back as soon as you get this. It really is an emergency. She was talking something about gypsies. Did she ever mention anything about gypsies that she might have not told us? Ok, this message is long enough. The point is: call us immediately. We're home. Thanks!"

"She didn't pick up, did she?" asked Sasha with a knowing nudge.

"No, but I hope she's really having a good time and hopefully she's going to check her cell phone very soon. But if Joe is in his romantic mood ... she's lost for tonight. Good for her, bad for us. Really bad for Nikki, because if anybody can help Nikki now, that would be Julie."

***

"Where do you want to go eat, babe?" asked Joe with the sweetest voice.

Julie was in heaven. She couldn't believe her ears. It was everything she always wanted from Joe. He was perfectly sweet and loving and caring and understanding and ... so ... so much like she always wanted him to be. After so long of putting up with all his "emotional unavailability", he finally reached his "perfectly emotional" destination. Great! What if it's all a dream?

"Honey, what do you think about a restaurant that I know near the water. We could watch the sunset, drink a glass of wine or water for you and have dinner. I want to talk to you, to hear you, listen to everything you want to say. I missed you. I want to spend as much time as possible with you" finished Joe and hugged her really tight, then passionately kissed her running his hands through her hair, touching her face and following his touch with hot small kisses.

"Yes, sure, that sounds fantastic. But maybe we should stop fooling around and going to dinner, so we can actually eat, and enjoy a sweet conversation, some wine, a virgin cocktail for me and what it looks like is going to be a beautiful sunset."

"You're right" said Joe between two smooth kisses on the left side of her neck. "And when we come back, we can cuddle for a long long time. I just want to feel you near, hold you tight" whispered Joe into Julie's ear.

Julie's head was spinning. She did not need any wine to feel tipsy. She was in relationship heaven with Mr. Right. She knew he was capable of being a perfectly loving partner. Finally, yes, she worked on this for so long, hoped, cried, fought and it finally arrived ... everything she wanted in a lover. He was so attentive, so loving and caring.

They walked out of his house, went towards the parking lot where he had his car, hand in hand. Before they got into the car, he softly touched her face with both his hands and kissed her. Julie's knees gave way, but he was faster, as he moved his right arm around her waist and held her up.

"You're not going to faint on me, are you?" he asked with an affectionate smile that warmed her up in the chilly fall night. "Are you sure you're not hungry?"

"I'm not hungry" replied Julie.

He looked at her, his voice got serious when he asked "Are you pregnant?"

"Of course not," quickly lashed out Julie. "You've asked that so many times. Do you have some sort of an obsession? Do you have a kid somewhere I don't know about?" said Julie offended. Then she finally looked at his confused face and added "No! I am not pregnant. I do not want children because I am not ready and probably wouldn't be a good mother. So, don't worry, I am not pregnant. Plus, I've been on the pill since I got my first period, my body wouldn't even know how to produce an egg."

"Julie, you would make a perfect mother, seriously. Never doubt that. You are so great, understanding and nurturing" said Joe trying to regain control.

Julie did not say anything. She was actually thinking about maybe getting off that pill at least for a month and letting a higher power decide if she should get pregnant or not. She loved Joe more than she loved anybody else in her entire life. She loved him more than she loved herself. Joe had this softer side of him that he decided to show her tonight, a vulnerable, loving and caring side. He would make such a great dad, and she would be the mother. They would make a perfectly normal and loving family, like the ones you see in the movies.

But what if he would hate her for lying to him and getting pregnant? Maybe he would take her baby away, considering her past, but then again, with her grandfather's money, she knew she would get to keep her child. Then she would be a single mother, a great single mother, maybe one of the best single mothers out there. But Julie wanted the whole perfect family picture, so the father had to be part of it.

She dreamed about Joe being that man who would fill in the husband and father to her child's figure, but as much as she dreamt about the idea of all that happening, there was a part of her that only wanted this entire dream to come true when both of them were ready, when he was ready to be vulnerable at all times with her and let her love him the way she wanted to love him and him love her the way she wanted and deserved to be loved. She could lie to herself all the time about his feelings for her and come up with reasons for his immature actions and the rude way he was treating her. She was able to rationalize anything when it came to him, but for some reason, she wanted him to want this baby as much as she did, with the whole loving family as the big picture.

It was clear to her that he did not want to take responsibility for anything that ever happened in his life. He always loved to blame everybody else for anything that didn't go his way. He wanted her to get pregnant without him asking her to, so in case things did not go the way he wanted them to go, he could just blame her for tricking him and make himself a martyr. He wanted to have no choice in every serious matter, so he could blame others. He even talked about of couple of reasons why they 'had to' get married, so he'd be pushed into it.

Moving in with him, marrying him and having a child with him would be so easy, should she choose to lie, cheat and push him into it. But they would not be happy. Julie wanted more than anything to be happy, hopefully with the man she loved so much. But no matter how much she loved him, against all his clear emotional problems, no matter how much she rationalized every mean thing he did to her, there was this strong part of Julie that did not let her compromise her happiness more than she already had in the almost two years they've been dating. She tried to fix him, so they could be the perfect couple she always dreamt of and then, they could get married and have children. Her dream would come true.

She looked at him and felt like she was getting so much closer to the destination, to his heart, for real this time. The last two years were full of pain and disappointment. Every time she called him and he did not pick up the phone. She couldn't rely on him for anything. He would only call her whenever he felt like it. He met all her friends and family, but he never introduced her to anybody important to him, none of his close friends or family. He did tell her he was emotionally unavailable, but that was a bunch of crap as she saw him change overtime slowly but surely.

Julie was prepared to wait until he was able to completely open up and literally ask her to marry him and have his child. She was dreaming about that moment, every long hour. The only thing she was scared about was that she might be all dried up and stopped loving him by the time he'd be ready. Every time he hurt her now it seemed to hurt less and less. Was she still in love with him or just stubborn? Julie shook that idea away and smiled back at him.

"Thank you for saying that, but right now I'm not ready to have a child. I wouldn't worry about me getting pregnant. I was just enjoying your kiss so much that my knees went soft on me. See what kind of power you have over me? You must love that, don't you?" said Julie weakly to deflate the whole seriousness of the subject that was brought up.

"Hmm, so that's what my touch does to you, my dear lovely Julie" said Joe smirking and touching her again.

They got into his car and started driving to the restaurant.

It was already dark outside, but she could still hear the water clicking against the shore, when they got out of the car in front of the restaurant. It smelled like the ocean, but the second they entered the building, the strong aroma of garlic penetrated her nostrils making her salivate intensely.

"Garlic, baby. I know how much you love it, that's why I brought you here. Surprise!" announced Joe proudly. "And look at those great couches they have. Do you mind if we sit on a couch instead of at a table, or if you want to sit at a table, that's fine with me also."

"It's ok, we can take a couch," said Julie smiling to the hostess.

"Come on sit next to me, I want you close to me," said Joe pulling Julie so close to him that she lost her balance and fell right into his lap. They both started laughing and he kissed her again. "You know that I love you, right?"

Julie stared at him.

"Do you want to hear it again? I'm sorry I don't say it as often as I should. I love you! I love you Julie!"

"I love you too, Joe! You are ..."

"Can I get you anything to drink?" interrupted a cute brunette waitress.

"A bottle of your best white wine, please, and a bottle of Don Perrier for the lady. We're going to look at the menu in a minute" replied Joe dismissing the waitress.

He usually was very flirtations with the waitresses, but it seems like tonight he only wanted to dedicate all his time and sweetness to Julie.

She wanted to record every minute of the conversation, every compliment he was paying her, every word he was saying. She couldn't believe it, she couldn't digest it and she desperately wanted to remember all that was said the second day, and the day after, and the day after that.

It was all happening, but she couldn't really believe it. It was such an amazing night.

After they fed each other dinner and kissed not worrying about who was going to see them, they walked outside for a romantic walk on the shore. The cold breeze made Julie shiver. She had left her coat in the car and was only wearing her backless green chiffon dress.

Joe stepped back and took her in his arms. "Maybe we should return home, honey. I don't want you to freeze." Then he picked her up and took her to his car, put her in the driver seat and said "I never let anyone drive my car, but I had a lot to drink and you had water all night. Do you mind?"

Joe wanted her to drive and admitted that he had too much to drink? Julie couldn't take it anymore. This was turning out to be the perfect night and he was proving out to be Mr. Perfect.

Once they got in the car, he started to search for a song, and when he seemed to have found the one he was looking for, he started singing along serenading Julie. He grabbed her right hand and started kissing it lightly.

Julie couldn't recall how they got to his place, but apparently, she got there and was able to park and get to his bedroom. The dress got on the floor way before she could even say she wanted to go home. She thought she should have gone home and not spend the night given the way she left the girls, but she stopped thinking the minute Joe's lips touched her neck, while his hands skillfully unzipped her dressed and slipped it right off of her.

***

Lizzie was sitting next to the phone hoping for Nikki or Julie to call.

"Are you still up?" asked Sasha yawning as she opened her eyes. "Apparently, I fell asleep on this uncomfortable couch. Was the movie good? How did it end?"

"Don't worry, I didn't pay too much attention to that movie either. It was a waste of money. We should have just watched some cable or HBO, but we had to find something on demand. "

"Oh, come on, we needed something to take our mind off what's going on and comedies used to work for us before, but I guess it all grows old after a while. And Julie wasn't here to defuse our little bomb called Nikki."

"Well, "said Lizzie, "I hope both of them are enjoying themselves, and are safe!"

"I get it, you're worried about Nikki's physical safety and Julie's heart. Oh, you are so sweet! And even if I'm half asleep I can still see how real your love for all of us is" commented Sasha hugging Lizzie.

"Now you should go get some sleep" added Sasha.

"No, I can't sleep. I'm just going to read a book or something, but you should go to sleep because you have a full day tomorrow."

"You are right. I wish I could stay awake, but my personal drama today took everything out of me."

"Don't worry about it. Just go to sleep and if anything, new happens I will let you know. Have a good night" said Lizzie blowing Sasha a good night kiss.

***

"Honey, I could cuddle with you forever. We are so perfect for each other. I don't want to fall asleep, just stay awake and touch you, kiss you, smell you. Talk to me please, just say anything. I love to hear your voice honey."

Julie's heart was melting. She didn't want to go to sleep either. Was this the day that will change their entire relationship, the entire way he looks and feels about what they are actually having? Julie was hoping that was the case with all her heart. What else could it be? He was finally giving into her and all the love she's been showering him with for such a long time.

"I love to hold you like this. Stay close to me tonight, please."

"Ok, I will, I promise. Just go to sleep now, honey" whispered Julie massaging Joe's right wrist.

"Sleep tight, honey" said Joe planting a kiss on her head. " I love you!"

There was a sweet silence and then Joe whispered into Julie's ear "We're going to be together for a very long time, aren't we?"

She stopped breathing. Did she hear that right? She couldn't ask. She didn't want to break the spell.

Chapter 6

A little movement woke her up. Joe was getting out of bed and to the bathroom.

Julie hoped he'd be back to bed afterwards, because it was so dark outside. It couldn't have been later than four thirty or five in the morning.

Ten seconds later she heard the shower running.

"Oh well, I guess I'll just get up as well," she said out loud jumping out of bed. He always does it. He wakes up really early in the morning, and can almost never go back to bed.

Julie was wondering what kind of skeletons he might have in his closet that he was not talking about, that won't let him sleep too well at night and make him jump out of bed very early in the morning.

The door to the bathroom opened and he emerged into his walk-in closet with a dark green towel around his waist. His wet body was sexier than ever and Julie's mind flashed back to the hot, passionate, orgasmic sex they had just hours before.

If she had more courage, she would just jump on him right then, but she knew better. She knew how dry and "back to business" he was in the morning, like they never shared anything close to the intimacy they melted into the night before.

After almost years of being together she felt like she knew him so well. Maybe that's why he was building up a wall between them – he was too afraid to be vulnerable especially with someone as sincere, loving, and nurturing person like herself.

Julie's mind wasn't giving her a break. Nikki's words were hunting her "How are you ever going to be happy with him if you always have to take care of him while nobody takes care of you? If your mind doesn't stop rumbling when you're with him, he's not for you! He will never make you happy. He is supposed to be your oasis, your little island of love, joy, care, not worry, fear, and agony. Stop thinking so much! Just feel and your heart will tell you what to do. Your heart wants you to be happy and your mind is a judgmental, arrogant, rationalizing dictator, who will find ways to control you, sabotage your happiness in order to pump hot air into your ego. Stop being stubborn, listen to your heart and stop your arrogant mind that wants to win no matter the consequence. And who deals with consequences? Your heart! Wise up! Stop thinking! Start feeling!"

Tears were coming down her face. She knew what she was supposed to do but couldn't bring herself to do it. "I'm so weak when it comes to him! Why? Oh God, help me!" whispered Julie to herself.

"Why are you up? Go back to sleep! I just have to do this thing", said Joe coming out of the closet startling her.

"I forgot to tell you last night, but I need to meet with a friend of mine for breakfast" lied Julie, giving into her urge to run away and leave him behind before he leaves her behind, just like always, morning after morning, day after day. He had already left her before she woke up, the second he opened up his eyes and got out of bed. She felt it and was just trying to protect herself by running away from it.

"Do you need me to call you a cab?" offered Joe. He seemed so serious in the morning. Sometimes Julie felt she was some kind of a prostitute, a booty call. But he was so sweet at night...it was like an addiction – she knew it was bad for her but couldn't stop herself from falling for it over and over and over again. No matter how much she went through pain and hurt and disappointment when it came to their relationship.

"I'm good. I always find one faster once I'm out in the street" said Julie grabbing her coat, giving him a quick kiss and rushing out the door.

While looking for a cab and going down the street, her mind wasn't stopping. She wasn't crying anymore like before when she felt pushed out of his house, she just wanted to get home, run away.

"I'm a screwed-up addict, if not drugs or alcohol then with this dickhead! Why can't I just do the right thing for myself? I love him. Do I? Do I still love him and I just can't give up and move on? Why am I so stubborn especially when it comes to a wrong thing like this one? I want my ego dead. All I want is to learn humility, that will keep me honest to myself and happy" said Julie out loud while hailing a cab.

"Great, I'm talking to myself now. I'm not just a pathetic loser, I'm crazy too. Maybe that's it! I'm just crazy" added Julie running after a cab that was stopping to drop somebody off.

It wasn't easy to run on high heels. Her left heel got jammed in a little grid and she was going face down, when a strong arm caught her and lifted her up on her feet. She looked up and a green-eyed handsome man was smiling at her. "Your cab is waiting, beautiful lady!" He said and opened the door for her. She got in and recited her address staring at her hero. She felt embarrassed.

The female cab driver smiled at her and said: "Wasn't that just the nicest thing? What a gentleman! Him, I would definitely take home to my daughter!"

The door was shut closed and the car started moving.

"Yes, I wish my boyfriend would be like that, but he's clueless, totally clueless. Man, I can pick them! And then I can't let go!" she found herself confessing to this complete stranger.

"We always go back to what we know. Doesn't mean it's right for us, but it's familiar", replied the cab driver.

Julie felt compelled to say to that "We are creatures of habit, says one of my best friends."

***

Sasha was running down the stairs with her laptop bag, a backpack and a big presentation pad under her arm. She was holding on to the rail jumping two stairs at a time, she turned right to get to the next flight of stairs and ran into someone.

"This is just my day!" she heard Julie saying.

"Julie, thank God!" exclaimed Sasha moving her pad out of the way. "Did I hurt you?" but she didn't stop to hear her answer before she began her tirade: "Nikki just bailed on us last night. She said something about some gypsies and us being in the way of her spiritual enlightenment. She didn't give us time to say much, and apparently everything we said was wrong because it just seemed to push her more and more away from us. And you weren't there to help us! You always know what to say, but you weren't there and she disappeared and we called you and left you lots of messages. Her cell phone is off. We didn't know what to do, where to look. She really looked all serious and crazy. It sounded like she was going to leave us for good this time. She usually calls after she calms down, but this time, she didn't. Lizzie has been sitting next to her phone all night long."

"Ok, calm down! I'll take care of this. Where are you going at this hour?"

"I got a call from work. My boss needs me to change this one thing to the presentation and I have to get to class by eight" answered Sasha.

"Your boss is a freaking vampire! She sucks you dry. Let her make the freaking change. You're just an intern, she gets paid to work there. Plus, you put together the whole thing – pretty much. She should kiss your ass and wake up at 4 AM to make that change herself!"

"Julie, I don't have time for this! I know, you're right but sometimes that's the way the world goes. It sucks, but I'm an intern with huge aspirations, so my effort has to be as huge as well. I can take it! I love what I'm doing and someone will see it eventually."

"Not your boss for sure," threw Julie back.

"Maybe, maybe not. I have to run now!" said Sasha and started rushing down the stairs again.

"Oh, how was your night?" asked Sasha stopping for a second to hear Julie's response.

"It was a fairytale. He's my Mr. Perfect. I'll tell you later."

"Sweet, see you later! I'm happy for you! Call me if anything new happens."

"I will. Go now!"

***

The bitter sweet aroma of coffee was coming from the kitchen. It smelled like a coffee shop. The morning breeze was flapping the blinds making a constantly irritating soft noise. But it did not seem to bother Lizzie who was snoring with her head on the kitchen table and several different mugs of coffee all around her.

Julie closed the kitchen window as silently as possible, moved slowly towards the table and grabbed the mugs of coffee and put them all in the sink. She was debating if she should wake Lizzie up and send her to her room, but she seemed so comfortable she didn't want to wake her up and ruin her sleep.

So, she went to her room, picked up the lilac fleece blanket she had folded on her armchair and wrapped it around Lizzie as lightly as possible and then just stood there staring at her snoring and smiling in her sleep like a content kid who was dreaming about getting her favorite present for Christmas. She did not want to break her out of that sweet dream, so she grinned and turned around to go to her room and start making some phone calls to find Nikki.

Her room looked a bit messy, with several outfits spread all over the bed, her flannel teddy bear pajamas on the floor, next to her closet, and the clothes she wore the day before thrown next to the hamper. She was in a hurry the day before to change and get to Joe's, as he surprised her with his call, as usual.

Julie was cleaning up her room while planning out the way she was going to get a hold of Nikki or find her. She was going over the little information she got from Sasha.

"I guess I'm just going to take my chances and call Nikki first", said Julie out loud while folding her pajamas and placing them in her closet "then, considering I have no idea what she was saying when she was talking about gypsies I will just have to go around and talk to some of her friends," she paused and seemed to think about it for a second, "Nick might be just the friend I'm looking for. I'm going to start with him after I call Nikki."

She picked up the cell phone, took a deep breath and dialed Nikki's number. It went directly to voicemail. She did not want to be found. Great! Well, at least she might listen to her voicemail when she was ready to hear from them.

"Hi Nikki, it's Julie. Sorry for having to leave like that last night. It was rude of me. We had plans and I completely abandoned all of you guys and went to Joe's. I am sorry. I love you guys more than anybody in this world, you are my family, but sometimes I just feel like I have to take a break, have my life, some experiences away from my family. It's normal and healthy and I know you understand me. I came home and wanted to talk to you about what had happened last night, but I guess you didn't spend the night home either. Ha! How about that? I guess you'll have a story to share with me too. I can't wait to talk to you. You are the only one who can help me out. Your advice is so insightful, it always amazes me. I trust you completely. All the love, awareness and spirituality you preach is so rare. When you are done sharing your gift with the lucky people, you're with right now, please call me. I can talk to Lizzie and Sasha, but it's not the same thing. You have a special gift and that gift brought us all together, you are the only one who truly listens to me and understands me and I seem to understand you. We help each other all the time and now I need your help, please. Just like me, you need to replenish your soul with new experiences and share your gift, so enjoy your time away and tell us all about it when you came back home. We are your home, we are your family, we know you and love you. Huge hug from us my dear. Love you!"

Julie put her cell phone down, set on her bed and took a deep breath. Where was Nikki? She usually left her phone on when she took her 'time away' from them. This time was different, why?

A knock on the door woke her up from her reverie.

"Julie, are you in there?"

"Come in Lizzie, I'm here. I was just leaving a message for Nikki."

"We did that already," said Lizzie "several times."

"Sasha might have mentioned that."

"Sasha, oh yes, where is she. I was looking for her when I heard your voice in your bedroom and came in to make sure I wasn't hallucinating."

"She had to leave. Her boss called her in the middle of the night to come and make some sort of a change to a presentation" muttered Julie with what seemed to be discontent. "She's exploiting our brilliant Sasha for nothing. I hope she'll wise up and give her a real chance and a permanent job in the office, because if anybody deserves it, that would be Sasha."

"She called her again? What's going on in that office? Is Sasha the only one who can make changes? Is she the only one working in that office? Or is she the only one working for free, so they work her to the bone for free? Isn't that exploitation?"

"Funny you say that; exploitation in the human rights department at the UN. How hypocritical would that be? Should we call the media?" commented Julie laughing at the idea. "You know how smart Sasha is. She probably put together most of that presentation, so she would be the only one who could fix it properly. This might be a good chance for her to get hired for real. It's her dream, she has to fight for it."

"That's true" Lizzie became all serious, set herself next to Julie and asked "So, what are we going to do about Nikki? Do you have any ideas? We can't just wait and see, right?"

"I was thinking of calling Nick." When she saw Lizzie's confused face she explained "It's that guy she does Kundalini yoga with."

Lizzie looked even more confused.

"That weird breathing yoga class we all went to in Brooklyn couple of months ago, at that Australian lady's apartment, gong playing ... You still don't remember?" said Julie looking at Lizzie's face for some sort of a sign of recollection. When she finally saw it creeping up on her face, she stopped throwing hints at her.

"Great, you remember!"

"Yes, I do. I do. That yoga session was a bit too much for my poor soul. But I do remember the two hot guys that were there. I went on a date with one of them, the lawyer guy. I thought he was the one: smart, handsome, wealthy, spiritual. What else can one look for? But apparently, he was too much into soul searching to be able to perform physically."

"Ouch!" laughed Julie. "You are looking way too hard for Mr. Right. You have to stop. There are millions of perfectly great men out there, just open yourself up and look around. I bet you won't know which one to start with."

"I thought I was opened. I am looking for love. And love will have to come to me. And it will. If I'm picky or not, it does not matter, what matters is that I know what I want in a man and I know sooner or later I will get it."

"I know you will" replied Julie smiling.

"So, let's go back to that yoga breathing teacher. Do you think he'd have an idea about Nikki's whereabouts?"

"He might. Last time I went to his yoga studio with Nikki, there were a group of gypsies preparing for a private class with Nick. I know that because Nick told that to Nikki and she was getting all excited and asked me if I could take a cab back because she wanted to talk to the gypsies. Remember she had a fantasy for the longest time about joining a group of gypsies, and travel with them and learn their ways, learn to have a clean heart, enjoy life and live in the moment. She made it sound so appealing that I would have joined them in a heartbeat as well."

Lizzie smiled back. "I bet Nikki will let us know if it's all she thought it was going to be ... if she really is with them right now."

"OK," said Julie, "now I just want to call Nick, but I don't have his phone number. I'm going to look for it in Nikki's rolodex. I always told her to upgrade and tech up, but now I'm happy she is one of those people who loves to have it on paper. Let's go to her room and find that number!"

Both of them walked into Nikki's purple room. The sweet smell of her favorite incent was impregnated into the walls, her purple curtains and numerous decorative pillows. The rolodex was on her small teak dresser, next to her laptop. Julie picked it up and started going through it. It wasn't under N, for Nick.

"Oh no, I can't remember Nick's last name. Actually, I don't think I ever knew his last name. I hope I don't have to look through this whole thing, she must have hundreds of contacts in here. Man, this girl really loves to meet new people, look at this thing" said Julie frustrated.

"His studio is named Breathe Life or Joy or something. I can't remember exactly, but I do remember it was breathing something. And don't ask me why I remember that, because I just don't know. It's one of those random facts that just got stuck in my brain" blurred out Lizzie in one breath.

" Maybe because you should remember to take a breath now and then while talking" laughed Julie at her. "That is genius though. Let's look under B ... br... breathe ... Breathe Love with Nick Bahri. This is it! Breathe Love! Yes! And there's a number on this card, perfect! Give me the phone!"

Lizzie ran to the kitchen and grabbed her phone that was sitting there next to her all night long waiting for a call from Nikki.

"Here you go" said Lizzie throwing it to Julie from the doorway.

Julie caught it and dialed the number. Nobody picked up, so she hung up and called again.

"I can't just leave a message. I have to talk to him."

"Hello. This is Julie, Nikki's friend, the one who wants to open an eastern medicine meets western medicine rehab. Remember me? I was talking to you about integrating your services into my idea? Well, anyways, I am not calling about that, even though I do want to talk to you about that some more once I finalize my business plan. Right now, I'm calling about Nikki, so please call me back as soon as possible. My number is two one two five three eight eleven eleven. Thanks!"

"So, what now?" asked Lizzie.

"Now we're going to his studio. There's an address here. Just let me call my professor to excuse myself from class. Nikki is my priority today!" replied Julie walking towards her room.

Almost an hour later, Lizzie and Julie found themselves in front of 'Breathe Love' studio. They walked in and went directly to the front desk. Behind the desk was a tiny very fragile looking young girl, dressed in white from head to toe. She almost looked like a ghost with a welcoming smile on her face. "Welcome to Breathe Love. May abundance, joy, and happiness accompany you on your life's path."

"Thank you" said Lizzie bowing her head just like the ghost girl did a second ago. "Is there a way we could talk to Nick. It's very important!" said Lizzie with as much seriousness as she could muster after bowing her head like that. "We're friends" added Lizzie quickly.

"Tell him it's about Nikki and it's very important" finished Julie.

It seemed like Nikki's name made an impact, because after hearing that the ghost girl bowed and made her way in one of the back rooms.

Five long minutes later she returned, smiled at Lizzie and Julie and said: "He wants you both to attend his class, free of charge and then and only then he will speak to you once the class is over."

Lizzie started laughing. "You are kidding me, right? What do you mean 'then and only then'? What kind of condition is that? It's insane. Is he crazy? I'm out of here."

"This one is not about you, Lizzie. Come on. We need to talk to him and he will understand how serious this thing is when he will see you and me joining that class. He knows what you think about his style of yoga. You made that clear to him last time you were here. Now let's go in and do it for Nikki. I will actually try to enjoy it" commented Julie grabbing Lizzie by her arm and literally dragging her to the room pointed out by the little ghost girl.

The class had started, so they silently snatched couple of lamb skins that were on a side and used them as mats, as everyone in that class was doing, to improve their aura, according to Nick. Nikki was always using a small piece at home that she meditated on.

After the class was done, spicy tea was offered to each participant. Lizzie was just happy to be done with it and was fidgeting, waiting for everybody to leave, stop socializing, so they could talk to Nick already.

Julie seemed to socialize and go with the flow which irritated Lizzie even more.

"So, what did you want to talk to me about," heard Lizzie coming from behind her. She turned around and Nick was standing right there, serene, gorgeous and happy. Only if she would cut that awful beard off and put him in some trendy clothes, he would probably be too perfect. Yes, something has to be wrong with him. Maybe it's all that meditation, and plus it kind of scares Lizzie off when he breathes and meditates with his eyes rolled over in his head. Yup, she peeked. She couldn't stay with her eyes close for thirty minutes and just breathe and meditate like everyone else. She was worried about Nikki!

"She took off on us last night and said something about some gypsies" answered Lizzie.

"I understand" replied Nick calmly.

"No, I don't think you do. She does take off like that now and then looking for new ways to improve her awareness or whatever she calls it, but this time she was really upset and turned off her cell phone. She never did that before."

"I see."

"No, you don't see. If you would see, you wouldn't be this calm. What's wrong with you. You are one of her best friends, aren't you just a little bit worried? Or maybe you know something we don't. Do you?"

Julie joined the conversation. "Is there any way you can help us Nick? Do you have any idea where she might be? We just want to know that she's safe. That's all. Can you tell us she's safe?" begged Julie.

"I'm afraid I don't know more than you do, but you can give her more than a night for her to come back to you. Let her calm down, find her way, experience whatever she's going through. You can't stay in her path or she'll hate you, you know that as well as I do. Maybe this time she had a revelation and she wanted to emerge into it as deeply as she could, so she cut her connection to her world. It's perfectly natural, safe and good. It will help her go through the process in an accelerated way."

"Or dig a hole under her in an accelerated way and use again!" barked Lizzie.

"It is not for you to decide. It is not your journey and there is nothing you can do about it anyway."

"Just tell us if you have any idea where she could be. Start with that group of gypsies you introduced her to last time you saw us" said Julie forcefully.

"There's nothing to say. I don't know much about them. I just introduced them to Nikki because she was genuinely interested in meeting a group like them. They only came to my class twice and then they disappeared. They paid in cash if I remember correctly, so I have no contact information I could help you with, even if I wanted to break my confidentiality agreement."

"What confidentiality agreement? Please, it's a freakin' yoga class; there's no confidentiality agreements" retorted Lizzie amazingly angry.

"You can't be mad at me, Lizzie, or yourself, or anyone else for that matter. It's Nikki's path and you have to respect that. Stop trying to control life. You have no control, life controls you! Just breathe" suggested Nick.

"Whatever!" pouted Lizzie.

"Let's get out of here and try Nikki's cell phone again. We'll find her, I promise" said Julie putting an arm around Lizzie in an attempt to calm her down and comfort her at the same time.

"And Nick, if you hear anything, please give me a call. Here's my card" continued Julie handing him a simple, white card with her contact information on it.

"I will, don't worry. It's out of your control. Let go!"

"It's easier said than done" commented Julie back, as they walked out of his studio.

Chapter 7

There always seems to be a shortage of cabs on the island of Manhattan every time one has an actual emergency. Where did they all go? The traffic was thick, but at least the cars were moving, going towards where they needed to go, in as much of a hurry as any New Yorker constantly moves. But there seemed to be no vacant cabs and Sasha had to be back at work in fifteen minutes. There was no way she'd get there taking the subway.

Finally, she saw one as she was crossing the street, so without thinking she just jolted through the cars, pushed into the people and forced her way to that cab that was going to take her back to work, to face the lady dragon, her boss.

She knew the presentation was over, but because she did not get any phone calls from her boss. Sasha was confident that the presentation went well and Diane, her boss, was pleased with the changes she made to the presentation early in the morning.

Sasha got out of the car, straightened her coat, took a deep breath and forced herself to move forward, enter the building and go for the elevators.

"If there's ever going to be a time for me to pitch my Eastern European project, now is the time, now, when she's still happy with me. Who knows what tomorrow will bring, especially for her, she's so emotionally volatile, tomorrow she'll totally forget she was happy with my work today."

As the elevator was making its way to the 14th floor, Sasha was going over her pitch in her mind, making sure it sounded convincing.

"It has to work. It will work! "Sasha whispered to herself taking another deep breath as the elevator stopped.

She rushed to her desk to pick up her brief PowerPoint presentation that she put together for Diane.

"Great! You are here. I want to talk to you for a minute," said Diane walking by Sasha's desk on the way to her office.

"Give me a second to grab something and I'll be in your office!" replied Sasha in a hurry. Then she closed her eyes, took another deep breath and walked into Diane's office.

Her boss was on the phone already, but she seemed to be wrapping it up, so she patiently waited for her to finish the call. Sasha's palms were getting sweaty. She really wanted this project to have a go.

"Sasha, the changes you made this morning worked perfectly" said Diane without the slightest inflection in her voice.

Was that a thank you? In whose world? Sasha had to take it as it was.

"Now I need you to work on the details with the people I met with this morning and see if there's ..."

"Can someone else do that?" interrupted Sasha.

"Excuse me!" blurted Diane flabbergasted, finally looking up at Sasha, who was still standing in front of her desk.

"I think I should be working on something much more important, that could have a monumental impact and put us back in the news before the year is over" dared to say Sasha as convincing as she could.

After a long moment of painful silence, Diane finally said "I'm listening!"

Sasha laid the short presentation on Diane's desk, opening it up to the first slide.

"Eastern Europe is the talk of the town recently. Everybody talks a lot about it, but there aren't enough real projects highlighting this newly opened part of the world. They are just waking up to democracy and we should be the ones to help them out, make them see, teach them how democracy works. Equality is not a real word in these countries, even though they did live under a communist regime for so long. Let's teach them what equality really means, in a democratic way" finished Sasha, turning page after page of graphs and data for Diane to look at in her presentation.

"I don't have the time for a full story right now. Leave the presentation and your notes on my desk and I'll go through them at a better time" said Diane, cutting Sasha off.

"There's something I have to do now, so please close the door after you" concluded Diana pointing the door to Sasha.

After Sasha got back to her desk, she picked up the receiver and called Julie.

"My Eastern Europe project has a good chance of coming to life!"

"Congratulations Sasha, that is huge! I know how much you've been working on this. Is she going to give it to you?" asked Julie enthusiastically.

"For now, I don't know how is going to work, but even if she cut me off in the middle of my pitch, I saw that nose twitch thing that she does whenever she gets interested in a project or idea of any kind" blurted Sasha checking her surroundings and making sure nobody was listening to her conversation.

Sasha could hear the happiness in Julie's voice "That is great! We should celebrate!" She was such a true friend.

"Yes, we should. Let's meet for lunch at Giorgio's. After that I have to come back to work and start updating my research on my Eastern

European project. Finally, one of my dreams is coming true!" exclaimed Sasha finally letting happiness invade her heart and fill it up with joy.

It was a delicious warm tingling sensation in her chest. It was so nice. She wanted more of that. Happiness and joy felt better than anything she ever felt in a very long time.

She grabbed her purse and was on her way to Giorgio's.

***

"It smells so good in here. I just want to eat everything they have" commented Sasha looking at the menu.

Julie smiled and gave her another hug. "I'm so happy for you. You got me excited. I want to help as much as I can, ok? If there's anything I can help with, you'll let me know, right?"

"Of course, I will. And I'm going to help you with that teenage rehab you're planning on opening after you're done with college" replied Sasha.

"What are friends for" threw in Julie and they both started laughing.

"Oh, it feels good to laugh. I haven't seen you laugh in a while" continued Julie.

"Maybe it's because I'm starving. I haven't had anything to eat since that slice of pizza last night."

"Then let's get something to eat, and fast" announced Julie with a smile and playful determination." Lizzie wasn't feeling too well after not sleeping almost at all last night, so she went home to bed, but she's happy for you. You'll see her tonight."

"No problem. I should have stayed up all night with her too, but I had to work today and go to class in the morning..." said Sasha, "I hope she'll feel better."

After they ate lunch, they walked to a close by pastry shop that was one of Sasha's favorites. The smell of freshly baked pastry made both of them drool even though they had just finished eating a delicious lunch.

"This might have not been the best idea we've had today" commented Julie, "but I know you love this shop and I had to make sure you feel celebrated enough today."

Sasha smiled at Julie, wrapped her arms around her really tight and kissed her on her left cheek. "You're the sister I've never had. Thank you so much."

Julie leaned her head towards Sasha and said "As your sister, I have to make sure you're not starving, and knowing you, if you're going back to work after this, you're going to forget that you have a stomach and just fill yourself up with coffee after coffee. Get anything you want. It's on me!"

"Well, if that's the case, I'll have the pastry chef himself. We could have him bake for us every day. And if he's cute, we'll buy him a tight uniform to use while in our kitchen" joked Sasha imagining the whole scene.

"It totally depends on how cute he is. Maybe he doesn't even need a uniform at all" said Julie winking at Sasha imagining an even better scene.

An older woman behind the counter was staring at them with a disapproving look on her face. "Anything I can get for you ... ladies?" she seemed to have pushed herself to say the last word.

Sasha blushed immediately and Julie started laughing.

"Ok, let's get something before this nice lady," said Julie emphasizing the word 'lady' while trying to be serious, "throws us out of her shop."

A cell phone started ringing and Sasha dug into her purse to find it. "Hello!?" she said and walked away from the counter.

Julie was watching her. It seemed like an important phone call. She waited until Sasha was done with the call and asked her as she was putting her cell phone back in her purse "Anything you want to share?"

Sasha looked at her while trying to grasp for air. Julie took her by her arm and pulled her out of the store. She was worried. "Are you ok?" asked Julie.

"It was my attorney, Mrs. Clifford."

Julie did not know what to expect. She did not know what to say, so she kept silent.

"My mom dropped the charges and we probably won't hear from her ever again according to the judge" muttered Sasha staring at the pavement in front of her.

"But that is good, isn't it? That's exactly what you wanted?" wondered Julie out loud, not sure what Sasha was really going through.

Sasha finally pulled herself together, looked at Julie, smiled and announced "This must be the best day of my life. I can't believe it! Is this really happening?"

"Yes, I guess it is happening and I am happy to be here with you and be a firsthand witness to it all. You deserve it all. I'm so happy for you!" declared Julie hugging Sasha.

"You are right. I should be happy. What's wrong with me?" asked Sasha confused.

"Ok, we're going in the store again and buying a ton of pastry. We're celebrating again! You are in shock right now, but it will finally catch up with you and I don't want you to be alone. You should at least have some delicious pastries with you" said Julie smiling sweetly at Sasha.

They walked into the store arm in arm.

Later on Sasha was in the small library they had in the building where she worked, pulling books after books on women's rights. Then she called couple of her friends from the UN offices in Geneva. It was the middle of the night there, so she left some messages. She was so excited she forgot about the different time zones.

"Maybe it's time to go home."

Chapter 8

S weet smell of cinnamon apple tea was welcoming Sasha as she walked in. She heard voices in the kitchen, so she dropped her stuff in the hallway and she rushed to the kitchen to celebrate her day with the girls. She had a cake that she grabbed from Whole Foods and was ready to show them all how happy and grateful she was.

The first thing she saw was Lizzie making tea and started skipping and yelling "I'm the queen of the day! Today is my day and nothing will take it away from me! Who wants cake?"

Sasha turned around to gloat at her audience and saw Julie with a bag of frozen peas on her face.

"Julie, did you trip or something?" asked Sasha half worried and half joking.

"Or something" replied Lizzie sarcastically, handing a mug of hot spicy tea to Julie. "Here, honey, it's your favorite. Drink a little, you're in shock, you need to let go!"

"I will after the cops leave. I can't be falling apart in front of them. I'm ok now" said Julie putting down the frozen peas and grabbing her tea.

That's when Sasha saw Julie's face. It was puffy and pink and it looked like she had a cut over her left eyebrow.

"What the hell happened here? Were you mugged? Cops are coming? What's going on?" screeched Sasha worried.

"You're going to find out anyway, the second the cops get here. You'll fill in the details then, so here are the main lines: Joe came to see Julie, she told him about Nikki, so next thing you know he's talking trash about Nikki and the rest of us – her roommates. I jumped in, it got out of hand and he was physically going to attack me when Julie got between the two of us. Joe punched her, I yelled and attacked him. Julie was on the floor and he went and kicked her in the stomach and said she's no better than her trash family. He pushed me against the fridge and then punched Julie couple of more times and called her names and he left as I was dialing 911" finished Lizzie and went to hug Julie.

Sasha's jaw dropped. This was a nightmare. It couldn't have happened, not to them, not today. Today was supposed to be a great day!

"Where the hell is that bastard? I'm going to kill him. Nobody treats the people I love this way. He's a piece of garbage. And after everything that happened last night? When he was Mr. Perfect he turned around and became Mr. Wife Beater?" said Sasha in disbelief.

"How was he Mr. Perfect? What happened last night?" asked Lizzie confused.

"Please, girls, I don't want to talk about any of it right now and I'd prefer if you didn't either. I just want tonight to be over and move on. I want to bury this memory forever" announced Julie and put the frozen bag of peas back on her face.

"Are you sure you don't need to see a doctor" asked Sasha "your face doesn't look too good and if there's any concussion or any kind of complication to your head or internal ... he did kick you!"

Julie took a deep breath before she answered "We'll see after I talk to the cops. I want that out of the way. Ok?"

"Sure. Whatever you want" replied Sasha.

"Thanks" snapped Julie as the doorbell started ringing.

Lizzie jumped off her chair and went to open the door. "Must be the cops!"

A female and male police officers walked in the kitchen followed by Lizzie.

"No way!" said Julie making eye contact with the male cop.

"Seen you before. Sorry I wasn't there for you tonight when you really needed me. What kind of hero I turned out to be?" said the cop Julie was staring at.

Everybody else seemed to be confused by the whole conversation going on, so Julie felt like she had to clear out the air. "He's my hero from this morning, who saved me from a nasty fall and stopped a cab for me."

"Ahh..." blurted Lizzie and Sasha still confused.

"Let's finish this please. I need to go to the hospital and rest. I need for this whole thing to be done with. Is that ok with you guys?" asked Julie with determination and continued "I'm ready for the statement."

***

Sasha hated the smell of hospital, but this was way too important to focus on her own uncomfortable feelings. It brought up bad memories from the past.

Lizzie and Julie came out from the room across the hallway. They seemed ready to finally leave.

"Hey, girls, I have an idea," said Sasha "why not take tomorrow off and go to our favorite spa?"

"I already made the necessary arrangements, so I don't want to hear a 'no' from any of you," continued Sasha with as much enthusiasm as she could muster after everything that happened.

Julie cracked a fake smile and replied "You might be right, but you need to make sure I have enough time to sleep, because they gave me some strong sleeping pills."

"No problem. I already thought of that and we're not supposed to be there until 11am!"

"You always think ahead. Sometimes I envy you and your big brain. But other times, I'm glad I don't think as much as you do, I'd probably go insane" said Lizzie getting into the conversations.

Sasha did not say anything to that. It was a long day for everybody.

"Let me get us a cab and we're out of here" muttered Sasha turning around on her heels and walking towards the exit doors.

"By the way. Is everything alright with you, physically? What did the doctor say?" asked Sasha looking at Julie.

"I was lucky," mumbled Julie, "...apparently, according to the doctor. Couple of stitches on my forehead and I'm as good as new" continued Julie forcing herself to make a joke. "I have to come back for a follow up in 10 days."

***

The alarm clock woke Sasha up. It was 5am and she was planning on going to work for 4-5 hours and meeting the girls at the spa.

She took a quick shower, got dressed, picked up her purse and laptop and left a quick note for the girls telling them she'd meet with them right in front of the spa at 11am.

When she got to her desk there were more than 10 voice messages waiting for her. One by one they proved to be exactly the messages she was expecting from her contacts in Europe at the UN, EU, UNESCO,

World Bank, and couple of NGOs. They were all excited with the project Sasha was putting together and wanted to help right away.

Sasha started making phone calls all over Europe. Finally, the time difference did not matter because she was up so early.

Eleven o'clock came by so fast. This project was coming together so handsomely; Sasha thought of pulling a selfish move and excuse herself from the spa day with the girls. Then she thought of Julie and the whole reason for putting this project together – to help women out. She had to go!

She grabbed her purse and rushed out.

"We thought you might not make it to your own spa day" said Julie when she saw Sasha jumping out of a cab right in front of 'Summer Solstice Spa' where they were supposed to meet 10 minutes ago.

"Sorry, to tell you the truth I thought about it," replied Sasha with a guilty look on her face, "because I had a very productive five hours of work. But I love you guys and I really need this as much as you do, too."

"You are a sweetheart," exclaimed Julie," I'm so happy that project is working out so well for you. I only want to talk about that and other great things that are going on in our lives today. No downers please" asked Julie taking Sasha and Lizzie's hands and squeezing them tightly.

"It's a deal!" followed Lizzie. "Let's get pampered!"

The moment they walked in, the receptionist recognized them and just handed them over to one of their girls who gave them bright white fluffy bathrobes and slippers to change into and showed them to their private locker room.

The girls were giggling already, following the girl with the bathrobes.

"Sasha," called Julie, "tell us everything about that project of yours. You've been dreaming about it for so long, I love your enthusiasm when you talk about it! Share some warmth and joy with us, please!"

They were taking their clothes off and putting the bathrobes on. "I love these things. I have no idea how they keep them so soft "noticed Lizzie brushing the sleeves against her face. "Do you think they buy new ones every week? Are they onetime use bathrobes? If they are I want to take mine home."

Julie laughed at her. "I'll buy you a brand new one any color you wish for just don't embarrass me and ask to take this one home, ok?"

Lizzie's eyes lit up. "Hmm, how about a peach bathrobe just for me? And matching slippers of course."

"Of course," replied Julie amused.

"Sweet! I love presents! It looks like today is turning out to be a spectacular day: spa, gifts ..." then her face turned serious "I wish Nikki was here with us!" added Lizzie with a sigh.

"We all wish that. Let's hope she's having fun wherever she is and let us have fun here for her! Just the way she likes it to be!" jumped in Sasha with a faint smile.

There was silence. Julie and Sasha grabbed the complementary hair bands on the brown marble counter and pulled their hair back in a simple ponytail.

Julie was the first one to talk. "Let's melt in that mud tub and I'll tell you everything about my business."

"Your business?" asked Sasha. "What business are you talking about?"

Julie seemed to be all fired up. "Remember the teenage rehab I dreamt of opening since we met?" After she paused to read her friends' reactions, she added "I guess, now is high time for me to start putting together the business plan for it. I'll be done with school in half a year and I need something to fill out my day and keep me as busy as possible until this whole Joe business is well in the past and history."

"Ok?" felt like saying Sasha, not sure what exactly to tell her.

"It's all good, I promise. You should hear all my ideas and I want your help with this whole thing, if you're still up for it, as you promised me couple of years ago" finished pleading Julie, biting her lower lip and staring at the girls.

"I'm here" exclaimed Lizzie.

"Count on me too" said Sasha immediately.

Julie seemed to start breathing again "Thank you guys that means so much to me. You are the best. Now let me tell you about my concept" then her eyes landed on the fresh lemon water on a small glass table to the side of the room and went to grab a glass of it. "First let's get a little bit refreshed, we all need it!"

"Oh, yes. Before I tell you about my project, I want to run this one thing by you"

"What thing, Julie?" asked Sasha intrigued.

" It's not a big deal, but my general psychology professor, Mr. Burton, told me I should apply for a master degree and go for my PhD in psychology."

"Really, he said that" inquired Lizzie lifting up her right eyebrow. "Isn't he the professor that you were telling me about with all the awards?"

"Yes, that's him" replied Julie.

"If he said that to you then you know you have to do it. You have a talent and we are not the only ones to notice it. That is amazing. Why didn't you tell us about this before?" asked Sasha.

Julie seemed embarrassed "Because I didn't want to do it. Joe didn't think it was such a great idea and told me my professor just wants to get in my pants, that's why he told me all that."

"Joe is a selfish moron. I thought we're done talking about him. He's not worth any of our time and energy. Let's refocus!" blurted Lizzie.

"I say, you should go for that PhD!" said Sasha.

"I second that!" added Lizzie quickly.

"But what about my rehab? I have to figure out how to balance that, my school, my personal life, my recovery and my volunteer work?" verbalized Julie trying to make sense of it all and come up with a way to make it all work out.

"We are going to help you!" declared Sasha. "We're already helping with the recovery part, keeping each other on the right track, you have no personal life as of last night, you're done with school in less than half a year, and won't start your PhD Program for several months after that, we already told you we'll help with the rehab you want to open, and you might have to give up some of that volunteer projects for couple of years. It's all going to work out! I promise!"

Julie looked up at Sasha "You are perfectly right. I can do this. I have you guys to help me out, just in case. I can do this and I'm going to do it!" exclaimed Julie with determination and finished up her glass of lemon water.

"Now let's enjoy today and this gorgeous spa!"

***

"Did you see how fake Julie was? She could barely enjoy today. The only times when I really thought she was ok, were when she kept talking about that rehab, so we better be prepared to help her out and push her to do it every single day" whispered Lizzie to Sasha, so Julie couldn't hear.

"Come on Lizzie, you can't expect miracles. They were together for two years and she put a lot of herself into that relationship. Truth is that he definitely made it easier for her with last night's disaster, but it will take time for this wound to heal."

"Nikki would be so good at making her feel better. Only if she knew what's going on, she would come back for sure" added Lizzie.

"We should talk to that cop, Mike, that came to take her statement last night. He seems to be into her. Maybe he'd help us, or at least tell us what to do, legally, to find Nikki," said Sasha.

"That guy is very cute! If Julie doesn't want him, I'll take him" joked Lizzie.

"What are you girls whispering about" asked Julie getting close to them.

Lizzie didn't seem to have anything to hide "We're talking about Mike. That cop hero of yours. He is so handsome and so smart and sweet and he seemed to be into you. How did you manage to pull that off with a black eye and swollen face? It's just not fair!" joked Lizzie again pouting.

"I'm going to see him tonight actually," said Julie.

"No way! Already? You move fast girl" said Lizzie smiling.

Julie smiled back "It's not that! He wants to follow up and I want to ask him if there's a way we can search for Nikki."

"Honey, you read my mind" said Lizzie amazed. "I really hope he can help us."

"Ladies," they heard one of the spa employees calling them softly, "your massage tables are ready. Please follow me."

"Oh, yes, now that's what I'm talking about. I'm so tense, a massage is exactly what I need" muttered Sasha, moving along with her friends, towards the massage tables.

Chapter 9

"I completely understand what you ladies are going through, but there's nothing you can do. Nikki chose to leave, she's not a minor and you are not her relatives" told Mike to all three of them sitting at the kitchen table in their apartment.

"It sucks! I want to know where she is, if she's alright. That's all. She can stay there for as long as she wants to, wherever 'there' is!" barked Lizzie in despair.

"Yes, it does suck and I'm sorry" replied Mike.

"And there's really nothing we can do? Or you can do?" hinted Sasha without taking her eyes off Mike.

"I see where you're all going, but there's nothing I can do. Not legally."

Julie interrupted "We're not asking you to do anything illegal ..." she paused and then added "just off the record."

"What have I gotten myself into?" said Mike trying to be serious. He looked at all three of them staring at him across the table, begging without words.

"Well, alright. I'll see what I can do, on one condition" he said.

Julie jumped in and declared "Anything! You name it!"

Mike turned towards Julie and simply said "Dinner and a movie! Tomorrow night. I'll pick you up at seven!"

"When you say 'you', do you mean all of us or just me?" asked Julie knowing fully well the answer to that question. She was just trying to buy herself some time to think about it.

Lizzie and Sasha were silent. Julie looked at them and knew exactly what they wanted her to do, but they couldn't really ask of her. It wasn't like she was selling her soul to the devil or promising sex. It was just a dinner and a movie. It will help Nikki and might take her mind off Joe.

"And you don't mind that I look like a boxing champion?" inquired Julie as her last try to move out of this uncomfortable position and give him a chance to change his mind.

"Not at all. I know what to expect once your face comes back to normal. I saw you before this whole thing happened, remember? And you fell right into my arms. It's a sign that we at least have to give it a try."

"A try? What are you talking about? I was just beaten up by my boyfriend less than 24 hours ago. Are you totally insane?" threw Julie in amazement. "It's only a dinner and a movie, for Nikki, that's all."

"I might be insane, you're right; I've never done anything like this in my entire life. I feel stupid and uncomfortable doing it, but somehow it just feels right. I can't explain it. You'll just have to trust me on this. I rarely have this feeling, but when I do and I act on it, beautiful things come out of it."

"Great! You do sound insane. But in your insanity, you sound like Nikki, and I am doing this for her, so maybe you're right and it is some sort of a sign, even if it sounds totally wrong to me" finished Julie.

"Stop thinking, Julie! Give that mind of yours a little bit of a break" interrupted Sasha." That's what Nikki would say anyway. And you always seem to listen to Nikki."

"Fine. You all win!" announced Julie standing up and talking directly to Mike. "I'll see you tomorrow at seven. "Then she turned around to go make some tea and as she heard Mike getting up and saying goodbye to Lizzie and Sasha, she quickly moved around on her heels and added "And please don't forget to have some sort of news on Nikki."

When she swiftly turned around to deliver her last statement, Julie's hair bounced like a golden cascade taking Mike's breath away. He seemed to need a minute to recollect himself. "I'll do my best!" he was finally able to verbalize.

"Goodbye ladies. I'll probably see you tomorrow" he said, walking towards the door.

"Thank you for everything" replied Sasha as she closed the door behind him.

"Julie, this is truly unbelievable. Forget what I said earlier today about your personal life being over for now. Mike is such an amazing guy and he's quite smitten with you" exclaimed Sasha as she was walking back into the kitchen.

Lizzie's face was beaming. "You are such a lucky lady. Just take it and run with it. Don't think about it for too long. He'll help you bury the memories of Joe so fast; you'll forget the past two years ever happened."

"I don't know," said Julie, turning around to face her friends. "I'm getting some weird vibe from him. I can't quite put my finger on it."

"Maybe is the 'good guy' vibe that you are definitely not used to. No judgment here, but you know you have horrible taste in man. They all somehow turn out to be some sort of losers. And this one might be your final break through. He might be the prince. Enough frog kissing for you!" declared Lizzie with a smile on her face.

"You think" asked Julie going into what the girls called 'the thinking mode'.

"Stop thinking. Just feel. Thinking got you in trouble until now. I think it's time for your heart to do the thinking for a change, see what comes out of it!" said Lizzie trying to shake Julie out of her over analytical way of dealing with everything.

"It would be great if you could stop your thinking at the 'what's best for Julie' part, but you speed right by that landmark and rush to 'what's best for everybody else' and find excuses for the most heinous behaviors" tried to help Sasha. "Nikki always tells you that!"

"Yes. That's right. I'm going to stop overanalyzing everything, or at least I'll try. Thinking takes me back to Joe anyway, so I'm trying to run away from that as fast and far as possible. Mike will be a perfect distraction" concluded Julie, putting the mug of hot tea in front of her on the kitchen table.

"Do you have any of those sleeping pills they gave you at the hospital yesterday?" asked Lizzie. "If you need more help to fall asleep just let me know, because I have an entire collection of meditation and relaxation CDs. And they helped me out during my worst times."

"That's so very sweet of you Lizzie, but I don't think I'll be needing much to fall asleep tonight. I'm exhausted. Thank you for the relaxing spa day and for letting me talk about Joe for more than I should have."

"Anytime sweetie," replied Sasha softly, "and remember what we talked about. Once I'm done with my Eastern Europe project, I'm going to help you with your business plan for your rehab. Just think about what sets it apart from the competition and we'll start from there."

Julie hugged both Lizzie and Sasha, grabbed her cup of tea and went to her bedroom. "You guys are the most amazing people I've ever met in my entire life. I love you! "

"We love you too!" said Sasha and Lizzie in unison.

"Good night, ladies" finally said Julie and closed the door to her bedroom.

A gorgeous bouquet of roses and lilies was the first thing that Lizzie saw as she opened the door for Mike.

"How sweet of you, really, you shouldn't have!" exclaimed Lizzie opening her arms to receive the flowers.

"If you don't mind, I'll bring you a rose next time. These are for Julie" replied Mike with a sweet low and sexy voice.

"Stop flirting with me, it's not right" said Lizzie jokingly, leading Mike to their kitchen where Sasha was eating a sandwich.

"Don't worry," said Sasha while chewing a good chunk of that sandwich she was holding with both hands, "Julie is in her room getting ready. She'll be out in a few minutes."

Lizzie pulled a chair for Mike and invited him to join them at the kitchen table. "So, sit down and tell us what's new. And yes, we always gather up around the kitchen table. It's an Italian thing, even though none of us are Italians ... that we know of."

Mike smiled and said "Well, I am Italian, so this is very comfortable for me. My question is: where do you ladies put all that food, because all of you have an amazingly fit body."

"You are too much of a gentleman" replied Lizzie. "You should see the strict diet we go through right before bathing suit season. Now it's cold, so we can cover it all up."

"That's very hard to believe. I had to fight my way up here through the crowds of men lined up at your door, all the way down the street. I had to pull my badge and scatter them, or you girls will get the fire marshal on your head for having too many people in such a small place, blocking the stairway. "

Sasha barely finished chewing and said "You are one funny gentleman; I'll give you that!"

"Ladies, stop flattering me. I can't take it. I'm a very shy guy."

"Shy is fine by us, but if you like to beat up women, you're a dead man" said Sasha becoming all serious.

Mike did not say anything after that. The joke went too far. Clearly, they were still obsessed with what Joe did.

"I was just informed, couple of hours ago, that Julie is not pressing charges against Joe. Should I say something to Julie? What was she thinking? I feel obligated to shake some reason back into her" concluded Mike, visibly worried, putting his left hand through his thick black perfectly brushed hair.

"Don't say anything, please. She knows what she's doing. That's her way of dealing with it. She wants to let it go and after burning all his pictures and letters and throwing all his stuff out this morning, she informed us, that she doesn't want to know he exists. She's wearing black, as a sign that he's dead for her. We're not allowed to bring up his name," said Lizzie. "We respect that. Whatever she needs to get over this whole thing."

"Understood!" muttered Mike. "But if it makes you feel better, I persuaded Joe to move back to Miami this morning. He already got a ticket and I told him I'll have my colleagues there keep a close eye on him and they all hate women beaters. "Then he looked at Lizzie and Sasha and added "Don't worry, everything was legal. I dug up some bad stuff on him and he was more than happy to move to Florida as soon as possible."

Sasha was the first one to break the silence "Thank God! He is finally gone!"

"Who's gone?" asked Julie as she walked into the kitchen. She was looking amazing in a double-breasted fuchsia coat she had bought from JCrew couple of days ago, paired with same color high heeled boots. It was hard to pull off colors like that, but it seemed to compliment her really well. She looked adorable and sexy at the same time.

Mike stood up and gave Julie the flowers. She took them, smelled them seductively and kissed him on the cheek. "Thank you. Very thoughtful of you!" Then her mind jumped and thought of Joe never giving her flowers and resentment and anger started surfacing, when she caught herself and brought herself back to the present.

"Sasha, could you be so kind and put these lovely flowers in a vase and in my room? Thanks" said Julie quickly giving the bouquet to Sasha.

"Mike has no chance" thought Lizzie smiling at both of them. Apparently, the black attire a thing of the past she had on all day

"Ok, you two, you better leave or you'll be late for dinner" said Lizzie slightly pushing both of them out of the kitchen.

"Can you believe that?" asked Lizzie after closing the door behind Julie and Mike. She rushed to the kitchen and looked at Sasha. "Do you think it's alright what he did to Joe?"

"Why not if that bastard did other ugly stuff like that to other people. He deserves it. Did you hear that Mike dug up other bad stuff about him. It must have been something pretty bad for Joe to comply so readily and move out of New York and go all the way to Florida. It serves him right!"

"I guess. Now let's forget he ever existed, just like Julie asked us."

***

"That was one of the best movies I've seen this year. Usually an open ending bothers me, but this time was perfect. I can imagine that he actually makes it back, with the kid and she's so happy to see them alive and well that she forgives him" said Julie with conviction.

"You are too kind. Even though I'm a guy, if she were my sister, I would have nailed the bastard if he ever decided to come back. But he died anyways" said Mike, then he looked towards Julie who seemed hurt by his brutal honesty and had to add "...but the boy definitely makes it back to his mom and says that his dad died saving him"

"Much better! He's a hero, so she forgives him" replied Julie.

"Hero, yes. Forgive him, no."

"Oh, come on! Everybody forgives heroes. Heroes are only remembered by their last actions, by their sacrifice. She definitely forgave him" concluded Julie putting her foot down.

Mike looked at her determined beautiful face, smiled and gave in "OK, she forgave him. But surely because he turns out to be a hero" had to add Mike.

She smiled back in agreement. "And in the sequel, he comes back, because a mad yet genius scientist finds him barely alive and finds a way to heal him."

"Oh, so in the sequel he's Robocop, part human, part machine. That's totally romantic" said Mike with a chuckle.

Julie poked his ribs with her elbow slightly irritated, but definitely amused, "Cut it out. How dare you destroy my romantic fantasy so cruelly? I thought you were a gentleman!"

"You were the one who decided that I was, I never confirmed it. And I'm not saying I'm not one either, but I'm probably somewhere in the middle" replied Mike taking her hand and putting it on his arm.

"Such a gentleman move. I love it! Your sonnet reciting, love poems writing, dueling for my honor ... these are the only missing parts towards becoming a full gentleman" announced Julie smiling whole heartedly.

The wind started blowing hard messing up Julie's hair.

A small branch from a nearby tree fell right in front of her startling her so badly that she jumped backwards.

Mike picked up the branch with his right hand, lifted it up, put his left hand behind his back, one foot in front of the other and attacked the tree with the branch pretending it was a sword.

"My lady, let me protect you from this tree's bad manners. En guard tree, for I am here to save my lady's honor" said Mike poking the tree with the branch.

Julie was laughing so hard; she was tearing up. "Ok, ok, I have to take it back! You're a gentleman alright. Nothing is missing, just stop it or I'll die laughing."

"I would not want you to die, not now, not ever" replied Mike and stopped and stared right in her eyes.

Julie forgot to breathe for a second and got lost in Mike's stare.

"Are you for real?" whispered Julie.

"Yes, I am. Let me prove it to you" replied Mike, then pulled her close to him and softly kissed her lips. His hand touched her face wiping the laughter tears.

She slowly opened her eyes, pulled away embarrassed and asked "How about that ice-cream you promised me?" breaking the spell.

"Nothing will give me more pleasure than to indulge with you in one of the best ice-creams in New York City and I know just the place" announced Mike winking at her.

"Let's go then! What are we waiting for?"

They started walking again having casual conversation, talking about the movie they just saw.

"Lizzie is the romantic one. She would probably agree with my happy ending."

Mike turned towards Julie and confessed "I don't really believe in happy ever after – not in my line of work, not after I see what kind of horrific things people do to each other every single day."

"I understand," said Julie.

"But I do know guys who still believe in romance, even though they work in my field" replied Mike.

"You see, there's still hope for you" commented Julie with a head nod.

"You might be right. Never say never, right?"

"Never say never" repeated Julie.

Mike seemed to be thinking about something that was far away. She couldn't read him.

Then out of a sudden, he said "You know what, my friend, that I told you about and Lizzie might be a match made in heaven!"

Julie's eyes opened wide with surprise "Really?"

"It definitely sounds like it!"

"That would be so great. Lizzie is such an optimist, believing in the perfect man and perfect romance, I was worrying that she'll give that up if a guy wouldn't show up in her life and soon!" said Julie with enthusiasm. "Let's set them up"

Mike chuckled "That sounds so sneaky! I don't usually set people up, but if you think we should do it ... let's give it a try!"

"Great! When?" asked Julie.

"Wow! I don't know yet, let me talk to John. That's his name, John."

"Give me a call when you know," said Julie.

"I will! As a matter of fact, we might do a double date, so another date for us. How does that sound?" asked Mike.

"Perfect! Just a second! A second date for us? I thought we're not dating!" said Julie and pulled away. "I can't date, I thought I made that clear!"

"No problem. It will not be a date for us, just a get together. If we're there too, it won't be a blind date for them, which I know John wouldn't agree to."

"Nor would Lizzie" replied Julie quickly.

"Ok. So, we'll hang out!" said Mike.

"Hang out" confirmed Julie. "Now let's get to that ice-cream place! I'm drooling just thinking about it!"

Chapter 10

John gave a quick wink to Mike and both Julie and Lizzie saw that awkward approval signal.

"I guess he likes what he sees" had to say Lizzie not knowing how to react. "Now I just wonder if he's mature enough to like what he hears, because I have plenty to say, especially after that wink."

"Oh no, do I hear a challenge? Did he dare you with one wink?" asked Julie jokingly.

Lizzie smiled at Julie's comment. "I might be taking things too seriously, aren't I?"

"Just a little bit" said Julie putting her hand in front of Lizzie and closing the distance between her thumb and index finger just to show her how much she was taking this wink thing to an extreme.

"You're right. I do expect way too much from men in general. I want to finally find the perfect guy, so I can get married and live happily ever after like my good friend Zoe and so many others like her."

"When was the last time you spoke to Zoe?" Maybe things have already changed.

"Don't be so cynical, Julie. Why would they change? They might have had their fights, but it's normal. Just like we have fights. It's perfectly normal to go through different stages in any kind of relationship, especially with the man that you're meant to be with for the rest of your life. People have to adjust to everything, especially loved ones and especially to the ones they know deep down in their hearts that they will spend the rest of their lives with through thick and thin."

Julie halted, put her hand on Lizzie's arm and said "I hope we're not going into the 'soul mates' discussion tonight."

"No, no, no. Of course not. I was just talking … to you. I would never bore anybody with anything like that, especially men. They are all scared of discussions like that" commented Lizzie.

"For a good reason!" underlined Julie.

"You are right. It adds an awkward pressure and it's not fair, not normal and we don't know these guys that well. I would never bring anything like that up anyway. I promise" added Lizzie trying to convince Julie.

Mike and John were waiting for them to reach the table, then they stood up and Mike introduced John to Lizzie and Julie before they pulled the girls' chairs to help them sit down.

"Two perfect gentlemen. Not something you find in Manhattan that easily these days" noticed Lizzie with an appreciative smile.

"I told you," said Julie.

John was the first one to ask "What would you ladies like to drink? We apologize but we were thirsty and ordered some wine for us already."

"We're not drinking, so you boys can have wine and order us some tea, if that's ok with you" replied Julie.

"No problem. Anything you beautiful ladies wish," said John.

Mike was just sitting back relaxed in his chair letting John order the tea and get acquainted. After a little while he interrupted "John has an amazing vineyard in Napa. It belongs to his family. Apparently, he grew up there and has known how to produce perfectly delicious wine from his early teenage years. He has people running his wine business while he plays the detective in New York City."

"My cop days are almost over" commented John. "I miss the simplicity, calmness and beauty of the hills of Napa. It took me a little while to figure out what I really wanted to do with my life, but now I'm convinced I want to spend it away from this crazy life on this tiny, noisy and crazy island of Manhattan."

"I hear you" said Lizzie nodding her head and smiling at him. "There are so many times when I just feel like running away from the ugly noises of the city to the invigorating sounds of the wind in the middle of nature."

"You two seem to have the same strange idea about life and the way it should be enjoyed" said Mike and then added "If I don't feel the pulse of this live city and its urgency every day, I feel dead."

"Really?" asked Julie with a confused look on her face.

"Not to say that I wouldn't enjoy being in the middle of nature now and then, but I do need to come back to my city or I feel left out, kicked to the side by life. I love to be part of the action!"

"And that's why you're a cop and a damn good one too" commented John. "I should know. This guy right here," he said pointing at Mike, "saved my life more than I'd like to remember."

"So, you're not just my hero, apparently you're everybody's hero!" said Julie appreciatively.

Mike smiled and preferred not to say anything.

He was so mysterious, so dangerous and amazingly kind, thoughtful and courageous, all in one. Julie's eyes rose up at him "And on top of all that, he's so handsome and sexy!" she thought, her gaze meeting Mike's eyes. She had to look away and fast. What was happening to her? She tried to shake away her thoughts and said "So, John, tell us more about your vineyard and your childhood. It sounds so innocent."

"My childhood or my vineyard. Which one sounds innocent?" joked John.

They all started laughing.

"Both!" had to jump in Mike.

"Oh, come on, buddy, don't help me look like a dork in front of these gorgeous ladies. I don't need any help from you, thank you very much" replied John.

"Far from it!" commented Lizzie, maybe a little bit too quickly.

"John, you might have a supporter here. Come on, amaze us with the description of your perfect childhood and promise us to take us to your vineyard soon, so we can enjoy your story and look forward to see what you're talking about" pushed Mike.

"You are definitely welcome to visit me anytime" said John inviting them all. "Let's go to my vineyard in couple of weeks. We'll figure it out, but don't forget to bring a good book to read in my hammock under the big old oak trees and walnut trees that I have in the backyard. It's like heaven!"

"I think the best book to bring to a vineyard would be our AA book" muttered Lizzie and started laughing with Julie.

John seemed to be a little bit confused.

"It's not that we're not drinking tonight; we don't drink, period" tried to explain Julie, but John's facial expression still seemed to not convey understanding of what was said, so Julie tried again "We're alcoholics, in recovery of course."

John finally started chuckling. "I wasn't expecting that because of your young age, but I need to apologize for my own ignorance. I guess I'm not the only one who tasted wine from a young age."

They all started laughing at John's last comment.

***

Couple of days later, Sasha was in Diane's office, looking in her rolodex for a contact that she couldn't seem to find in the electronic file of her boss's business cards. While grabbing a piece of blank paper on Diane's desk to write down the phone number she was searching the thick rolodex for, her eyes dropped on a presentation that she wasn't familiar with.

"I thought I knew all her presentations, as I work on or do most of them" thought Sasha.

She grabbed it to take a better look and while she flipped through the first couple of pages, the blood in her face drained and she looked pale like a ghost. She couldn't help herself but go through the whole thing, page by page.

Diane walked in and when she saw Sasha with the presentation in her hands, she barked at her "What are you doing sneaking in and going through my things?"

"You mean my things" barked Sasha back emphasizing the word 'my'.

"What are you talking about? How dare you?" screeched Diane.

Sasha threw the presentation at Diane and said as calmly as possible "This is my project that I pitched to you last week, my work, my passion, my life, and you take it and put your name on it?" She didn't finish saying all that and her eyes were attracted by a colorful glossy brochure that had "UN for the Eastern European women" written on it in bold letters.

Not waiting for permission, Sasha grabbed it and read it in front of Diane. "This is the mockup of the brochure for the Eastern European Women Rights conference that I envisioned, but with you as the main speaker and my presentation as your work!?!" Sasha was flabbergasted. She couldn't believe what was happening to her.

"After all the hard work I've done for you for so long. I let you take credit for so many projects that I built from ground up for you. And don't get me wrong, I enjoyed doing it and I was grateful to have the opportunity to do it and thankful. But this, this is my life, this is my baby project. My name should be somewhere on this damn brochure and definitely on my presentation" and Sasha emphasized again the word 'my'.

Diane went behind her desk, cleared her throat and said "Sasha, I do appreciate all your work. You are a very smart, hard-working girl, but in order for your dream to come true, you have to let someone with credentials put their name on your work. The information will be received better from a well-respected and known expert, like myself. "

"It's a good argument, but it has a lot of flaws in it. The first one is that you, with all your expert credentials, couldn't make the impact that a passionate person on this subject would be able to make, not even close."

Sitting down in her chair, Diane didn't even look at Sasha when she said "I don't have time for this. Leave me alone, I have to make an important phone call."

The conversation was done. Sasha knew that. She walked out of Diane's office feeling blown to pieces. What could she do? Where could she go? To the head of the department? Would that be appropriate?

She couldn't think clearly, so she grabbed her purse and her laptop and decided to go home. "I'll talk it out with the girls and figure out my next step. I don't want to do something stupid, not right now. This is too important to me."

When she walked in their apartment, she smelled something burning. Her senses woke up and she was alert and running towards the source of the smell. It was on the balcony, in a pot and burning. Julie was sitting next to it.

"It's time to let go of Joe. I'm burning the rest of our photos that I just dug up" she explained staring at the pot in front of her that had partially burnt pictures in it that were being quickly consumed in their entirety by the fire that seemed to have started devouring them from the corners inward.

"So, you lit them up one by one" said Sasha stating the obvious.

Suddenly, she knew what she had to do. "Julie, do you mind postponing this burning ritual for another couple of hours? Let's do this as a family. I have stuff I want to burn and I bet Lizzie has something as well. This will work much better done in a group. It will help us release all those bad energies. Remember how we did this with Nikki? Let's do that again."

Julie's blank expression disappeared. She looked back at Sasha and confirmed "And when Nikki did it, it worked for all of us; whatever we had to release we were able to release."

"Great then. Let's go and buy a big bucket, so we can do this the right way. I'm going to call Lizzie and let her know we're having a 'cleansing ritual' later, so she comes home early after she's done with work at the gallery" announced Sasha, searching for her cell phone deep in her purse.

"Ok, I'm going to change and get ready to go with you and buy that bucket and anything else we might need, like a pint of ice cream for each one of us at the end of this whole cleansing thing. We're going to need it!" added Julie walking towards her room.

"You do that!"

***

They went to the store around the corner and got a big bucket, matches, couple of fragrant candles and a lot of ice-creams.

"Tomorrow, we have to go to the gym," said Sasha smiling.

"Yes, we do. I actually really have to because I've been celebrating daily with ice-cream for the last couple of weeks."

Sasha looked at Julie and laughed. "You've been having a lot of things to celebrate for then. It was more than worth it. Congratulations!"

"Congratulations to my growing butt, if I don't go to the gym daily for the next couple of weeks to balance off all that celebrating" replied Julie pointing to her behind.

"Come to think of it we've been having a good deal of things to be thankful for lately. There were bad things as well, but the good things seemed to overcompensate for the bad ones" said Sasha with her eyebrow raised and nodding her head like she just discovered something interesting that she hadn't seen before.

"Except for Nikki disappearing, I totally agree with you."

"Yes, Nikki, I totally forgot about Nikki for a second. I wonder where she is and what she's doing right now. I hope she's ok," said Sasha.

"She is. You know her. She feels an urge to just go, but she's always alright and she always comes back. I bet she'll be back in no time" said Julie trying to convince herself at the same time.

"By the way, did you talk to Lizzie?" added Julie.

"Yes, and she's on her way home, right now" replied Sasha.

"Then let's take this party home" said Julie, handing Sasha the oversized metal bucket they had just bought. "Are you ok caring this home?"

"Of course, I am. It's not as heavy as it looks" replied Sasha, grabbing the bucket.

"It's not heavy, but it's definitely uncomfortable because it's so big."

"No worries. If I need to, I'll ask you to switch. Is that ok?" asked Sasha.

"It's more than ok. Just ask."

"I will. Now let's get going and prepare this whole ritual and have it all ready by the time Lizzie gets home. She said she wants to participate, so I'm glad we bought this huge bucket, we'll need it. I have things to burn as well," said Sasha.

"Wow, that is great. I won't feel like the only loser in the house who needs to let go of things."

"Julie, nobody's a loser for having to let go of things. People are losers for not wanting to let go of things. We all need to let go of things on a daily basis" said Sasha putting the bucket down and giving Julie a hug.

"I know. And thank you for the hug" commented Julie." You seem to be able to let go of things much faster. I admire you for that."

"Some of us are better than others at doing so, and some things that happen to us are so powerful that we need help to let go of them. But the important thing is actually realizing you have to let go and having the courage to do so. It takes a lot of courage!" added Sasha as they were walking down the street back to their apartment.

"We are a bunch of courageous women, aren't we?" asked Julie expecting Sasha to agree with her.

Sasha was able to see right through that questioning statement and nodding she replied "We definitely are courageous, the most courageous bunch I've ever met."

Both of them walked silently for the rest of the way home. It was a freezing night, but the thoughts and bags they were caring kept them busy and warm.

Lizzie was already home, waiting for them, with a book in her arms. "Hello! Welcome home. So, are we doing this or what?"

"Yes, we are doing this. Here, hold this" said Sasha handing the bucket to Lizzie. "Take this on the balcony, please!"

"I'm going to my room to grab all the things I want to burn to help me let go of Joe once and forever" said Julie putting the bag with the candles and matches on the table. She took the ice cream out of the second bag and put it in the freezer. "We bought some ice-cream to seal the deal after we're done cleansing!"

"Great idea!" exclaimed Lizzie opening the balcony door and putting the bucket right in the middle of it.

Couple of minutes later, Julie showed up on the balcony with the matches and the candles. She took one candle at a time, lit them up and placed them all around the balcony, in a circle.

"Look what I found" said Sasha showing them the little container of gasoline that they used before when they did a cleansing ritual with Nikki. "There's still some left!"

"Perfect! It's freezing here. This is going to be a good fire. It will help us let go of our ghosts and keep us warm all at the same time!" exclaimed Lizzie, taking the container from Sasha's hands and pouring some of it on the book she had already placed in the bucket.

"Is that your last book that you're setting on fire?" asked Julie.

Lizzie was staring blankly at the book that was slowly consumed by the fire. "Yes, that's the last book I wrote. It was jinxed. It had no success compared to the first one and I was never able to write another one since then."

"I understand, but you also have to understand that it is a great book. The kids you read it to loved it. You are an awesome writer. The children's books you write are adored by every kid I know. Your literary agent and publisher just dropped the ball on it. It wasn't you or your writing."

"I agree with Sasha. If there's anything you should burn, it should be your agent and your publisher" added Julie.

"My published book that I'm burning represents them. You are right. Tomorrow I'm going to cancel my contract with them" announced Lizzie.

"Good for you!" said Julie.

"And tomorrow I'm going to start writing a new book. I don't know what it's going to be, but I'll just have to start writing again. Starting is the hardest part!" said Lizzie.

"Isn't that true for everything!" muttered Sasha.

Julie was holding a pile of things in her arms. She stepped closer to the bucket and started throwing one thing at a time in the fire.

"My pictures with Joe," she said throwing in picture after picture.

Lizzie and Sasha were staring at the smiling faces disappearing as the fire consumed those photographs.

"Plane tickets from our San Francisco trip! I was so in love back then. And he seemed ..." and Julie stopped herself before she had a chance to finish her thought. "I guess he wasn't as in love with me as I thought he was."

A bright yellow T-shirt followed the plane tickets. "He brought me this T-shirt from Puerto Rico, when he went with his best friends. He did not take me with him, but according to him I was on his mind all the time. Bastard! He always told me that but never took me anywhere with him. What did he think, that I'd embarrass him or something?"

Lizzie and Sasha knew better than to say anything. They let her talk it all out.

"I hate him for never giving me a chance, but always dragging me along to think that there's going to be a possibility of that happening in the near future. I'm such an idiot! How could I let this happen? How could I let him take advantage of me like that? And for so long!"

There was complete silence. The fire was crackling, breaking the silence from time to time. Julie's face was full of tears. She was staring at the fire, hating him, hating herself and going through this hateful emotion until she finally felt like she was ready to let it go.

"Joe, I gave you power over my feelings, over my happiness for two years, and I'm still giving you that power now. I'm still giving you power to hurt me, to be afraid and not believe in the possibility of real love. I guess I have to forgive you, so I can forgive myself. "

Julie grabbed Lizzie and Sasha's hands and finally said "I have love and I deserve love. I will love myself and I will not give anyone the power to hurt me ever again. Joe Caltani, you are dead for me!"

"Congratulations!" exclaimed Lizzie and Sasha at the same time.

They all watched the fire for another minute, then Sasha stepped closer to the bucket and threw a brochure with her boss's face on the cover. "I hate you Diane, you stole and ruined my dream. I need to let go of my hate for you. I gave you power to hurt me and I shouldn't have ever done that. I promise I will never let that happen again."

"What are you talking about?" asked Julie. "What did she do now?"

"She took my idea, my presentation on Eastern Europe and she put her name on it."

"Are you kidding me?" asked Lizzie.

"Nope, I saw this brochure on her desk this morning and I confronted her" replied Sasha.

"And?" asked again Lizzie pushing for an answer.

"She pretty much told me there was nothing I could do and to be happy that my idea will be presented to the world by an expert, like her."

"That is bullshit!" yelled Julie. "There has to be something you can do. We'll figure it out!"

"I was thinking the same thing, I just needed to calm down before doing anything crazy," said Sasha.

Lizzie gave Sasha a high five. "Good job! Don't you worry, we'll take her down!"

"I know I will somehow, one day" said Sasha and took the photo she had in her back pocket and threw it in the fire.

It was a picture of her mother. No one said anything, they all knew way too well what that was all about.

"Sorry mom. I have to let you go now, for good!"

They all just stared at the fire and the rhythmic dance of the flames. It was hypnotic. None of them moved until the fire lost all its fuel and slowly died in the cold air of late fall. The winter was near. There were still golden leaves on the trees on their street but they were already dead, the trees were just holding on to them for as long as they could, not being able to let go, bare themselves of all the beauty and colorfulness of the summer and fall days and gracefully receive the winter days.

The winter has its own still and white beauty. It numbs everything. Nature goes to sleep for couple of months, until spring brings it all back to live again with beautiful blossoms and butterflies and singing birds.

Chapter 11

The guy in a multicolored shirt grabbed Julie's wrist and threatened "You are mine. I am going to make you mine no matter what. I am what you need!"

Julie was pulling herself away from this awful man. She couldn't see his face, but she knew he was ugly and scary. "If you won't let me go, I will scream!"

"You can scream as hard as you want, princess, but all you're going to scream for is for more!"

"You are disgusting!" yelled Julie and hit him as hard as she could in the left sheen.

He let her go and she started running, but for some reason she couldn't run fast at all, she was barely moving and she couldn't understand why. She could barely see as well. Her sight was fuzzy, but her mind was very clear. She had to run away from this man.

Julie struggled hard to see where she was going. She saw a boat on the lake a hundred feet away from her. She just needed to get to it and row away from this man, but her feet weighed like a ton, she couldn't move them. He was catching up to her and she felt hopeless and scared and started screaming.

The next second she was sitting up in her bed, covered in sweat.

Julie's throat was all dry. She needed a glass of water, so she got herself out of the bed and moved towards the kitchen. It was five am, but after that dream she didn't know if she could go back to sleep again.

Sasha was in the kitchen grabbing a muffin. "Hey, why are you up?"

"Bad dream!" said Julie. "Why are you up and all dressed up?"

"Work emergency" replied Sasha.

"Again? What does that boss of yours want from you?"

"It wasn't my boss who called me. That's why I'm going!" said Sasha rushing out the door.

The moment Sasha got to work, there was a memo waiting on her desk. Apparently, someone tried to get a hold of her the day before, but she turned off her cell phone after she left work because she was too upset and didn't want to talk to anyone.

"Diane Griffin was in a car accident today, early afternoon. Unfortunately, she's in a comma. Effective tomorrow, all her projects will be taken over by Mr. Stalvin, who's going to delegate Mrs. Griffin's projects as he sees fit. All Mrs. Griffin subordinates should report directly to Mr. Stalvin's assistant, Mrs. Johnson."

"Oh, no! I hope she's all right. Did I do this to her?" Sasha asked herself out loud and answered her own question "No. This accident happened before our cleansing ritual. It wasn't me. Well, I hope she's going to be ok. Now I should go and grab my project from Diane's computer before someone else decides to take it as their ow

"Tell me a little bit about the project! Convince me I shouldn't fire you for accessing information you don't have access to for a good reason" barked Mr. Stalvin.

What was the head of the whole Economic and Social Council doing here at this hour?

Sasha stared at him, trying to focus on what she was going to say next. This was it, this was her shot for promotion or for getting fired. She had a choice. Now she had to make the best of it, ignore the fear that this imposing, brilliant man was inspiring in pretty much every person she knew in that office and tell him about her project.

"There's evidence that in most countries in transition, like the ones in Eastern Europe, women take over a disproportionately high share of costs of systemic changes while their access to opportunities remains low, according to studies made by the World Bank Institute. In these countries, work opportunities are distributed in a very uneven way, of which gender is a major dimension and change is not an option in a political climate where women are vastly underrepresented in new decision-making structures at any level.

My project proposes ways of reversing these negative trends in gender equality and respecting human rights of individuals – what United Nations fights for in every part of this world."

"Do you have statistics, numbers, contacts, data and accurate information to back up your project?" asked Mr. Stalvin.

"Yes, I do. Starting from the World Bank Institute, to the United Nations Economic Commission for Europe, small NGOs in numerous Eastern European countries ..." was enumerating Sasha when she was abruptly interrupted.

"That's fine. I want to see a short presentation on my desk by tomorrow morning and if I approve it, you can coordinate the entire Eastern European Women's Rights conference. "

"And Ms. Brooks," added Mr. Stalvin, "I knew this whole thing was your baby. I know everything that goes on here. But great ideas are not enough, I want to see that you can handle the huge responsibilities that come with the position you're going to have."

"I'm positive I can do this. Thank you for the opportunity, Mr. Stalvin" replied Sasha.

A smile finally showed on his serious face. "I like your spirit, Ms. Brooks. And you can call me Martin."

"Martin, you can call me Sasha", she said with a slight smirk on her face.

She couldn't believe how this whole thing turned around. She felt like screaming from the top of her lungs. She had to play it cool though, at least until he left.

Sasha picked up the phone to give the girls the good news and tell them she was going to pull an all-nighter.

***

Lizzie smiled at Sasha's good fortune.

It was bound to happen, poor girl. She's been having a tough time since birth!

On her way to her room, Lizzie passed by the big oval mirror in the hallway and quickly glanced at her reflection. Her hand went through her hair for a second and she quickly decided it was time for a new haircut. Her bangs were getting too long and she didn't seem able to arrange her hair the way she liked anymore.

"It's time for a new beginning! Maybe a new haircut!" said Lizzie courageously to her own reflection, which seemed to immediately like her idea.

She went to take a shower and freshen up before going for a little adventure in the city.

The showerhead was pulsing at regular intervals sending jets of hot water right into her tensed shoulders. "I love it! It feels so good. I have to remember to thank Julie for buying this amazing shower head for me. Hmm, this does more than cleanse my aura or the shampoo out of my hair. This is heaven."

"All I need is a little bang trimming, nothing huge. Isn't it crazy how such a tiny difference can make such a remarkable change? My features seem to change over time when my hair grows. Just a small trim for a huge effect!"

Lizzie did not get to finish her thought when she was struck by a refreshing idea. Her hands stopped rubbing the shampoo in her hair and her eyes widened.

"Of course! A little trim here and there will completely change my book as well. All I need is to make the father figure in the story a bit more loving. Give him couple more lines and the entire story changes! Yeah!"

She barely managed to rinse her hair as she jumped out of the shower, grabbed her bathrobe and ran to her room to write down her brilliant idea before it went away!

Her laptop was on the white antique desk positioned right in front of the window which allowed a gorgeous view of the small park across the street. Lizzie loved watching out the window every time she sat in front of the computer searching for inspiration.

With the click of a button, she turned it on and threw herself into the off-white cushioned chair in front of it waiting impatiently to start typing. As usual, she put her left leg underneath her as she rearranged herself comfortably into the chair. This was going to be a long session.

Hours later, Lizzie finally got up from her chair only to run to the kitchen and get a glass of water and something to chew on.

The kitchen was empty. Perfect! She loved being home alone when she was in the middle of her writing. It kept her focused. It was a little bit stuffy, so she went to the kitchen window to open it a little bit. It was a warm day, probably one of the last one of this fall. The smell of freshly made popcorn made its way up from the street vendor in the nearby park.

It must have been late in the afternoon, as Lizzie could hear a group of kids laughing joyfully just outside the window. They were done with school for the day and now were playing tag. "You're it," yelled one boy immediately followed by a fast "Not so! You only touched my hood, that doesn't count," said another boy.

Lizzie walked to the window to take in the whole scene. None of the kids seemed bothered at all or angry, the little disagreement seemed to be very friendly.

The redhead girl dressed with a pale baby blue dress and white flowery cardigan, stepped in, put her hands on both boys and calmly announced "You're both it!" And sealed that with a cute giggle.

"Poor boys, they don't stand a chance. Look at her, she's a pro already!" decided Lizzie smiling at them from the window.

She gave them a last melancholic look and shook herself back to her own reality. Her book.

The refrigerator was her first target in the kitchen. As she was pouring some water from the cold pitcher with one hand, she opened the cupboard right above her head to grab a bag of dried fruit. There was no time for cooking. She had to keep on going as long as her writing muse was sticking around.

Armed with a full glass of water in one hand and a bowl of dried fruit in the other, she was on her way out of the kitchen when she lightly touched with her left elbow an apple from the silver platter on the kitchen table. That was enough for that one apple to go overboard, on the table and then roll on the kitchen table dangerously reaching the edge.

With a quick swoop, Lizzie caught the apple right before it fell to the ground, right after she put the dried fruit bowl on the table to free her hand. "Wow! That was fast! I am good! Matrix good!" said Lizzie grabbing the dried fruit bowl with her thumb and index finger, securing it against her body.

"Well, apple, you're coming with me, just like you clearly wanted to!"

"Are you talking to an apple?" chucked Julie from the doorway. "You should have come to my room; I would have generously given you some attention. No need to talk to inanimate objects, especially food, and especially right before you're going to savagely feed on it."

"I wasn't ..." tried to say Lizzie but was cut off.

Julie continued uninterrupted "Poor apple. One minute you talk to it, then the next you satisfy your beastly hunger by carving your teeth into it."

"Ha ha! Very funny!" replied Lizzie. "Now please don't talk to me, I'm in my writing mode."

Julie immediately grasped what Lizzie was trying to say and moved out of the way without another word, just a faint smile on her face. She was glad Lizzie picked herself up and started writing again. It pretty much meant no one will see her out of her room except to grab food and water until she was done for the day, week or month.

One time, while she was writing her first children's book, she was off limits for 11 weeks. They learned to stock the fridge and stop any conversations they were having while she was out of her room getting food. And it worked. Eight months later her book was published and had a tremendous success.

It was time for another book after the second one's fiasco, even though everyone seemed to really love that second book, for some reason it never made it and it demoralized Lizzie to such a degree that she stopped writing altogether.

It was high time for a change. Good for her!

Julie pulled out a chair, grabbed an apple and started staring somewhere outside the window. Lizzie's newly found creative energy seemed to have brushed off unto her. Maybe it was time to start putting together that business plan for the teenage treatment center.

"Ok, so why would my treatment center be different from the others. What should it offer to make it stand out and more importantly help those teenagers more than other treatments out there are able to currently," said Julie out loud to herself brainstorming.

"I'd like the idea of some sort of an Eastern and Western medicine synergy" continued Julie now playing with her hair deep in thought.

The next second she jumped off the chair and ran to her room. "I need a notepad."

After grabbing the first bright yellow notepad she saw on her dresser, she eyed the red pen sitting on top of the stack of books next to her bed and started writing feverishly: "Yoga will be definitely an important part of it. I should call Nick and talk to him about it in more detail."

Julie wrote "Nick - yoga brainstorm - lunch" on the notepad. Then she grabbed her cell phone to check her calendar. "Oh, this is so exciting! I can't believe I didn't start doing this a while ago."

***

"Your presentation is well written, informative and convincing. I'm impressed with the amount of data that you accumulated and the way you integrated it in the presentation, so that it doesn't seem overwhelming" stated Martin Stalvin.

Sasha was pleased. "Thank you, Mr. Stalvin." She was standing in front of his desk in his office. She was too nervous to sit down.

"Now I want you to coordinate with the other departments and make this whole conference happen. You have a year to put this together" finished Martin Stalvin.

"I won't let you down."

"I need updates, monthly. Just leave the files with Mrs. Johnson, she'll update me when necessary. By the way, I'm curious, what made you start an internship here?" asked Martin.

"There was a United Nations press release in March of '05 on women flooding the migrant streams in huge numbers. I read that for one of my Women Studies classes and from there on I knew what I wanted to do with my life. That's why I'm here and that's why my major is in Women Studies."

"I understand that, but why Eastern Europe?" asked Martin.

"I was pretty much raised by my nanny. She was from Romania and all that I became today was because of her. She was very well read and very smart, she's the one who introduced me to philosophy from a very young age" replied Sasha.

Martin laughed. "Instead of fairy tales, she was reading philosophy to you? That doesn't sound right."

"Maybe not to you," replied Sasha defensively, "but I enjoyed the soothing sound of her voice and later on I loved having philosophical conversations with her that took both of us away from the ugly realities of this world into utopia."

"Is she still around? If she was able to influence you so much, I'd like to hire her!" commented Martin with what seemed to be a very serious face.

Sasha didn't know what to make of it. Was he serious? Why would he be interested in her nanny? Was he making fun of her?

"Sasha, you're a bright, stubborn and very ambitions woman who knows exactly what she wants and is not afraid to go for it. I'd love to have more like you working in this department. It's exactly what this whole place needs" said Martin looking her straight in the eye. Then he turned on his heels and was gone.

***

"John is so amazing!" blurted out Lizzie as she was walking unable to contain herself, no matter the consequences.

"I guess your date went well then ... again!" Julie stated the obvious smiling at her. "Mike and I thought you might be compatible enough, but you two have taken the fast train to relationship highway. You crammed more time with each other than I have with Mike since the minute I've known him."

Lizzie giggled like a little girl. She was about to spill something important out. Julie knew the face way to well. "Should I ask Sasha to join us? She's in her room, wrapping up some work emails, or so she said an hour ago."

Julie couldn't believe her own eyes. She hadn't seen Lizzie so happy in a very long time, if ever.

"Stop, don't say anything! Don't move! Let me get Sasha!" said Julie while running towards Sasha's bedroom.

"Sasha! Lizzie has something important to tell us!" yelled Julie on her way.

Sasha's door flew open as she poked her head out. "Is everything alright?"

Julie grabbed Sasha's hand and pulled her towards the kitchen. "Ok, when was the last time you saw Lizzie like this? She's radiating love and joy and light and ... oh my! Did you just see that?" asked Julie in dismay. "Lizzie just lifted her left shoulder to her cheek, looked down, wrapped her arms around her and started swinging her body! And look at that grin!"

"Whatever this is, it must be good!" concluded Sasha.

"Come on! We're ready to hear it!" begged Julie.

Lizzie looked up, met the girls' gaze and blurted out "He said 'I love you! And I can't wait to have beautiful babies with you!'"

"Beautiful what?" Sasha was sure she didn't hear right.

"We're going to wait, of course, until I'm done with school. I'd like to open my own gallery or at least make a best seller out of my new book before ...but those are details"

"Ahh, very important details" pushed Julie.

Lizzie walked towards Julia and Sasha. " You will always be my family. And Nikki. Forever!"

"Forever!" underlined Sasha.

"Nothing has to happen soon. No worries. It's just that my dream finally came true. My man really exists and he found me!" proclaimed Lizzie.

"You found each other" cared to intervene Sasha.

Lizzie smiled and hugged them again. "I am so happy!", then after couple of seconds she added "I wish Nikki was here with us tonight!"

Julie broke away from the hug. "Oh, speaking about Nikki, Mike said he has some news and that he'd be here pretty soon to let us all know what he found out."

"Did it sound like good news?" inquired Lizzie.

"Kind of, I guess. I hope. He didn't ..." Julie couldn't finish her thought as the doorbell rang. "It must be Mike! Let me get the door."

"I found a lead on Nikki," announced Mike as he stepped into the girls' apartment. He was clearly proud of himself as he had the manly bounce in his step on his way to kiss Julie.

Sasha jumped right off her chair and started asking questions: " Where at? Is it really true? How do you know it's Nikki? Is it really Nikki?" without taking a breath.

Mike turned on his heels to face Sasha and visibly tried to stop laughing at Sasha's tirade. "A buddy of mine in Montana called me an hour ago to tell me that there's a girl who fits her profile in a spiritual yoga camp called "Lost and Found Souls" just outside of the small town where he works.

"Lost and Found souls? Is that supposed to be poetic or spiritual?" questioned Lizzie. It sounds to me more like a minimum wage kiosk near the information desk at the local public fair.

"Don't pick on it just because Nikki decided to stay there rather than with us," stepped in Sasha. " The important thing is that we found Nikki, thanks to you" and she jumped to give Mike a hug.

Mike raised his eyebrows in a quizzical manner. He looked like he didn't know what to do. He smiled, and patted Sasha on the back. " I'm glad I could help."

Julie smiled back at him. "He's amazing and my friends like him. Wow, is this really happening to me?" thought Julie now staring at Mike, Sasha and Lizzie with satisfaction mixed with a little bit of fear. "This needs to be true!"

"Let's go to Montana!" blurted out Lizzie.

Sasha's eyes widened " Yes! We should definitely do that! As soon as possible."

Lizzie ran to her bedroom while announcing to everybody very loudly " I'm grabbing my laptop. Let's find flights!"

As Lizzie returned with her laptop in her hands, all excited, Sasha's face turned serious. "I .... I .... hmmm" and then she started mumbling something under her breath. She didn't seem too happy about whatever she was saying there to herself.

"What's going on Sasha? Is everything ok?" asked Julie stepping closer to her lifting her arm to touch Sasha's dropped shoulders to get her attention as she seemed to go into her own world talking to the floor.

There was no answer.

"Sasha! Are you with us?" spoke up Lizzie after several awkwardly silent moments.

Sasha's eyes shoot up from the floor to meet Lizzie's slightly worried gaze. "Oh yeah, I was just trying to figure out how I'm going to go after Nikki with you guys when I have all these meetings scheduled back-to-back for my conference."

"I totally forgot about that," said Lizzie. "Honey, you don't have to come" tried Lizzie.

"But I want to!" said Sasha cutting her off.

"Trust me, you don't want to jeopardize this lifetime opportunity that was offered to you for this" Lizzie replied with conviction.

" I know, I know, but ..." tried Sasha again.

Lizzie did not let her finish her thought "Julie and I can handle this. Plus, you know Nikki would completely freak out if she saw all of us there. She would see it as an intervention of some sort and she would totally shut down."

"Is that what we're doing? An intervention?" Julie seemed to just realize.

"Well, isn't it? "questioned Lizzie.

"If it is, maybe we shouldn't go at all," said Julie.

Lizzie stared at her blankly. "What do you mean not go?"

"Our interventions have always spooked her and pushed her further away from us. She would smell it a mile away!" finished Julie.

"Yeah, you are right!" agreed Sasha "but we still have to do something about it. What should we do? I want to make sure that she's alright."

There was silence. They all seemed to go deep in thought.

Mike finally stepped in "Maybe it's not my place to say, but how about if I send my friend a picture of her, with your permission of course. He can make sure it is her and that she's ok. " As no one said anything, he continued "And then we can go from there. We don't have to decide everything tonight!"

Julie was the first one to react "I think that's the best idea I've heard all night! Thank you! You saved me again!"

Mike laughed and replied "You are welcome! Anytime! I am your hero after all. I'll save you always!" Then he looked straight at Julie and his gaze was serious. He made a step to close the distance between the two of them, gently touched her chin with his hand to lift her head up and made her look back at him.

Julie forgot how to breathe for a second.

He leaned down, cupped her face with his hands and touched her lips softly with his own. Slowly, he pulled away. Julie took another long second and then she opened her eyes again to look at him.

"I need popcorn and a soda" said Lizzie out loud. "This promises to be the best romantic movie I've seen this year" she added jokingly.

Sasha poked her. "What did you have to break that spell with your silly comment?" then she looked at Julie and Mike "That was so intense I could feel it! Wow!"

Julie blushed immediately and hid her face in Mike's chest. He put both his arms around her protectively.

"Ok" felt like saying Lizzie as she got up from her chair. "I'm going to take my laptop back in my room. No need for it now if we're not going to Montana after all."

Sasha took the hint and left the new couple alone. "I need to look over my project notes and I have this paper that is due tomorrow and ... yeah, I ... have to leave you guys."

"Thank you for finding Nikki, Mike" yelled Lizzie from her room before she loudly shut the door behind her.

"Yeah, thank you" said Sasha before she disappeared into her room.

"You're both welcome" spoke up Mike making sure they heard him.

"As for you, my beautiful lady" said Mike leaning his face towards Julie's again "I'd like you to thank me with your sweet lips."

She closed her eyes and let the world disappear around her. There was only Mike's body against her, only Mike's gentle breath on her neck and his lips, his warm soft lips purging their way from the sensitive little valley at the bottom of her neck up to her right ear and her face. It was a sweet torture that seemed to last forever until he hungrily searched for her lips and made her heart beat at unison with his.

When she came around and opened her eyes, he had a Cheshire grin on his face.

Julie quickly stepped on his foot as hard as she could and watched his grin turn into a grimace "Just to wipe off that stupid grin off your face!" Then she stepped away satisfied with herself.

He caught her right arm, swung her back around towards him, held her close and kissed her again.

The insistent loud vibration in his pocket broke the magic.

"You better answer that! It might be important!" whispered Julie breaking away from their passionate moment together.

Mike grabbed his phone lazily and looked at the caller ID. His face changed immediately. He wanted to hide the reaction but it was too late.

Julie preferred to pretend she did not see the sudden change. "Do you have to leave? Is it work?"

"Yes, sorry, duty calls!" he replied trying to plaster a fake smile on his gorgeous face.

"I hope is nothing serious! Good luck!"

Mike was walking towards the door when he swiftly turned around ran back to Julie, picked her off the floor and kissed her lovingly. Then with a sigh he slowly put her back on her feet, kissed her forehead and left.

Julie couldn't move from where she was. Overwhelmed with the feelings that flooded her she dropped on the chair next to her. "I'm falling for a decent guy! Wow! How is that for breaking a lifelong pattern!"

Ten minutes later, she slowly moved towards her room to get ready for bed.

Her cell phone had a blinking red light. She grabbed it to see what it was. "I already miss you!" said Mike's text message.

Chapter 12

The next several days went by really fast and Lizzie was rushing through making time for everything and everyone in her life.

There were three things that were urgent at this point: John, Nikki and finding a new literary agent and a new publicist for her new and improved book. The gallery had to wait and she was finding herself skipping more and more classes than she intended to at school.

"You need to be more careful! You're almost done with school, don't screw it up now!" cautioned her Sasha.

A call interrupted her thoughts. " Lizzie, it's me, Nikki. I'm coming home!" And that was the end of it.

Lizzie couldn't believe it. She checked her phone to make sure it was Nikki's number. It was. She didn't pay attention to the caller id when she answered.

She had to call the girls. But why did Nikki call her? She was usually communicating with Julie.

Lizzie shook her head while dialing Julie's number. It doesn't matter why! What's important is that she called and that she's coming home!

"Nikki called me!" yelled with content in the phone Lizzie when she heard Julie picking up.

Julie seemed to have gone mute.

"She only said that she's coming home. That's it!"

"Did she say when? Or where she is? Did she sound ok? Do you think she's mad at us? Does she know we've been spying on her? When did she call exactly? Did she use her cell?" asked Julie one question after another in rapid fire.

"I don't know anything but that she's coming home!"

Julie squealed at the other end of the line.

Lizzie smiled "Ok, so call Sasha and let her know. I'm getting ready to enter this place where Joanne is having her birthday. Don't wait up! I might not stay that long anyway ... but you never know!"

"Have fun! Be careful and stay safe! Call us for anything!" said Julie making sure Lizzie knows she meant it.

"I will! No worries, you know me! ... Have to go! Bye" finished Lizzie and hang up as she stepped into one of the loudest places she's been in a while.

She immediately spotted her friends next to the bar, where they said they would be.

"Thank you for coming Lizzie!" said a buzzed Joanna while hugging her tight.

"I'm glad to be here! So, what's on the menu?"

"Maybe who's on the menu" joked Joanne winking at her and leaving her surrounded by some people from the gallery while going in to hug and welcome other guests.

Lizzie was hungry. Hopefully this place has some good finger food. She looked around for a waiter for a menu. The dancing floor was packed with moving bodies bathed in flashing red, green and blue lights.

People seemed to be having a really good time, but none looked sober. Three loud girls were making their way from the mass of moving bodies to the bar laughing and doing their best not to trip over their heels.

Lizzie found herself missing those times, when she would go clubbing, dancing and laughing out loud, but then again, she was also drinking, binge drinking, drinking until she would pass out. Never having enough.

"Where is the waiter? I need some food. I'm starving" she said out loud trying to snap herself out of it while searching her surroundings with quick glances.

Something got her attention.

"Lizzie! What happened? You look like you just saw a ghost!" yelled Linda, one of Lizzie's friends' from the gallery, so she could make herself heard over the loud music that was inundating the entire lounge area of their favorite club at this late hour.

"What?" replied Lizzie, clearly shaken out of her reverie.

Joanne got closer to her and start looking in the direction of Lizzie's stare, searching for a recognizable face. Nothing. "Are you ok?"

"Just want to see something", said Lizzie absent mindedly while she made her way towards the focus of her attention.

"It can't be!"

The closer she got to the crowd of loud women with minuscule yet flashy tight dresses and thigh high latex shiny boots that were gathered around the dark booth closest to the ladies' bathroom, the more sure she was that the only male sitting at that table was the one she was falling for after several charmingly romantic dates.

"There's no way!" she told herself. "I'm mistaken for sure!" Lizzie said out loud to herself. No one could hear her in that infernal noise that sounded like music to her several minutes ago.

Couple of more steps would have brought her exactly in the lap of the man she had been staring at continuously while robotically moving towards the booth.

At the last second, the man got up and grabbed the blond next to him with bright red lipstick covering her overly fat pumped lips. "Teasing me with your naked pussy like that is driving me insane. I'm going to fuck your brains out and you'll love it, you little whore!"

Lizzie froze. She couldn't move and she couldn't look away either. He was standing right in front of her and she had no escape plan whatsoever.

He pushed Lizzie firmly aside and squeezed the blonde live blowup doll in front of him, guiding her towards the men's bathroom. The pink neon dress was fighting to cover the blonde's genital area, but to no avail. Lizzie stopped breathing wishing the ground would open and swallow her whole.

He didn't seem to acknowledge Lizzie at all.

"I don't know about you bitches, but I'm going to his vineyard in Napa if I have to suck my way there. You know?!" yelled a short-haired redhead stationed right next to Lizzie, making a loose fist with her right hand and bringing it close to her mouth in a back-and-forth motion.

Lizzie felt sick to her stomach. She was literally feeling like she was going to throw up on the table right in front of all those ridiculous women.

She had to get out.

Her lead feet seem to finally listen to her commands and lift off the floor, one by one, taking her to the safety of the wide-open street. At long last she could breathe.

Lizzie put both her hands on her knees while bending over trying to catch her breath and recover from the shock. The cold air penetrated her lungs and brought clarity to her overwhelming thoughts.

As the shock melted away, tears come pouring down her pretty face.

"How could I have been so wrong about him? Am I that desperate?"

Her body started shaking uncontrollably and she dropped to the ground, on the hard freezing cement, holding her knees as close to her face as possible with both her arms circled around them.

"Hey, lady! Lady! Are you alright?"

Lizzie barely heard the question. Everything seemed to be a blur and so far away.

"Do you need a cab?"

Chapter 13

Her chest was still hurting. Lizzie put her hand on the sore spot and tried to take in a deep breath. With the air that rushed in came the memory of the past night. The horrific images and sounds played in her head louder and louder. She could hear her rapid heartbeat. Her hands were over it trying to keep it in her chest. The tight grip around her chest and her throat made her want to scream for help, but couldn't get anything out but a pathetic low cry.

"I need to open my eyes, get out of bed and keep myself busy until this entire episode is well in the past", she told herself.

But the bitter sweet misery had a hard grip on her. She just couldn't and wouldn't let go.

She replayed last night in her head over and over again trying to understand.

"Maybe it wasn't him" tried a limp hopeful voice in her head.

"It was definitely John! Why lie to myself like that! If I were blind, I would have still recognized his voice and touch, when he pushed me out of his way to rush and have his way with that plastic whore."

"I hate him!" Lizzie decided.

"I hate his cretin face and retarded smile and sleek touch. I hate his silver tongue and all the dreamy sweet pictures of an amazing future that he painted in my mind. What a fake! What a disgustingly low creature."

Lizzie took another deep breath. "I hate him, I hate him, I hate him!!!" Tears were pouring down her face and she started sobbing "And I hate myself for letting him do that to me! I'm so stupid!"

She started hitting herself in the chest trying to punish herself and make the pain inside go away or at least replace it with the pain she was physically inflicting on herself. "Stupid, stupid Lizzie!"

Her cries became louder and louder. She grabbed a pillow and forcefully stuffed her cries in it, so she wouldn't wake up the girls. She wanted to be alone in her misery. She wanted to hate herself like she deserved before the girls would try to stop her and bend over backwards to make her feel better.

Lizzie did not want to put on a show for anyone. Her insides felt torn apart and it hurt like hell.

There was nothing else in this world, but she and her engulfing pain.

***

Julie was brushing her teeth, watching herself in the mirror and contemplating the long day she had ahead of her.

"Me, you, Cozumel and a long weekend! How does that sound to you?" asked Mike with a seductive smile coming out of the steaming shower while wrapping a towel around his waist.

"Just horrible!" joked Julie keeping a straight face. "Excruciatingly boring and long! But what can you do, I am a sucker for endless uncomfortable moments with guys I can't stand to be around, so ..."

Mike did not give Julie time to finish up. He started poking her until she was laughing and squirming around. "Stop it! It's not fair that you know how ticklish I am, yet you seem to be made out of stone!"

One second later Mike's lips took over her mouth, holding her face between his hands. She was melting. No more giggling. He lifted her up with one arm, picked her off the floor and without pausing his insatiable kissing, he took her back to bed.

His hungry lips were devouring her neck. Julie's eyes were closed, allowing her body to take over. No more thinking, no more smart remarks, no more talking. Those moments were so precious and sensual. His hands took off the towel she had wrapped around her and his fingers begin their lascivious journey on her petite naked body.

"Baby, I can never get enough of you! You're driving me crazy! Our bodies are perfect for each other!" whispered Mike with a low husky voice full of desire.

Julie's body got stiff. Those were the exact words Joe used to say while they were making love ... having sex ...whatever! Julie couldn't stop her brain from digging through all the painful memories.

Mike finally noticed the change. "Are you ok? Is it something I said?"

"No, not at all honey! That bruise on my ribs is still sore and I couldn't breathe for a second", lied Julie trying to sound as convincing as possible. Joe had no business interfering in her life anymore and she was not going to let him ruin this one for her.

"Baby, I'm sorry! I completely forgot. Let me kiss it and make it better! I don't want to do anything to hurt you. Ever!" said Mike looking her right in the eyes emphasizing the last word.

Julie pushed herself up to his face and kiss him. "I know honey!"

His cell phone started ringing interrupting the heavy moment. Mike did not seem to care and started kissing Julie again. "It can go to voicemail", he said at Julie's raised brow. She closed her eyes again abandoning herself to the sweet caressing of his lips.

The phone rang again. She tried not to focus on it as Mike seemed undisturbed, but when it started ringing for the third time in a row, she pulled herself away " You better take that! It sounds like an emergency!"

His face grimaced. He clearly did not want to pull himself away from her.

"Please!" begged Julie.

"Only because you want me to!" said Mike slowly lifting himself off of her. He walked around the bed towards the dresser where his phone was sitting. He picked it up, looked at it and concluded after 10 long seconds of silence "Well, duty calls again!"

There was a sad note in his voice, so Julie said "Honey, it's alright! People need you! I understand"

Mike looked at her and tried a smile. "So, does that mean yes to our Cozumel getaway?"

"Of course! Which weekend are we talking about?" asked Julie.

"This upcoming weekend!" replied Mike.

Julie was completely taken by surprise. "I don't know. I have to see..."

"Please, please, please baby! We need to get away from this craziness, from my job, from my cell ringing all the time! I want alone time only with you! Away!"

Julie couldn't say no to all that pleading. She couldn't remember if she had anything planned for the weekend, but it all had to wait.

***

Sasha was already in the kitchen microwaving a bowl of oatmeal when Julie walked in the door.

"Can't believe Nikki is coming back!" yelled Sasha enthusiastically and went in for a hug before Julie even had the chance to take off her coat.

"Yes, " she said absentminded, " I can't believe it either."

"Hello, Julie! What's going on up there in that pretty head of yours? You're not paying attention to anything I'm saying, are you?" said Sasha patiently looking at Julie and waiting for an answer.

It took Julie several seconds before she could break away from her own world, finally look up at Sasha and respond "Oh, just a little tiny minor thing ... with Mike"

"Do tell! I'm all ears, said Sasha sitting herself comfortably at the kitchen table with the hot bowl of oatmeal in front of her.

Julie grabbed a mug and some tea and tried to make herself busy while telling Sasha about the weekend away proposal from Mike. " It's kind of abrupt! And a lot!"

"Wow, girl! You haven't been treated right in so long that you have some sort of an allergic reaction to a nice romantic gesture! That is sad and pathetic!" replied Sasha.

"Right?" interrupted Julie. "It must be something like that." She became quiet again and stared at the kitchen floor but her mind seemed to be far far away.

Sasha gave her a long moment before she questioned "Does something feel wrong? Do you feel pressured in some way? I can always come up with a perfectly believable excuse for you and you won't even have to face Mike until you're ready again."

"Oh, no! Nothing like that! He is wonderfully attentive and loving and warm! Everything that I wanted Joe to be!"

"But wasn't!" finished Sasha for her.

The frigid reality of Sasha's words shook Julie to the core. She took the kettle off the stove and poured some hot water in her mug covering her spicy tea bag. The aroma lifted from the mug and infused the entire kitchen.

"Now that's a smell that will wake me up and get me ready for a great day every day of the week!" exclaimed Lizzie walking slowly into the kitchen.

Chapter 14

She was standing in front of the white building, took a deep breath and walked in. She wasn't sure what to feel, if she should be upset about them butting in her life or be flattered. She did not know if she was able to let go of what had happened and she wasn't sure how to handle it. Maybe she should go back; maybe this is where she should be. Let be and let God!

The moment she walked into the apartment; she knew she did the right thing coming back the moment she heard the chatting going on in the kitchen. It felt so good! All the doubts dissipated in a matter of seconds.

"Nikki! Oh, my God! Nikki, I missed you so much!" screamed Lizzie in disbelief tearing up and running to hug her.

Julie dropped her cup of spicy tea and froze for a short moment. They all turned towards Julie. She finally was able to say "You came back home!" with a cracking voice.

Nikki smiled, walked toward her and met half way and hugged her really tight. "Of course, I came home silly! Did you think I wouldn't? I love you guys! I always come back to you. I'm sorry I have to take a break now and then, but my feelings for you guys never change. I will always, always come back!"

Sasha came in to hug Nikki and Julie and announced "Group hug!" so Lizzie jumped in immediately and started hugging them all.

There was laughter and crying and hugging. Emotions were flying high in the girls' kitchen this early morning.

Finally, Julie broke away from the group and asked "Nikki, would you like some tea? I guess I need to make myself another cup anyways" she said cleaning up the shattered mug that she had tea in when Nikki walked into the kitchen several minutes ago.

"One of your spicy teas would be exactly what I need right now. Thank you, Julie! I love you honey" replied Nikki innocently with a sweet, calm voice.

Julie couldn't stop herself no matter how hard she tried and she burst into tears.

Nikki was confused "What's going on? Something is off" noticed Nikki. She stared at Lizzie and Sasha looking for answers, but both of them just stared at the floor not saying a thing.

"OK, what's going on Julie?"

Instead of saying anything, Julie just threw herself in Nikki's arms and started sobbing really hard. Nikki wrapped her arms around her slowly and tightly. Julie's sobbing became a hysterical cry and no one dared to say anything but sit and wait in silence until she was through. Julie dropped all her weight on Nikki and they slowly collapsed to the floor on their knees holding each other.

When Julie seemed to be out of breath and out of tears, Nikki grabbed the tissues that Sasha brought to the kitchen from her room and handed one at a time to Julie while slightly rocking her body.

"It's going to be ok. The worst is over! Whatever happened happened and it's done. It's over. Now it's time for healing" said Nikki in a soothing calm voice not wanting to put any pressure on Julie to say what she didn't seem like she wanted or could say.

Julie took one of the tissues that were gently handed to her and began blowing her nose. She was starting to calm down, trying to catch her breath.

"I, ...I..." Julie tried saying but she was out of breath every time she pushed to say whatever was on her mind. She couldn't even get a full word out. The dry sobbing was interfering with her wishes to speak and share her pain with Nikki.

"You - you need to recognize this emotional state you're in, validate it, bath in it for a little bit and then, when you're ready we'll let it go together. Ok?" asked Nikki caressing Julie's hair and kissing her on the top of her head holding her close.

"I ... I" tried Julie again.

"Shh, it's ok. No need for words for right now. Listen to your body, let it feel this emotion entirely."

"But Joe, he ... I" continued Julie catching her breath with every word.

Nikki pushed Julie's face away from her chest and up in front of her to face her. "I knew that much! Trust me, baby! I know you better than you know yourself. He could have been the only one who could have hurt you this much. You don't even give yourself half of the power you give him over yourself" muttered Nikki, pulling Julie's head at her chest again.

Julie did not fight it, quite the contrary, she just let herself relax into it and breathed deeply closing her eyes.

"Maybe you should start by telling Nikki about Mike!" suggested Sasha shyly.

A really loud burst was heard and Nikki and Sasha looked at Julie with concern. The hysterical crying was starting again. But to their surprise, Julie was calmly breathing deeply in Nikki's arms.

Not even a second later, Lizzie literally sprang out of the kitchen and into her room slamming the door behind her.

"What the hell is going on here! I'm gone for couple of weeks and you all fall apart!" said Nikki with a mildly accusatory tone looking at the only person in the room that had not started crying yet, Sasha.

"Julie, I get! I know the story. I was there" replied Sasha looking directly at Nikki. "Lizzie ... I thought she was super happy ... or at least she was last time I talked to her."

"You know what," continued Sasha, "you take care of Julie, I'll go check up on Lizzie."

"Team work. That's how it's done!" Nikki tried to lighten up the mood.

Sasha picked herself off the chair and walked over to Lizzie's room. She softly knocked on the door and asked "Lizzie, sweetheart, can I come in?"

There was no response. She waited another 10 seconds before she tried again.

"I understand if you don't want to talk to me about it, but all I want to do is make sure you are ok because I care." Sasha waited before she continued "I care so much about you! Please let me be a part of whatever's going on. All I want is to give you a hug and support you any way you'd like me too. Promise I won't push for anything that you are not ready to share."

The doorknob turned with a high-pitched squeak and the door opened slightly.

There was no one in the doorway.

Sasha figured Lizzie just opened the door to signal her in, but did not want to come out at all. She walked in and saw Lizzie two feet behind the door, on her soft carpet, lying there motionless.

"May I?" asked Sasha for permission as she set herself next to her.

There was no crying, no tears, but her eyes were red shot, her face was pale and she was looking straight at the pillow she was hugging tightly in her arms.

"Whatever happened in there to trigger this reaction in you was not intentional. You know that, right?" asked Sasha. "We do not want to hurt you in any way. We love you immensely. Please let me know you are aware of that."

Nothing.

"Can I touch you?" asked Sasha softly. "I would like to hug you if that's alright with you. Can you let me do that?"

Lizzie did not verbally respond, but slightly gave a faint vertical nod.

Sasha did not wait for any other kind of invitation. She threw herself at Lizzie and hugged her as tightly as she could and started rocking Lizzie's motionless body using her own bodyweight.

"Whenever you're ready to talk about it, just say the word. I'm here for you" said Sasha waiting for any kind of response. She didn't get anything. "In the meantime, we can just sit here quietly."

"Take as much time as you need" continued Sasha after more than 5 minutes of silence.

Lizzie's mind was racing. "What had happened? How did she lose it like that? Nikki just got home. Julie went through physical abuse from the man she loved and still loves and here she was making a scene over a bastard who broke her dream of perfect love."

She was embarrassed, but her body did not seem to listen to her rational. It was frozen and did not want to move or say anything.

"I hope I can just brush this off as an emotional trigger and relate it to my addiction past. No one will question that. But what if they ask for details or make me talk to my sponsor? I don't want anyone to know how stupid and desperate I am that I let myself fooled like that by the biggest jackass on the planet. And on top of it all, I let him hurt me this bad that my body reacts to outside stimuli like that?"

"Do you want me to bring you a blanket?" asked Sasha interrupting her thoughts. "You're shivering! You must be cold!"

Not expecting any kind of answer from her, Sasha unwrapped her arms and put her left hand down to support herself while getting off the floor.

Out of the blue, Lizzie's hand grabbed Sasha's and pulled her back to the floor next to her.

"Please don't go!" begged Lizzie.

"But I'm not going anywhere, I promise! I was just getting you a blanket" said Sasha softly in an attempt to not break the comforting silence that Lizzie had built.

"Don't!" whispered Lizzie "Just hold me, please!"

Sasha obeyed. "For as long as you need me to."

"I was debating in my head if I should even tell you what exactly triggered my idiotic and insensitive reaction and my first thought was to lie."

"Why would..." tried Sasha, but was quickly interrupted by Lizzie: "Julie finally found a good guy to get her over the Joe nightmare and she seems to be falling for him, hard."

"Isn't that good?" questioned Sasha with a raised eyebrow.

"Not when this hero of hers has disgustingly atrocious sleazy friends!" offered Lizzie.

Sasha was looking confused "Sorry, I'm not following you."

"Last night, I saw John, my John and Mike's best friend enjoying cheap hookers and lines openly at a club."

"No, ... no, no, no" started repeating Sasha her brain refusing to accept the reality of Lizzie's words.

"Yes, yes, yes!" corrected Lizzie.

Sasha's brain visibly shifted gears. "Are you ok? You seemed so head over heels for this guy" said Sasha with a sympathetic look on her face. "I am so sorry, honey!" and then she seemed to be at a loss for words "I guess it's better you found out sooner rather than later!"

"I guess!" mumbled Lizzie almost to herself. Then she raised her head and looked at Sasha again " But what about Julie? What about Mike? There's no way Mike can be a good guy with a friend like that. You should have seen how he treated those women ... like meat...worse...like garbage!"

Sasha had to agree. "Birds of a feather ..."

"Flock together" added Lizzie to finish the saying.

Sasha tried "I mean, there are some exceptions."

"Really? Should we hope for a rare exception for our Julie betting her health, mental wellbeing and her sobriety on it? "

Both of them set in silence for a while.

"Let's not be too hasty" concluded Sasha. "We'll consult with Nikki as well once she's up to speed with Julie's life and from the ongoing conversation that I can hear in the kitchen, it won't be long until that's done."

"Yeah, I guess you're right," said Lizzie.

Sasha looked at her and hugged her again. "How about you, baby? How badly did that asshole hurt you?"

"He disillusioned me...more than anything. My heart will recover. It always does. It sucks and I might need to scream, yell and cry until I'm healed, but as Nikki said "the worst is over", the damage is done, now it's time to focus on the recovery and the healing part."

Sasha looked at Lizzie without saying a word. She just hugged her tighter.

"Thank you, Sasha, for listening. I really appreciate it!" said Lizzie leaning into her hug.

"Anytime!"

"Let's go see what's going on in the kitchen" pushed Lizzie.

Sasha was compliant and was getting up "Are you sure?"

"Yes! Please! This is how I heal, not paying attention to my drama once I have processed what happened and decided I should move on."

"Your body, your life, your decision. But remember I'm always here for you" Sasha reminded Lizzie.

"I know. And I'm grateful for that!"

One more hug and they were walking out of Lizzie's room and into the kitchen.

Julie and Nikki were sitting at the kitchen table sipping on couple of cups of hot tea and chatting like the scene that just took place half an hour before never happened. Julie was calm.

"You look quite cheery, Julie!" exclaimed Sasha surprised.

Julie looked up at her, "Nikki is a miracle worker, as always!"

"Yes, she is", replied Sasha promptly going for a high five.

Nikki responded on the spot, then jumped up and grabbed Sasha's hand and pulled her in for a hug. "I missed you, baby, how you've been?"

"Good, you know, busy at work!"

"Yeah, Julie already filled me in on that whole Eastern European women project. Congratulations! This is huge! I am so darn proud of you!" said Nikki, going in for another hug.

Sasha was mute, taken by surprise.

"You more than deserve it, you worked very hard on it" continued Nikki, trying to drill the truth into Sasha's stubborn head.

"I totally agree with Nikki, Sasha! You are amazing. More amazing than any of us. This project, your work is going to be global! How cool is that?" came in to help Julie.

Lizzie went in for the kill "You are the smartest, prettiest and more accomplished woman that I know, especially at your age."

"I don't know about 'the prettiest' part, but you can take smart and accomplished. As we all are already painfully aware, I am the 'prettiest,'" joked Nikki.

Lizzie and Julie started laughing and Sasha and Nikki joined them in an instant.

The atmosphere was light again. Back to the moments they used to have before Nikki's disappearance. Things seem to be going back to the normal path again.

"So, what was all that Cozumel talk that I overheard on my way here," asked Lizzie, looking straight at Julie.

She bit her lip for a split second than answered "Mike invited me to go with him on a long romantic weekend. Just me and him. Away from his work and his constantly beeping phone."

"I don't think that's such a good idea," started Lizzie in a very serious tone of voice. She did not seem to just state a vague opinion, but vehemently make her true feelings and beliefs known.

She clearly got everyone's attention fast.

"But why?" asked Julie. "I thought you liked Mike and were all for me forgetting Joe and moving on."

Sasha interrupted "Is he making you forget about Joe?"

"Mostly, yes! It's just too soon for me to completely erase him from my memory, but Mike is doing an amazing job at replacing him and his touches and his smell and his kisses ...and ..."

"Ok, then" concluded Nikki. "I say you should go then."

"No doubt about it" added Sasha.

Julie's eyes moved to Lizzie. "Lizzie?"

"You should not listen to me right now, I'm not in the best state of mind...
I guess," then Lizzie turned around to leave the kitchen. A split second
later she turned back on her heels and said "But I still think you shouldn't
go, because it's too soon. Your relationship is really new, you've been
through a lot and you don't really know this guy. "

"Well, that's partially why I'm going. To get to know him better and see
where this thing is going" replied Julie.

"Maybe. But I know you and I know how vulnerable you are right now
and how fast you're falling for this guy and I want to make sure he's not
anything close to Joe. That's all!"

Nikki's face went livid. "No one's close to Joe. He's a monster. I just wish
I was here."

"You really think so? Because ..." then Lizzie stopped and looked at
Sasha's face. She was begging her not to say it. She took a deep breath
and finished "well, as I said. I'm not at my best right now."

"Care to share?" jumped in Julie.

"No. Not yet. But I will, soon. I promise."

"Whenever you are ready, you know we're all here" confirmed Julie with
a reassuring smile.

"Yes, I know. Thank you"

Chapter 15

"There were no tickets left for Cozumel Airport, so I got us two tickets for Cancun. We'll get a cab to the ferry in Playa del Carmen. Hope that's ok with you, baby!" said Mike to Julie while picking her luggage off the curve.

"I'm not worried at all with any of those details. Better yet, I guess this way I get to see Cancun and Playa del Carmen" replied Julie with a smile on her face while getting in the cab that Mike got for them.

"Cancun is definitely a place to see, but I don't know exactly what Playa del Carmen is all about"

Julie took Mike's hand into hers and pulled him close to her for a quick kiss. She was so happy. She never wanted this feeling to end. "Apparently Playa del Carmen is way cool. Nikki went to a summer Spanish school at a place called Solexico, if I remember correctly. She was raving about it for years and trying to get us to go. Her Spanish is amazing, so if we ever have time, I'd like to check it out if that's ok with you."

"Anything you wish, my dear" came Mike's reply breathed softly on her lips while his left hand was cupping the lower back of her head and his right making its way behind her back bringing her closer to him. The soft touch of his lips made Julie forgot all about her Playa del Carmen plans, especially the ones that included school.

She was holding on to her passport that she forgot to put back in her purse with one hand but she quickly used her free hand to dig right into Mike's gorgeously thick hair. She grabbed a hand full of hair and playfully pulled at it. Mike's pleasure moan came deep from his throat. "If you keep doing that, we might not make it to the airport in time, as I may have to ask this cabbie to pull out at the first motel he sees."

Julie's satisfied grin made Mike smile. "I see, I guess this was your plan all along."

"Not necessarily. I do want to make it to Mexico. We have 3 days of bliss waiting for us. No point in rushing this when we can fully enjoy it in paradise! And I am not planning to leave that bed at all this entire weekend. Now that's what I call a paradise," whispered Mike into Julie's ear.

She started blushing glad that he did not say it out loud so the cab driver could hear it. Some kissing is fine and probably normal, but their private plans had to be just that...private.

"Too bad for my miniscule sexy leopard print bathing suit. I was hoping to show it off at your side" whispered Julie back.

Mike's eyes were bulging in a way that made Julie burst out laughing.

"Yeah, now I'm sure I'm going to get to wear my newest piece of garment that I just purchased especially for this trip" said Julie flamboyantly.

"Oh, we should have done this a long time ago."

Julie laughed "We haven't been together that long, honey!"

"Why didn't I find you years ago!" said Mike with a melancholic look on his face.

Julie was trying to understand the whole mood change. But before she could ask him about it he shook it off and with a smile on his face he said "But you are here now and you make me so happy! I've never been so happy in my entire life!" then he pulled her closer to him and kissed the top of her head.

She felt safe and loved. Life was finally giving her a lucky break.

***

All the handouts that Sasha prepared were passed to everyone in the room. She gave them couple of minutes to look over the bullet points of her presentation while she was breathing as deeply as she could visualizing herself successfully completing this presentation. Her hands were sweaty and she closed her eyes to steady herself.

Mr. Stalvin was in the first row waiting for her to start. He was never a patient man and she knew it. Well, ready or not, she had to go for it. This was her baby; this was her dream and she was more than prepared to make it happen. She only had to speak out loud, in front of everyone and make them quiet and keep them interested in what she had to say. Piece of cake, right?

Sasha's head started spinning.

"Aheem" was heard from the front of the room and the chatter vanished within seconds. She knew Mr. Stalvin gave her the go. It was now or never. She had to jump in head first.

Come on, just say the first words...the rest will follow. She told herself. Look at the piece of paper in front of you, nothing else.

"Hello everybody and thank you for showing up to my ...I mean to our first meeting. This event that we are planning is of the biggest importance and I'm glad that most of you volunteered to work on this project. For the ones that did not have a choice, thank you Mr. Stalvin for making them - I bet they are a very important addition to my team, and I will make sure that this will be the best project you've ever worked on. Or at least the food that I'll be providing for all our brainstorming sessions will be delicious."

She heard a few laughs in the back of the room and her shoulders started relaxing slowly.

" I know you have all read the presentation that I made for my department head and pitched to the senior management - and she signaled with her head towards Mr. Stalvin - if you have any questions on it, we will be having a separate meeting later in the day. Please write down all the questions and ideas and bring them along. Right now, all I want to talk about and focus on is the meeting that we will be having tomorrow with a bunch of deep pockets as we need their support immediately in order to start moving on this project."

Things seemed to be going alright. The mass of people in front of her seemed to be honestly interested in what she had to say. It was not as hard as she thought at the beginning. Apparently all one needs to do is jump in and think afterwards when it comes to public speaking.

"Tomorrow, before we ask anybody for their support, why not close our eyes, breathe and rethink the whole campaign from the sponsors' point of view. Forget why you signed up for this.

"Why do they think of giving money for this particular campaign?"

"What attracted their eye?"

"What are they hoping to see? Where do they think this campaign will go?"

"Where do we fall short?"

"Let's ask them and let them build our campaign for us. We won't need to sell it anymore. If it feels like it's their baby as well, they will put lots of money in it with pleasure and enthusiasm.

We all win!"

"That's brilliant!" she heard someone saying. She didn't know her team yet, so couldn't identify who it was.

Couple applauses were heard in the back and then they made their way to the front of the room.

Sasha was smiling while catching her breath. She couldn't believe this was happening to her.

Mr. Stalvin approached her "From here on, I need updates only on a weekly basis. Do not come to me unless there's an emergency" then walked away.

She was completely overwhelmed. Was she going to be able to pull this off? This was huge!

Several people came to the front of the room to introduce themselves to Sasha.

***

"Why should I accept you back in the program when you disappeared again without giving us notice or a reason of any kind?"

"Dean Jackson," replied Nikki "I would love to be given the opportunity to finish my program at your school. I know I have repeatedly taken off for weeks at a time, but as you said in our first-year speech, we all have our muses and all have our demons that feed us the art that's within us. I respected you from day one because of that speech, because I knew that you understood firsthand the struggles of a true artist at heart."

"Unfortunately, even though I know your huge potential and I know in my heart you are the most talented artist I've ever had the honor of having in my program, I can't overlook those absences without some sort of penalties."

"All actions have consequences" admitted Nikki. "I know and I'm prepared for them."

"If I expel you, you will lose your scholarship and I know how much you need it. We knew from the start about your corks in personality as you so honestly laid them out for us in your application. But you were so talented we chose to take a chance and gave you a full scholarship."

Nikki immediately jumped in " Which I'm very grateful for."

"Are you? Sometimes I don't know. And we can't really make any exceptions for you. It wouldn't be fair to the other students."

"I know and I'm not expecting you to make any exceptions for me" added Nikki.

"So how do you propose we solve this?" asked the dean.

Nikki was already prepared for this question: "I've been working on a private collection that I want to exhibit on school grounds first at the beginning of next year."

Dean Jackson's attention was focused on the idea immediately. He knew exactly what she was offering. With her talent, her first official exhibit and on campus grounds would bring a ton of positive publicity to the school, the program and himself directly. This meant more money, donations, applications and definitely a raise for him."

He knew he couldn't play her in any way. She was really aware of what she was doing, no reason to toy or even negotiate with her: "Your talents and your quick mind saved you again. I need the presentation on your collection on my desk first thing Monday morning- with pictures of any finished pieces. You are excused. But this will be the last time! You have less than a year left of school. Please try to keep it together for everyone's sake."

"I will dean, I promise! Thank you for your time!"

Nikki walked out of the dean's office with a smile on her face. She knew this will only push her to actually start on her idea with the "Love flood" collection. She needed this creative work more than she needed to finish school or air to breathe at this point. This collection will save her life. This collection will save her soul.

She already knew what her first piece will be, she just had to decide on the medium. All the times when she woke up Sasha from her bad dreams, she imagined a child being brought back from the claws of a nightmare by a vigilant, loving and nurturing parent and hugged back to sleep with sweet kisses on their forehead and gentle rocking.

This was going to be it. The beginning of her collection. Was it going to be a painting, charcoal, watercolor, sculpture or maybe a simple photograph. This was all up in the air for right now. All to be decided at a later time, but soon, very soon.

Chapter 16

Papa Hog's Scuba Diving sign was visible from far away. Especially when she knew what she was looking for. Julie was strolling down the beach in her sexy bathing suit with a light see-through dress and a huge hat to save her fair skin from the baking sun.

He saw Mike waiting for her with a huge smile on his face. He had two tropical looking drinks in his hands, topped with tiny umbrellas and pineapple slices.

"The blue virgin drink is yours, baby "he said handing her the tall glass. "It's some sort of berry soda. I made sure there wasn't any alcohol in it."

"That's very sweet of you!" said Julie taking the glass in her hand. " I was waiting for you. I thought you would come back after taking that call. Didn't you promise me to have your cell phone shut off once we got to Mexico?"

"Baby, it's shut off. I'm sorry. Those guys at work tried their luck and got a hold of me. But I told them I'm off limits now and look" he swiftly let her take a quick glance at his phone "I shut it off."

Julie felt a bit silly. "Sorry, honey. I don't mean to be naggy or anything."

Mike kissed her softly. "You are not naggy at all. That phone was a bother to me as much as it was to you. That's why I preferred to take it outside. Sorry for not coming back. I had to walk it off. Work news gets me all heated up. But I'm glad you got my message and met me here."

"Are we going to scuba dive?" asked Julie trying to change the subject and move on to a happier conversation.

"Only if you're comfortable with it? But I would definitely love to see that sweet ass of yours in that bikini in the water. Now!" said Mike with a playful tone touching her lower back and slowly moving towards her barely covered butt.

"Mike!" she squealed, slapping his hand away. We are in public. It's not appropriate." But she couldn't move away from his touch.

"How about moving out of the public area then?" And before Julie could answer Mike had already picked her off her feet and he was carrying her towards the small romantic cottage he rented on the beach not far from where they were.

"Aren't I too heavy?" questioned Julie. "You've been caring me for quite a while."

As Mike was laying a kiss on her awaiting lips, he lifted her body higher closer to his face and buried his face into the nook of her neck. "I love keeping you as close to me as possible. At all times!"

She had nothing to say in return just gasped for air as his chest was crashing hers while inhaling the smell of her freshly shampooed hair.

Before she knew it, she was gently settled on the soft white bed in their little paradise home. His eyes were looking at her adoringly. "I love you!" he said without taking his eyes off of her.

Julie stopped breathing for a second. Did she hear him right? Did he just say he loved her? Was that possible? So soon? Was it true? His eyes were saying yes. She trusted him completely.

"I love you too!" replied Julie, tears streaming off her face. "You make me so happy!"

"I've been the happiest man on the face of the planet since I've met you. You need to be mine forever! I love you Julie! I love you so much!"

Julie pulled his face close to hers and touched his lips with her wet feverish lips.

"I want you baby! I want you as close to me as possible. At all times!"

He complied, helping her take off her flimsy dress. His hot lips started a passionate fiery trail down her neck while his hands were cupping her small firm breasts, releasing them from the tiny leopard print triangles. His tongue touched her nipples, one at a time sending electric shock waves through her body. Her lower back lifted off the pristinely white bed arching in pleasure while his tongue was circling each breast slowly but with determination.

"Make love to me honey! Please take me now!" moaned Julie touching his face and his strong back.

"That's exactly what I'm going to do my love!" Mike whispered to her as he was making his way down to her bellybutton.

Julie never knew how erotic this slow kissing down her body could be. But she couldn't take it anymore. She felt like she was going to explode. She needed him in her.

"Please" she begged as her back arched again as his fingers were expertly discarding the bottom piece of her bikini. His hand barely touched her femininity and her breathing started racing. Her mouth opened wide trying to desperately grasp for air while at the same time releasing a guttural moan.

"We're almost there, baby. You are so beautiful! You are perfect!" Mike said swiftly ditching his shorts and moving on top of her. She immediately felt just how much he wanted her too. The evidence was poking at her inner thighs.

Her legs immediately wrapped around him pulling him into her.

"Not yet!" he said breathlessly. "I want to make sure that you are ready for me my love."

Julie opened her eyes and looked him in the eyes "I'm ready for you honey, please. I need you in me" she begged. And he obliged her with a rapid yet smooth penetration that she felt deep down in her core.

He moved slowly at the beginning but as she pulled him into herself by lifting herself to him the thrusting grew more precipitated until she started screaming at the peak of her pleasure and he followed her promptly.

Both of them were still catching their breath when Mike said "Stay close to me. The night has just started."

Julie's laughter filled out the room. "That's exactly what I was hoping you'd say."

***

It was dark and the only sound in the room was the rhythmic wash of the waves against the shore. She reached her arms across the bed, but could find nothing. Julie's eyes opened double checking the information that the touch of the empty bed was giving her. Mike was gone again.

Her heart sank. Why can't I just be happy all the time? Why am I worrying so much? So, maybe he went to get a glass of water or a quiet stroll on the beach. The moon was casting a hypnotic glaze over the rolling ocean surface.

He loves me and I have to trust him. I do trust him! I guess the only one I don't trust is myself. I'm the psycho with trust issues and all sorts of horror scenarios in my head. I need to get over myself and believe in him, believe in me, believe that this is really happening and it's beautiful.

"I wonder what time it is?" she said out loud, looking around for a clock. She did not bring a watch with her. He asked her not to. "This is going to be timeless, baby. It's a vacation, a time to build amazing and unforgettable memories that we'll get us through tough work days to come. Watches, clocks and cell phones are prohibited!"

She listened to him.

But he did bring his cell phone with him. And he left it on. Didn't he take a call during the day and had to walk away from her when he took it? It was nice of him not to bother her with work details, but nothing about him could be boring to her at this point. She wanted to hear him work, she wanted to hear him play detective, solve puzzles and murders, stopping terrorists and whatever else he was doing. She wanted to be a part of it all. After all, she was his and he was hers, right?

The beach was covered in silence. It was unusual. People usually partied until early in the morning in resorts like this. Maybe it was really late, or early. What time was it again?

Julie reached to his nightstand to grab his phone and look at the time. The phone wasn't there.

"Not again! And at this hour! He promised no work!"

Now she was mad. If he couldn't keep his promise with this, at this point in their relationships, he will never do it. Didn't she read in x number of books that the way a guy treats you at the beginning of a relationship is the way he will always treat you? Julie didn't agree with the statement in its entirety, but was fairly sure that if he wasn't respecting his commitments to her right now, he: 1, will never do; and 2, doesn't really care and respect her as much as he should.

Julie was on a roll. There was no way she was going back to sleep now. She got up to get a glass of water. The silky robe was on the rocking chair next to the window. It was a cool night with a light breeze. She was happy she had left the window open. She pulled the light see-through white curtains aside to let the breeze in. It was dark outside. The moon's light cast a strange shadow of the palm tree in front of her window. The ocean was caressing the beach with its soothing waves.

The entire scene hugged her soul. She instantly relaxed.

"I am not thirsty. I'm just going to go back to bed" decided Julie and just dropped her body on top of the bed listening to the sound of the waves rocking her back to sleep.

Suddenly there was some quiet shuffling outside of her window. Her heart skipped a beat and she stopped breathing listening to whatever or whomever was outside her opened window. And her hero was not here to save her this time.

She was quite certain she heard couple of men speak in Spanish in a whisper. Julie was desperately looking around for anything that could be used as a weapon. Her eyes were scanning the entire bedroom and what seemed to be beautifully white and romantic and cozy during the day with Mike around, now became a helpless useless death trap that was only offering, flowers and soft cushions to throw at the possible attackers.

The whispering grew louder. There were definitely more than two men out there and they were moving towards her window. She jumped out of the bed and in her heist, she pushed against her nightstand making a loud cracking noise.

"Great Julie, now they won't be surprised when I hit them with a pillow in the face!" she told herself stabilizing the nightstand again. That's when she saw her weapon.

"Amor...si me llamas amor,

Si me dejas amarte, mi bien yo te voy a adorar,

Las estrellas ..."

The loud singing startled her. Then guitars jumped right in accompanying the voices.

It took a second for it to make sense, but when she figured out what was happening, she couldn't stop laughing at herself. "I'm so freakin' paranoid and he's such a wonderfully sweet man. What have I done to deserve him?"

The Mariachi band went on singing their love ballade.

"Contigo voy a soñar con que subes

Contigo voy a pasear en las nubes"

Julie was already at the window smiling, watching Mike pretending to sing and opening his arms to express his love. When he went on one of his knees and pulled a rose from the inside of his jacket, she opened the French doors of their cottage and ran into his arms.

"I love you baby, please move in with me" he asked handing her the rose.

Tears of happiness started rolling down her face that she didn't want to contain, not anymore.

"Yes, honey. With all my heart, yes. I will move in with you."

Julie forgot about the mariachi and she stopped hearing the music all together. It was just her and Mike, happy and in love.

He stood up, scooped her up and walked towards the cottage.

Julie was fully in love and happy and she wasn't afraid of any of it anymore.

"Baby, why do you have a lamp in your hand?"

Chapter 17

The coffee shop was full of people and everyone seemed to be talking and moving at the same time. It reminded Sasha of a hive more than anything else.

Ryan was supposed to be waiting for her at a table next to the window facing the park. Sasha hoped he would have all those books and helpful reading material that he was talking to her about after class the other day.

Somehow, out of the entire commotion in that place, she was able to distinguish Ryan's raised hand waving her in. Sasha couldn't stop herself from admiring that well-built arm. Then her eyes slowly moved towards his torso. His body was so appealing. How come she wasn't able to see that until now?

When she saw his eyebrows raised in a questioning yet confused manner, she realized that she had just stopped moving in the middle of the mayhem around her and just stared at her classmate in disarray.

"Wow, I better come up with something for my visible paralyzed gaping stance before I make a fool of myself," Sasha told herself while forcing her legs to move towards Ryan.

"Yes, I get that a lot. Don't be embarrassed. And I've always wondered why you never did that before. You eluded me for almost four years now, no matter how hard I tried to parade myself in front of you" confessed Ryan when she reached his table.

Sasha was blushing. There was no point in lying anymore, he caught her red-handed. "You've been parading in front of me?" she asked laughing. "Why would you do that?"

"Why wouldn't I? You are the most gorgeous girl in our class and I've been dying to know you a little bit better, but you've always seemed to be in a rush, running in the class at the last second and jetting out the moment we were excused after class."

"Yes, I am a very busy girl," flirted back Sasha.

"Maybe so, but I'm glad I was finally able to get your attention somehow even though I had to partner up with you for the final project and you always pick the toughest titles on the professor's list."

"What can I say," said Sasha smiling "I like a good challenge."

"Well, I hope this one will earn us an A. You don't know how hard it was to sneak those files away from my dad's office. We better go somewhere and make copies of what you think is crucial for our project, so I can put them back before he notices."

Now Sasha was really curious "And may I ask who your dad is?"

He hesitated for a moment.

"Or is it one of those, 'I have to kill you if I tell you'?" joked Sasha giving him time to consider what he was going to say.

"Have you heard of Richard Bernstein?" asked Ryan cautiously.

Sasha thought about it for a second. There was a Bernstein who won a huge trial against an energy preserving conglomerate a few months before. It was all over the news. She remembered it because she made a note of his name as she wanted to interview him for her UN conference. Apparently, the heads of the conglomerate were so greedy that they made all their hiring HR personnel find out directly or indirectly if the women interviewed had small children or were thinking of having any in the near future and rejected their application on the spot under false pretenses. It was a huge scandal and the CEO of the energy titan was a close friend to the US president. No one thought Bernstein would win, even though he had just as impressive connections as that CEO.

"As in Plural Synergy's David? Wasn't that what he was called after he took that "goliath" down? No freakin' way! That's your dad?" Sasha was not even trying to hide her surprise.

Ryan's lips tightened for a split second and then he grinned back at her "Yup, that's him! The one and only!"

"I would love to meet him if that's possible" blurted out Sasha without even thinking of how she should diplomatically approach the subject.

His lips immediately puckered and he took a step back.

"I mean, if that would be ok. It's for an international conference for the UN that I am putting together for next year. It's on women's rights in Eastern Europe and I believe what he did for those women here in our country -which is considered to be the most advanced from every point of view- will be a powerful foundation for a similar movement in that area" pitched Sasha trying not to sound too much like a salesman.

When she saw him now making a move, she tried "It's ok if you don't feel comfortable asking him. I understand. Parents can be difficult and too busy for their own children sometime."

Her slick manipulation tactic worked.

"No, it's not a problem. I can definitely ask him about it for you and I'll let you know what he says."

Sasha was pleased. The torturous years in her mother's house where she perfected her manipulation skills have finally paid off "Thank you. You're amazing!" And she went in for a hug catching him off guard. "You're a super friend!"

Ryan's lazy smile seemed to be stuck to his face. "You're most welcome. Friend" and his eyes locked her gaze while his arms did not let her go from the hug that now developed into an embrace.

Sasha was not comfortable with the entire situation. "I'm probably overthinking again. Chill, it's just a hug, robot!" she told herself trying to calm down as she moved away from him and into the chair opposite to his at the table, he reserved for them.

"Ok, let's look at what you've got. I'm dying to see what's in those files. I see an A coming already!"

Ryan pushed the files on the table towards her. "That's the best news I've got today. After you accepting to see me, of course."

"Smooth," commented Sasha with a faint smile on her lips. She already had the files in her hands and was skimming the pages of the red folder on top of the pile. "I wonder how much of this we can use and quote without getting you or your dad in trouble," she spoke her thoughts out loud.

"That's a question for Larry, my dad's attorney. I bet I can consult him on this without my dad knowing that I actually took those files."

Sasha's jaw dropped open. "Here's the CEO's testimony. Oh my God, this is huge! I can't believe I have this in my hands!"

"Most of the stuff in there should be public information anyway, it's just hard to get to."

Without thinking Sasha reached out and grabbed his hand in the excitement of the moment while her eyes were still glued to the plethora of information and data she had in her lap. If Ryan's dad would give her the permission to use some of this for her conference, the entire event would be a resounding success.

Her brain finally caught up with the mindless gesture and she moved her eyes to their hands that were locked together. A familiar tightness gripped onto her chest and she felt she couldn't breathe. She pulled her hand away but his wouldn't let go.

In desperation she looked up and muttered the word "please", to which he gently lifted her hand to his lips, softly kissed it and opened up his hands to release hers.

"I'm sorry! I don't know what came over me!" apologized Sasha looking down. She couldn't face him. What the heck happened there? He'll think I'm a freak.

"No apologies necessary," said Ryan visibly trying to ease her guilt. "I'm known to be straightforward especially when there's something or someone, I know I like and would want close to me. "

Sasha said nothing.

"I hope I wasn't too pushy!" Ryan added.

" It's not you, it's me!" replied Sasha softly.

Ryan's burst of laughter startled her. "Are you breaking up with me already?"

She joined him with a soft laugh. Her mind was still racing like a scared mouse and she was trying to calm it down. She looked at him smiling. He was handsome! And her craziness hasn't seemed to send him off running yet. Was he her knight in shining armor ready to fight the monsters of her mind and win the battle to her heart? Her gaze moved to his perfectly sculpted chest. "Oh, I hope so."

***

Nikki's face lit up. This was it. This was the picture that will frame her collection. She could feel the rush coming over her immediately. It was the perfect moment on a perfect day. The sun was about to set sending gold and amber diffused rays through the red and yellow leftover leaves behind the couples' bench.

Camera was ready. Nikki's heart was beating fast. Everything just lined up again for her for this project giving her the ultimate seal of approval and green light that she was expecting. It came just like always and this time she was ready for it.

The old couple was snuggled against one another borrowing from each other's body heat. But something else was keeping them warmer than those coats. The complete abandonment and adoration coupled with the visible comfort with one another that only dozens of years of living together can bring, made the undeniable love connection so strong and potent that it was palpable to every living thing in the immediate vicinity. Even the couple of pigeons and the chipper squirrel seem to gravitate around them.

Click, click - Nikki started her photo shoot craziness. She was not going to let this precious and unique moment not be immortalized and accessible to the billions of souls out there that need to see it and to feel it for themselves.

The sun evoking couple was obviously locked in their own universe, far away from all the mortal creatures around them. They were immortals. And they looked like it too.

Nikki's face seemed to have borrowed the peaceful serene smile on the couple's face, as she moved on to snapping shots of the little boy with a head full of curls sharing his precious ice cream with his puppy that he was trying to keep warm with his oversized handmade scarf.

"I'm probably going to make a painting out of this one" decided Nikki. " My collection will be done in different mediums, just like life is. Just like love is."

Dean Jackson, I'm going to blow your socks off!

Chapter 18

The trip back was pretty much uneventful. Except for the flight attendant with a bright pink hair band who was trying a bit too hard to please Mike, it went quite well. To Julie's astonishment, Mike did not pay any attention to that flirty flight attendant. His eyes were just for her and his hands were caressing her and holding her hand throughout the entire flight. Julie felt seen and loved.

"I am going to pick up our luggage while you go to the restroom. Or do you want me to wait for you?" asked Mike and put a soft kiss on Julie's forehead.

"Sure. No, that is fine. I'm going to go to the restroom and I will find you at the baggage claim. I promise I won't be long."

"Well, that's nothing that any airline can promise when it comes to luggage and picking it up after a flight. Five bucks says that you will be faster than our luggage" said Mike with a laughter.

Julie said nothing, but her face was beet red.

Mike chuckled, "Really, I can make you blush so easily?"

"It's just that I'm taught not to talk about anything that comes close to bathroom related stuff. I can't even joke about it. It's bad." Julie's head was bent forward looking at the ground at her fidgeting feet.

His right hand with his palm halfway closed gently lifted to her chin and pushed upward making her look straight at him. "You should never ever be afraid to talk to me about anything. Or be embarrassed or ashamed. That silliness has to stop. Please!"

"I know," said Julie looking straight into his eyes." My girls have tried to get me over these little quirky taboo subjects that I grew up with, but it's not that easy to get over. It's like a bad habit. But I promise that I will do my best."

Mike gave her a big hug then looked at her and smiled." I love you; you know!"

Julie smiled back but said nothing. Her face was giving all the reply that Mike ever needed.

"Let's do this!" announced Julie. " I will beat those bags by at least half an hour!"

" I hope it won't take that long for our bags to come through."

***

Sasha was going through all of the papers that she had in her lap. This was definitely going to be an A plus paper. She didn't even need Ryan to help her out at all. She was going to finish this paper on her own before sunrise. This was nothing compared to her work, or any project that she had to do in the last year or so for Diane, her boss.

" I hope Ryan will not mind if I don't make him a part of this. Maybe I should call him, and ask him?" said Sasha out loud to herself.

Then she grabbed her cell phone and dialed Ryan's number before she let a second thought stop her.

"Hey Ryan, this is Sasha. I couldn't stop going through all the material that you gave me and I've already set up a structure for the entire paper that we are supposed to hand in. I know we still have a lot of time until this paper is due, but I have a lot on my plate at work and right now I have all the energy and motivation and enthusiasm to do it. So, if you don't mind, I'm just going to go with it and I might ... even ... be close to finishing it by next Tuesday when we decided to get together and brainstorm for this paper. I hope this is okay with you. If not, please let me know asap. Okay, have a good night."

Well, thank God it was his voicemail. This way I can do whatever I want to do. So, I'm just going to go ahead and dive right into this paper.

She didn't get to finish that thought and her phone rang in her hand. It was Ryan. She had to pick up.

"Hi, Ryan. I just left you a message. Did you get a chance to listen to it?" asked Sasha.

"Yes, a part of it."

Sasha rushed in "I hope it's ok, I just ..."

Ryan didn't let her finish her thought, "Actually, it's not ok. I do want to be part of 'structuring' or whatever you called what you are doing right now. It's my paper too, and to the contrary of whatever impression I might have given you by mistake, I do like to earn my grades ...especially the good ones."

"I apologize, Ryan, if I gave you the impression that I don't appreciate your input. It's not that at all. It's just that I had all this in my hands and fresh in my mind and have the drive to do it right away ... and ...and ... I'm used to working alone at stuff like this."

"No apologies needed. I understand. As long as you understand me and let me help."

Sasha thought about it for a second, "I feel like doing it right now and I can't really ask you to come and meet me every time I feel like working on the project. And other times I'm really busy and I don't see how we could make this work. I don't want you to feel ..."

Ryan jumped in again, "Then let's meet now. We can make it an all-nighter. And by tomorrow we might have the entire thing done. Or almost done. I don't mind you putting the finishing touches on it as long as I was a big part of putting it together. How does that sound?"

"That's great! And I don't have to feel guilty for keeping you out of it either. It's actually perfect."

"So, where should we meet? Your place or my place?" asked Ryan.

Sasha's left eyebrow rose, "Neither! Let's meet in the Social Science lab. I know the assistant professor who works there and she keeps that lab open at night. I'll give her a call to make sure. Meet me there in 20 minutes!"

"Do I need to bring anything?"

"Nope, I'll grab a pizza on the way. There is soda and water in the lab in a small fridge behind the first counter."

Ryan laughed, "I guess this is not the first night you spend in that lab."

"No, it's not. What gave it away, the pizza or the exact location of the staff's goodies fridge?" asked Sasha with a light laughter.

"I'll never reveal the secret" promised Ryan. "See you in 20!"

"Ok. Bye" said Sasha before she put down her phone and started piling up all her organized piles of materials and files that she had already went through all evening long.

On the way out of her office, she grabbed her laptop bag and turned off the light.

While waiting for a cab she dialed the pizzeria that she had in mind:

"Giovani, sono io Sasha."

"Bella, che piacere sentirti! Come posso aiutarla?"

"A grande pizza, te prego!"

"I'll have it ready for you, just the way you like it. But I need 10 minutes" said Giovani on the other end of the line.

"I'll be there in 10. Grazie mille!" thanked Sasha.

"Arrivederci, bella!"

***

"You got here before me. And you got the pizza too!" said Ryan surprised while putting his bag on the ground, next to the table where Sasha had the pizza and her laptop set up.

"I know my way around. You were the one who said I seem to be always in a rush. Well, I know all the shortcuts as well. It cuts down on time. You would be shocked."

Ryan smiled coyly "Nothing shocks me anymore when it comes to you. You seem to be a superwoman! Beautiful, successful, super intelligent ... I feel like a mere mortal around you."

Sasha blushed, "And you sir, are no mere mortal. With your looks, your brains and the charisma that true mere mortals only wish and pray for every night before bed ... the world is surely at your feet."

"Now it's my turn to blush" replied Ryan closing the gap between their bodies. "I thought you never even knew I existed."

"Oh, I knew," said Sasha fast. "I've been more than aware of you and your powers from the first day you showed up in class. You were like a jar of honey for all the pretty bees on campus. Even guys seemed to hover around you at all times. How do you breathe with all those people on you?"

"Not without difficulty, I assure you" whispered Ryan next to her face.

"Really? Because you are only one person and you make it hard for me to breathe with you so close to me" Sasha barely pushed those words out of her in one long breath. Her heart was beating fast and she felt uncomfortable in a strange way. Did she want this or not? She was confused. But she did want to touch those beautifully sculpted arms, his torso and that perfect chin ... and look at that silky hair - just the way it was flowing it invited her to touch it. It was hypnotizing.

"So, how about it?" asked Ryan, breaking the spell.

Sasha had to snap out of it faster than she wanted to "About what?" she asked confused while trying to pull her thoughts together. He had moved back and was staring at her clearly waiting for a response for some time.

"I asked about dinner. If we could start with that pizza because I'm starving"

"Oh," Really? He had a full conversation with her while she was contemplating his breathtaking body and she didn't even hear a thing? She heard about things like that before, but she never believed them to be true. How can someone be so far away from what's happening right in front of them? Strange.

She looked at him. He was still waiting for her reply.

"Oh, sure. Let's eat! This pizza is to die for. You'll lick your lips and your fingers not to lose any of its flavors and goodness to a napkin."

Ryan raised his arms palms up enthusiastically "So what are we waiting for? And I brought the perfect chaser." He pulled two packs of beer on the table. "The best of the best" he smiled.

"I'll stick to water, but thank you" said Sasha and jolted off her chair to go grab a bottle of water from the fridge.

"I understand if you're not a beer girl. I came prepared. Here's a bottle of my dad's best brandy. It will be perfect for digestion" he said winking at her.

Sasha got back in her chair, grabbed a slice of pizza and replied "Ryan, I don't drink at all. I don't like the taste of alcohol." She lied, but preferred it that way. People didn't need to know she was a recovering alcoholic and addict. It was her cross to carry and no one else's.

"Whatever you say, Sasha. But just in case, I'll put this in front of you. Its aroma will drive you crazy and once you taste it, all that 'not liking the taste of alcohol' will evaporate into the past with all the cheap nasty alcohol you might have tasted before."

"I really don't want it in front of me, Ryan. Just the smell makes me dizzy. It's bad, it's like an allergy or something," she continued to lie. But she knew she could not have that brandy glass in front of her. It was too alluring.

"I've never heard of brandy allergy" replied Ryan with a laughter.

Sasha's nostrils opened up when Ryan shoved the glass right underneath her nose. "Come on, it will help you relax. You are very tense. And we have a whole night of work in front of us."

She stopped listening to him, all she saw was the bottle of brandy and her mouth was watering just inhaling the vapors from the glass that was right at her lips. Maybe a tiny sip would not hurt. After all, she used to be more into drugs than alcohol. That's what she had a problem with.

Ryan grabbed her left hand and put it around the glass of brandy that he was holding in front of her. "Here, you deserve it. You worked hard today and the day is not over! You need a break!"

"Yes, I do need a break" thought Sasha. "Just a tiny one. I deserve it!" She took the glass and poured the amber liquid into her mouth.

That same second, Nikki's loving face popped into her head. "Whatever you need to do to take care of yourself honey, but don't forget that I'm always here for you." She wasn't admonishing her, like Sasha thought she would. Then she heard her mom's cracked satisfied laughter. "You stupid junkie! Thief!" she was hissing in her ears. Then she saw Nikki holding her and caressing her hair after she would wake up screaming from her nightmares.

Next thing she knew, Sasha was spitting the content of her mouth all over the floor.

"What the hell?" yelled Ryan in dismay.

Sasha grabbed her water bottle and forcefully rinsed her mouth as she was walking out of the lab and towards the restrooms.

"I'm ok. I'm ok" she was yelling back to calm Ryan and herself down.

"I'm ok" she repeated over and over again to herself while looking in the bathroom mirror at her own reflection.

Then she set herself down on the floor trying to collect herself.

"Should I call Nikki? Should I call my sponsor? Should I just leave? No, I have to finish this. Ryan will think I'm a freak and then the entire school will find out and think I'm a freak. What if they find out the truth? Will my work be in jeopardy? I worked too hard for this? I can't lose it now."

A thousand thoughts were whirling around her head. She couldn't escape the mental chatter and it was so loud it literally hurt her head.

"Ok. Alright!" she heard herself yelling to the empty bathroom walls. Her voice hoarse. "I am going to pull myself together. Go in there, finish this project and deal with this tomorrow with my girls!"

As she came out of the bathroom, she saw Ryan waiting for her with a bewildered look on his face.

"I told you I was allergic. I'm a freak of nature."

Ryan laughed and came in to hug her. " I was so worried! You are no freak. Sorry for pressuring you like that! I'll never do it again. I promise."

"Thank you! Now let's attack that paper! We need to finish it tonight!" said Sasha pulling herself away from the embrace. She was still working on feeling comfortable with it.

***

The minute she got to the baggage claim, Julie was able to spot Mike right away. He was too tall and too handsome not to stand out. Julie smiled – he's all mine and he loves me.

By the time Julie eventually got to him, Mike had already pulled out his cell phone from his backpack to turned it on. He was quickly scrolling through all his messages. Clearly the honeymoon little vacation was over. Julie sighed.

" Hey honey, I guess I was faster," giggled Julie.

Mike took her hand and pulled her next to him, kissed her on top of her head and answered her." Just what you expect from the trusted airlines. I've got an idea: what if you and I reward ourselves for such a good behavior and for the patience that we exhibit right now waiting for our luggage and order your favorite meal from that follow your heart restaurant, some ice cream or whatever desert you want, get my masseuse to come and work those tight neck muscles that we gained on the flight back and then just relax. How does that sound to you?"

The smile on Julie's face spread from one year to another. " That sounds perfect. I love it!"

"That's a deal. I gotta call my masseuse right now." Mike saw the yellow striped suitcase coming down the chute. It was Julie's. While she went to grab it, his phone rang. His face switched to serious right away.

"Julie, honey, I have to take this," and he walked away to the other side of the room full of people.

Julie had a bad feeling about it." I bet his work again or something like that" said Julie to herself trying to sweep it away." I really don't need his full attention every second of the day. I'm not a baby. Come on, Julie, grow up!"

The other two bags followed pretty quickly. Julie pulled them off and into the cart to move next to the window, waiting for Mike to finish his phone conversation. He will see her when he is done. All she needed to fantasize about was that massage.

Julie's hands were clutching around her neck and tight shoulder muscles. "Yes, it's definitely time for a massage."

While contemplating the frenzy of all those people and cars moving through the busy airport, a stern hand touched her left shoulder. She jerked back and looked to see who was touching her.

" It's just me," said Mike. The severity on his face was still present." Baby, I don't know how to say this, please, please, forgive me. I have to get you a cab to take you home. It's my job. It's a very complicated and dangerous case and it needs my immediate attention. Hope you understand."

Julie took his hand in hers," I completely understand. Don't worry about it. Go save the world. I will be okay. Unless you haven't noticed, I am a big girl. Just go. I will hail a cab."

Mike grabbed her face into his hands looked into her eyes and then delicately kissed her open lips." Thank you, you are an angel. I will call you as soon as I'm done." Then he grabbed his bag from the cart and he disappeared.

After staring at the space that he had previously occupied a moment ago, Julie decided to get herself moving. She missed the girls. It was time to go home. She had so much to tell them, now that she was moving in with Mike.

Chapter 19

It was dark already and none of the girls were home. The entire apartment was silent. No movement, no noise. Lizzie wasn't sure if she had woken up from her sleep or if she was still sleeping. She forgot the last time their apartment was this quiet.

The air that was rushing through the open window was cold and unfriendly. The street lights were throwing a diffused milky glow through her snowy sheer curtains into her bedroom lending right on her laptop that was sitting on her white desk.

"Hmm, very clever," said Lizzie. "I guess I have to take it as a sign and put myself in front of the computer and maybe I'll finish my book tonight."

She lifted her head off the pillow and listened attentively for any faint noise in the house that might alert her to her friends' presence.

"Wow, I can be so sly sometimes. I almost fell for it" Lizzie admonished herself. "I'm just hoping for any kind of reason not to do this. Consistency is my middle name. Consistency in procrastinating!"

Lizzie shook her head in disapproval and pushed out from under the covers. Her feet immediately found the snugness of her favorite fuzzy slippers the moment they touched the floor. The feathery feeling covering her bare feet traveled quickly from her toes to the crown of her head and she closed her eyes to savor the moment.

"Sometimes it's better than an orgasm," Lizzie whispered her secret to the still surroundings.

She pulled the chair away from the desk and set in it before she had a chance to change her mind. With one finger she turned on her laptop. This was it. She was going to sit in front of the manuscript for as long as it takes. All she had to do was write one paragraph. Only one!

"That's not that hard, right?" Lizzie tried to convince herself. She knew that once she wrote that first paragraph, she won't be able to stop for a while and finish at least one chapter if not more.

"I only have to round up the story. One chapter is all that it takes," Lizzie was talking directly to the manuscript opened in front of her on her laptop.

For some reason her last words made her freak out a little and she felt the urge to get up and go to the bathroom, or maybe get something to eat ...and close the window, because it was too cold. Maybe see if they have any ice cream in the fridge.

"Hey, you're not going anywhere. No running away from this" Lizzie caught herself just in time. "As I said, one paragraph, only one. That's all I'm asking. I can do this!"

And with a deep breath Lizzie's hand quickly typed "Life is fun when loved by family."

***

"I've never been able to put together a paper this fast. You are quite amazing at this" said Ryan appreciatively to Sasha who at this point was on the floor on the only carpeted area of the room, with all the books, and files spread around her, her laptop in her arms and Ryan right next to her.

Ryan continued, "I'm a little bit confused. Have I helped at all or was I just your sounding board?"

"You were of great help. The middle chapters, the case comparison and the last paragraph that encompasses the entire paper were all you! Now we just need to put more meat on this skeleton and we shall have a perfect A plus paper" replied Sasha convinced.

"Excellent! I feel so much better now that you said that!" replied Ryan. "You are a genius. A gorgeous genius. You should see yourself now. It might be " and Ryan quickly looked at his watch " almost 4 in the morning, but you look so ravishing."

Sasha looked at him not knowing what to do or what to say. "I think all that beer clouded your judgment."

"Not according to what you just said earlier" Ryan opposed. "How could I have helped write this paper if I had a beer fogged brain. You're contradicting yourself my dear."

"Ok. Maybe I just can't trust your words right now, because it is 4 o'clock in the morning and I haven't slept or showered in almost 24 hours, so it's hard to believe that what you say it's true."

Ryan grinned "Let me be the judge of that. And by the way, you smell intoxicatingly appetizing."

"You sound like a vampire," laughed Sasha.

"Maybe I am" replied Ryan, as he leaned in and put a soft kiss on her neck.

Sasha trembled from her core.

"You like that?" And it sounded more like a statement rather than a question from Ryan's tone of voice.

His right hand swiftly pulled the pencil that Sasha used to pin her hair to the back of her head. Her jet-black smooth hair fell on his hand. He groaned with pleasure and with his left hand took her laptop and pushed it away from them on the floor while his lips came into contact with hers.

Sasha couldn't respond in any way. She didn't know if she liked it or not. He was such an amazingly looking guy and she hadn't been kissed like that in so long. She didn't want him not to like her, but she didn't know if she was as prepared as he was to move so fast.

He used a gentle forcefulness to push her back while he positioned himself on top of her. His kissing grew passionate and a bit forceful, pushing her to make the next move.

What was her next move? Was she going to give in? Was she going to let this passion drown her? Was she ready for that?

In the middle of her thoughts, she heard a familiar sound. A zipper. She did not remember having any zipper on her clothes. Then she felt one of his hands fiercely trying to unbutton her pants. She quickly snapped out of it. That was it? That was all the romance she was going to get? He was just going to pull her pants off, now that clearly his pants were undone with the help of the quick zipper, and push himself into her? No!

She pushed him off "No!"

"Ryan, I said No!"

It didn't seem to register with him, as he was frantically pulling at her pants.

"I said No, Ryan!" she yelled in the cold still air of the empty room.

He looked up at her for a brief moment. His face was contorted with an animalistic desire. He didn't seem to grasp the meaning of her words.

Sasha used her hands to push him off and was squirming her body underneath him trying to escape.

"Get off of me, brute!" she screamed.

Ryan came up and stifled her loud cry with his mouth. Sasha could taste the beer in his breath. She felt like throwing up. She couldn't breathe, his tongue was deep in her mouth muffling any noise she was fighting to get out.

She used her left hand to pull his head off by his hair and with the right hand she scratched his face. For a second, he lost his grip and yelled in pain, and she used that moment to push him off of her and get up to run.

Ryan's hand grabbed her before she could stand and pulled her down by her shirt ripping it off of her. "What the hell's wrong with you? Now you want it, now you don't? And why the fuck did you scratch my face? Are you a fucking animal? I'll show you what happens to animals and you'll love it"

Sasha was kicking as hard as she could with her legs and her arms, flailing all over the place. Oh, now she wished she had taken a self-defense class, but she never thought this could ever happen to her. She was always so careful, so aloof, so unfriendly to all strangers.

Somehow, she got a good amount of space to get enough momentum and ran the bed of her right hand into Ryan's nose. She had seen this move a thousand times on tv. Maybe tv violence was not all that bad. He screamed so loud and so deep from the bottom of his throat that Sasha thought she broke his neck. Blood came rushing down his nose and a few drops fell on Sasha's face.

Ryan took both his hands to his bleeding nose yelling "Fucking bitch!"

Sasha managed to stand up and kicked him as hard as she could in the stomach before she ran out the door and she didn't stop running. It was only when she finally got the courage to stop that she saw the way people on the street were looking at her. She probably looked crazed.

Her back was hurting her. She looked down and saw that she was only wearing one shoe. How did she run all this way in one shoe without noticing the difference? Her pants were unbuttoned and a side was almost completely torn off.

She looked at her hands and there was blood on them, her bra was showing from the ripped shirt.

But what was all this blood on her hands from?

Sasha couldn't focus. She was exhausted and just wanted to go home. It was the only safe place she knew in Manhattan or anywhere in the world right now.

A cab stopped abruptly next to her. Sasha jerked away. Maybe it was him. He found her. She had to run.

"Sweetie, let me take you home now" a calm warm female voice said to her from the driver side.

Sasha cautiously looked in the cab and saw the woman looking at her with kindness. There was no one else in the car.

"I promise I'll take you anywhere you want. We'll go as slow or as fast as you feel comfortable and you can tell me which way to go and we can stop at any point. I promise. Here's my cell phone. Call your family and have them on the phone with you at all times. Ok?"

Sasha's fear was not allowing her to move.

"Tell me your family's phone number. I will dial it for you and put it on speaker, so they can direct me to your place. Ok, sweetheart?" the woman continued softly.

"Ok!" was all that Sasha could say.

Chapter 20

The strident noise that cut through the darkness was most unwelcomed. His hand groped through the objects on the nightstand trying to get to the annoying ring without opening his eyes. When he finally brought the phone to his face, he recognized the number and picked up without hesitation.

"Mike, I'm sorry to wake you up so early in the morning, but we have a complicated situation here and we ... I... need your help, please!"

"Julie, are you ok? Is everything alright?" asked Mike concerned.

"It's not me" answered Julie promptly to calm him down.

"Nikki?" was his next guess.

"No, Nikki is here with me. It's Sasha!" and the moment she said her name Julie's voice started trembling with poorly contained need to cry. Mike could tell she was swallowing her own tears, trying to be tough, tough enough to make this call. It was very important to her, he could tell.

"Is she physically alright?" asked Mike trying to get more information. Julie seemed to not be able to articulate much.

"I guess so, I ... we don't know" scrambled Julie without much force.

Mike heard a commotion, some muffled noises and then he heard a different voice at the end of the line "Mike, it's Nikki. We need you to come to our place immediately! Sasha was sexually assaulted.

"Jesus" was all that Mike could say.

"We don't have any details. She's in a cab with a lady who called us. Lizzie is on the phone with them right now, giving her directions to our place and keeping Sasha company."

Mike jumped out of his bed and was putting on whatever clothes he found first.

"I'll be there in 10 minutes. Don't let her shower. Touch as little as possible. I'm going to have a friend that we work with, a psychologist, come with me. Let her know that I'm coming, once you have her in the apartment. She doesn't need any more surprises right now. She needs to trust you."

"Mike, thank you!" said Nikki courtly and hung up the phone.

Then Nikki turned towards Julie, gave her the phone and put her arms around her. "Honey, we need to be strong for her! Mike is on his way."

Julie looked at Nikki thankfully and shook her head signaling that she understood. "I'll do my best. I promise."

"I know you will," said Nikki. She took Julie into her arms. She still didn't have enough details of Joe's assault on Julie, but this entire thing could not be easy on her. It's a good thing, Mike is going to be close by.

"We're coming downstairs to get you," said Lizzie into her phone. She turned around to the other 2 girls "She's here. Let's go down!"

Lizzie opened the door in a rush, then turned to Nikki and asked "Can you please bring some cash for the cab ride?" Then she turned back on her heels and ran downstairs as fast as she could, followed closely by Julie and then Nikki.

***

"So, what do you think Janice?" asked Mike pulling his co-worker into the hallway.

Janice didn't hide a thing "This might be tough, Mike. The pictures we took and her broken statement ... I don't know. I already sent a team to the lab where the whole thing took place. But ..."

Mike jumped in "I know, I know, he's Richard Bernstein's son."

"Don't get me wrong. We both know that we can build a case on what we have here, including his blood on her shirt, but it's a 'he said, she said' case and no one was in the lab with them. How can we prove both of them were in there to begin with? How do we make her credible?"

Anna, the newest legal consultant in Mike's department joined the two in the hallway. "I just got a call and had to check with the girls and unfortunately what I just found out is true."

Mike turned towards her and asked impatiently "What are you talking about?"

" You know her mother suing daughter year after year trauma? It will only shake her testimony. They will use a psychiatrist to say she's emotionally unstable and it's going to be hard to fight that."

"But we have the cab driver's testimony as well. Do you think that will help?" asked Mike.

"I have to gather more info before I can say more on this case"

"Ms. Belding?" Julie announced her presence.

"Yes," Anna said taking a step to the side, so Julie could join their circle.

"This is Mrs. Clifford's business card. She's Sasha's lawyer. She might be able to help you with more details on those cases you were asking about" said Julie handing her a polished bright white elegant card.

"Thank you, Julie." Then Anna looked up at Mike and Janice, tapped the business card against her fingers and pursed her lips. "I have to go back to the office and start working on this case. Call me with any kind of new info as soon as you get it. Thanks!" and without waiting for their answer she took off.

"I have to go back to work, too, if I still want to keep my job. But Janice here is the best at this kind of cases. Trust her completely," said Mike and gave Julie a hug before he followed Anna's footsteps. "Call me if you need anything," he yelled as he was rushing down the stairs without looking back.

There was silence for a moment. Janice was looking at Julie, but said nothing. Then she put a fake smile on her face and said "Let's go inside, Julie. I still need to ask all of you a lot of questions."

Chapter 21

It was only a week later, when Sasha decided to take control of her life, yet again. "It's just like all the other trials I've been through with my mom. This time with a scumbag that is not my family, so I can't and won't let him make more of a victim of me then he has already done. I'm going to classes today" announced Sasha bright and early on that Tuesday morning.

Nikki gazed at her for a second, trying to feel her energy. "It definitely feels like you're ready to move on and take charge."

"I'm coming with you to school today, "proclaimed Lizzie. "And please don't argue with me. I'm not going to budge."

Julie disagreed. "I'll be the one to argue with you. Today you have an appointment with your agent at 10 and you're not going to miss it. No more self-sabotaging, not matter the reason."

"This is not self-sabotage. This is important!" Lizzie fought back.

Nikki came in to help Julie " Do you recall asking us to promise you not to let you miss this opportunity no matter what? This is us doing just that."

"Plus, I have the day off today, so I'll be joining Sasha on her adventures today" said Julie while forcing herself to look excited.

"At least promise to meet me for lunch or a snack at the gallery later today. I want to hear how the day is going for you gals" begged Lizzie.

"I'm actually planning on coming by your gallery around 2 o'clock, right after my sketch class. There's something I want to run by you," said Nikki.

Lizzie's eyes brightened. "If it is what I think it is, I can't wait!"

Nikki smiled "I don't know what you're talking about."

"It is! Oh my God, it is what I'm thinking off!" Lizzie was bouncing off the walls with joy. She went and hugged Nikki and then Julie and Sasha. "Oh, Sasha. This is going to help you too. You'll see. I'm certain of it" announced Lizzie.

Sasha finally smiled herself. "Your joy can be pretty contagious. Keep this up for today and you'll certainly land that deal with your agent on this book."

"Oh, yes. My book." Lizzie looked concerned again.

"You'll do great" assured her Sasha. "It's an amazing book. Thank you for letting me read your manuscript. It was the reason why I chose to reboot my life today" said Sasha, stressing on the words "the reason"

Julie and Nikki both jumped in at the same time "What? Sasha got to read the manuscript and we didn't? How's that fair?"

Lizzie wasn't fazed even a bit. "She needed it more than any of you. I thought it might help take her mind off things" said Lizzie looking at Sasha's sad face "And to get her feedback. She always had amazing feedback for me."

"And we didn't?" asked Nikki pretending to be serious.

"Sorry, I didn't mean it to sound that way?"

"Don't apologize for life's curved balls" quoted Julie.

Lizzie's jaw dropped. A second later her nostrils started inflating.

"Oh-oh. I think you pissed her off" Nikki pointed out. "Lizzie! Just think what papa bear would do?" Nikki couldn't stop but laugh as Lizzie was coming after her, face contorted.

Julie jumped in between the two of them. "Come on, Lizzie. We couldn't help ourselves. Especially after Sasha miraculous change of hearts that we could feel last night."

"We asked what moved her out of the darkness this time and she pointed to your manuscript that was lying on her bed. We didn't mean to snoop, but it was right there in front of us" added Nikki.

"And you didn't think to ask if you were allowed to read it? Did I give it to you specifically?" blurted out Lizzie.

Sasha was done with the drama. "Lizzie, grow up. We love you and we love your book. It doesn't matter how they got to read it and it's not like they hacked your computer when you weren't home."

Then she continued "And you girls should have asked first and not taking advantage of my momentary weakness. It's her book after all."

"You're right," said Julie. "We apologize Lizzie. I wanted to stop, and ask, but after the first page, I was hooked."

Nikki's head nodded approvingly.

Lizzie took a deep breath to calm herself down. Then another one. And another one. She moved her eyes from the kitchen floor to each of the girls taking in the words and the energy. "You really think I have a shot with this book?" she busted out not able to contain her new found enthusiasm.

"For sure", "Definitely", "It's a done deal" answered the other three girls at the same time.

***

The wind was cold this morning and blowing in quick powerful bursts. All the leaves that were forgotten on the ground from the previous sweeping were thrown against passersby. Everyone who chose to walk this morning had their bodies slightly tilted forward in a sturdy attempt to fight the wind and move faster towards their destination.

Sasha and Julie had their scarves wrapped all around their necks and up, covering their faces to their noses not wanting to inhale any of the flyaway debris that the wind was stirring up from the ground.

They finally got to Sasha's university. With quick steps, they walked in, took a few steps to the right of the entrance and stopped to pull themselves together.

"Your hair looks like a neurotic rat's nest," joked Sasha pointing at Julie's hair. "I've never seen it like this."

Julie immediately unraveled the entire scarf, plunged her hand deep into her large green purse and produced a brush. "That's because I never walk in winds like that. I like to upkeep my image."

"I like to upkeep my image," repeated Sasha with a stuffy British accent while tilting her head slightly backwards and raising one eyebrow.

Julie busted out laughing which made her stop brushing her hair. "I did not sound like that!"

"Of course, not darling! Now make sure your hair is perfect and put away that bloody brush before you give your perfect hair secrets away! Really, darling!" continued Sasha the charade.

"Ok, ok, you got me. I can be a bit snobbish when it comes to my hair."

Sasha stared straight at her, "A bit?" Then laughed. "I know for a fact that half of your oversized bag is full of hair care products."

"I know, I know" agreed Julie. "It's actually becoming a problem these days. Now that the fashion industry decided to re-introduce the tiny purses. What am I ever going to do?"

"Decisions, decisions! Should I stop carrying a beauty salon in my purse or should I stop obsessing about my perfect hair," mused Sasha out loud pretending to be Julie.

"I'm glad my obsessions amuse you" muttered Julie. Then put her arm around Sasha and said "Now it's time to attack your problem, heads on! Ready?"

Sasha took a deep breath, pushed her chin up and replied "Ready!"

Ryan was not in class that day. Good! But all his friends were there giving her dirty looks.

"Slut!", "Lying bitch", "Crazy piece of shit" were some of the compliments they all showered her with from the moment she started walking down the hallway.

Julie was right next to her, "Are we back in freakin' high school? I thought popularity contests and small brains were not allowed past high school walls."

"He is the captain of the lacrosse team. What did you expect? Popularity contests don't stop even in nursing homes," said Sasha.

Julie laughed thinking about it "Oh, yeah. remember when we volunteered at that Nursing Home last Valentine's Day and the residents chose the King and Queen of hearts?"

"As I said. It never ends. We seem to be a peacock species more than anything else. Look at me, look at me, my fathers are all up and pretty!" said Sasha lifting her hands next to her shoulders and spreading her fingers to impersonate a peacock.

"Disgusting whore! Why don't you stop lying, you pathetic clown!" yelled a curly blonde whose face was covered in a rainbow of bright makeup.

"Look who's talking!" yelled Julie back. "Do yourself a favor and find a mirror, bozo!"

"Please don't do that Julie!" begged Sasha. "Don't put gas on fire! You won't be able to be here with me every day and I'll have to clean up after you!"

"Clean up after me?" asked Julie confused and pissed. "Your asshole classmate assaulted you and now he's using his best friend as an alibi and hides behind his daddy's ass and all I'm doing is being on your side, and you have to clean after me? Me?"

"Lower your voice, please," begged Sasha again. She stopped and leaned against the hallway wall. "I'm sorry I lashed out at you."

Julie reacted fast. "And I'm sorry I raised my voice at you! This entire situation is overwhelming."

"I overheard Nikki say that this might be some sort of déjà-vu for you with Joe, so I understand how hard this might be for you and I really appreciate you being here, supporting me" barely whispered Sasha.

Julie stepped next to Sasha, leaned against the wall herself and answered "The thought occurred to me too, but to tell you the truth, you fighting this, and especially against this Titan, makes me feel like you're fighting for me too and it makes me stronger " said Julie grabbing Sasha's hand in her own. "Thank you for fighting for me Sasha and thank you for giving me a second chance to fight my Joe through you."

Sasha looked at their holding hands and a single tear rushed down her cheek. "Thank you!" was all she could mutter.

"Let's go to the cafeteria and grab a coffee to jump start us for the next class," said Julie. "If I have to go through more history classes with you, I'll need shots of espresso lined up in front of me so I don't interrupt the captivating lecture with my loud snores.

"Coffee it is then" said Sasha with a faint smile on her face.

The line was too long, so they decided to just grab a chair and relax for five minutes in a corner, next to the window, away from all the noisy crowd.

"Thought you might need some coffee," said a female voice that was approaching their table. Sasha and Julie turned around to see if she was talking to them. She was. A tall blonde with big blue eyes and impeccable taste in fashion was walking towards them, looking straight at Sasha.

She put the three coffees she was holding on the table in front of them and introduced herself "Hi, my name is Donna. I'm a graduate student at this university and I have two things you'll definitely be interested in."

Julie's eyebrow was raised in disbelief and confusion. Sasha was just curious. But neither of them said a thing.

"I guess you're Sasha, " Donna addressed Sasha directly with her right arm extended for a handshake.

Blinking couple of times to regroup herself, Sasha came out of her reverie and shook Donna's hand, "Ahh, yes. I'm Sasha. Nice to meet you, Donna."

"And I'm Julie, Sasha's almost sister" followed Julie, extending her arm for a handshake.

"Almost sister?" asked Donna confused, but didn't seem to be too interested in an explanation.

Julie gave it anyway "Like sisters."

"Ahh, I understand" replied Donna then turned towards Sasha. "I only have a minute, but I saw you giving up on standing in line and hiding in this corner, so I decided to talk to you now."

"Ok" said a confused Sasha. "Oh, and thank you for the coffee"

"My pleasure" said Donna and then quickly went to the point. "The two things I was saying you would be definitely interested in were the coffee and the fact that Ryan pulled the same stunt with me over a year ago. I want to help you anyway I can. Just let me know."

Sasha was too blown away to react, but Julie was there for her. "That's great!" then she tried again "I don't mean that is great that it happened to you too, but that you're willing to help and that you offered."

Donna said reassuringly "I completely understand your meaning, don't worry. "

"Do you know that Ryan's best friend is lying for him giving him an alibi?" blurted out Sasha out of nowhere.

Donna looked back at her "Yes, they do that for each other. I think the official story is that they were practicing for their next game and that's where he was and that's how he broke his nose."

"Wow, you are up to date" said Sasha impressed.

"Always am when I'm interested in the subject" replied Donna swiftly. Then she got up "I'm sorry but I really have to go. Here's my contact information. Please call me anytime" then she stopped, looked at Sasha, grabbed her hand and said "I will help you! I'm sorry it had to happen to you too! I wish I could have stopped it myself!"

After Donna made her way out of the cafeteria, Julie finally said to Sasha "And that just happened, right?"

Sasha was shaking her head in disbelief "Can you believe it?"

Chapter 22

Her eyes were bulging and she couldn't breathe. A plastic bag filled with credit cards was suffocating her. She could barely concentrate on what was going on. The mascara was running in thick black lines down her face and she had a gun right next to her right temple. On the gloved hand that was pulling the trigger was written in blood red letters "Your Bank."

Nikki was staring at the oversized picture that was taking the entire southern wall of the art gallery that Lizzie was working at. She couldn't pull herself away from all the details that the artist drilled into that piece.

"So, you find consumerism fascinating?" asked Lizzie approaching Nikki.

"Yeah. Especially when you have to spend money to buy a picture as big as your wall that says that spending money is going to kill you! Why not spare yourself the drama and go directly and buy a gun!" commented Nikki still glaring at the immense picture.

"It conveys a clear message and you would be surprised how many pieces like this one we have sold lately. Some say they buy it to remind themselves, or their wives or whatever. Others for a chuckle. I had two investment bankers buy several pieces as gifts for their favorite bankers" explained Lizzie.

"It's not a laughing matter. This is sad. True and therefore very sad" replied Nikki seriously.

Lizzie took a moment before she continued. She knew she had to give Nikki a moment to go through this negative emotion to get it out of her system - she always asked that from all of them. "It is, but sometimes we have to laugh at this crazy world."

"Maybe," replied Nikki "Or maybe we should focus only on the good stuff."

Lizzie had been waiting for this moment the entire day. "Like let's say a 'Love Flood' collection would bring about?"

Nikki smiled feeling her enthusiasm. "Exactly!" She was finally able to walk away from that wall. "Is there a chance I can talk to the owner? I brought couple of my pieces to support my pitch, but I think your gallery could use a little more love."

"And so does the world," added Lizzie barely containing her elation.

"But before you do so, why don't you tell me how the meeting with your literary agent went this morning!" pushed Nikki before Lizzie could run upstairs to her boss's office.

"Oh yes, my meeting. Well," Lizzie said trying hard to play it cool while looking down and around, but not in Nikki's eyes. She knew her fake coolness wouldn't last if she looked at her.

"Lizzie?" Nikki said putting both her hands on Lizzie's arms.

Lizzie couldn't hold it anymore and busted out with as much enthusiasm as a girl who was just asked to the prom by the love of her life "I just got a call minutes before you walked through the door. They are going to publish it!" She was radiating!

"Oh yes, I knew we were due for some good news! This is going to brighten up our day, and week and month!" laughed Nikki jumping up and down hand in hand with Lizzie like two teenage girls.

"I'm sorry to interrupt this happy occasion, but the boss wants you upstairs", said Lizzie's coworker.

"Oops," she said laughing and covering her mouth at the same time trying to conceal her extreme happiness for a moment.

"I hope I didn't get you in too much trouble," Nikki said without any worry in her voice.

"Neah! Especially not after we're going to get her the next biggest exhibit of her career with your collection. Why don't you follow me upstairs. I think it's time you've met the owner of this gallery" concluded Lizzie showing Nikki to the upstairs office.

***

All the four girls were sitting around the dinner table in their kitchen, chatting away.

"I love our pizza nights," said Lizzie grabbing another slice.

Julie immediately dropped a handful of salad on her plate, right before the slice landed on it. "A bit of a balance would be helpful."

"Thank you my dear," came the consciously suave reply.

Nikki smiled looking at the two of them interacting. "A year ago, you would have gone for her jugular, Lizzie, for telling you what to do or how to eat."

"A lot has changed in the past year, hasn't it?" contemplated Lizzie.

Sasha jumped in "Oh yes, more than a lot. I can't believe all those events fit into a year."

"And we're still here" concluded Julie.

"Yes, we are." Lizzie smiled, "And now it's time for me to give you my good news, as promised."

"Drum roll, please," joked Nikki.

"They are publishing my book!" exclaimed Lizzie jumping out from her chair with excitement.

Julie and Sasha followed her and came to hug her. "We are so proud of you!"

Lizzie was glowing, "Oh let's not forget Nikki's big news! Nikki?" she raised her eyebrow at her giving her the international 'it's your time to talk' signal.

"My Love Flood Collection will see the light of day at Lizzie's gallery beginning January 13th of next year."

Nikki was the only one who was still in her chair, so the other girls rushed to her and pulled her up and kissed her and hugged her.

"Believe it or not, I have some good news too," interrupted Sasha. All eyes went to her and no one was breathing anymore waiting for the miracle. "Another of Ryan's victims came to me today and she's offering to support me, testify and whatever else I need. "

"Are you kidding me?" yelled Nikki. "That asshole has done this before and got away with it?"

Sasha replied "Let's focus on the positive. Donna, that's her name, and Mrs. Clifford have already got in touch and Mrs. Clifford called me to tell me that we stand a good chance now."

"She said what? Holy cow! This is huge! Sasha, it's amazing! I'm so happy for you!" jumped in Lizzie.

"Thank you!" said Sasha. "Now it's time for Julie to get a little miracle of her own, and our family is complete."

Julie was quiet, she grabbed Lizzie and Sasha's hands, looked up at Nikki and announced "I'm moving in with Mike."

They were all dumb folded.

Nikki was the first one to snap out of it "As long as this is what you want and it makes you happy, I guess you got your own miracle as well."

"It does make me happy, but I didn't know how to tell you girls before ... and with everything that has happened since I came from Mexico..."

Lizzie interrupted her "So, you knew since then and didn't tell us anything"

Julie defended herself "Well, I didn't know if it was the right move. And it felt like the timing was inappropriate with what happened to Sasha and ... I'm sorry guys. I love you, but I need to do this for myself."

"Can we still stay in your apartment?" asked Nikki.

"Of course, you can. As a matter of fact, I'm keeping most of my stuff here, I'll need days off from Mike. I think it will be good for us to have some time away now and then. And sometimes he has cases that take him away, so I'll take advantage of that and spend some time with my family, you guys."

"We are happy for you, Julie, really! We're just being a bit selfish, right girls?" said Nikki, looking at Sasha and Lizzie for approval.

"Yes, we are so happy for you," joined in the other two girls who were quiet for a while.

"Guess what day is this Thursday?" asked Nikki.

Lizzie looked confused, "I don't know. Did we plan something we forgot about?"

"We didn't plan anything, that's the problem" answered Nikki. "And it just dawned on me too!"

No one said anything for a few seconds until Lizzie blurted out "Freakin Thanksgiving!"

"How did we forget?" questioned Julie out loud.

"Wow, time went by really fast" acknowledged Sasha. "Ok, let's figure this out tonight and make all the necessary planning, so tomorrow we can make it happen. Thanksgiving is only a day away!"

"Holly Turkey, we almost forgot Thanksgiving" said Lizzie and they all started laughing.

***

"Why did you wake up so early" asked Sasha. "Oh, I see!" she added admiring Julie's perfectly fit and expensive running outfit.

Julie grabbed her iPod from the kitchen counter "Have to work out early today if I want to do it at all. I have two classes this morning that I definitely have to attend, Mike and I are meeting at Restoration Hardware to choose a dining room table, now that he won't be eating alone"

Sasha smiled at her comment. "Good for you, Julie. " Then she followed her to grab a banana from the counter. She stopped, looked at Julie and continued "You know that I'm happy for you, right?"

"Yeah, Sasha. I do," said Julie raising an eyebrow and turning her head towards her. "Why do you even feel the need to assure me of that? Is there something more, something you're not telling me?"

"Oh, no! I'm just so absorbed by my own drama that I know I can be forgetful or mean to say things and then don't say them" Sasha shook her head. "I'm just kind of double checking that I've told you that. That's all."

Julie smiled back at her "You have! And thank you!"

"One question though" had to say Sasha.

Julie was heading for the door already but turned around again, "Yes?"

"How can you sweat in those ... perfectly amazing looking clothes?" finally articulated Sasha.

Julie looked down at her clothes. "They are workout clothes!"

"I know, but they look so bright and fit and ... expensive!" added Sasha.

"Aha, that was the real question. The money!" smiled Julie completely understanding Sasha's dilemma. "They feel right, I can sweat and it doesn't retain the wetness, my skin breathes ... and I look good" decided to add Julie. "I like looking good. I hope that's not a crime in your books!"

"No, it's not. And I understand, I just had to ask."

Julie winked at her and opened the apartment door. "Are you ready for the day?"

Sasha walked through the open door. "I guess I have to be!"

***

Walking into the apartment in the middle of the day was not something Sasha was used to. Between work and school, she never seemed to have enough time to show up at home before sundown.

"Please make yourself at home Donna!" Sasha put down her bags and coat and went towards the kitchen cabinets to grab the mugs and heat up some water for some spicy hot tea.

Lizzie walked into the kitchen. "I thought I heard some noises. Was just making sure it was made by friendly intruders before I knocked you out with my deadly yoga foam roll."

Donna got up from her chair and introduced herself "I'm the friendliest intruder you'll ever have to paddle with your foam roll. My name is Donna" and she extended her hand so Lizzie could follow suit.

"Ah, Donna, I've heard a lot about you already" said Lizzie recognizing the name from Sasha and Julie's conversations. She put the purple foam roll on the couch and shook Donna's hand. "Nice to meet you, Donna. I'm Lizzie."

"Let me guess. You're Sasha's other almost sister" deduced Donna.

"Funny! I haven't heard that 'almost sister' thing in a while," said Lizzie with a smile. "We used to call each other that years and years ago when we first met."

Sasha added a third mug to the two she had out on the counter. "I hope you'll join us for a warm cup of tea. It's getting really cold out there and this will do the trick, so we can unfreeze our minds and heat our souls up. "

Lizzie laughed "Nikki should hear you quoting her. She'd be quite impressed."

Sasha shared the laughter. "Yes, she would. Don't tell her. Her head is getting bigger and bigger already with all the praise you and your boss are giving her. "

"Yes, and this morning her dean called her to do just thing. And to offer her their gallery for Nikki's Love Flood's first public appearance. Too late dude! Ha!" mocked Lizzie. "Nikki's collection is going live at my gallery first!"

"Wow, galleries and deans fighting over a 'love flood'? This sounds intriguing. I'd love to see this collection myself" interrupted Donna.

Lizzie turned to her and assured her "You're helping Sasha a lot, right now. Nikki and all of us are more than grateful, so be sure you'll have one of the first invitations to this momentous event."

"I won't miss it for the world" replied Donna smiling at Lizzie.

"Not if you know what's good for you!" countered Lizzie smiling.

Donna smiled too. "You guys are a friendly bunch. I'm glad to have met you, even though the circumstances are not quite pleasant."

"To say the least" agreed Lizzie.

"Tea is ready" announced Sasha. "I need to be back at work by three, so if we can start with that statement, I'd really appreciate it."

"Sure," said Donna, grabbing one of the mugs full of hot tea that Sasha lined up on the kitchen counter for them.

"We'll have time to bond later, I promise. And I'm sorry for rushing this" added Sasha.

"No worries. I completely understand" Donna reassured her.

Lizzie took her tea, turned on her heels and announced "I'll leave you two alone. I have couple of emails to send and then I'm off to do all the shopping for our Thanksgiving dinner."

Sasha touched her arm, "We all really appreciate you taking the afternoon off for this. So sorry we couldn't be of more help."

"Yeah, yeah. No worries, you'll help cook it and the cleaning is up to you guys. I'll be rubbing my stuffed belly and watching you clean the dishes" joked Lizzie already rubbing her belly for visual effect.

Before Lizzie left the room, Donna suggested "I could help you out, Lizzie. My afternoon is free and I can't think of anything else I'd rather do."

Lizzie gave her a bewildered look "Nothing else you'd rather do?"

"Nope!" Donna stood her ground.

"OK, then!" said Lizzie raising her eyebrows, thinning her lips and lifting her hands. "The more the merrier. But with one condition."

"What? Carry the heavy loads and walk four feet behind you?" joked Donna.

"No, though tempting," smiled Lizzie, "You should enjoy the feast we're going to prepare with the goodies we get today."

Donna looked confused.

Sasha explained "We are inviting you to our Thanksgiving Dinner looks like."

"Yes, we are!" said Lizzie making sure it didn't just "look like"

"Thank you, both of you, but I already have plans" countered Donna.

"So? Cancel them!" said Lizzie decisively.

"That wouldn't be ..."

Lizzie interrupted her, "Well, then, you can't help me shopping today then either."

Donna took a minute and then broke the silence, "Ok. I'll make sure I'll make it to your dinner."

Lizzie smiled victorious. "It's settled then. Sasha, now she's all yours."

***

As Julie was walking into the store, she saw Mike relaxing on a leather recliner.

"Oh, honey, you have to try this. I have one just like it at home and I don't think I'll be able to share it. Even with you" said Mike inviting Julie to sit in his lap.

"So, then what's the point in me trying it?"

Mike turned her face towards him, put a soft kiss on her lips and answered "I've just decided that we're going to get you one as well."

"Great," said Julie smiling, "I can see us in 30-40 years from now. Two old farts watching TV in our recliners, fighting over the remote control."

"Oh no baby, no fighting over the remote."

"Oh right," said Julie, "because the man always has the remote."

"No!" corrected her Mike, "You will have a remote, our kids will have one, but I will have the one to rule them all!" announced Mike with a deep throaty voice.

"Yes, your precious," Julie joined in doing her best Gollum impression.

Both of them started laughing and Mike hugged her tightly in his arms. "You're so much fun! I love you!" he whispered in her ear.

Julie loved hearing that. She was not sure that she would ever get tired of hearing it. "I love you, too, Mike!"

"You do?" Mike played dumb. "Here's a gift for my lady," he said handing her a silver box wrapped with teal ribbon.

Julie took it, then looked at Mike. "Come on babe, open it up."

She did and then took a breath. "The key to your apartment."

"Our apartment," corrected her Mike.

"Our apartment," repeated Julie her heart filled with so much joy she was sure she was about to wake up from this wonderful dream.

Mike kissed her again. This time, he took his time and wrapped his arms around her again. He was real. This was all real. Julie couldn't stop her tears.

"I'm sorry, Mike, I'm just happy! These are happy tears!" she reassured him.

Mike took her hand, kissed her on the top of her head, then lifted both of them out of the recliner. "If that key made you happy, let's see what a real dining table will do you."

Julie laughed and followed Mike's lead to the store's dining room.

Chapter 23

"The sweet potatoes are ready to be served," said Sasha, putting them on the table in front of everyone.

Julie rearranged the green beans with almonds and the mushroom stuffing platters, so the sweet potatoes could fit. "I don't think we've ever had so much food on this table. All of a sudden it looks like a miniature dining table."

"We never had so many guests at once either" acknowledged Nikki.

Mike grabbed Julie's cloth napkin from her chair, so she wouldn't sit on it and when she was comfortably back in her chair, he laid it on her lap and gave her a kiss.

"Ohhh, that's so sweet of you," said Nikki. " If I drop my napkin, would you do the same for me? I'd be more than thankful" she added batting her lashes at him.

Mike laughed and Julie sent Nikki a killer look. "He might do it. He's a gentleman and a hero. My hero!" announced Julie kissing him back.

"This is a bit too mushy for my stomach, guys. Let's slay the turkey and bring peace to my digestive system" said Josh, one of Nikki's friends she decided to invite to their Thanksgiving dinner.

"Just because you have no romantic bone in your body, does not mean that romance is dead" replied Julie defensively. "I bet Nikki would love to see one of those 'sweet' gestures from you, Josh. Whatever your deal is this time around, I don't think it makes Nikki as happy as she deserves to be."

"None of your business," threw Nikki cautiously.

"No really," continued Julie. "What the hell is going on with you two. On and off and back and forth … When you clearly love each other. I haven't seen you in what? A year? Maybe more? Now you show up again into her life, our lives and have the audacity to ask all of us to pick it up where you left off last time. We're not your puppets!" finished Julie with a high-pitched voice.

"Enough!" said Nikki loudly, hitting the table with her fist. "No one needs an explanation of what I choose to do! Unless I offer it! You are my friends, my family! You only need to support me no matter what. That's it!"

No one said anything to that. They all seemed preoccupied with the empty plates in front of them.

"Are your dinners always this much fun?" asked Donna, but only so Sasha and Lizzie could hear as they were both sitting next to her.

"You haven't seen anything yet!" said Lizzie and smiled at her reassuringly. "Don't worry, they'll get over it in couple of minutes. Like it never happened."

"We're dysfunctional like that" added Sasha. And all three started laughing at her comment.

Sasha just remembered something, so she felt like she had to announce it to the entire table. "Hey everyone! I want to thank you for being here today, sharing our plentiful Thanksgiving dinner. Before we start carving into that big deliciously looking bird, thank you Donna for bringing it," Sasha said smiling at Donna, then she turned back to the entire table, "I'd like to let everyone know that Mrs. Clifford found an attorney who would take my case. This guy, not only is the best in the country, but he has taken Richard Bernstein to court before and he won!"

" Oh my God, that's the best news I've heard in a long long time," exclaimed Lizzie.

"That's fantastic," added Mike.

"The bastard won't know what hit him!" jumped in Donna.

"We definitely have a lot to be thankful for this year," said Nikki. "How about going around the table and giving everyone a chance to say what they are thankful for this year and then we can commence this feast." She didn't finish saying it and her stomach growled loudly.

Everyone laughed.

"I guess we all agree, stomachs included," said Josh not seeming to be phased by what had happen several minutes before with Julie.

***

After dinner they were all sitting in the living room enjoying a cup of tea and talking about current events and engaging in a card game that the girls remembered from their rehab days. They were all laughing and chatting. The atmosphere was light and peaceful.

"Sasha," Mike said addressing her after checking his cell phone. "My colleague just gave me some good news."

"Really? Let's hear it" replied Sasha immediately.

"It might sound weird at first but please bear with me" advised Mike.

Sasha didn't know what to say but she braced herself for the strangeness of the information Mike was going to give her. Julie jumped at her side, putting one arm around her shoulders in a comforting and protective posture.

"This Ryan is too clean. Too fishy. Either someone expunged his records clean or he's keeping a very low profile, too low. Something's totally wrong" warned Mike. Then he looked at her concerned, "Are you ok? I'm not done, I told you it will sound completely wrong and not helpful at first, but"

"But what," interrupted Julie a bit freaked out by the news herself.

Mike smiled calmly at both of them. He took a breath in and regrouped his thoughts, so the explanation would immediately ease both their angst. That's when he noticed that the room was in complete silence. They were all listening.

"This only tells us something is very wrong and just made us more curious. Now we're going to dig so deep, we'll find even how much zit cream he used in secondary school. Whomever did this, made a huge mistake. They should have left some little things here and there, but a perfect record ... he just set the best of our dogs on the hunt for every piece of information that ever-made part of his life."

Sasha's face was showing the confusion that was clouding her mind.

"In simple words: He's screwed! Big time!" concluded Mike, hoping that would bring some relief to her. It did.

A single tear ran quickly down her cheek. She said nothing. Julie put the other arm around her and gave her a long hug. "This is good!"

"It's fantastic news," Donna broke the silence among the rest in the group.

Nikki jumped in "And with Donna's testimony and that fancy lawyer, you have nothing to worry about, honey! This is an easy win! I promise. I feel it! And I can see it"

Sasha's face finally broke a faded smile and she looked straight at Nikki to get confirmation from her facial expression that what she was saying she really believed in. Nikki's face was radiant.

"And so, it is!" Sasha murmured.

"Yes, because we all know that if Nikki can see it, it will happen. We've lived with her long enough to know this. She's our good witch!" joked Lizzie joining in.

Sasha went back to worrying. Her face was mirroring the conflict that was going on in her mind.

"What now?" asked Nikki. She was always able to read all of their faces faster than anyone. She seemed to be more intuned with them than they were with themselves sometime.

Sasha tried to dismiss her bleak thoughts, but she knew she couldn't fool Nikki. "Nothing big, just trying to figure out how I'm going to pay this top-notch lawyer. He has to cost a fortune."

Nikki came next to her, took her hands into hers and firmly said. "The bastard will pay for everything. But until the trial is over, I will give you the money I got from the gallery as an advance for my collection."

Lizzie joined them, "And I will give you the money I got for signing the book."

"But guys, you don't have to" replied Sasha.

"No, we don't have to, but we want to," said Julie. "And you know you can always count on me when it comes to money, especially for stuff like this."

There was a second and a third and a fourth tear finding their way down Sasha's cheek. "I love you guys!"

Donna was next to Josh. She didn't want to interrupt the moment, but couldn't help herself. "This is sort of beautiful and freaky at the same time. Are they always like this?

Mike and Josh said at the same time "Worst, I'm afraid" and started laughing at the coincidence.

"It's time for some slow dancing," announced Mike as he quickly chose a CD from the impressive collection that the girls decorated half of the living room walls with and popped it into the player. Then he looked at Julie, smiled and reached his hand towards her. She jumped up and closed in the gap with one step.

"I really need a hot bath, if everyone is ok with that," said Sasha softly. "Need some alone time."

"We understand, " replied Nikki. "Go take care of yourself, honey!" She gave her a hug and then Sasha disappeared down the hallway.

Josh grabbed Nikki's hand and swirled her around into his arms. "I want some me time as well. With you."

"Very smooth," smiled Nikki.

Listening to the music and watching the couple dance, Lizzie was swaying side to side smiling. Donna popped in front of her, offered her hand and asked with exaggerated politeness "Would the beautiful lady do me the honor of considering dancing with me on this melodious music?"

Lizzie laughed and got up, "I accept your invitation, my dear gentleman! Or should I say gentle woman!" And then she laughed at her own joke.

"You look amazing tonight!" whispered Donna in her ear.

Lizzie smiled and complimented her back. "So do you."

"And you pulled an amazing Thanksgiving dinner. I'm glad you convinced me out of spending today with my awkward family" commented Donna. "My family has no idea what to do with today, so they give the help stupid gifts. I bet they'd prefer the day off to spend it with their families."

"I'm happy that you came and especially that you helped me do all that shopping yesterday. You saved my ass" thanked Lizzie.

"Anytime, Lizzie."

"Thank you for helping Sasha, too" added Lizzie quickly.

"That's a given. But if there's more that I can do, please let me know," said Donna.

Lizzie was pondering and then she just let her thoughts flow out "I hope this is not too personal, but how did you get away from Ryan so easily. I read your statement. I mean, he's handsome and popular and all that. Did he get the chance to charm you a little bit like he did Sasha?"

"His first and biggest mistake was that he did not pay attention to details or to me really. He was trying hard to peacock around me, but to no avail. He should have dropped it."

"But he didn't" concluded Lizzie.

"No, and I was not interested at all" added Donna.

Lizzie seemed confused, "At all, at all? Even Sasha gave into his charms and she's the most cautious and picky girl I know."

Donna stopped the dance for a second and looked right in Lizzie's eyes, "Lizzie, I'm gay!"

Lizzie was dumbstruck. Her mind stopped functioning all together. She was following Donna's steps and dancing, but that was only her body. Her mind did not react at all.

"Is that alright with you?" asked Donna.

She was uncomfortable, you could see it easily on Lizzie. She had a thousand questions and didn't know how to ask them. She smiled politely.

"You can ask me anything. I promise I won't get offended" offered Donna.

"Does Sasha know?" was the first thing that shot out of Lizzie's mouth.

Donna simply replied "Yes. I briefly mentioned it to her because she was asking the same question you were asking about Ryan."

"Was she ok with it?" was the next question.

"Meaning what?" asked Donna. "If I can help her with Ryan knowing that I'm gay?"

Lizzie didn't say anything. The question clearly came out wrong.

"Do you have a problem with me being gay?" finally asked Donna.

Lizzie shook her head vehemently. "No! Not at all. I'm sorry if my question implied that at all."

Donna smiled back confidently, "Good!"

" I really enjoyed spending time together yesterday and today," said Lizzie truthfully.

"Me too! More than I've enjoyed spending time with anyone in a long time" replied Donna, slowing the rhythm. The song was almost over. " How about I take you out for dinner and a movie tomorrow or Saturday?"

Lizzie didn't know what to say. She didn't want to seem that she was dodging her now that she found out she was gay, but even if she really connected with her from the first moment she saw her, Lizzie didn't want Donna to get the wrong impression.

"Dinner and a movie? Like a date, date? Or hanging out?" asked Lizzie for clarification.

"Whatever suits you," replied Donna. "I'd love to take you out, but if you just want to hang, I'm good with that too."

"Ok" said Lizzie. "I ... can I let you know later?"

"Later?"

"Yes! Actually, no!" Lizzie was trying to clarify the situation. "Listen, I've been straight all my life. I'm straight. I never kissed a girl, not even to experiment. I was never interested. I like boys. Men! I love men!"

"I understand," replied Donna.

"But I also like spending time with you, too. We connect in a weird way" added Lizzie.

"I agree on the connecting part" offered Donna.

"Ok. I guess that's all I wanted to say!" finished Lizzie.

And the song was over as she said her last thought. Donna pulled her a bit closer, took Lizzie's face into her hands and kissed her.

Lizzie couldn't stop it. She saw it coming, like a train rack, but just stood there like a deer in the headlights. Was this really happening? Did they just destroy what could have been a beautiful friendship? Was anyone watching? Why did it feel good? Was she that kiss deprived? Oh, man, she had to find a man fast!

When Donna pulled her head away and dropped her hands from Lizzie's face, Lizzie finally got a hold of herself and got out of her head.

If anyone saw them, they were doing a good job at pretending everything was normal. Was everything normal?

"Really? Come on!" Lizzie heard Julie saying in a seemingly annoyed tone of voice.

Oh, so she did see. Lizzie was trying to come up with something to say fast. Then she saw Julie and Mike going towards the door.

"Sorry, guys, duty calls!" announced Mike as he opened the door.

"You should have turned that phone off for tonight. Just for tonight" begged Julie, but she knew she was a bit out of place, so she pouted like a little girl. "I know, I know. Being a cop is a 24/7 job."

Mike kissed her and turned fast to run out, but he ran into a muscular bearded guy that was standing right in the middle of the doorway.

"What the..." exclaimed Mike.

Nikki jumped right from behind Mike, "Nick, glad you could join us!"

Nick seemed to be as surprised as Mike. "Oh, thank you for inviting me."

Nikki grabbed his hand and pulled him into the living room. "Perfect timing! Julie can drill your head about her rehab that she wants to open where she wants to integrate yoga and stuff. She'll tell you all about it. But first, let's get you some food. There's plenty!"

Chapter 24

I don't want to be. I can't be gay. That kiss did not mean anything to me. Then why do I keep thinking about it? And touching my lips with my fingers all the time like I can still feel it lingering hours and hours later. What the heck is wrong with me? I've never been attracted to a woman before. Why now? Is that how it works? Does it just pop into your mind one day that you actually like people of your own sex now?

Lizzie was too confused to be able to stand still. She needed answers and she needed them now. She walked out of her room not knowing exactly what or how she was going to get those answers.

With the eyes focused on the ground, softly speaking out loud to herself she walked into the kitchen.

"Did you say something?" she heard Nikki's voice.

Lizzie lifted her head up and shook it violently from side to side, "No, no! No! I was not saying anything!"

Nikki stepped towards her worried, "You look freaked out. More like a crazy person. What happened?" As she said that Sasha walked into the kitchen as well and was looking at both of them trying to assess the situation.

"Lizzie, it is ok! You can talk to us" said Nikki with a soft calm voice. "Whatever it is" she continued, then waited to see Lizzie's next move before she reached out and grabbed both her shoulder in her hands not knowing if she was safe to go in for a hug, but making the attempt and letting Lizzie close the gap if she wanted to.

Couple of seconds later, Lizzie turned her gaze from the floor towards Nikki and whispered. "I can't be gay!" and then started shaking and bursts of loud cry came out with a flood of tears. She collapsed on the floor in front of Nikki.

Sasha threw herself on the ground next to Lizzie, "Why are you saying that? What happened?"

Nikki knew. She saw it happen the night before but did not say anything then. "It was just a kiss," she said comforting Lizzie with a tight hug and kissing the top of her head. "I kiss girls all the time. That doesn't make me gay! And I kissed a bunched of frogs hoping they would become Prince Charming and that doesn't make me zoophilous either."

Lizzie cracked a tiny smile. "But I think I liked it."

It took Sasha a moment to understand what the heck had happened while she was asleep. Then she put it together. "Donna!"

Both Nikki and Lizzie looked at her at the same time. "Sorry, I'm catching up!" apologized Sasha.

"Yes, Donna!" confirmed Lizzie. "And you knew and didn't tell me."

"It didn't seem relevant" replied Sasha." I've had so much to deal with lately, I can't keep track of what I've said and to whom."

"What am I going to do now?" asked Lizzie begging for an answer to her dilemma.

"Go along with it, slowly, and explore the possibility" suggested Nikki.

"How about my dreams of perfect love and family and kids?" cried Lizzie.

"You can have all that!" said Nikki reassuringly.

"But ... but how? I mean, if I'm gay ...I can't ...we can't" sputtered Lizzie.

"Yes, you can. And you're not gay. At best, you're bisexual. And if you decide that the love of your life is a woman, you can adopt or get sperm from a donor" came in Sasha with a logical explanation to her drama.

Lizzie didn't say anything for a moment. "But in my dreams, there was a wedding and a man by my side who held me through thick and thin for the rest of our lives. It was so magical." She was daydreaming again, visualizing her oldest girlie dream.

"You can always have that too" reassured her Nikki. "But you're jumping the gun," she said making sure Lizzie was paying attention. "It was just a kiss."

"Yes, but she wants us to go out" whined Lizzie.

Nikki smiled "So, go out. Have fun. Let it flow naturally, but let her know your feelings from the start, so neither of you will be hurt later on."

"I agree. It's only fair to do so, for both of you" added Sasha.

Lizzie's face was reflecting her thoughts perfectly. She seemed to be putting all that was said in balance, considering both sides. "You are right," came the answer. "I already told her how I felt, but I'm going to hang out with her and see what happens next."

"And don't be scared. Don't throw amazing opportunities away just because they didn't come to you the way you expected them to" said Nikki knowing Lizzie fully well. "Don't half ass it!"

Lizzie took a breath, looked at Nikki and said "No half measures!"

"One of my favorite things that I learned through 12 steps!" added Sasha.

Both Lizzie and Nikki looked at her and laughed. "You overdo it though. You're a workaholic in all aspects of your life," said Lizzie.

"How about no half measures when it comes to relaxing and having some fun too!" suggested Nikki.

"But that's how I have fun, through my work" defended Sasha.

"You're a work in progress," commented Nikki. "But you are perfect just the way you are right now."

"Thank you" said Sasha bowing her head in gratitude. She knew Nikki meant everything she said. She always did.

They all got up the floor.

"Julie said she was coming this evening for a brainstorming session with us" Nikki informed the other two.

"Brainstorming on what" asked Sasha. "Apparently I missed a big part of the evening yesterday.

"Yes, you did" confirmed Nikki. "But you needed that alone time, so we'll fill you in."

"Great. Thank you!" replied Sasha.

"Well, where should we start" pondered Lizzie. "Oh yeah, I kissed a girl and I liked it" sang Lizzie.

All three started laughing.

"We already covered that part" said Sasha still laughing.

"Mike had to leave early again," jumped in Nikki. "Work," she responded to Sasha's raised eyebrow. "I don't know how Julie puts up with it. It seems to call him at the wrong times, all the time."

"And Julie still went to his apartment?" asked Sasha.

"Their apartment," corrected Lizzie. "Yes, she did. That girl is in love. You can see it on her."

"And he is too" added Sasha.

"Yes, he is. Very much so" agreed Nikki.

Lizzie didn't want to spoil the moment but she couldn't help herself, "It might all be an act."

"What are you talking about?" Nikki asked incredulous. She couldn't believe that Lizzie, the only one of them who was always dreaming about the perfect man and perfect love was fighting this beautiful reality. Then it dawned on her, "Are you jealous, Lizzie?"

"What?" snapped back Lizzie shocked. "Of Julie's happiness? Are you insane? I love Julie."

Nikki wanted to snap back, but Sasha intervened. "I completely understand" she offered trying not to see Nikki's shocked facial expression. "It's John, right?" she confirmed with Lizzie, who only nodded her head.

"What about John? And who's John again?" Nikki wanted to know.

Sasha looked at Lizzie waiting for her approval to continue telling the story to Nikki. She whispered "Go ahead."

"John is Mike's best friend and he turned out to be a worthless scumbag!" announced Sasha to a blown away Nikki.

"What do you mean? What exactly happened?" wanted to know Nikki.

"He was going out with Lizzie, made her fall in love and then she saw him drinking, doing coke and fucking prostitutes out in the open at a well-known club. Don't think you need more details than that" continued Sasha.

Nikki had to give herself a minute to absorb the new information. When she was finally ready to talk, she addressed Lizzie directly "Has he tried to contact you since then? Did he see you in the club?"

"I don't think he saw me. He was too high and was rushing to the restrooms to fuck one of the whores he was with. I heard the conversation. I knew exactly what was happening. He walked right by me, but I bet he didn't even notice me."

"That piece of shit!" exclaimed Nikki not able to control herself. "I'm sorry you had to go through that, honey!"

Lizzie took a deep breath in a desperate attempt to not fall back into that abyss that John created that night in her soul. It was deep, black and more painful than anything she had to go through for the longest time. "To answer your other question: Yes, he has tried to contact me, but I did not answer the phone."

Sasha turned towards Lizzie, "You didn't tell me that."

"Yeah, like you don't have enough shit to deal with in your life. All you need is my crap!" replied Lizzie.

Nikki reacted first, "Has Mike asked you why you're not picking up his calls? He must have complained to him."

"Nope. Not once" answered Lizzie.

" That is strange!" concluded Nikki. "And even for Mike to have a best friend like that! That tells you a lot about who he really is."

"My feelings exactly," said Lizzie.

"Why didn't you tell Julie?" asked Nikki confused.

"Bad timing" answered Sasha.

"There's never good timing for something like this" barked back Nikki. "You should have told her."

"Well, my bad," replied Sasha. "I asked Lizzie not to say anything yet."

Nikki started passing through the kitchen playing with her hair. "Well, what's done is done. Now we need to figure out how to tell Julie."

"Is there a chance Mike could be exactly who he seems to be and John is just a lost soul he feels like protecting because they grew up together?" tried Sasha.

Lizzie didn't seem to agree with that hope at all.

"Well, miracles do exist in this world, but it's hard to justify their friendship if their vibes don't match at some levels. And then the fact that he didn't ask you Lizzie why you don't call John back... He must cover for him. Like this is something he normally does" said Nikki out loud." There's too much darkness around this whole thing. I have to pay more attention to Mike next time I see him."

"But he does seem to love Julie, Nikki!" exclaimed Sasha.

Nikki looked up, pondering "Yes, he does!"

Sasha did not feel comfortable with all the tension so she had to change the subject.

"Ok, so what else?" asked Sasha eagerly. "What else did I miss last night?"

"Nick came and Julie started talking to him about her rehab plans. And both of them got so excited over it." Nikki stopped for a second trying to remember if there was anything else. "That's what the brainstorming session is about. FYI!"

Sasha smiled, "That's fabulous news! I'll be there. What time?"

"Six o'clock" replied Nikki.

"No problem," said Sasha. "Now if there's nothing else, I need to go jump in the shower and get ready for the day."

"Are you going to be able to make it?" Nikki asked Lizzie. "Aren't you going out with Donna today?"

"Because I was freaked out, I pushed for lunch and Christmas shopping" replied Lizzie. "I'll be here at six for sure."

"That's it," concluded Nikki.

Sasha remembered something, stopped and looked at Nikki "How about Josh? Did you guys have fun?"

Nikki smiled. She was so sweet to include Josh. "Yes, we had plenty of fun!" Her face was radiating with joy.

***

Donna already had three bags in one hand and couple more in the other. "I'm almost done with my Christmas shopping," she let Lizzie know.

"You are a fast shopper," said Lizzie. "My hat's off to you!"

"Thank you" said Donna enjoying the compliment.

Lizzie was overwhelmed by Donna's ability to make up her mind. Shopping was an art for Lizzie. She liked to go and get immersed in the possibilities before she even knew what she wanted to buy and for whom. And then, when the time came to buy, she was panicking not being sure what exactly to buy so she could make the receiver of the gift as happy as she was buying it for them. It was always a cumbersome process that required days of preparation, lists and mall trips.

"How do you know what other people want for a gift?" asked Lizzie curiously. "You seem very confident in your picks."

Donna smiled. "It's a talent of mine!"

Lizzie didn't seem to be satisfied with the answer, so Donna explained "I like to pay attention to the people I care about. So, I usually know exactly what they like and dislike. And I keep my lists short. I'm not superhuman, I can't remember all my friends, so I keep to my family and closest friends. That's it."

"Oh, I know what you mean. Because I buy gifts for everybody. Even the barista that prepares my coffee almost on a daily basis," said Lizzie.

"It's a sure way to kill yourself slowly. That's an overwhelming task, and it ends up stressing you out and depleting you of fun and energy. Isn't gift giving supposed to be fun and fulfilling?" asked Donna rhetorically.

"Maybe, for some people like you" replied Lizzie. "You are so confident in everything you do. Even picking gifts for your loved ones. A task that takes me days and weeks, takes you minutes - and that's mostly because it takes the counter girl too long to swipe your credit card."

"Do you want me to share some of my magic with you" asked Donna with a smile on her face.

Lizzie wasn't sure what she was offering. She hoped Donna was talking about Christmas shopping and nothing else. Was she? Lizzie's thoughts were spiraling down and she couldn't stop them. She didn't want to have to make a decision right now. She enjoyed Donna's presence. Lizzie found herself a bit nervous before she had to come and meet with Donna not knowing what to wear, not to give her the wrong impression, but still to look casually sexy and beautiful. Maybe even desirable.

Donna was reading the signs." I was talking about helping you with your Christmas list."

"Ahh, yeah. My Christmas list" mumbled Lizzie barely present.

"Ok, Lizzie. Listen! I love spending time with you, but if I make you uncomfortable in any way, just let me know. If you want me to leave, I will. I like you too much to hurt you or confuse you. And hopefully you don't feel any kind of pressure coming from me at all. Because there's no pressure, regarding anything." clarified Donna.

Lizzie jolted out of her reverie "Oh no, no! I don't feel pressured. And I do love spending time with you too. Time flies by so fast. I can't believe we already spent what ..." and Lizzie looked at her watch and did the math "wow, five hours together!"

"Good. Because I feel the same way" replied Donna.

"Thank you for being so wonderful. And understanding" continued Lizzie. She wanted Donna to know how much she appreciated her. "I feel like I can open up to you and not feel judged, which is so rare."

"It's another of my specialties," replied Donna jokingly.

Lizzie smiled. "You blow me away with all this ...this ... confidence you have in yourself. And you're so smart and wise and ..." She wanted to say attractive but she was too scared to say that out loud. What the heck was going on?

Donna interrupted her thoughts. "Let's sit down at that cafe on the second floor and I'll help you with ideas on Christmas gifts? What do you say?"

"If you can help me out with that and I can walk out of here with at least couple of gifts in my hand, then you are a miracle worker" proclaimed Lizzie.

"Haven't I given you one of my business cards - Donna - the miracle worker?" joked Donna winking at Lizzie.

***

It was already dark by six o'clock. The wind was blowing hard and it was the first freezing night of the year.

"Maybe it will snow tonight to soften things up a little bit," wished Lizzie.

"It's that time of the year already!" said Julie smiling and looking out the window through the darkness of the night.

Nikki set herself next to Julie and gave her a yellow notepad and a pen. "Let's do this!"

Julie smiled, gave Nikki the notepad back and pulled her laptop from her bag."I'd like everything saved electronically, if that's ok with you."

"Maybe it's just me, but when I handwrite stuff, it seems to come easier to me. All the ideas seem to flow better" she said then looked at Julie and noticed her disagreeing smile. "Ok, ok. We're all different. What works for me might not work for you. I got it. I'll shut up now."

"I don't want you to shut up" replied Julie. "Unless we're still talking about notepad versus laptop."

Nikki smiled, "Roger that!" Then she continued "So, what's the name that you dreamed of for your rehab? Let's start from there. If you have anything."

Sasha butt in, "Name can come later, too."

"Wow, you can tell you've never had to write a book or a business proposal" interjected Lizzie as well. "Name and motto and all that usually come later after you build the entire concept around it."

"Or the other way around," jumped in Julie.

"What do you mean?" asked Lizzie.

"I already have a name," announced Julie proudly.

"Ha! See, the hardest part is over!" said Nikki. "Let's hear it!"

"Solstice!" announced Julie. "It means turning point!"

"How appropriate!" exclaimed Sasha. "It's actually perfect. How did you get the idea?"

"Remember the day we went to the spa and start talking about my rehab idea more?" explained Julie.

Nikki looked confused.

"Oh yeah," replied Lizzie. "You weren't here Nikki!" she said so she could get Nikki over her confusion.

"The name of the place is Summer Solstice Spa, and I just loved the way Solstice sounded. I played with it for a while and then when I discovered that it meant 'turning point', I knew it was the name I was looking for" further detailed Julie with enthusiasm.

"It's perfect!" agreed Nikki. "So, what did you and Nick talk about last night?"

"How yoga and meditation could be integrated into my program along with the 12 steps and western medication" explained Julie.

"So you're going to make a fusion of the eastern and western medicine kind of thing?" asked Sasha.

"Yes! I will encourage more eastern, and I will incorporate healthy eating, juicing and homeopathy. There will be chiropractors, acupuncturists, massage therapists, reiki healers, you name it ..." added Julie.

Lizzie was feeling the enthusiasm, "Are they going to be on staff or contracted?"

"Contracted first!" answered Julie.

"Is the treatment going to be standard for everyone - like 2 massages a day, 1 acupuncture session, one AA meeting - and all structured? Or customized?" asked Lizzie.

"That's where I need your help" confessed Julie.

"It definitely needs to be customized, but there has to be a main structure off of which you branch out a little bit for each resident according to their needs" offered Sasha.

"Yes, that sounds great!" said Julie typing notes of what everyone was saying. "Keep it up, I love where this is going."

"First you should talk to a nutritionist, the best money can buy, with a lot of experience in their field and hopefully some extensive experience in addiction. Hire them as a consultant. Talk to many and choose to hire the best. The one who talks to your heart!" said Nikki.

Lizzie went off on that same idea, "Then find the best homeopathic clinic and see what works for them. How they prescribe treatments, with whom, what's their basis and why they think one form of treatment works better than the other."

"Yes, talk to the experts in every field. The ones who have a high successful rate. See what works for them and then combine their best ideas" chimed in Sasha.

"Then I'll mix my spin on things, bake it, top the cake with a delicious cherry and I have my one-of-a-kind rehab" announced Julie excitedly while typing everything in her laptop.

"And the best yet," said Nikki.

"Talking about juicing, I just got a big bottle of apple and carrot juice from the organic juicing place down the street. Let me bring it. It's toasting time" announced Lizzie.

They were all in high spirits. Julie's excitement and enthusiasm was sweetly contagious.

Nikki finally understood what Sasha and Lizzie said about timing. She couldn't take this happiness away from Julie. Not tonight.

Chapter 25

It was wet and cold and she couldn't tell if she liked it or not. She had a good feeling about it but she didn't know why. Nothing around her looked or felt like something one could be happy about. The smell of fungus penetrated her nostrils. She reached out and touched the stone walls. Where was she?

She groped in the dark trying to find a way out, maybe a door, maybe an answer. Anything. She didn't feel like she wanted to run away from this entire experience. It felt comfortable, familiar, loving in a strange way.

Her breathing was shallow but she didn't feel like she had to breathe in more depth. Everything felt right. This stonewall was cold but it felt good under her fingertips. There was a longing to get outside. She knew she had to find the way out even if she felt comfortable in this place. Maybe what it was about to come would be better. Or so something inside of her told her that.

She made a step, then another, then another step. She finally closed her eyes knowing that the sight sense would not be of any help, it would just drain her energy. So, now she could focus all her energy onto the only sense that could help her — the touch. She reached out again. Another stone wall. She was not going to give up. She knew that by now. She decided she was going to find the door so, without pausing even for a second, she had the other hand reach out and now with both hands she was touching and moving her fingertips up and down the wall and following what her senses were telling her. One more step. Her right-hand finally met a wooden surface. The left hand followed. She kept her right hand still, so she wouldn't lose the door somehow, while her left hand was looking for the doorknob. It had to be a door.

It was a door. She turned the doorknob and pushed and the door opened up. It opened to a beautiful landscape. The invigorating smells and sounds of a sunrise in the middle of the countryside moved her soul. She could smell the newly cut grass soaked in morning dew, waiting for the rays of the sun to come and dry it all out so it could be stored away as hay for the winter. There was an orchestra of different sounding birds chirping away, welcoming the new day.

Nikki was welcoming this new day as well, with life, promises, love and perspective.

But where was she? Where was this wonderful place? She had to step out and try to recognize it.

She then saw a wrinkled, kind, radiating with love familiar face. It was her grandmother. And she was smiling at Nikki full heartedly. Then she came up right next to Nikki and she just grabbed her hand and Nikki could feel the energy going right through the palm of her hand. Her grandmother was sending her love.

Nikki's grandmother turned and looked at her land with pride. She allowed Nikki to feel all that love she had for the thing that kept her alive, healthy, and full of joy. Both of them started walking towards the closest field that was covered with some sort of grain that Nikki couldn't recognize. The second they got there, her grandmother looked at Nikki, hugged her, then knelt down on the ground and kissed the grains. She was an explosion of light that warmed Nikki up to her bones. It felt like heaven.

Nikki was awake. She knew what she had to do. She quickly scribbled a note to leave on the kitchen counter for the girls to see. She wasn't disappearing this time. She had a vision and she had to follow it. It was all for the love flood collection. She hadn't felt so much love, freedom and joy in a very, very long time.

Nikki had to immortalize this feeling. The world had to have a glimpse of it. Anything less than that and the feel that her collection hoped to give people would be lost. It wouldn't even touch people's souls the way she wanted it to touch them. She wanted to transform them to make them feel more love, gratitude, and appreciation.

Grabbing her camera and a small duffel bag that she hastily filled with clothes and a couple necessities, she looked around to make sure that she got everything she needed. Especially the note for the girls.

She had to go.

***

Lizzie walked back in their apartment thinking about how much fun she had with Donna, again, checking out the new Ethiopian restaurant around the corner. She knew where the best food places were and was very versed into the world's cuisine. The food was amazing. They didn't even need utensils. Delicious fun moments that Lizzie was still smiling at when she ran into Sasha.

"What are you smiling about?"

"Nothing" said Lizzie. Then she smiled again, stopped and corrected herself "Everything"

Sasha was interested " I bet it's Donna. Anything you'd like to share?"

"I wish ... I wish" Lizzie started saying but couldn't find her words to finish her thought.

"Don't wish anything" said Sasha shaking her head from side to side "Just enjoy it!"

"I am! Trust me I am! But ..." stopped Lizzie midsentence again.

Sasha didn't say anything. She let Lizzie put her thoughts together before she continued "I'm not ready to talk about it! I don't know much and don't want to think about it at all. Just enjoying Donna's company. She makes me feel ... so good, and fulfilled, light and giggly ..." tried to explain Lizzie. Then she smiled again looking somewhere far in the distance clearly reliving some fun memories.

"Please remember that I support you a hundred percent!" said Sasha.

Lizzie broke herself away from the memories and came back to present fixing her gaze on Sasha giving her a warm smile "I know. Thank you!"

"Anytime!" replied Sasha.

Lizzie took off her shoes and coat and moved past Sasha towards her room. "Do you have any idea when Nikki's coming back? I saw her note this morning."

"No idea" replied Sasha slightly frustrated. "I can't remember the last time she went to visit her grandma in Ireland. You know Nikki, she can stay forever or a second and be over it."

Lizzie laughed at the image. "Yup, that's Nikki alright." Then she opened the door to her room and dropped off her scarf and coat.

Sasha followed her and leaned against the doorway. "I just hope she'll be back soon."

"Before your trial, you mean?" asked Lizzie understanding her completely.

"I'm not that selfish!" replied Sasha.

"Noone said you are. But it's a huge deal. She should be here" acknowledged Lizzie.

"Well, she has some time for that. I just would like to have her here for Christmas. It's our favorite holiday!"

"She will be. She's always home for Christmas," said Lizzie with conviction. "What do you mean by some time? I thought your lawyer said it starts immediately."

Sasha pulled a folded piece of paper from her pocket and handed it to Lizzie. "Apparently it was postponed due to the defendant's acute medical condition."

"A psychopathic rapist should be locked away behind a thousand locks, not taken to the hospitals to attack unknowing innocent nurses" said Lizzie unfolding and scanning the short notice. "Cancer? terminal stage?" yelled Lizzie. "What kind of sick joke is this?"

"His dad is powerful, but not God! I don't think he has the power to give him cancer and then take it away!"

Lizzie stared at Sasha "No, but powerful enough to come up with shit like this" she pointed out lifting the paper in front of them.

"I don't think it's a fake. Not even he can get away with something like that" said Sasha "or at least that's what my lawyer said, because I didn't buy it either when I saw this."

Lizzie didn't say anything for a little while. Then set on her bed, looked up at Sasha and asked "How are you feeling about this?"

"I don't know yet. I want him dead! And I don't feel guilty or ashamed of it"

"I want him dead, too. But this is too easy. He should suffer and pay for everything he has done first. Cancer is too easy....and final stage! Straight bullet to the head. Too easy!" concluded Lizzie.

"Do you think I caused this?" murmured Sasha almost in a whisper.

"I hope so. But I don't think you're that powerful" then Lizzie smiled at her joking "but if you are, can you make it so we can win the lottery? Couple of millions of dollars for each one of us would do fine."

It worked. Sasha smiled. "Yeah! Coo-coo idea. I'm no death angel or my mom wouldn't have had the chance to hurt me so much through the years."

"You would have never killed your own mother. Maybe put her in a loony bin" Lizzie smiled imagining the scene. "Can you imagine your mom in a straitjacket, with her perfect coiffure all up in a frizz."

Sasha laughed at the image "Only that would have thrown her over the edge."

"Yup! That's true." And both of them laughed until they were tearing up.

Sasha wiped her tears from her face. "But seriously, do you think I might have had something to do with this? I can't stop thinking I probably should say a prayer for him, but I feel like throwing up when I think about him. All I want for him is pain and suffering. I just can't seem to be able to lift myself above those dark emotions and I'm afraid they will take me down with them. I need light in my life!"

"But you do need to let yourself go through those emotions as well. It's the only way to let them go, by letting them wash through you, just like Nikki always says. Allow yourself to take as much time as you need to. Or else you'll carry them with you indefinitely."

"Hmm! It's easier said than done. I just want to not hurt anymore," said Sasha.

"Think of them like growing pains. They are uncomfortable but necessary for your growth process."

Sasha looked at Lizzie with a sparkle in her eyes "Growing pains! That's brilliant! That's a beautiful and helpful way to look at it! Thank you!"

"Anytime!" replied Lizzie amazed for a second at her own wisdom.

Chapter 26

Big fat white flurries were floating down from the clouded sky. Everything was white and pristine. Even the air was crisp and refreshing. The big limo that Donna arranged to pick them up from the airport was already waiting for them.

"You have to thank your family for this luxurious treat Donna," said Julie as she was moving in next to Mike in the car wrapping his arm around her to keep her warm, loved and safe.

Donna smiled. "We barely use this cabin and it's a pity. They are glad that someone gets to enjoy it."

"Well, we are going to enjoy it alright," said Lizzie with a big smile on her face. "I am ready to kill that bunny slope!"

Sasha laughed, "If it doesn't kill you first!"

"I'll make sure the bunny slope won't attack her," reassured Donna putting a tentative hand on Lizzie's knee. No rejection.

"Well, as I'm the only guy in here, I will have to go into the woods, chop some wood and build us a fire," announced Mike.

"Just don't fight any bears with your bare hands, please. You are mine now and I'll have to kill anyone who even puts their paws on you" retorted Julie.

"Woohoo, a little bit possessive there, aren't we?" joked Sasha.

Julie pouted and put her thumb and index finger closely together, "Just a tiny bit."

Mike laughed and hugged her even closer.

"Don't want to destroy the romance in here or anything, but we have a staff and the cabin is ready for us, fire, hot water, food and everything" interrupted Donna.

"We are royalties for the weekend. I love it!" exclaimed Lizzie. "Thank you, Donna!" she said excitedly putting her hand right on top of Donna's hand that was resting on her knee.

Sasha broke the moment "Look outside guys! It's so majestic! You never get to see this on our crowded island!"

"Too bad Nikki is not here. She would have loved this!" commented Lizzie contemplating the mesmerizing world outside the comfortable limo.

The road was cut through a thick forest covered with glistening snow. Everything looked frosted in a state of peace and serenity, frozen forever while more snowflakes were dancing their way to thickly covered branches.

***

How the heck do people move with those logs attached to their feet? Skis are huge! And those plastic boots are not helping either. How can you feel comfortable in them. It's like they are wearing you instead of you wearing them. They take you anywhere they want you to, they control the situation and you just slide into them and let them take you for a ride.

"My body does not speak ski!" lamented Lizzie after falling for the twentieth time trying to slide down the bunny slope.

Donna was smiling warmly and gave her a hand to help her prop herself back on her feet. "You're doing just fine."

"Fine? What does that mean? Fine" asked Lizzie with visible frustration and dropped herself back on the groomed snow.

Donna didn't take it personally, "You're doing exactly how everybody is normally doing at this point".

"So, I'm not the last clumsy kid that no one wants to pick on their team, but I'm not the captain either" translated Lizzie.

"Something like that" responded Donna and then seeing Lizzie's hurt feelings plastered all over her cute red nosed face, she explained "When I had to learn, my parents were watching and expecting me to be a professional right from my first try. I expected that from me, too. So, I pushed. I did great at first, but after a little while when I started getting tired and I couldn't focus anymore I face planted in the snow in the weirdest position ever invented. And just like that, from superstar I became a super failure in only couple of hours."

Lizzie was laughing "I'm sorry, I don't mean to make fun of your failures as a kid, but I'm just imagining those face plants."

"Thinking back, they were hilarious, "said Donna, "but back then it felt like my life was ending."

"I'm glad to find out that you're not perfect in everything you do. At least not right from the start. That you have to work on it like the rest of us" confessed Lizzie.

Donna grabbed Lizzie's right hand and with a swift nudge pulled her off the snow. "I know I come across like that sometimes and that can scare people away. I'm glad you're not one of them."

"Not far from it either," confessed Lizzie.

Donna looked a bit disappointed so Lizzie continued with her confession in hopes she would make Donna understand, "My mom is an uneducated loser, my dad makes all the money in the house. She never went to college and never had a real career, or a passion of any kind. And she hired a nanny too for me and my sister. So, I had two opposite role models as parents. I never wanted to end up like her, so I always fought for my dreams no matter how they seemed out there - like publishing a book at the age of 19."

"At 19? that is very impressive! Wow, now you make me want to prove myself to you" said Donna amazed at Lizzie's accomplishment.

A row of two- and three-year-olds who could barely walk in normal shoes, were gracefully skiing around both of them like it was the most natural thing to do.

Lizzie laughed at the entire thing, "I hate them! Look at them. They make it look so damn easy! It's hard! It feels like they are all looking and laughing at me."

Donna laughed again. "Don't worry. It's a natural feeling. We all hate them at the start."

"Don't you feel like blowing their way so they can fall over? I know kicking them sounds evil, but ...," said Lizzie.

"Not evil. Very natural, trust me. But you'll get over it ... in couple of seasons."

Lizzie looked confused, "Couple of seasons?"

"Yes. Unfortunately, this row of ducklings will show up on the intermediate slopes too. You can't get rid of them that easily. By the time you're advanced intermediate, you'll love seeing them around. You'll even find them cute, doing their 'pizza and French fries."

"Pizza is my favorite right now. But it doesn't seem to help me stop too much" complained Lizzie.

"That's only because you're not doing your snowplow correctly. But you'll learn, don't worry." Donna set herself next to Lizzie. "Are you ready to go again?"

"Thank God you're not my sister!" muttered Lizzie.

Donna looked confused "Which sister?"

"I'm not talking about the girls I live with" explained Lizzie shaking her head vehemently. "I actually have a blood sister."

"You do? That's great? Younger or older?"

"Older. Her name is Josephine. And she is perfect" said Lizzie with a trace of envy.

Donna caught that. "So, now that you know I'm not perfect, at least I don't remind you of your sister who you seem to not care for too much."

"I do care. I love her. She just ..."

"Is too perfect" finished Donna for her. "Just like my brother. I always felt like I was in competition with him for my parents' affection."

"I know exactly how you feel. I once even kissed her boyfriend when I got drunk just to take something from her" confessed Lizzie then looked at Donna to read her reaction.

"Wow, we are both screwed up at a weird level" replied Donna.

Donna laughed. "I guess we are. Are you ready to finish this round. I'll get you some hot cocoa and a Nutella crepe when we get to the bottom of the slope."

"Deal," said Lizzie and rearranged her skis to point downward. She wanted to get there as fast as possible. Donna will help her stop if she can't. She was sure of it. Donna was her soul mate. She would never let anything happen to her.

***

"I am so sorry you didn't get to ski today either Julie. I know how much you love it" said Sasha concerned, putting her skiing boots away, "Are you feeling better now?"

"Perfect. I might even go for the afternoon session. Is everybody coming back to the cabin for lunch?" asked Julie.

"No idea. I forgot my cell in my room and I didn't run into anyone on the slopes."

Julie was rubbing her stomach, "I wish I didn't eat that fish before we got on the plane. Who the heck orders fish at an airport bistro? I deserve this."

"Yeah. Food poisoning is no fun. It's strange that you only started throwing up yesterday morning. When I get food poisoning, especially from seafood, I am dying within hours from the meal," said Sasha.

"Well, I decided to ski this afternoon. We are leaving tomorrow morning and I didn't even get to play in the snow yet. I won't let this happen" concluded Julie.

Mike came through the door at that moment shaking loads of snow off his hat and shoulders. "Man, it's beautiful out there. How are you feeling honey?"

Julie ran to him and gave him a kiss. "Much better. I'll join you after lunch."

"Really? That's fantastic. I was getting lonely at one point. And you told me you're a fantastic skier. I found some amazing slopes that are almost deserted. Can't wait to take you with me and show them to you. You'll love them!" Then he threw his jacket on the ground grabbed Julie in his arms, lifted her up and kissed her properly.

"Lunch is ready!" announced a middle-aged blonde woman who was working as the chef in Donna's family's cabin.

"Perfect timing! I'm famished!" said Mike rushing to take his skiing boots off.

Right at that moment Lizzie opened the entrance door laughing and screaming at the same time and then dodged the rapid snowballs that were fired from the outside. Two of them smacked Mike right at the base of his head.

"Bull's-eye," yelled Donna laughing. "Wrong target, but perfect shot!"

Mike turned around as the snow was slowly melting down and sliding underneath his sweater. "You're going to pay for this, so dearly, our lovely hostess. The lunch that your staff has prepared for us will only fill up my tank and I will take you down."

Lizzie was on the floor laughing hard, covered by crashed snowballs.

Donna walked in, "You're on!"

"My lovely girlfriend will join me. So, it's going to be Julie and myself against you and Lizzie, here who seems to be unable to peel herself off the floor at the moment!" said Mike looking at a Lizzie who was laughing uncontrollably and holding on to her stomach as she was rolling from side to side.

"You should see yourself," said Lizzie barely being able to stop laughing for a brief moment just to articulate those four words while pointing at his wet collar and back.

"You should see yourself when we're done with you" countered back Mike with conviction and a smile brought on by a vision of his future victory.

"I say Bring it on" challenged Donna.

"We shall! Make sure you're ready" replied Mike then turned back on his feet and started towards the kitchen.

"If Julie's joining us that means she's feeling better?" asked Lizzie rhetorically while Mike was still in her line of sight.

"Better than ever. And ready to fight!" said Mike loudly so he didn't have to turn back. He was too hungry. He wanted to get to the kitchen as soon as possible.

Chapter 27

There was too much noise in the hallways, so Donna quickly passed by the Sociology lab and headed towards the stairways.

"Too many bitches like you in this world," yelled a stringent voice. "You're a fucking witch, that's what you are! "

Donna was sure none of that was directed to her, but her curiosity got the best of her and turned her head towards that voice, so she could see who the poor victim of that poisonous attack was. Oh no, shit! She had to do something.

"Hey, you hysterical illiterate! Go fuck your redneck boyfriend and beg him to sell a hog to pay a poor freshman to do your school assignments because your white trash ass is not going to last long in this school with your shit for brains!" yelled Donna vigorously making her way through the crowd till she got to her target. She stood tall and menacing inches away from the girl with stringent voice. She was staring down at her with vicious laser sharp focus. The crowd went silent.

Donna was not the one to step back. The other girl did, turned around and pushed her way out of the crowd, "Out of my way, morons!" The crowd slowly dissipated.

"You didn't have to do that"

"You are welcome. And yes, I did have to do that. I don't know why you don't do it yourself! I know you have it in you. I've seen it. What happened Sasha, why didn't you fight back?" asked Donna perplexed.

"I didn't think it was worth my time or effort. If it weren't that one, it would be another one."

"Do you get harassed like this all the time now" questioned Donna. "Have you filed a complaint?"

"No. I thought it would go away once the trial started and people would see I was not the aggressor but the one who was aggressed. Now that the whole thing was postponed..."

"I get it. Well, it's your life. You choose how you want to handle it. But know I'm here for you. "

Sasha faintly smiled at Donna, "Thank you!"

"Well, winter break starts tomorrow, so I guess you won't have to make a decision about this right now," said Donna.

"True, thank God" muttered Sasha in relief.

"Are you going home? I'm actually heading there to pick up Lizzie. We're going to see that new elf movie." At Sasha's surprised face Donna added, "I know, I know, but Lizzie loves animations, so..."

"Thank you for caring so much for her. And to make her happy," commented Sasha.

"My complete pleasure," replied Donna and her face was lit up with what Sasha could only imagine would be some sort of happiness, joy maybe.

"Well, you two have fun. I'm going to work. There's still so much to do for my conference."

Donna's eyebrow raised in recognition, "Yes, Lizzie told me a lot about it. Eastern Europe and women rights?"

"Yes, put in a few words" answered Sasha happy to see the impact.

"I'd like to hear more about it" said Donna with real interest.

Sasha was pleased. "Anytime. Maybe at the Christmas dinner that we're having at our place. I know you're coming; Lizzie told me you will."

"I'll definitely be there" confirmed Donna. "I have to run now. I don't want to keep Lizzie waiting."

Sasha smiled understandingly, "See you at the Christmas party then. And thank you for today."

"See you then"

"And please," added Sasha, " can we keep what happened today between the two of us? I don't want to upset the girls any more than necessary. I've brought too many rough moments to this year already."

"Got it" said Donna winking at her. "My lips are sealed."

***

Julie was in the mall running like crazy trying to get the best Christmas gifts for all her friends. And for Mike. And for Donna. It was exhausting. And she wasn't feeling too good either. Couple more things and she was done for the day. If she wanted to add more gifts, she was going to do it online.

Plus, she had a meeting with Nick in twenty minutes to finalize the ideas on the yoga part of her business plan for the rehab. Only that thought made her giggle. She was finally going to do this. Her dream will become reality.

Smiling at her future plans, she checked the directory for Bloomingdales. They had an amazing selection of scarves and Donna seemed very fond of scarves. She had a different one each time she saw her since the day she met her. It had to be the perfect gift for her.

The food court was right on her way and she was hungry. Maybe a quick stop to grab a bite to eat would do the trick. Not too much because she was going to have to eat with Nick as well, just something to tide her over.

Sushi, a spicy tuna hand-roll sounded just like the thing she was looking for. So, she got in line next to the sushi bar and while waiting she checked her phone to see what everyone was up to. You have to love Facebook. It keeps you up to date with people's lives even when you don't feel like or think you have the time to keep in touch. It was such a brilliant idea.

"I feel like a stalker" had said Lizzie once when they were talking about the genius of social media.

Julie laughed thinking back at Lizzie's opinion. She was right. We all are stalker at some level. Her smile turned into a grimace and her grimace into horror. Julie hunched over; her free hand automatically pushed against her mouth. The herbs and spices mingled with the sweet flavor of frying fish was one of those beloved smells that out of a sudden went rogue on her.

She frantically looked for the restroom sign, but could not see one in the near vicinity. Finally, her eyes laid on what looked like a restroom sign fifty feet away to her right. She dashed for it. All Julie could think about was the sour taste in her mouth. Her stomach was revolting and contracting violently putting a ton of pressure on its contents and it seemed that the only escape for all that was up and out through her mouth and nose.

It was too late; she was not going to make it to the bathroom. So, she eyed the next best thing and landed with her face on top of a large trashcan. Her hands were grabbing hold of its edges in a desperate attempt to not fall into it as her stomach was hurdling everything she had to eat and drink for the last several hours.

When the convulsions finally stopped, she tentatively took a breath. Nothing happened. Her lungs expended glad to have some oxygen. She was okay. Julie finally saw the two women who were hovering around her, one holding her hair away from her face, the other gathering her bags that were spread all over the place.

"Are you feeling better," asked the woman who was holding on to her. "Here's a tissue," she added handing one to Julie.

"Thank you," mumbled Julie embarrassed.

"Do you think you can make it to the restrooms? We'll help you out" asked the second woman. To Julie's confused face she added, "You need to clean up a little."

Now Julie was really embarrassed. Did she look as dismantled as she felt? A complete mess? All she could do was whisper "yes" and then force herself back on her feet and walk toward the restroom that she had previously dashed for but never made it.

She washed her face and rinsed her mouth. When she felt back in control again, she told those two nice and helpful ladies that she was good and after she promised them, she was going to head straight home, they left her alone to her own thoughts.

A single and simple question that one of the women asked her was still ringing in her head. Of course, she dismissed it immediately, but now it came back to haunt her. She needed to find out.

Julie grabbed all her bags and rushed out of the mall. She wanted to get into the first cab as soon as possible. One yellow car stopped right in front of her and a man with a rolled yoga mat came out of it.

"Damn!" She forgot about Nick.

She was going to call him and excuse herself. She was in no shape to meet with him, or anybody else for that matter. She knew exactly what she was going to do and she had to do it right away before Mike got home.

***

"Those pictures go deep into your soul grab a hold of what's good inside of you and bring it to the surface!"

Nikki turned around to look at whomever uttered those words. They had to be intended for her photos that she was looking at on her laptop while waiting to board on her flight back home to New York.

Right behind her lazily leaning against a glass wall was a tall, handsome man with a charismatic smile. His eyes were deep blue and couple of dark bronze locks were playfully disobedient which gave him a slightly unruly air.

Nikki smiled swiftly and turned back to her laptop. He was way too cute to talk to. Was he really talking to her? His words were not simple. He could have said "Nice pictures," or "Did you take those photos" or something as dull as that but he didn't. Her pictures seemed to have had the same effect on him as they have on her. Is that possible? Is that real? And he's so gorgeous. It feels unreal.

"What the hell is wrong with me?" asked Nikki furiously under her breath. "I've been spending way too much time with my girls and I'm catching their male insecurities."

With that, Nikki turned back towards the handsome stranger and introduced herself. "I'm Nikki!"

"Sam!" he said leaning towards her to shake her outreached right hand.

"It takes a pretty self-confident man to recognize deep feeling and say it out loud!" replied Nikki immediately without any other introduction.

"That I am" simply replied Sam and pointed to the seat next to her, "May I?"

"Only because you're so breathtakingly beautiful and you seem to get my art" consented Nikki.

Sam chuckled, "And I love it that you speak your mind so openly!"

"I'm nothing but sincere. Too sincere sometimes! I end up hurting people's egos" confessed Nikki. "I only regret it when I hurt my friends, my family. But I can't stop myself from saying what I truly believe. It's like a curse."

"If egos' what you hurt, keep on doing it. They have no real value in this world. They just bring all of us down!" declared Sam theatrically gesticulating to further prove his point.

Both of them laughed. "I one hundred percent agree with you" said Nikki mesmerized by this impossibly handsome man, who got her so totally and completely. It felt like they were sharing a brain and a heart.

"Do you mind showing me some more of your work?" asked Sam with the cutest enthusiastic smile Nikki had ever seen. He looked like a little boy in a candy store right then. And it was all inspired by her own work for her Love Flood Collection. It worked exactly as she saw the collection working and it wasn't even close to being done.

Nikki was more than happy to share her treasure with this kindred soul. "Are you on the flight to New York as well?"

"Yes, I am."

"Perfect," answered Nikki. "Then we have quite some time to take you through my vision of this entire collection."

"It's a collection? I see. This is serious, not just a hobby. That's the most inspiring thing I've heard yet."

Nikki was blushing. "Keep it up and my head might get so big they won't be able to fit it in the airplane."

"As long as it's not your ego," joked Sam and they both laughed.

Chapter 28

Mike came into the house not knowing what he was in for. He dropped his bag on the floor next to the door and called Julie's name before he took off his coat and boots. It was snowing outside and he brought a bunch of that fluffy snow with him to prove it.

"Honey, I have a surprise for you!" he yelled trying to figure out where she was before the snowball in his hands melted.

Julie's head poked from behind the recliner. "I bet it won't beat my surprise for you!" she said lifting herself off the recliner to face him.

Before Mike launched the snowball at her his eyes fell on the small white plastic stick that she was holding in her hand. He knew exactly what that was and he knew exactly what the surprise was. His hand dropped next to him and the snowball fell out of his hand.

Julie didn't know what to do next. Was he angry? He was so quiet. He was never quiet and so still. Did she just give him a heart attack. Is he panicking?

"I mean, what the hell was I expecting?" Julie said in a whisper. Two seconds later tears were pouring down her face and she was shacking uncontrollably.

That was when Mike seemed to break out of his statuesque pose and react. In two long strides he was next to her reaching around her and pulling her into his arms. "Baby, we are going to have a baby?" he asked even though the answer was clear.

"I took three tests already and they are all positive" complained Julie. "I never expected...We never ... did we?"

"I always tried to be careful. You're too young, not even done with college" said Mike chastising himself.

"I'm done with college in 5 months!" replied Julie, then her face caught up with her thought "I'll be showing!"

Mike took her worried face into his palms and lifted her head towards him. "Honey, we are going to have a baby! You and me ...a baby...our baby!" Then he started smiling happily and hugged Julie tight.

Nothing seemed real for Julie for a little while, not the plastic stick in her hand, not the positive result and definitely not Mike embracing this idea more than she did. Was this really real? Was she ready for this? Was she going to be a good mo...

"You are going to be a great mother!" said Mike guessing her thoughts. "Believe me, I know! I know these things. I see a lot of mothers of all kinds out there on a daily basis and I can judge how good or bad they are in an instant."

"Maybe, but you're a little bit biased when it comes to me. I'm none of those strangers to you. And you don't know my entire past" Julie mumbled the last part.

Mike kissed her on the lips, then on her nose, just the way she liked, then on the cheeks and forehead. "Baby, I don't need to know your past. I'm in love with the Julie you are now, not the one from last year or two or ten years ago."

"Now you sound like Nikki," Julie complained faintly. "I love present Julie, not future or past Julie" said Julie mimicking Nikki's eloquent gestures whenever she was talking 'wisely'.

Mike laughed. "Honey, I love you more than anything. And I already love our baby."

"Well, glad you do, because I ..." Julie couldn't finish her sentence. She couldn't finish her thought for that matter. She couldn't even think abortion. But why? She did not want to end up like her parents. They started too young and they screwed up big time. She needed time to cement this recovery thing first, didn't she? From what everyone says at the meetings, no one ever heals or cures, they are all in recovery for the rest of their lives. Was that the case? If she had to live one day at a time, was she going to make a kid do that too? Isn't that too much to ask from anyone? Especially a baby, your own baby?

"I see that your head is spinning around some nasty ideas," said Mike picking her up and slowly laying her on the sofa. "I'm going to make us a nice fire. I know how much you love watching its flames dance in the fireplace. It will relax you and take your mind off anything that makes your forehead crimple up like that." Mike kissed her on top of her head and grabbed the key for the storage unit to go get some firewood.

"I'll be back in a minute. How about you think of baby names until I come back" continued Mike and returned to where she was lying, put a soft kiss on her soft slightly pursed lips and added "and a nice massage is waiting for you. My treat!" he winked. "I love you! You make me so happy Julie!" then he left to get that wood.

Julie was left with her thoughts and worries. Baby names? She couldn't get passed the fact that there was a baby to talk about in the first place. Did he say massage? Ahh, that would definitely be so relaxing and fun. Yes, but massages usually lead to, and she couldn't. It's probably not good for the baby to have sex now, or was it? Who was she going to ask? None of her friends have babies yet and her family is ... forget about that stupid idea!

"I see that you're still roaming around in that pretty little head of yours," came the unexpected voice behind her. She looked up. It was Mike. Who else would it be?

"About that massage," started Julie.

Mike smiled, "Yes! What about it my greedy little monkey!" a lascivious grin laid all over his face.

"That's exactly what I wanted to talk about," she said looking straight down in her lap at her fidgeting hands.

"Let me guess," said Mike finally putting two and two together, "You are worried about the baby and ...intimacy"

Julie's face confirmed his suspicions. She still couldn't look up.

"Baby, there's no danger or harm to the baby! Ha!" he laughed. "Baby, baby! I just caught myself. Maybe I have to stick to calling you anything else but baby... now ...that we're having our own baby."

His laughter and joy were contagious. Julie finally smiled and reached for a hug.

"That's my girl" Mike comforted her.

Then the phone rang ... again.

Julie sighed. Why does that damn phone have to ring all the time at inopportune moments? When the baby comes, he'll have to get rid of it, at least while around the baby.

It seemed like he could read her thought. He picked up the phone and turned it off completely.

Julie was happy. She had his undivided attention.

***

"Santa Claus is home!" yelled Nikki as she walked through the door.

Sasha poked her head out of her room. "Santa Claus is a girl?!"

Nikki laughed. "You might be right! Only a woman could be as generous as Santa Clause!" She put all her bags on the ground next to the kitchen and took off her boots.

"So, how was it?" asked Sasha coming out with a big purple towel wrapped around her head tying her fluffy robe around her waist.

"Just got out of the shower?" asked Nikki.

"Yup! I was really cold when I got home and was sure a hot shower would do the trick faster than anything else" explained Sasha.

"And it did, didn't it?" asked Nikki pointing at her robe and slippers.

"Just what the doctor ordered" smiled Sasha.

Nikki smiled back and dropped herself in the nearest chair. Her thoughts were far far away but were definitely keeping that smile on her face. Sasha was curious, "Tell me about your trip! It looks like it was successful"

"What makes you say that?" asked Nikki coming back to Sasha and the present moment.

Sasha pointed towards Nikki's face, "That silly and satisfied smile that you've had on your face since you got in."

"It started like an amazing adventure and it ended like a fairytale," said Nikki contemplating something beyond the wall she was looking at.

After couple of minutes Sasha decided to break the silence. "Are you going to tell me about it or I'm I supposed to just see right through you and into your head because apparently you're far away from me into your fairytale land."

"The Love Flood collection is going to be extraordinary. I've got so many shots from two different continents already, at different moments with different protagonists by telling the same love story. Love is definitely all around; you just have to be open to see it. And I opened myself to it just by stepping into this project and it didn't take long until love came knocking at my door." Nikki stopped there and smiled again.

"Are you trying to tell me that you're in love?" asked Sasha a little bit confused. "Is it possible? My Nikki really in love with just one guy?"

Nikki's smile confirmed Sasha's suspicions.

"God! Who is this mythical creature?" asked Sasha jokingly but mesmerized at the same time. "Where did you meet him? When? Is he from here... I mean, is he from New York or at least from the United States? He is human, right? One of those humans that I can see..."

"Yes, he's human," laughed Nikki. "I think I already kissed a lot of frogs; don't you agree?"

"So, he's your Prince Charming!" alluded Sasha. "I want to know everything there is to know about him. Or at least everything you know, how about that?"

Nikki was still not present and unresponsive.

"Come on Nikki, please, please pretty please! I need this more than I need fresh air right now! Please?!" begged Sasha.

Nikki's eyes fell on Sasha, "Okay. Let me start with the end. He's coming to our Christmas dinner tomorrow. Happy?"

"Very much so!" said a giddy Sasha. "It's like Santa Claus himself is coming to our Christmas dinner! I can't wait! This is so exciting!"

"Now, to start with the beginning, he approached me in the airport on my way over here. He completely understands my art, and we seem to be on the same wavelength. It's like he's cut from my own flesh and blood. But he's so much hotter than me, than any guy that I've ever dated or met. And he seems to be into me too. What can I say!?" sighed Nikki, "the flight over the Atlantic Ocean went by in a blur, in a wonderful second!"

Sasha smiled wide from ear to ear. "I cannot wait to meet this guy!" Then a bothersome thought crossed her mind, "How about Josh?" she said out loud with a tortured face.

Nikki laughed. "Oh my God, that's not an afterthought. I mean, Josh is a very charismatic and sexual guy, but there's no substance to what we... had. It was only sexual." Nikki was sighing "The best sex of my life, actually" then she shook her head "Up until now though. I'm sure of it.

Sam is going to trump Josh and any other guy that's ever crossed my path."

"Well, yes, because you actually think that you are having some intense feelings for this guy. Other than sexual, right?" analyzed Sasha, her face an intense red.

Nikki jumped up, went to Sasha and hugged her really tight." I feel your energy! You're loving this as much as I am! Thank you! You are a true friend!"

"Thank you. You are brightening my Christmas and my life," replied Sasha while hugging Nikki back.

That had lasted for a good five minutes. The door opened and Lizzie was home. Her face lit up when she saw Nikki "I am so happy to see you! Just in time for Christmas, as usual!"

"You know I would never miss Christmas dinner with you guys. And this time I came a day ahead so I can help you out with the cooking."

Sasha got out of her chair and joined the conversation "It had to be this year, right Lizzie?"

"What do you mean?" asked Nikki turning towards Sasha, confusion written all over her face.

"What I mean is that this year we don't have to cook because Donna is bringing the entire dinner. All homemade. She has an entire staff that does that for her family so this year she decided she's going to ask them to cook more so we don't have to. Isn't that spectacular?" asked Sasha happily.

"It's just perfect. Let's do lots of baking then," said Nikki.

"Good idea," thought Lizzie out loud. "Our home will smell like cookies, ginger and cinnamon! It's Christmas all right!"

"There is another Christmas miracle that Nikki has to tell you all about. And his name is Sam" said Sasha winking at Nikki.

"Oh, this must be good. Please let me put all my stuff down, and I'm coming right back to hear all about it. Judging by Sasha's face and your lightness and enthusiasm this is going to be good. Give me a second please!" pledged Lizzie running to her room.

Chapter 29

The Christmas carols were filling up the air dancing with the cookies, cinnamon and ginger enticing aromas. There was a plethora of candles all around the living room and dining room area that were helping out the two big candles in the middle of the table and the Christmas lights on the tree lit up the room.

As she promised, Donna brought a lot of delicious food that was now just waiting to be served. Apple cider was being warmed up on the stove and everybody was getting ready for dinner.

"Sorry for making you wait," Julie excused herself. "Mike and I had to pick up one more thing on the way over."

"Really?" asked Lizzie jokingly. "If I knew I had to wait an extra two hours for you while I was drooling all over this amazing food," I would have gotten that one thing for you."

Julie's face went into baby mode, her lips pouting, had bent slightly forward and to the side and her beautiful eyes looking up over her jet-black eyelashes. "It was not a gift for any of you that we were getting. It's a last-minute surprise!"

"I hope it's a good surprise but then again there can't be any other but good surprises on Christmas!" interjected Donna.

Mike couldn't stop but chuckle when he saw Julie's pleading eyes towards him," Can I? Please?"

All Mike could do was close his eyes and slightly signal yes with his head. At this point they had everybody's attention.

Sasha couldn't wait any longer, "Drum roll please!"

"We're going to have a baby!" announced Julie and then took a deep breath as if what she just said took all her breath. She couldn't afford breathing anymore waiting for everybody's reaction.

"Holy shit!" Nikki was the first one to react. "Are you planning on? Or you are pregnant already?"

"It's a done deal" announced Mike coming closer to Julie and grabbing her hand to show support.

"But when? I mean how far along are you?" asked Lizzie puzzled. "I thought you were always careful."

Julie couldn't say anything. She felt attacked. She didn't want to defend this. She was pregnant. And she was happy. And Mike was happy. Why couldn't they just be happy for her?

Mike stepped in, "According to our calculations it was that trip we took to Mexico! We've always been careful, very careful. I guess we were just swept away couple of times... or more on that fun vacation!"

Sam was the first one to break the silence and he addressed Julie without even being introduced to her yet, "Are you happy?"

Julie's eyes finally lifted from the ground where she was drilling a deep hole already with her laser focus on looking anywhere else but to the people she loved. "Yes, yes I am! Very much so!" Then she let her head lean on to Mike's chest and smiled, "We are so happy!"

Mike kissed the top of her head and wrapped both his arms around her waist then looked at everybody else and smiled. Joy filled his gaze. "We are deliriously happy!"

"Then we are happy for you!" Came Nikki's response as she walked towards Julie and Mike to give both of them a hug.

Everybody followed her suit and within couple of minutes everybody forgot the embarrassing moment after the announcement. They were all laughing, talking about baby names.

Lizzie who always wanted her own child and family was fighting the ugly feelings of envy and jealousy that were creeping up and prohibiting her from enjoying this moment and being truly happy for her friend. Sasha pulled her to the side and gave her a hug. "Soon you will have your own family as well!"

"I love Donna! I've never loved anyone as much as I love her. I knew I was falling for her but didn't want to say it out loud because more than anything in this world I do want to have children!" confessed Lizzie in a low whisper.

"So then you never told Donna what your feelings are for her?" asked Sasha.

"No. How could I when the next thing out of my mouth would have been that I have to let her go so I can have the one thing I want more than love: children!" replied Lizzie with quiet desperation.

"First of all, you're not giving up on love. Children will give you that. More than you have ever dreamed of. But most importantly, right now you need Donna, you need to figure out who you are! Donna seems to be a huge clue in your life's puzzle. You have to let this unfold naturally. See what happens! Worst comes to worst and you two will go to a sperm bank. You will still have your children too! I promise!"

One single tear rolled down Lizzie's cheek. "You are right! I hate myself for even having those thoughts!" Then she shook her head "You are definitely right. I can have it all no matter what. Thank you for pulling me out of my stupid narrow-minded mystery."

"Anytime my dear" said Sasha and gave her a tight hug. "Let's go look before anybody realizes that we're gone."

Right that second, Sam pulled out couple of bottles out of his bag and announced. "Let's celebrate this moment with some virgin champagne! Oh, and by the way, my name is Sam!"

"We all know who you are, Sam!" said Lizzie back, "we are the tightest family you'll ever meet!"

"And they are not joking!" laughed Mike looking at Sam. "They will all know what you have done the second you're done doing it. It's like they share a brain."

"And the heart!" added Julie.

Donna pushed herself in the middle of the crowd and announced out loud "It's time for dinner! This delicious food is waiting to be devoured. Let's not disappoint it."

"Or all the starving children in China, right?!" said Mike. "Was I the only child their parents use this line on?"

"Who said here that special?" questioned Julie with a laugh and gave them a quick kiss and pulled him towards the dining table.

Sam poured the sparkling cider in everybody's glasses then raised his glass and wished "Merry Christmas everyone! Thank you for letting me be part of your special group on such an important occasion! Now someone who knows everybody needs to make a toast before we start gorging ourselves with all this holiday food and cheer."

Julie stood up, picked up her glass, looked at each and every one around the table, smiled and began "Thank you everybody for being part of our lives in the last four years or so. This is our fourth Christmas together," she said looking at Sasha, Nikki and Lizzie. "And I hope it won't be our last one now that we're all going to be done with school. Sasha has a future in Geneva now, once her project is finalized. And we all know it's going to be a success! Nikki always on a quest for higher power, muse, love and art! And Lizzie, with her second book in the printing right now and slowly but surely figuring out her new life, identity and power to give and receive love. Then there's me!" Everyone laughed while the girls were wiping their tears. "I will do anything in my power to complicate my life more than anyone in this room in a second if that's possible. But while doing that and planning my new business, my rehab, a dream that you girls helped me build, considering a PhD and finding love -more accurately stumbling into love- now it was decided for me that I'm bringing a new baby into this world!" Julie touched her belly. She was getting emotional. "I love you all and you all need to promise me that we'll get around the Christmas tree together next year! You are my family, my life and my sanity. Merry Christmas!"

"Merry Christmas" replied everybody in unison.

***

"So, Sam," said Lizzie approaching him. "I understand that you are a travel writer."

"And a photographer," corrected her Sam.

"It must be a charmed life" continued Lizzie. "Going all over the world, experiencing all those cultures, and all you had to do to repay life for this beautiful dream was to share what you were experiencing with the rest of us through your articles."

"And photographs," corrected her again Sam.

"Right!" replied Lizzie sternly, then added with seriousness "it sounds like you're a nomad. And Nikki is known to be attracted by nomads with a charmed life like yours. But if you ever hurt her, I will never stop until I hurt you too. "

Sam laughed. "Are you serious? Is this a Godfather scene that you put all the boyfriends through?"

"Pretty much. But only because we mean it" came the answer from behind both of them. Sasha was slowly making her way towards them.

"You seem way too cozy way too fast and even if we do believe in true love, we want to make sure that this is the real deal."

"Okay. You girls are amazing and you proved that to me tonight. I would never do anything to hurt Nikki or any of you. Ever! If I ever learned anything from my travels was to appreciate the real value of a human and the life experiences that we go through. I would never interfere with the natural course of anyone's life unless my intentions were deeply rooted in my soul." He looked at Lizzie and Sasha and simply stated the fact "I am in love with Nikki. Foolishly, completely and irrevocably. It has never happened to me but I welcome it full heartedly."

"I'm blown away!" replied Lizzie. "Start the truth I felt a connection like he used to describe yours with Donna but I fought it. I envy you for your courage and clarity. But know that we're watching and were not head over heels in love with you like Nikki seems to be."

"I never expect less from you guys. I would never hurt Nikki because I feel very protective of her."

Sasha put a hand on his shoulder. "It sounds like you will fit right into our neat family."

"I'd be honored!" replied Sam with a bow.

Lizzie was smiling, "You got the right attitude. I like you! Now it's time to join the group. And don't forget to use that duct taped old camera that you've been caring around all night long."

"It's a classic Nikon. Nikki understands. It's a thing of beauty. Just imagine what this camera has seen" replied Sam picking up his camera into his hands in an idolizing way.

"Sure. Whatever. As long as it takes pictures and you don't have to burn a light bulb every time you take one picture!" said Lizzie walking away towards Donna.

Sasha put an arm around Sam's shoulders and declared, "I think you and me will be best buds!"

"I have the same feeling!" replied Sam with a smile.

Nikki was staring at both of them from across the room. Tonight, was the night of miracles, love, and supportive togetherness. It was a real Christmas after all!

Chapter 30

"Christmas was beautiful at your place. Thank you for making me the honor of meeting your family" thanked gratefully Sam. "Before we go on this fun expedition to see where love shows up again and pile up more and more beautiful pieces to your collection, I'd like to ask you to come with me to one of my closest friends' New Year's Eve parties."

Nikki smiled and put the camera over on her head and over her shoulder in slow-motion trying to remember if she promised to any of the girls that she would spend the special night with them. Nothing came to mind, and they would understand anyways. "It would be my pleasure!"

Sam lifted his right fist above his head and pulled it slightly down in sign of victory. "I was afraid that this was too much to ask on such short notice! This makes me really happy! Wait and see, you'll be blown away! And definitely don't forget your camera!"

He seemed to be so excited for both of them that Nikki touched his arm in an attempt to rub some of that positive energy onto herself. Sam stopped, looked at her with his exotically shaped blue eyes and without any hesitation he dropped his lips onto hers, very softly. They barely touched; his sweet breath was caressing the sensitive skin of her lips. The corner of her mouth began to shake in expectation.

His eyes were looking for contact from her own eyes. She couldn't look at him. She felt too embarrassed by her body's quick response to his touch. But she didn't have the power or the will to pull herself back either. He was not the guy that she wanted to take charge with from the start, like all the others in the past. She needed him to do it. Nikki finally let go of control.

She looked up at him, owning her desire. A guttural moan came from deep inside of him. He kissed her, but this time he put in all the passion that was burning from within. Nikki felt the instant connection. and it was more than carnal. She had found him, finally.

The loud sound of the extra lens hitting the ground broke the magic for a slight second. Enough for both of them to snap out of their shared euphoric moment.

"That was incredible!" exhaled Sam. He touched Nikki's face to make sure she was real and present just like him.

"Now that's something everyone should experience at least once in their lifetime or they lived in vain!" exclaimed Nikki ecstatic.

They both smiled.

Finally, Sam kneeled down to look at the dropped lens. "It's intact."

"That's more than I can say about myself right now," commented Nikki.

Sam came back up, "I'm so happy we waited to know each other like this. Normally I'm in and out of a relationship before the plane even takes off."

Nikki started laughing and nodding, "I know exactly what you mean!" After two more seconds of silence, she asked "So, should we stay and get acquainted with my boudoir or go and find love!"

"Who still says boudoir except you? I love it!" reacted Sam with a chuckle. "But seriously, after what we've just experienced, I'm leaning toward going deeper into this thing that we're building right here, whatever it is. What do you say?

"Finding love it is then! What woman in her right mind would decline that offer!"replied Nikki wrapping her long baby blue scarf around her neck.

***

Sasha was doodling on the notepad in front of her while talking to Lizzie and Donna on the phone. "Seriously, I need to work from now until March nonstop if I want this conference to be all it can be. And it will be! This is my life! The only good thing I have in life besides my girls!"

"We just don't want you to feel left out in any way. There's plenty of rooms at my parents' estate, so if you change your mind, you'll know where to find us," confirmed Donna.

"Thank you, guys! But this is it! This is the moment of glory for me, when I make it, I can say "fuck y'all" to all the shit in my life! This is it!" affirmed Sasha with conviction. "There will be plenty of other New Year Eve's for us to spend together. And please one of you, or both, explain this all to Julie, so I don't have to go through the third degree again for choosing to work on New Year's Eve!"

"I will make sure Julie and Nikki are updated by the time you get home tonight," assured her Lizzie. "I'll keep some of the lasagna I've brought over in that glass container in the fridge. Don't forget to eat it! You need nutrition for all that brilliance!"

"Ha! You're amazing! Thank you! I'm actually a bit hungry right now, so I'll go grab a bagel or something to hold me over for another couple of hours!"

"Take care of yourself! That's your number one priority, always. So, you can do the rest and show the world what a hot shot you are, like we already know!" said Donna.

"I am a hot shot!" yelled Sasha louder than she initially anticipated. She looked around, but the office seemed deserted.

"You're sexy and you know it!" confirmed Lizzie singing a popular hit that was all over the radio recently.

They all laughed.

"Okay, then. I have to go, be sexy with my bagel and all," said Sasha.

"We don't want to know the details," joked Lizzie. "I'll see you next year then!"

"Yes, next year!" echoed Sasha. "Have a Happy New Year! Both of you!"

"Much love, Sasha!" said Donna. "Bye!"

Chapter 31

The smell of spring was already in the air. How was that possible? Just a week ago there was snow covering everything and everyone. But the sun was shining bright, you could hear some birds singing, and people had left their heavy coats at home. Most had a light jacket or just a sweater on. It was amazing how nature would switch on you in such a dramatic way in such a short period of time with no notice at all. It was amazing, shocking and really scary! But fun and joyful if you knew how to enjoy what was given to you.

Most of the stores were already wrapped in red, white, and pink. Hearts and cupids were all over the place.

"Wow, can you believe it's almost Valentine's Day already?" said Lizzie to Donna grabbing her other hand and smiling at her. "Any special plans for a special someone?" hinted Lizzie barely hiding a smile on her face.

"Hmm, I don't know any special someone." Then Donna waited for Lizzie's response. "But I do have the perfect someone next to me!"

Lizzie was falling. Was falling hard. She wasn't familiar with this feeling, but it exhilarated her. Was this what love was supposed to be? What did she have before, because she never had this? It felt fulfilling. It felt safe. It felt kind and generous. And so euphoric!

"When was the last time you spoke to Sasha?" asked Donna interested.

Lizzie had to think for a second, "I .... don't even know. I mean, I talk to her over the phone now and then, and we text each other, but I barely get to sit down with her anymore. I guess she pretty much moved into her office!"

"I know she's going to kill it! She must be amazing at what she does. And she's so dedicated!" said Donna with appreciation.

Lizzie was shaking her head into a whole heartedly yes. "The United Nations will not know what just hit them. She's going to rock this out of this world!"

"Well, now that Ryan is pretty much out of the way...she needs to only concentrate on that project. That's her baby! That is the one thing that I can tell, since I've known her, that brings her joy, purpose, and love! Except you guys, of course!" said Donna putting one of her arms around Lizzie's shoulder.

Lizzie rested her head on Donna's shoulder and sighed. Yeah, you got it exactly right. Love how insightful you are! I love a lot of things about you!"

Donna didn't want to say a thing. She did not want to break the spell. She did not want Lizzie to take back what she had just said. She actually wanted to hear more. She was head over heels for Lizzie and she could see that Lizzie was cracking her own shell slowly and letting Donna in. She was going to have all the patience necessary. Lizzie was worth it!

"Ha! Three more weeks and my book will be published! It's such a miracle! I guess it just came at the right time. It was definitely timing! Some other book that was scheduled to be published was cancelled. Lucky me!"

Donna leaned her head against Lizzie's head and whispered, "And lucky me!"

"Let's go home," said Lizzie. "I need to meet with Nikki and I know she's going to be in for a couple of hours before she goes to that photo shoot with Sam."

Donna seemed to be curious, "So, what do you think about them? Is this as magical as everyone else thinks it to be?"

"If you would have known Nikki for as long as we have known her, you would have known this is a magical miracle! And he seems to be the manifestation of her deepest desires. He seems to be perfect and that frightens her as much as it exhilarates her."

"It seems to be a magical year for all of you guys," replied Donna taking in consideration the events of the previous year.

"Yes. It seems that way, doesn't it?" said Lizzie contemplating everything that had happened in the last few months. "Ok, let's get a cab. I want to get home before Nikki leaves."

***

"I have a surprise for you," announced Sam to a surprised Nikki.

"I love surprises! What is it? Maybe a romantic weekend just the two of us somewhere far far away... Valentine's Day is tomorrow, isn't it?"

"That it is. And I have a surprise for you related to that, but the surprise I'm talking about right now has nothing to do with Valentine's Day," replied Sam.

"Oh, now you really made me curious. It has to be good! What is it? Can I get a hint, a little clue?" begged Nikki. She was getting closer and closer to Sam trying to ride that high that she always had around him. And the closer she would get to him physically the more joyfully, light-hearted and expansive she felt. Her own skin was smothering her.

"Oh, no, no, no! No sexy time for you!" joked Sam mimicking Borat's accent, a well-known satirical character that became popular in the last years.

"I was not going for that! Just a little touch, that's it! I promise," said Nikki batting her eyelashes.

Sam couldn't stop but laugh. He reached out, grabbed her and pulled her close to him and gave her one of the bear hugs that she was so addicted to.

"Instead of the photo shoot, I thought it was time for you to move to a new medium," announced Sam.

Nikki's eyes got bigger and she was staring at him waiting breathlessly for what he was going to say next. Was she ready to move on to the next medium? Was she supposed to finish with one and move to another? Or move in-between them? She trusted Sam's judgment. She knew that. So, the tense feeling gave way to a serene smile. Now was time to get excited again.

"Sculpture baby! One of my friends has a studio not far from here. You never told me if you ever tried sculpture, but I think it's time for you to try it. And I will be there every step of the way. Making fun of you. And letting you make fun of me. Let's have fun with this!"

Nikki jumped and wrapped her hands around his neck. "You make me so happy. It's frightening sometime!"

"I feel exactly the same way. And all I can tell myself is 'stay in the moment, enjoy this paradise!'"

"So, I'm your paradise!" said a smug Nikki jokingly.

"Yes, you are! Now don't let it get to your head, gorgeous lady and future brilliant sculpture genius!" said Sam before he kissed her with hot passion that felt to be never-ending.

***

Sasha was in shock. She couldn't believe her eyes. She didn't know how to react. Should she call? Should she go visit her? Should she just lay low and say nothing and hope she'll never see it or hear about it? One thing was for sure: she had to go tell the others before she decided on her next move. She grabbed her coat, slipped back into her shoes and left all her work spread all over her desk without a second thought and ran to the elevators. She had to get home fast!

There was nobody on the streets. The day had not started yet. It helped to get home faster.

Running up the stairs with the newspaper in one hand and pulling on the rail with the other in hopes that it would propel her and quicken her step, Sasha got to the door, looked for the key and barged in with as much noise as she could.

She went to the hallway and started yelling "Nikki, Lizzie, you have to see this! Please wake up! Come on, please! Please, please, please!"

"Nikki!" she said knocking on her bedroom door loudly, and then she moved couple of steps to Lizzie's door, "Lizzie! Lizzie, wake up! It's urgent!"

She heard noises in both rooms and then both girls came out struggling to shake off the sleep that was fogging their mind.

"What is going on" asked Nikki worried when she looked at Sasha's face.

Sasha said nothing. She grabbed both their hands, pulled them to the kitchen, signaled for them to sit down next to each other and plopped the newspaper in front of them on the kitchen table.

"Happy Valentine's Day to Julie, my husband's addict pregnant mistress!" was written in huge title font on the cover of the social section.

Lizzie stopped breathing, "Is this somehow related to our Julie? What kind of sick joke is this?"

Sasha preferred not to answer. "Read!" she commanded.

"She's a lost soul. A desperate lonely and broken kid who latched herself onto my husband with her sad story. She was lurking in the night hunting a generous spirit to save her from her nightmare life. And she found my poor good-hearted husband who confused his job as a cop with his mission in this world for a second. It was enough for this coke addict to dig her claws into my family's heart and future, rip it out and shred it to pieces. Or at least try to.

I am 14 weeks pregnant, just like she is, but our baby will have a father and a future. She's condemning hers to the horror of her own childhood.

Her mother and father gave her and her sisters and brothers coke when she was only seven years old. The white powdered parties that went on in their house were famous at the time. Her grandfather, a generous billionaire with deeper pockets than God himself, kept them all out of judicial problems, but could barely contain the rapid disaster that was engulfing this family.

Julie's teenage years were spent in a colorful diversity of rehabs where family days were spent with paid staff. Her grandfather's private jet would only land in the same zip code when he had business in town. Money to cover her and her family's rehab lives were sent through one of his accountants.

The poor white rich girl, has to tough it out now in an all-paid Manhattan penthouse with three of her closest rehab screw ups who do not seem to get out of the court house for more than couple of months at a time. And grandpa just foots the bill for that coo coo's nest!"

Nikki grabbed the newspaper and bunched it all up before she stormed to the trash bin, lifted the cap and threw it out. "That's enough! I don't want to see the rest! Too much poison out of that evil viper!"

Lizzie was shaking, "It's all my fault! Only my fault! I could have prevented this entire thing if only I would have said something!"

"This is not your fault in any way," yelled Nikki at Lizzie which startled her. "How the hell can any of this be our fault?"

Sasha knew what Lizzie was referring to, "Lizzie," she said waiting for her to make eye contact, "This is not your fault in any way! You couldn't have known! None of us could have! You were just protecting Julie!"

"And look at the great job I did in protecting her!" lashed out Lizzie.

"Well, then blame it on me, I told you not to say anything, "replied Sasha.

"What the hell is going on here?" asked Nikki. "See how this viper already made us blame each other for her own venomous acts? We can't let her win like that! We did nothing! Let her stew in her own garbage!"

Lizzie took a deep breath, looked up at Nikki and revealed their little secret, "John, Mike's best friend, whom I dated for a while proved to be a scam bag."

"I remember! So, I gather that you said nothing to Julie" concluded Nikki.

"No. Not a thing" confessed Lizzie.

"It was really bad timing!" came in to help Sasha.

Nikki was lost in thought for a moment. "It's like I always say - You always can tell a man's character by the people he hangs out with most"

"And John is his best friend!" added Lizzie. "I feel so guilty! It was definitely my fault for not telling her anything for such a long time, but you came that night and then their trip and ...." Lizzie did not want to bring this up but was part of the timeline "... and then Ryan happened." She immediately looked at Sasha to see her reaction.

"Then Donna and the holidays, the baby news ..." continued Lizzie.

Nikki stopped her, "It's not your fault at all. It's his fault only. He fooled us all!"

"That miserable prick!" called out Sasha. "What a low life! And they moved in together! How the hell can he live a double life like that?"

"And what was he thinking? That he can keep all of this a secret for eternity?" cynically asked Lizzie. "And to think that I was jealous of Julie for getting pregnant with her perfect man" she continued making air quotation signs with her fingers when she said 'perfect'.

They all went silent.

"She's 14 weeks pregnant," stated Lizzie, "just like Julie!"

Sasha looked disgusted, "The asshole left Julie pregnant and then went home and fucked his wife and left her pregnant too!"

"I don't even want to think about it!" said Nikki dismissing the thought with a quick wave of her hand.

"Poor Julie!" commented Lizzie, "She's going to think about that and then each and every moment they spent together and every word he ever muttered. It was all a lie!"

"We have to tell her about this entire thing, but we have to contain the entire situation" concluded Sasha.

"We'll get her here and bring her sponsor up to speed and have her on speed-dial" Lizzie started putting together the plan.

"Yeah, her sponsor can't be here or else she'll freak out!" agreed Nikki.

"Under which pretext can we bring her here as early as we can this morning?" asked Sasha trying to brainstorm the best idea.

Lizzie's face lit up like she just had the mother of ideas, "That's why he was always disappearing and getting phone calls at all weird times while blaming it on work!"

You could see blood running into Nikki's face. Sasha could tell right away that she was going to explode and braced herself for impact.

"Damn it, Lizzie! Let's focus on Julie! Forget about that piece of shit and pull yourself out of this fucking down-spiral. That's Julie's near future and we need to be here lifting her up and not sinking with her for all of our sakes."

There was silence again. Nothing was said for a good while.

"Ok. I'm going to call Julie and tell her that I have news from my lawyer on Ryan's case and that I need someone to talk to asap and need all of you here" announced Sasha pulling her cell from her pocket and dialing without waiting for approval from any of the girls.

***

The annoying buzzing sound woke Julie up. Who was calling at this hour? They can wait! Julie pushed her head back on the pillow and close her eyes yawning.

The buzzing continued. She wanted to ignore it but she didn't want it to wake Mike up. She grabbed her phone with one hand and quietly got herself out of bed and shuffled to the bathroom. The phone started buzzing again.

Okay, okay. What the hell is going on?

"I hope something's burning," Julie said instead of hello.

Sasha was taken by surprise. "As a matter of fact, something is definitely burning!"

Julie leaned against the sink and looked at herself in the mirror touching her puffy eyes with one finger. "Man, I need more sleep. This pregnancy is taking a toll on my body!"

"Focus Julie, please" begged Sasha. "I need you. I need you badly. Can you please come to me?"

Julie finally snapped out of her sleeping state and automatically responded, "Of course I'm coming! I'm leaving now!"

She knew this was important. She could hear it in Sasha's voice. But Sasha was always the kind of person to wait until the proper time rather than ask for help exactly when needed. Julie knew this was no joke. She slipped into her Uggs, grabbed a coat and her purse and closed the door behind her as softly as possible.

It was only in the cab when she realized that in her hurry, she grabbed Mike's coat. "He'll live! I'll be back by the time he has to go to work anyways!"

When she got to the building, Julie jumped out of the cab and ran upstairs as fast as she could.

Everybody was waiting for her. This was definitely serious, more serious than anything they've ever went through, and they went through a lot.

Her mind was racing, her heart was beating fast, and when her hands touched her belly in a protective way it reminded her to calm down for the baby's sake. Everybody was alive. Everything else can be handled.

Julie set herself down on the sofa next to Nikki and braced herself. This was going to be big she knew it. "Bring me up to speed please!"

Nikki took her hand, looked at her and began "This is going to be very hard to say and to hear. We need you to stay as calm as possible. Think of the baby!"

"So, somebody did die!" murmured Julie breathlessly. "Is it mom? One of my brothers?" She asked looking for clues before anyone said the name out loud. "Not my grandpa!" No one seemed to want to look at her straight in the eye. "It is grandpa, isn't it?" she barely articulated. Despite her family's lack of affection, her grandfather was the only one who sent her flowers every month just because, gave her gifts like this apartment on each and every birthday and never forgot the important moments of her life. He was the closest thing that she ever knew to a loving relative.

"Julie, please calm down! Nobody died!" reassured her Nikki.

Sasha and Lizzie left their chairs and set themselves down on the floor next to Julie.

"What the fuck is going on?" Julie was freaking out.

"Mike is married and his wife is pregnant!" blurted out Lizzie not giving anyone a chance to sugarcoat it in any way. She had to know and the wait was too much of a torture for all of them.

"Wait! Mike..." Julie said while a thousand thoughts were rushing through her head at the same time "My Mike? ... Wife? What kind of wife? .... When? I ..." Julie just couldn't put it together, it was all too much. Everybody was looking at her, talking to her, rubbing her hands, but she couldn't understand what was going on. What exactly were they saying? She couldn't think. She couldn't breathe. She needed air. There was no air in the room. How are they able to breathe? She was suffocating. She grasped her neck and stood up. She had to go to ... Where was she going? Why couldn't she breathe? She collapsed and everything went black.

***

"Welcome back!" said a concerned yet grateful voice. It was Sasha.

Julie looked around and recognized the sterile environment of a hospital room filled with flowers, cards and balloons to hide the death sentence behind it. Her hands immediately went to her belly.

"The baby is okay!" reassured her Sasha.

"What happened?" Julie asked and as a response she started to feel the heavy throb in her head. She lifted her hand to touch it. It was bandaged.

"You fainted and hit your head on the way down! We weren't quick enough!" explained Sasha.

"How long have I been here for?" asked Julie, while memories of the moments right before she lost her consciousness came back to the surface. "Shit! I'm going to throw up!"

Sasha grabbed the pan next to her bed and shoved it under Julie's contorted face. She helped her sit up, pulled her hair away and gently rubbed her back while Julie was emptying her stomach contents.

"You were out for a little bit over 24 hours. We started to get worried. Your sponsor came to visit you and she told us that this is how you usually cope with very emotionally stressful situations."

Julie lifted her head up, wiped her mouth with a small towel she found next to her and motioned to Sasha to take that pan away. "I want you to tell me everything right now. Not waiting for anybody else. Short and concise and don't hide anything from me, please!"

"But I think it would be wiser if..." started Sasha, but was interrupted by Julie.

"No! No thinking! I need to know now! Please Sasha!"

Sasha knew she had no choice. If it were her, she would probably want it exactly the same way, "His wife is a journalist and wrote a nasty piece on you, on us. That's how we found out." Sasha waited for any kind of response or question from Julie. Nothing came. Julie was staring at the Jell-O on the tray at the foot of her bed.

She continued, "She's 14 weeks pregnant, just like you. They live in a big house on the east side. He was living a double life. His best friend John was the only one who knew about it. Lizzie found out weeks ago that John was as big of a douche bag as Mike. We hoped that Mike was the real thing that's why we didn't say anything. Donna and Lizzie already picked up all your things from Mike's place. Your grandfather stopped by yesterday and left this cute bodyguard to make sure Mike will never bother you again. Nikki is booking us a trip to Costa Rica as we speak."

Julie was quiet. She continued to stare at the Jell-O.

"That pretty much covers it!" said Sasha after a few minutes of silence. She set herself on the bed waiting for Julie to react. Nothing. She was just staring and her mouth was closed tight.

After more than 45 minutes of waiting, Sasha moved to the chair next to the bed and kept herself busy rearranging the pile of magazines that were on the small rollaway table next to her.

"We're all booked up!" announced Nikki as she walked in the room looking at Sasha.

"She woke up!" announced Sasha. "She's been like that for the last hour after she asked me to tell her everything." Then Sasha's eyes moved to Nikki, "And I did!"

Nikki set herself next to Julie and hugged her. Julie let herself be hugged and then laid back on her pillow and started sobbing. "Good Julie! Let it all go through you. Do not stop it! You're healing!"

"I'm going to talk to the doctor and see when we can get out of here!" said Sasha on her way out of the room. " Then I need to go finish up the last details for the conference so I can join you guys for the first week in Costa Rica."

Chapter 32

The inviting blue waters were peeking through the thick green canopy filled with little acrobatic monkeys that were well known to quickly jump on tourists' backpacks and pull their hair.

Lounged in comfortable cushioned chairs, the girls were sipping on frescos made out of a verity of tropical fruits that were growing so lavishly in the area.

"I told them not to put ice in it," complained Lizzie. "It's like Mexico, you never drink tap water and you never get ice!"

Nikki was laughing wholeheartedly, "Lizzie my dear, you just finished your second glass of Refresco in less than ten minutes. What do you think they use in those watered fruit smoothies? Pellegrino?"

Lizzie immediately put her drink back on the table. Then she grabbed it again, "Well, I've been drinking these delicious concoctions since we got here and a week later, I seem to be okay, so I'll stop paying attention to the crap I read online and enjoy this experience as much as possible."

"So brave of you!" commented Nikki sarcastically leaning back into her chair and tuning into the sound of the ocean breeze and animal life in the surrounding forest.

Sasha put her laptop down, got up and announced, "I'm going to check on Julie!"

"Here. Take a smoothie to her room. She has barely eaten anything since she left the hospital. Some vitamins will do her good." Lizzie got up and poured a big glass of the fruity drink and gave it to Sasha.

"Are you going to tell her that tomorrow you have to leave?" asked Lizzie.

"I'll play it by ear, see if she's in a talkative mood. I hate that I have to leave!"

Nikki jumped in, "You've been working for too long and too hard to make this conference happen. There's no way you're going to miss it! It's your baby! She'll understand."

"You think?" asked Sasha staring at the pink glass in her hand.

"Better yet, she'll kick your butt if you don't go!" reassured her Nikki.

"Ok, here goes nothing!" said Sasha half joking half serious. She opened the French doors and walked into the spacious house they rented for the month. Julie's room was past the living room and to the right.

The door was still closed. She knocked softly and let herself in. It was pitch black in the room. As she bumped into something she couldn't identify she whispered a swear and when she heard a movement in the bed, she identified herself. "It's just me! Wanted to see if you're still alive!"

All she heard was an affirmative sob.

"I have to get myself some blinders like these. They are perfect for the job. They totally blinded me!" tried Sasha to joke. No response.

She felt her way toward the head of the bed and set down, next to an inert Julie.

"I brought you a delicious fruit smoothie that we've been indulging in for the last week. I'm going to leave it here on the nightstand," Sasha said as she groped in the dark in search of the promised surface and sat the drink down.

Sasha could hear Julie's shallow breaths. Somehow it comforted her to know that she was still breathing and not given up on life all together. She had been like a zombie for the entire week. She dressed herself at the hospital and followed them through the airport and the customs, talked to the appropriate authorities but never said a beep to any of them. Nikki was calling this "the purging silence" step. Was she even paying attention to what was going on around her? Sasha wondered.

"There's no easy way to say this, honey, but I have to go to Geneva tomorrow morning. My conference starts in less than 10 days and they desperately need me. It breaks my heart to leave you like this. Hope you understand. Once the conference is over, I'll be back. Lizzie and Nikki are going to stay here with you."

There was nothing. Just shallow breathing.

"Please, Julie, say it's ok for me to go. I feel so terrible leaving you right now" confessed Sasha. She didn't know if it was wise to touch her or not, so she kept her hands in her lap waiting for some kind of response. Anything.

Nothing. Not even a turn. Or a whisper. Or a soft cry.

Sasha finally got up and said, "I'm so sorry to let you down like this. Please try that drink that I left on the night stand. Do it for the baby if not for you. We love you!" Then she slowly found her way to the door, her eyes used to the dark by then.

***

"So, what now?" asked Lizzie. "Should we get a doctor and put her on an IV? She's scaring me!"

"Let her grief in her own way!" said Nikki. "It's her path, it's her grief, it's her own way of going through it and letting it go."

Sasha didn't agree with Nikki, "But she's pregnant! This can't be good for the baby! What if she kills it? That will definitely kill her if not eating won't."

"This entire situation is freaking me out!" said Lizzie. "We need to do something! It's been a week and all she had was fruit! I read somewhere that if a mother is anemic there will be problems with the normal growth of the placenta."

Nikki sighed, "For a moment I forgot about the baby. You are right. We do need to intervene!"

"But how?" asked Lizzie hysterically.

"After I drop you off at the airport tomorrow," said Nikki to Sasha, "I will find a doctor who is willing to come here and do whatever it takes to keep her fed and hydrated."

"What about me?" asked Lizzie. "What am I supposed to do? I can't just stay here with my arms crossed waiting for the inevitable."

"Someone has to stay here with Julie," explained Nikki.

"You're right. And you speak Spanish so you can find help faster than I could" agreed Lizzie.

"Everything is settled then" confirmed Sasha. "Don't forget to keep me posted!"

Lizzie's nod assured Sasha that she'll be kept in the loop while in Geneva.

"I feel so guilty for leaving like this. Right now!"

Nikki jumped up and two short strides she was next to Sasha, "You have to go! For all of us! We all put our lives on hold because we can. You can't! This is it for you! You have to do this, for all of us. And especially for Julie! It will destroy her to know you killed this once in a lifetime opportunity just to sit around with us and sip Refrescos waiting for our beloved sleeping beauty to piece together her heart!"

"Nice pep talk!" jokes Lizzie. "But I totally agree with what she said. You have to go!"

"This still doesn't feel right" said Sasha covering her eyes with her hands in frustration. She took two deep breaths and said "I'm going to pack now."

"That's the spirit!" recited Lizzie like a cheerleader. "I'll help you! I'm getting bored here. Nikki, you can have the nature all to yourself for now."

Nikki said nothing. She just pulled the rope that was tying up the hammock, grabbed a pillow from her chair and laid back in it.

***

The sun was ready to come out from behind the horizon. The birds were chirping like crazy and the wild life in the surrounding little forest came to life gradually but in a fast rhythm.

Sasha couldn't sleep all night, so she decided to go outside on the huge elevated porch and take a moment before all the Geneva craziness would start. She looked down at her cell phone. One more hour and then she could turn it on and with it switch herself back into work mode. She was excited and scared at the same time. This was what she's been working for and dreaming about for such a long time. She didn't care what else happened in her life, this was it. This will repay her somehow. This will make her hell life worthwhile.

The only thing she felt guilty about was Julie. Every time she thought of her and the way she'd seen her the last several days a crushing pain squeezed the air out of her lungs. She wished she could take the pain away from her and drown it in work. It was one hundred percent tried method and it worked every time for Sasha.

She was only scared about the time when everything will catch up to her, like Nikki predicted. But Sasha loved her job and as long as she worked until she drew her last breath, nothing will ever catch up to her. Ever! Her personal life can lag behind indefinitely and forever. That was the plan anyway!

Geneva and the beginning of her true life were one hour away! She couldn't wait. Just the thought put a big grin on her face!

A faint sound drew her attention behind her. She turned to see what it was. "Oh, Julie, you scared me! I thought it was a monkey or some other animal that usually shares this porch with us on a daily basis." She was talking too much. She knew that. Just because she felt guilty for smiling a moment ago thinking about Geneva when Julie was right behind her tortured in pain. She looked down trying to hide it all.

"Sorry!" crooked Julie. "Didn't mean to startle you ... or to snatch you away from your happy reverie that seemed to have put a smile on your face."

Now Sasha really felt guilty. Damn it! She caught all that.

"No need for all of us to be locked away in Julie's hell. One of us needs to go out there and bring some sunshine and hope in our lives. Like the dove with an olive branch."

Sasha didn't know how to respond to that but she finally looked up to see Julie. It was a miracle that she was up and outside and talking. It didn't matter what she was saying or how guilty it made her feel.

"I'm so glad to see you here, out of that dark hole you call a room" said Sasha compassionately. "I missed you. We all missed you!"

"I wanted to make sure I saw you before you left. I don't want you to feel bad for leaving me here" Julie said looking around for the first time and seeing the splendor of a breathtaking Costa Rican sunrise. "Wow! It's actually beautiful here. Sorry I didn't come out earlier to spend some time with you before you had to leave."

"Don't worry about it!" jumped in Sasha. "I'm glad you're here now! It means so much to me!"

"And it means much more to me that you took the time that you did not have to come here and keep my sad self-company."

"I'm sorry I can't stay longer," Sasha apologized.

"And I am sorry I can't come with you! I was looking forward to Geneva, the shopping and all of us being together again on a European trip with you leading what I know to be the most important UN conference of the century!"

The tears in Sasha's eyes were blurring her vision. "You are such an amazing friend!" She opened her arms asking for permission to hug her.

Julie was the one who wrapped her arms around Sasha immediately, "You are the best friend anybody could ever wish for! I love you! Thank you for being here."

"Thank you for having me in your life!" replied Sasha hugging Julie as tight as she could. "I love you too!"

The moment was interrupted by a loud stomach growl. They both started laughing and grabbing their stomachs.

"Was that the both of us at the same time?" asked Sasha.

"Don't know about you, but all this emotional crap I've been going through took me through the hell desert and back. I'm so hungry I could eat the neighbor's cow ... that's assuming we rented the house without a cow!" joked Julie.

"And she's back!" retorted Sasha. "Let's get some food in you. And I could use some breakfast too."

***

The capital of peace, with all its humanitarian tradition and cosmopolitan flair, caressed by nearby Alpine peaks, Geneva was sure to impress any living soul that passed through its old yet modern Swiss charming streets.

"Jane and Derek!" called Sasha. "The two of you will be in charge of all the NGOs. Make sure you have the most accurate and up-to-date list of all those that are coming. We don't want any last-minute surprises."

"We are on it," replied Jane.

"George and José," called again Sasha. "My list says we have 34 youth groups from all over the world attending this very conference. We went over the specifics last night. Make sure all details are in place."

"Speakers," fumbled Sasha. "Who's in charge of the speakers?" She was starting to panic. No speakers, no conference! What the hell! How could she forget the most important thing of all? This was it! It was going to all fall apart! And she was convinced that she could pull this international event together on her own in such a short period of time. Who was she kidding?

A voice pulled her out of her misery, "You put me in charge! Hence it's been all confirmed, reconfirmed and doubled checked." She recognized Mandy's annoying voice. Her personality had always clashed with Sasha's, but she was always very efficient, detail oriented to the extreme of being very anal and extremely demanding from everyone including herself. If she said all was good, it was all perfect!

"Security, tech team, volunteers, logistics... You name it. It's all under control. We've been over all this a thousand times, Sasha" confirmed Sean, her assistant.

"This is the dress rehearsal. Want to make sure it all fits perfectly in its designated spot. We've worked too hard for it not to run smoothly," replied Sasha.

"As smooth as it will ever be able to. Any conference has hiccups, but we've seen it all and dealt with it all and if something new shows up, I'm very confident that we'll be able to handle it," reassured her Pete, the only guy in her entire department who's been putting together conferences for the UN for over three decades. She trusted him completely.

Sasha finally breathed. "Good! Let's get a good night sleep! The show is tomorrow."

Usually, during beautiful sunny days stolen from the frozen claws of winter, New Yorkers go to the park or take a walk just to take advantage of the vitamin D filled miracle.

Being in Costa Rica, far away from what New York Times predicted to be one of the toughest and longest winters, was a welcomed gift of life.

"Geneva must be freezing this time of year, "said Lizzie out loud." I'm so grateful to be here enjoying the sun." She closed her eyes and started listening to everything around her. The salty breeze coming from the ocean was invading her senses. She could almost taste it on her lips.

She loved how she felt caressed by the gentle whisper of the wind.

"You're right Nikki, I can feel the godliness of this element of nature. It loves me right now. And just because it has the strength to destroy everything and everyone I know; it doesn't feel the need to show off."

"Like so many of our so-called friends, back in Manhattan," commented Julie.

"That's only because other people release their ownership to their own power and freely give it away to those scared and empty scarecrows who think they need it to prove something to their mom, dad or whomever took their own power away when they were little," added Nikki.

"Empty scared souls ..." echoed Julie.

Lizzie jumped up shaking her arms vigorously in an attempt to shake off whatever was crawling on her. "Whoa, too heavy! Too much with a heavy again! Can we go for a bike ride or something? Some endorphins will do us good!"

Nikki was the first one to answer snapping out of her reverie. "Yes, that's an excellent idea!" She pushed herself out of her beloved hammock and grabbed both Julie's hands, pulling her up from her chair and her misery.

Julie opened her mouth in protest, ready to oppose Democratic vote of mandatory endorphins pump up, but then she remembered the promise she made to the girls and especially to her baby. "I love you baby," she said out loud using her freed hands to rub her ballooning stomach. "I'm doing this for you and you are doing this for me! Together we'll beat depression... And empty scared souls!"

"Hah, ha, no!" Exclaimed Nikki. "No pressure like that on any of you! Now let's just see what new animal we see today."

"Maybe try that place that we saw the other day on the way to the clinic. I'm definitely getting hungry with all this sitting around," joked Lizzie.

"Sitting around is dangerous! Can get you bored, depressed and fat in no time!" Commented Julie. "Look at me!"

"Are you calling your baby fat? That's not nice!" Replied Nikki jokingly.

They went back in the house to change clothes and get the necessary sunglasses, hats and money.

"Can we please walk today? I like to be on my own two feet if you don't mind!" asked Julie putting a pair of sneakers on.

"Walking it is, "approved Nikki.

***

I close my eyes and I see you!

I travel to events to immortalize them and in every frame, I see you!

I take my body to a sports bar to brag and have a beer...and I see you there too!

I take a shower; eat my dinner and I see you again!

You're with me always and forever.

I miss you even when I see you!

I love you!

Sam

Nikki's heart was full of joy. She couldn't breathe exhaling all this love that she was receiving daily from Sam.

It was hard to believe it was all true. Why now? Why Sam? Why Nikki? What did she ever do to deserve such a fairytale?

Of course, she preached believing in the fairytale and happily ever after to everyone who would listen, but she never really thought it would happen to her. To her friends? Her best pals – for sure. But not to her. She never banked on it.

She had to see the world before she settled. If she ever settled. Wasn't that her dream? Always? To travel the world, learn from it about love, joy and happiness and then share it and give it freely to everybody? She always wanted to be that. The messenger of love and joy.

Why all that! Maybe because she felt she needed to learn what that was. Love! Joy! Happiness! What was all that? Wasn't that what everyone wanted but never seem to fully get? Everybody was self-sabotaging their own love and happiness every day, all the time. She never heard of anyone staying happy or in love forever. Why was that?

She wanted to find the answer and the solution and to bring that 'forever' to the world. It was her mission in life!

And now... Sam happened!

How did he happen? He brought, awakened and brightened feelings into her that she never thought she had.

What she thought was love before, and happiness, were like visibility in the murky waters of a swamp. Now she could really see! She saw him too. Everywhere! She felt him. Everywhere! She wanted him. All the time!

A joke, but beautiful sunrise, an incredible story, a dream...he was the first solo she thought of sharing all that with. Anything and everything. Forever!

But will this worldly forever last? It was so magical. It had to last! For her, for him, for everyone.

She had to go back and search for the cure. So, she and everybody else can have 'forever' when they find their Sam.

***

The strange noise of a foreign bell woke Lizzie up from her afternoon nap. The sun was already setting in the breeze that had been comfortable and welcome before it was chilly and slightly unpleasant without a sun to warm her skin to a nice toasty level.

There it was, the strange bell rang again.

"Hold your horses! I'm coming! ...yo.... coming!" Lizzie tried all the Spanish she could muster while her brain was still in dozing off mode.

She shuffled her bare feet to the front door and without thinking about it she opened the door to a most colorful arrangement of flowers she had ever seen, big as the whole door frame. Yellows, magenta, blues and greens, orange, peach, white and red, purple splashes all over the overwhelming bouquet.

"It's breathtaking!" Whispered Lizzie gasping for air." Who said Costa Rica isn't the most hospitable place on the face of the planet must have been blind! Gracias, whomever you are! Come right in!"

"If I were a vampire, you would have been sucked dry by now and your lovely friends would have been next," joked a familiar deep voice from behind the multicolored waterfall of flowers. "You invited me in so earnestly!"

"I would happily give my life for this splendid display of flowers," replied Lizzie with a smile.

"I hope your friends think the same way you do," said Sam trying to balance his gorgeous burden.

"Let me get the one friend that I know will be mostly impressed," said Lizzie running toward the back patio.

"Is this Noah's Ark for flowers? Is there something I wasn't told and plants are going extinct?" Nikki said coming from the opposite direction.

"Only if you leave them behind for weeks at a time... Especially in this fragile state... At the beginning," replied Sam finally setting them down on a round glass table that was shoved to the wall couple of nights before when the girls felt like sugar high dancing after eating too much chocolate.

Nikki's face lit up. " Who are we talking about now?" She put her left hand on her waist to the side and pushed her hip to the right.

"Me," admitted Sam and in two long strides he reached her, pulled her close to him and kissed her to make up for lost time.

After Nikki balanced herself and regain some control, she half nagged him, "I thought I told you this was a girls' trip only."

'Yes, you did. And I respect that. But it's been over a month and when you're coming back to New York, I have to go to LA ..." Sam tried to rationalize.

"Sam, don't fall into that trap. She wanted to see you as much as you wanted to see her. She was just worried about me," came Julie's voice from behind Lizzie.

"How are you, Julie? These are for you!" said Sam pointing at the flowers.

"You are amazing! I've never seen such a magnificent show of natural beauty. They can bring a suicidal woman from the edge of the bridge," smiled Julie and came in for a hug.

"That was my intention. But I made sure there were no bridges around, just in case of flower failure."

Julie laughed. Her first real laughter in so long. It felt so good, like the dirty windows of a rundown dark warehouse were finally broken and the sun inundated the place with its joyful, bright rays. She could finally breathe without putting her hand over her chest in on unconscious way of pointing to the pain that was blocking her and keeping her prisoner.I think we should all go out and celebrate tonight," said Julie." Unless the two of you prefer to go alone."

"No, no! We should go. All of us. Yes! Celebrate ... your first breakthrough," said Nikki with confidence and excitement. She could see the sudden change in Julie.

"We'll be ready in a quick second," announced Lizzie directing Sam to the large flat-screen TV in the living room then she followed Julie and Lizzie to their rooms.

***

"What were the chances to get some jazz music with this mouthwatering food," commented Lizzie, munching on the lemon and garlic marinated grilled asparagus.

" If I'd known the food was this delicious, I would have insisted on daily takeout during my ...recovery," added Julie with a wide smile on her face. "Jake loves it to," she said touching her belly in a most maternal way.

"Guys if you don't mind, Sam and I will leave before dessert."

Lizzie smiled understandingly." Of course. But Julie and I will devour the entire dessert menu and enjoy the scene and the music for a while longer."

Nikki and Sam got up, but before they left Sam assured the ladies that everything was paid for so they only had to enjoy themselves as much as possible." No second thoughts," he said.

"Did you see the two guys at the table to your right?" Asked Lizzie in a whisper after Sam and Nikki were gone. "Is it too soon? Ohh, that was so stupid of me," apologize Lizzie feeling guilty.

"Can I turn and look?" Asked Julie and her question and childish curiosity made Lizzie feel better instantly.

"Why not?!" She smiled and took a sip of her water with lemon.

One of the guys had a dark suit on, expensive shoes and a salon haircut. He looked to be in his mid-40s and exuded power. His friend was dressed more appropriately for the location, jeans and a dark gray T-shirt that showed hints of the marble chest and stomach underneath it every time he reached for something on the table or brought his fork to his mouth. And what a mouth with brilliant white teeth and generous lips. He caught both of them looking. He smiled and nodded his head covered by luxurious black hair with a slight wave in it. The other gentleman followed suit. Then they returned to their conversation.

Julie and Lizzie couldn't muffle their giggles of little girls being caught drooling over the most popular guy in school.

"Good thing that Donna is not here. She would be so jealous," said Lizzie and continued laughing.

"Lava cake para usted," announced the waiter who showed up next to their table unexpectedly. Lizzie and Julie's attention was just that fickle. They completely forgot about the two delicious men sitting at a nearby table and focused on the mouthwatering American dessert.

***

It was time to walk, to move, just got out of this whole mess that was swallowing her with every waking minute. The nap did not help.

Julie went to look for Nikki. She knew that Lizzie had gone to bring some groceries, mail some postcards and people watch close to the center of the town. She loved doing that. She won't be back for a while.

Nikki wasn't in the house or on the porch. Julie listened for the sounds of the shower. Maybe that's why she couldn't hear her calling her name.

Nothing. The silence was eerie. Yup! She had to go. She wouldn't get lost. They've walked in the area for couple of weeks now. She won't stay long, so they wouldn't worry. Maybe leave a quick note.

It was hot outside, so Julie decided to put on the best sundress she had. She was going to look good. For the baby.

Her bulge was visible now, but the sundress was able to conceal it.

Julie grabbed a white hat with huge rims and a small bottle of water and was on her way up the coast.

It was usually quiet on the narrow trail that she chose which was leading to the cliff where the girls took her couple of times to witness the most vibrant warm colored sunrise. They actually had to yank her out of her bed, but it was worth it. If her memory serves her right, it was a very secluded area away from all the touristy traps and chatty vacationers. That was all she wanted. To be alone with her thoughts, but outside in the sun looking over the ocean, letting the splashing waves crash and clear away her pain.

She had to let Mike go. But every time she said his name – even in her thoughts – all she could think about was his unbearable betrayal. How could he? She felt his love. She knew he loved her. But he also loved his wife, who he kept secret from her. And she was pregnant. Same week as her. Was it the same day? Not possible. According to Julie's calculations she got pregnant in Mexico. But he left her at the airport on their way back, claiming he had a work crisis. Was that the night when he conceived another baby with his wife? While texting her the same evening that he already misses her... While being inside his wife, looking at her, touching her, kissing and caressing her. Was he having as much pleasure thrusting with her like he did with Julie? Was he telling his wife he loved her right before and after climax, like he always told Julie? Those thoughts made her sick, but she couldn't push them away.

Julie barely saw the white courageous birds who were feeding themselves by plunging straight down into the water like an arrow, closing their wings closer to the body right before entering the water at full speed.

She used to love watching this entire show. Not now. All she could see was Mike hugging his wife, kissing her forehead, promising her eternal love, forgetting Julie's existence... And his baby's... His other baby. A bastard baby! They were probably both laughing at her and her illegitimate child.

Julie felt a sharp poke in her stomach. She immediately snapped back and touched her belly protectively. "I'm really sorry baby! All my misery can't be good for you. I know and I'm sorry. I promise I'll do better!"

A loud thud followed by a big splash got her attention for a split second. She looked towards the water to see the source of all that. There was nothing, but the waves slamming their powerful drive into the rock below, exploding into 1 million pieces that fell back in the wetness below to be part of the ocean once again.

It was a never-ending cycle. Nature did it all the time and pulled itself together fast without complaining, whining and cutting itself completely off from the rest of the universe, like humans do when they break into pieces.

It seemed to be so normal, so casual and non-consequential for the ocean, atmosphere and plants, even animals. No whining, no 'poor me' act.

"Humans are so pathetic," said Julie out loud criticizing her own species.

A febrile splash moved her gaze towards the water again.

The little hand that smacked against the surface of the blue water went down under swallowed by the following wave. Was she imagining it?

There it was again!

Julie jumped up and look down at the beach to see if there was anyone there, closer to those tiny hands that must have been a child's.

She saw the young couple. They were kissing each other tenderly, both laid-back on a salmon-colored blanket, oblivious to the world. Next their blanket, towards the water, there was a myriad of colorful plastic sand toys that for sure were meant to keep those little drowning hands busy. But those tiny hands were so far away from those toys by now.

"Hello! Your child is drowning! Hellooooow!" Julie yelled in desperation from the top of her lungs. "Help! Help her!" She tried again pointing at the spot where she last saw those baby hands flailing in the salty air just an inch above the water.

Was this a dream? Was she invisible? How come no one could see or hear her?

Well, if it was a dream, nothing permanent was going to happen to her, Julie decided. But she had to do something.

She took her shoes and hat off; she threw her water bottle to the ground and next thing she knew she was airborne.

"I'm going to die! There's no way I'll survive this jump! The cliff is too high and the rocks below ...." Julie finally understood that she was not dreaming. It was all real and she had just made the decision that was going to end her life.

Maybe it was for the better! She was calm. The end was near but she wasn't afraid anymore.

A glimpse of a photograph that was never taken flashed before her eyes. It was a happy curly baby boy with gorgeous blue eyes and rosy cheeks in the arms of a beautiful brunette woman radiating joy and bliss.

It was she and her unborn baby.

She knew it right at the exact moment when she hit the water and plunged the bottom like those white birds she was watching before.

The dive into the water felt chilly on her skin. Pricked her with a thousand needles at once and woke her up to consciousness. It hurt!

She was going to fight! The last image she saw before the ocean water covered her jolted her to life.

Julie opened her eyes. All she could see was bubbles floating up in the light blue water. It confused her she knew her mouth was not open. She wasn't breathing. She was going to fight to go back to the surface. But then, why the bubbles? Her mind was racing, but she had to live and pushed that aside and made her focus on her own survival.

When she finally stopped going down, she looked up to the surface and frantically started kicking to reach that point.

Her arm brushed against something and she freaked out for a second. No fish that wasn't looking to eat her was going to come that close to her.

Before her mind started filling with the multitude of predators that could be considering her their next meal, her eyes automatically switched from looking up to searching the object of her fear.

She froze. It was a sweet child from her future picture. But the hair seemed longer than the child looked bigger. And she was staring at Julie not moving at all.

Julie instinctively put her hand around the child's waist and pushed them both towards the surface with renewed strength.

***

"You were very brave out there," assured Julie the little child who refused to let go of her hand and go into her wide-open arms.

The young couple were throwing thank you' s in English, Spanish and French were overwhelming her. What was more overwhelming was that they looked more scared than grateful, exchanging frightened looks every other second. Then they looked around to make sure nobody saw what had happened with searching eyes. Julie did not understand the scene, but she was happy that somehow, she had the strength to pull both of them out.

"It wasn't your fault! I tried to let you know, but you couldn't hear me!" Julie couldn't understand their frantic exchange. It was too fast and it changed from English to Spanish to French and back to English again.

"What matters is that she is okay now!" Julie tried to appease them, if not for their sanity at least for the little girl's sake who was clinging on to Julie scared for dear life.

After another quick exchange between the two young parents, the woman opened her arms for the little girl, "Come on my darling! We're going home now. You're going to be just fine!"

The man helped her pull the kid from Julie's arms while thanking Julie again "God bless you for what you did today. You have saved us! Thank you!"

That was the only time the girl started reacting, "My angel, my angel!" She called out to Julie reaching her tiny hand towards her.

"Yes, she is an angel!" the mother agreed. "Angel will always be with you, but now we have to go back to the house."

Julie didn't know what to do.

The father offered, "I will take you back to your place. This is a private beach and the only way out is by our place. It's the least I could do for all you've done."

"I can walk," Julie said and looked down. Her white dress must have got caught on something before she jumped or maybe in the water, as it was torn on one side exposing her hip and thigh.

Ahh, must have been the white dress that made a little child confuse her with an angel.

Her eyes finally met the man's worried face. Okay. A ride would be appreciated," she said wanting to somehow end this guy's misery. He probably wanted nothing but to be with his wife and young daughter right now and she was stealing those precious moments from him.

When they got next to the impressive white villa with extensive gardens, an infinity pool and what seemed like tennis courts from where the cars were parked, she jumped into the Jeep that the father opened the passenger door to and looked up at the ivy-covered balcony to the side of the house.

"Angel, angel!" called the little girl. Then the mother came to take her back inside. The mom took the little girl in her arms and waved a brief goodbye to Julie before they disappeared into the house.

Julie's eyes were filled with tears. She could still hear the little girl calling her angel.

***

The image of the curly baby boy in her arms and the little girl whose name she never got were Julie's catalysts to sanity.

One week after the incident she was ready to go home. She went back to the house to visit the little girl, but she was told that they had left the next day after Julie pulled her out of the water.

Too bad. She really wanted to get to know that sweet little girl who jolted her back to life. Julie owed the girl her life just as much as the girl owed Julie hers.

They were forever intertwined.

Chapter 33

"You're looking at the new UN Ambassador to Eastern Europe Women's Rights division. I am a UN Ambassador! Can you believe it?" announced a dark gray suited Sasha, the second she saw Nikki and Julie at the airport.

"No one deserves it more than you do Sasha. You will do important things out there that will go down in history," said Nikki hugging her tight.

"Congratulations!" chimed in Julie. "Just don't forget about us, the little people."

Sasha laughed and hugged Julie as well." You could never be little people to me or to anyone in this world!" She stepped back to take a better look at Julie. "You're absolutely beaming! What has happened since I left you on the deck in Costa Rica?"

Julie blushed. "I apologize for my behavior back then. I forgot to look at this world and life and see it for what it is -a miraculous experience!"

Not believing her ears, Sasha's eyes were literally bulging out in an inconspicuous attempt to understand what Julie was saying.

Nikki laughed at the entire scene, "You have some catching up to do!" she said grabbing one of Sasha's bags. "Has Julie had an angelic encounter of some sort!"

"Look who's talking," replied Julie. "Nikki and Sam just signed a contract with a travel magazine for a monthly column ... or feature article ...

or something," enumerated Julie in confusion ..." So now they get to travel and discover and create art based on their new experiences. Did I get that right?" asked Julie turning towards Nikki who seemed to be engrossed into finding the quickest way out of the craziness of the international terminal.

"Pretty much. I just have to finish my BA first and give a final form to my Love Flood collection."

Sasha couldn't stop herself from pointing out, "but you will be done in a couple of months or less. Are you ready for this commitment? More so, are you really ready to commit to it with Sam?"

"Why not?" Jumped in Julie. "I would take that god of a man at any time, even with this huge bump," she said protectively arranging one hand on top and one on the bottom of the rounded belly that was now obvious.

Sasha put her hand on Nikki and stopped her to look her in the eye. She didn't look away, "Yes, I feel the blissful connection to the core of my being. I don't know how I got this lucky, but I've never felt so happy and light in my entire life. I'm not walking anymore. I'm floating and gliding. Everything is easy and ..." Nikki was trying to find the best word to describe it "... sparkly."

"There are times when you think tiny bluebirds will start flying and chirping their little happy songs around her like in those musical cartoons with blissed out princesses," commented Julie. "It's joyful and annoying at the same time to be around her, but my little Jake loves it!" she said touching her bump again. She was clearly profoundly in love with the baby inside of her.

It wasn't hard to get a cab anymore. Everything seemed to fall right into its place at the right moment.

"Where's Lizzie?" asked Sasha as she pushed her small bag in the backseat of the cab with her.

"She and Donna are in LA. Her book took off couple of weeks ago. She's doing more book tours than she did with the last one. Lizzie still can't believe it, but she's going through the motions and Donna is there to pinch her every time she thinks she is dreaming " clarified Julie.

"Wow! I go away for three weeks and you all reach the stars while I'm gone. Talk about fast miracles" Sasha said pointing at Julie mesmerized at her 180 degrees change from the pale, anemic and depressed face she left behind when she went to Geneva.

"Look who's talking! Our own UN Ambassador!" exclaimed Julie.

"Because of the new and shiny title, we'll forgive you for having to stay an extra twelve days in breathtaking Switzerland." I can't believe you didn't take advantage of the opportunity and visit that amazing country," said Nikki. "It's always been one of my favorites!"

"Your extensive traveling experience at your baby age still blows my mind," commented Sasha in awe. You've been to Switzerland?"

Nikki nodded her head with false shyness.

"Where haven't you been, Carmen Sandiego?" asked Julie rhetorically.

"Carmen Sandiego is a novice compared to me," joked Nikki. They all laughed as they were sure it was true.

"How about you Julie?" asked Sasha skillfully delaying her little announcement.

Julie was taken by surprise. "What about me?"

"From what you told me on the phone last week, you're graduating early. Still going for that PhD?"

"Nope!" said Julie with conviction." I've actually spent more time with Nick and Diatrice from my grandpa's office. My business plan is almost complete and I'm going to get a loan next Tuesday."

"Diatrice is from your grandpa's office?" asked Sasha.

"Yes," answered Julie and before Sasha could ask her the next question she clarified, " And yes, my grandpa offered me the money, but I declined. I want this to be my baby!"

"Don't you have one already? Too many diapers at once!" Joked Nikki.

Julie laughed. "I'm up for the challenge. Plus, I have all of you to help me babysit both of my babies, don't I?"

"Of course, you do!" exploded Nikki with enthusiasm. "Sam loves babies, he'll pay you to let him babysit little Jake."

"So, he's a little baby boy," concluded Sasha from the conversation.

"Yes," said Julie smiling and lovingly touching her belly again. "Didn't I tell you that already?"

"First I heard of it!"

"What!? You have something against babysitting little boys?" joked Julie. "Everything works the same, I promise ... well kind of."

Sasha took a deep breath and pulled herself to the edge of the seat so she could see both Nikki and Julie, "I'm moving to Geneva!" she announced.

She let it sink in. She had nothing to add, the decision was already made. She knew she should have called the girls before she accepted it, but everything happened so fast and she accepted the position without even asking any details. It was her fault, but if she had to do it again, knowing now that they wanted her to move to the UN headquarters in Geneva, Sasha was sure she would have answered the same way. " Hell yeah! And thank you!"

"I guess I saw this coming," said Nikki," breaking the silence." How else would you be a UN Ambassador without being in the belly building of the UN."

" Plus, all the traveling you'd have to do especially to Eastern Europe. It makes sense," added Julie deep in thought.

The atmosphere changed completely in the small inside of the cab and it was palpable.

"I'll be in the New York office multiple times a year," Sasha said trying to offer an appeasing upside to the entire situation.

"I've seen you work. If you're in the New York office it will be to work. It won't matter if you're here or in Geneva. We won't be able to see you," pointed out Julie tears bursting out uncontrollably followed by smuggled sobs.

Nikki swallowed hard and put both her hands around Julie." You will be so busy with Jake and your new business, Solstice, that you won't even notice her absence."

Julie didn't seem consoled.

"She will call daily and come home for every holiday, won't you?" Nikki asked drilling her eyes into Sasha with a pain ridden facial expression.

"Yes, I will. I promise!" replied Sasha. "You are my family! I love you all, but I have to do this and I hope you can find the strength and understanding to support me!"

Sasha's words touched Julie's heart immediately." Sorry, honey. I think it's the hormones. I seem to cry from nothing these days even when I get good news," she said grabbing Sasha's hands into hers." And this is good news! It's great news!" Then she forced a smile to prove her point. It didn't really work.

"I'm sorry too," apologized Sasha." I should have discussed this with you first."

"And if we would have been against it, would you have said no to this unbelievable opportunity of a lifetime?" asked Nikki rhetorically.

Sasha's stare moved to her own hands, "No, I guess not!"

"And we would never have asked that of you," reassured her Julie wiping her tears with the back of her hand.

"I love you guys!" Said Sasha cracking an apologetic smile.

"We love you too!" responded Nikki cupping her hand under Sasha's chin and forcing her lips into a fish pout. "Say you love us again!"

"I wuve you!"

They were all laughing.

Chapter 34

Sasha's move was tough on all the girls, especially Nikki. She never expected anyone else to leave their 'nest' except herself so the fact that Sasha had to go shook her down to the core.

She always thought that the girls were always going to be there for her when she returned from her 'escapades' with a smile on their faces and loving hugs. Nikki got used to all that by now and probably took it for granted, because Sasha moving to Geneva created havoc in her mind and her belief system.

"What the heck is real anymore and lasting?" Then she looked at the little girl using a flower as her umbrella laughing – it was the first concept Sam and Nikki put together after their rookie sculpture class. It was the cutest and most joyful and loving drawing she ever created and Sam was there for the conception, inspiring it, building it together.

Sam – he offered so much love freely, without seeming to ever get tired of it. He was smiling at strangers and within couple of minutes he could make them feel enough and appreciated. It was amazing to be a part of it, just to see how much a person can transform the day for anyone they see on the street just with implicit attention to anything they have to say. Simple validation for who they were and a real smile, maybe a hug or a meant handshake. That was all.

Nikki believed she attracted Sam, by starting her Love Flood collection. She wanted to see the beauty and love in everyday life and monotonous routines and routes and bring all that love and joy back to the people.

She wanted her collection to inspire people to accept love to enter their lives and enjoy it ... like Sam seemed to be able to do so easily.

He paid so much attention to Nikki. When they were together, she was his number one priority, but in a very carefree way. Nikki didn't feel pressured in any way. All she felt was love and being loved, important and enough.

Sam taught her to accept herself and love herself.

She had to give all that back to the world. She had to find a way to spread that love and make it last. For Sasha, for Lizzie, Julie and her baby, herself, Sam ...for everybody.

Her family was uprooted with Sasha in Geneva and Nikki's world felt unstable once more. She wanted that narcotic feeling of safety that the apartment in New York with the girls, her family, used to give her.

Love and happiness were supposed to be forever, not only temporary. Where did we lose this balance?

Nikki had to find that out and discover a way to bring it back to humanity for everyone's sake.

She had to find it.

She had to leave.

***

Julie walked into an old and grandiose building downtown New York. She had her file ready and was sure she was going to walk out with a needed loan for her business.

"I came to see Mr. Weinberg. I have an appointment. My name is Julie Sorel," she said to the receptionist she encountered on the fourth floor where she was directed to.

Sitting and waiting her turn, Julie was fidgeting. Maybe she should have let Lizzie come along. No, this was her business, her baby, her dream. She was growing up now. She did not need a babysitter. There were so many offices there and cubicles, but the noise level was curiously low except for the fax, copy machine and ringing phones.

The door in front of her opened up and a man in his late 50s with a blue shirt and suit pants invited her in. Julie followed him. The hairless spot on top of his head was visible even from her modest height. Do any of those bankers soaring investment bankers have a full head of hair? Julie asked herself. This must be a very stressful job, and boring, she concluded.

"Please sit," Mr. Weinberg asked politely.

"Thank you," replied Julie choosing the closest chair to his desk thinking that would be the easiest once she had to point to the details in her business proposal, which she laid in front of her and gave a copy to Mr. Weinberg. Her hands were shaking. She wanted this to go right for so many reasons ... mainly survival of her dream and her happiness. She didn't want to suffocate her baby Jake with all her misplaced attention. She needed more focus in her life for her and the baby's sake.

"Before you even start, Mrs. Sorel"

"Ms. Sorel," Julie corrected him.

" Ms. Sorel," he repeated and coughed lightly," your grandfather asked me to meet with you and I respect him very much. He is a giant in our industry. A brilliant man."

"I don't understand what this has to do with my grandfather," Julie interrupted him." This is all me. My grandfather has nothing to do with it. Can I just please start to tell you about my business, my idea," Julie said emphasizing the word 'my'.

"I read the business plan already," explained the banker handing her back the folder she put in front of him. I'm sorry but if your grandfather..."

Knowing the possible words that were going to come out of his mouth, Julie jumped in to save the life of her dream, maybe even herself. "Please give me a chance to show you."

"Sorry, Ms. Sorel. It would be just a waste of time for the both of us."

"Please, I need this! How can I convince you?" Started Julie then lost her voice recognizing the libidinous look on the older guy's face.

"Maybe we should talk more over dinner."

"The hell we will, you disgusting pig. I might have had some daddy issues before but let me assure you, pigs like you helped me get over all of them. Fast!"

Julie jumped out of her chair, grabbed both folders that contained her business plan and stormed out. But before she did, she turned around and showed him the finger. "That's all you'll get from me; you piece of shit. I didn't see any family pictures in your office. At least you had the decency to rid the next generations of assholes like you."

He was furious at this point and shoved her out of his office while telling his assistant to call security. " If it weren't for your grandfather and your situation," he said pointing to her belly, "I would throw you in the street myself."

"Why don't you, pussy? What are you so afraid you're going to lose? Your boring job and life? You garbage! Leave those poor innocent ladies be," she said pointing at all the cubicles in the hallway," they deserve better!"

He slammed his door shut while two men in uniform picked her off the floor and in the elevator.

What the hell just happened? Maybe she overreacted a little. Or a lot. The man was a chauvinistic pig, but she shouldn't have projected and let loose of all her suppressed hatred for misogynistic men like him that had hurt her over her lifetime. Well, he had it coming one day. Why not from her. But what about the loan? No, she never stood a fighting chance. He might even call other fellow bankers to warn them about her.

Julie's shoulders dropped, her gaze was stuck to the floor, her dream shattered. The security men felt her resignation and put her down. They were flanking her to the exit doors.

"Angel, Angel!" She heard a sweet voice from afar. It sounded like a dream. Now she really was going crazy.

Then something touched her hand. It was a small hand. She looked towards the tiny person that was smiling at her. Memories flooded her. She was speechless.

"Joy, honey" she heard a masculine voice coming from behind. She knew that timber. She heard it before. But where? She turned around with the girl holding her hand. The man was right next to her, his imposing stature, his deep blue eyes hypnotizing her.

He smiled in recognition.

"Where do I know you from?" asked Julie confused.

"Costa Rica. Jeremy's" he responded. "You and your friend giggled at an enormous pile of chocolate cake."

Julie blushed. Oh no! How embarrassing.

"Daddy, this is the Angel! I told you she doesn't live in heaven like mommy," said the little girl's twinkling voice.

He knelt down to pick his daughter up. His eyebrows were pushed together. Was he stressed by something? A memory? Me? I hope it's not me! Thought Julie and tried to untangle her fingers from the little girl's grip.

"You are an angel!" He finally said looking straight at Julie with a serious face." I've been looking for you."

"Actually, I'm Julie."

"Angel," he said again in unison with his daughter.

Julie didn't understand what was going on.

"Sir, I'm sorry sir, but we need to escort this lady to her car," interrupted one of the security guys.

"I don't have a car," replied Julie." They are kicking me out, they are just being polite ... I guess."

"Kick you out?" The little girl's father chuckled. " What did you do? Try to rob the bank to get your chocolate fix?"

"It's a long and boring story," said Julie feeling pulled by the elbows by the hunky men to her side. " I'm glad I got to see you again, sweet little Joy! You have such a beautiful name!" Julie said bending to touch the girl's rosy cheeks.

"Why don't you tell me this long and boring story of yours," he said. Then he turned to the security guards and pulled out his wallet.

"We know who you are, sir, but Mr. Weinberg " try to explain one of the guards.

"Mr. Weinberg works for me and so do you. Don't worry. I'll take care of this," he said putting a firm hand on Julie's arm." She has a story to tell me about my own employees."

"Thanks to my daughter's almost misfortune, that I only found out a few weeks later, I can vow for this lady's character," he continued. "Angel" he said turning towards Julie and emphasizing the strange name again. "I bet I can learn a lot from her."

Julie was dumbstruck. Who was he and why was his little girl calling her angel all the time?

Chapter 35

"That was the craziest Fourth of July that I've ever had," confessed Donna." Thank God he convinced me not to go to the Hamptons! You girls make unforgettable holidays!" she said looking at the photographs Lizzie had on the coffee table next to her Jake scrapbook.

Lizzie laughed," yes, I guess we do. Jake couldn't have picked a better day to get born. What an awesome birthday date!"

"With nationwide fireworks and parties. He'll never be alone on his birthday!"

Too bad Nikki wasn't there for it. She would have probably kept us all calmer," mused Lizzie.

Donna touched Lizzie's face with both her hands and pulled her in for a hug. "We'll hear from her soon. It's been three months already since she last called to check in. Has she ever disappeared for longer?"

"Not since she'd moved in with us. It worries me. And her note was confusing and idealistic..." Lizzie's eyes were filling up with tears "... and immature. What is going on in her mind? Sometimes, I swear I just ...." Then she stopped herself from saying it.

"It's Thanksgiving already," tried Donna, "Maybe she'll surprise you all! Isn't this her favorite holiday?"

Lizzie was playing with the photographs in her hand absent-minded.

Donna tried again. "You guys knew who she was from the start, right? That's what you told me. Why did you think she'd change? Maybe it's you that changed, Lizzie!"

"No shit, Sherlock!" Lashed out Lizzie pointing at the two of them standing in such an intimate position.

Donna said nothing. She knew what was going on. She just had to let it pass. The summer went by in a blur. Julie finally opened her Rehab center by Halloween and everybody put a lot of time into that to happen. They all needed a project to take their minds off Nikki, who seemed to do her best not to be found.

The phone rang and Lizzie picked up.

"Sasha, are you done? I got the cutest toys and outfits for little Jake and I'm going back to the apartment in an hour. Meet you there? "

Donna liked Sasha being back, even if it was just for a couple of months to work from the New York office on a highly charged political issue. It was clear how much she loved her job, but it was clear as well how much this perfect timing meant for Julie and Lizzie, now with Nikki gone to cure the world of 'short-term relationships'.

"What was that? Where?" Lizzie asked precipitately. " Did you call Julie? without waiting for a response she offered: "I bet Donna will be okay with looking after Jake till we figure this out."

Donna was now worried. Something big must have happened.

"Let's meet at the apartment and come up with a plan," said Lizzie and hung up the phone with a preoccupied look on her face.

"Can I know what's going on? Why did you volunteer me to take care of Jake? Not that I mind, but Julie never"

Lizzie finally looked straight at Donna and said, "Nikki. Sasha just got a lead on Nikki! We have to go get her."

***

"Nikki!!! God no, Nikki!!! Break the window, Nikki!!!" You could hear the desperation and horror in their voices. But Nikki was the only one who had already given in to her inevitable death. She knew it, they knew it, but they were still hanging on to some crazy idea that a miracle would happen and she would be saved. Nikki looked at them and finally understood how much she loved them all.

Lizzie was still stopping cars in a frenzied attempt to find someone who could do something about the whole situation. She was not going to give up. As long as she could still see the car on top of that cracked ice, she was going to fight for everybody's life in that car, Nikki's above all.

"Oh, dear Nikki, what have you gotten yourself into this time. I'm so sorry I wasn't strong enough to stop you from running away with that bunch of losers. I knew they were too high to even know which way they were actually going. They didn't even have boots on, just freakin' flip-flops in the middle of the winter, pretending they didn't feel the frozen winter air because "their spirits will keep their bodies safe for as long as they still want to continue their journey in this mortal world". I guess their spirits concluded they are lunatics and decided to bail on them. End of the journey for them! Maybe, but not for Nikki. Not as long as I'm here and I can do something about it!" Lizzie said out loud while jumping in front of every car that was crossing the bridge in hopes someone will know what to do, or have enough rope for her to safely get to that car with a hammer and free everybody from that awful death. Especially Nikki. She saw Nikki's face as she turned and put both her hands on the back window in an attempt to reach out as the car was flying off the safety of the road. She couldn't erase that sheer panic she could read all over Nikki's beautiful face.

Lizzie shook her head and started yelling off the top of her lungs "Does anybody know anybody who can help them and can get here faster than the fire department or the police? Can you think of something that can help? Come on people. This is a life and death emergency happening right here in front of your eyes. Wake up! Think! Help me! Help them!"

Her throat was hurting from screaming. Nothing happened. Nobody said anything. Nobody did anything but watched the car that had Nikki in it slowly sinking into the river.

"What a bunch of idiots. Watching this like it's the circus. Like this was some kind of entertainment. Maybe Nikki was right, maybe the world is doomed, especially if these people right here were representatives of our human race. God, I'm starting to think like her and look where all that "thinking" got her. I need to be productive. Come on, think, what else can I do? Maybe throw rocks to crack a window? But the car is too far and I can't see any rocks on this stupid bridge. Ok, what else? I need another idea. Come on, Lizzie, think! Think!"

Julie and Sasha were on their cell phones frantically trying to get some help, any help, fast. They were staring at Nikki both with tears in their eyes trying to send their love and hope and not to look as freaked out as they were. Wasn't that what Nikki always said to them? That she can feel the emotions of other people when they are looking at her? Let's hope she really does.

Sasha exclaimed "She just needs to hang on until help comes. She needs to know that I have decided to move back. I'll be working from the New York office. It's been already approved."

Julie stopped her yelling on the phone and stared at Sasha. "Are you just saying that now?"

"No. I wanted to surprise you all. I'm coming back home!"

Lizzie's eyes were filled with tears. "Oh my God, we are going to be a family again!"

"We've always been! But now we'll be all back together again," said Sasha.

"All we need is Nikki now!" whispered Julie looking at the rusty piece of metal that was holding Nikki prisoner.

Lizzie pushed her body against the side of the bridge, bent over it and started yelling "It's really here! Look Nikki! Love is lasting! Look at us, your mission is complete! Please come home to us!"

"I'm going to miss you all! See you in our next lives!" whispered Nikki almost to herself as she closed her eyes and accepted what was coming with as much serenity as she could muster. Sam's serene face appeared in front of her as she kept her eyes shut.

"Sam! I want to say goodbye to Sam! That's all I want!"

"Where's my cell?" asked Nikki knowing nobody will give her an answer. She started jamming her frozen fists into her pockets hoping to find it. Nothing there was big enough to be a cell phone. Her mind started racing, "I just need my cell and one last call to Sam. Just one last call!"

A tear started trickling down her left cheek. "Please, I just want to say goodbye to Sam."

She could hear the thin layer of ice giving way under the weight of the car. Soon, the frozen waters of this cold river she used to swim in every hot summer day while still a child, will take her away forever from the people she loves and cherishes. How strange, that some of those clichés, that this society she's been running away from all her life, are proving to be right. Wasn't it said that right before you die the most important moments of your life flash before your eyes? That's what was happening to her, at this very moment. She finally understood how much her family and true friends actually love her. And she always "knew" she was alone. How wrong she had been.

It wasn't too easy to tune out the other four people in the car that were still trying to get out, banging the frozen windows of the tiny little old Volkswagen with their bare hands and feet. Their hauling cries were ripping her heart apart.

"Stop it!" Nikki yelled. "Joel, Anna, Crystal, Ben!!! All of you, stop and accept it! This is the end of our lives in these bodies. It's ok. Death is a wonderful thing! It's like an escape from the limits of this world. Weren't we looking for an escape from this mundane world, from its selfish, self-destructing inhabitants? What changed? We're looking death in its eyes! Don't turn around and close your eyes. Don't fight it. It has us in its grip. Now let's smile back at it, so it'll make the transition easier for all of us."

Nikki was trying to convince herself as well, by saying all that out loud. Did she believe it?

Somebody's foot smacked her right in her nose. She couldn't tell anymore whose feet were where. Arms and legs were flying agitated in the almost nonexistent space there still was in that car. Their bodies were all crushed together like sardines in a can, but when they picked this small car, they didn't think they might need more space to gain enough velocity to smash a window in case one of the tires of this old coffin would just literally fall out of its place, making the car jump off the bridge and into the river. Yeah, they didn't see it coming. Maybe the price tag should have been a clue. Maybe driving a car- that was cheaper than her last meal- on snow packed roads should have given her a hint. Well, not that they could have afforded more anyways. They spent all their money on that sweet stash for the party tonight. They were so sure that this cheap car was a sign from divinity. It was a sign all right, a sign that it was time for all of them to go to heaven, if any of them believed in such a place.

Her nose was bleeding. Nikki remembered her hands being frozen solid but with all this "last breath" agitation, her blood was flowing rapidly all throughout her body. What was the point of trying to stop the bleeding? It was such a normal reaction to reach for the first piece of cloth she could put her hands on and try and stop the bleeding.

"Funny!" thought Nikki. "I'm going to die any second now and I'm wasting my time and energy trying to stop a nosebleed. Isn't that how life usually goes by anyway? We waste our time taking care of the small immediate and trivial things automatically, without even thinking, while the actual important things in our lives tend to be left to chance? And then if life doesn't turn out the way we want it to be, we complain and blame everybody else except ourselves."

A noise penetrated the madness in the car and Nikki's hand went right to the source of that sound. Finally, her cell phone. She looked at it and her heart stopped beating, it was Sam.

"Nikki, my love! Thank you for picking up"

She couldn't say anything, she didn't want to ruin the moment and the unconditional love, gratitude and miracle she felt and heard in Sam's voice. He was her miracle. Her one and only. He understood her. He let her go and gave her the freedom she thought she had lost. But he was still there, waiting for her to come back. She had a home to go back to. She had Sam. She would always have Sam. Why did she ever leave when she had everything right there with him? She was blind before, always searching, never believing she had actually got to her destination - life. Life is a destination and a journey at the same time. Nikki knew she had to stop searching and start living and enjoying! She had arrived. Her blindfold was finally lifted. But was it too late for her?

Then she turned around and looked at the girls on the bridge. They were so close, yet so far away. All of them were frantic but trying to hide it for her sake. She could see it. She could feel it. They loved her unconditionally.

She had all that. What does she have now? Regrets that she was so blind to her own magnificent life, to all the beauty, precious moments and loving friends around her. She should have given her new cell phone number to the girls as well. What was she thinking cutting herself off from them like that.

Nikki had to die with that regret, with all the people she loved close by but unable to help her at this point. They had tried, all of them, so many times, but she never took their reached-out hand. She always turned her back on them and looked for something more. Always more. She came back and then ran away again with that searching thirst scorching her throat. Nikki always knew there was more out there to be had.

Happiness, bliss and eternal love was just in reach. Now she finally understood. She always had that, but always ran away from it in a sick and twisted way of self-sabotage.

Now she understood, finally. But it was too late.

"I'm sorry Sam," was all she could mutter. "Please tell the girls that I love them for always!"

His voice changed immediately, "Nikki, honey, please talk to me!" The seriousness in his voice shook her up.

"I'm staring at my own death, Sam. I thought it would be peaceful, but I have so many regrets."

The slight yet final and deadly crack in the ice underneath the car was deafening. She could see Ben and Anna's mouths and eyes wide open with panicked fear. Crystal and Joel were crushing her. She couldn't hear anymore. But she could see. She was seeing her death gripping her by her bare feet. Its grip was freezing cold, climbing patiently higher and higher to her heart.

This was it. She knew it. She felt it. It was her time.

She said nothing. Tears were rushing down her pale face. Everything seemed to have slowed down. There were flashes. Time stopped to be continuum. It was random pictures of what she would have called the present. She couldn't even hear her breathing anymore. Maybe because that had stopped to.

"Fight Nikki! Damn it! Fight! Fight for me! Fight for us! Always!"

The incomprehensible noise coming from the tiny flat box she was gripping to her ear finally reached her overwhelmed mind and when something smooth, cold and hard yanked her into her left shin, she instinctively reacted. She reached to her shin and grabbed the metal tool that had no name for her.

The water was so clear and freezing cold. She tried to pull her feet up, but Crystal had pinned her to the corner. With a sudden move she smacked Crystal in the face and twisted her body towards the back of the car, staring decisively at the back window armed with the heavy tool. The freezing wetness of the water had reached her waist. It was now or never!